"If you like a dark, dangerous man, a spirited heroine, and sultry New Orleans nights, *Creole Nights* is a must read. I loved it!"

—Rexanne Becnel

PASSION'S PERILS

René captured Elina's chin, forcing her head up so her mouth was so close to his she could feel his warm breath when he spoke. "You're like the cotton plants in the fields—all prickly and proud on the outside, but on the inside soft as silk. When I ignore the barbs and reach deeper to find the real woman, I find more willingness than the woman will admit to feeling."

Elina's eyes closed involuntarily as his mouth pressed teasing kisses along the warm skin of her chin and cheeks, and his fingers snaked around to stroke her nape. She felt his other hand slip down to cup her hips, and her eyes flew open. In that moment, she caught a glimpse of his confident smile, and that gave her the strength to resist him.

Her pride wounded, she slapped him. He released her, one hand rubbing his cheek as his eyes flared with anger.

"One day you'll tire of having the barbs prick you," she told him. "I hope and pray that day comes soon, so I can be free of this house and of you."

"*Creole Nights* is a dynamic read...the perfect book to sit back and enjoy!"

—*Romantic Times*

Other *Leisure Books* by Deborah Martin:

MOONLIGHT ENCHANTMENT

CREOLE NIGHTS

Deborah Martin

Book Margins, Inc.

A BMI Edition

Published by special arrangement with Dorchester
Publishing Co., Inc.

Printed in the United States of America.

To my good friends Brenda Howard, Mary Lou Fuenzalida, and Rexanne Becnel, who gave of their time to critique the novel.

To all the wonderful folks in SOLA, especially the historical group.

And to my own Rene, bits of whose heritage are threaded throughout this novel. This one's for you, babe.

Prologue

"Why were you in that place?" Elina Vannier asked her brother, Alexandre, as he drove the carriage out of the small town of Creve Coeur.

He frowned, but kept silent.

His refusal to answer increased her pain. "With Mama newly in the grave, I thought you'd wait a decent amount of time before . . . before beginning your amusements again."

"I had to see to some important matters," Alex said. The grim set to his mouth reminded her of their absent papa, whom Alex resembled. Although she and Alex were twins, they looked nothing alike. While she had their mama's auburn hair and green eyes, he looked Creole through and through, his French and Spanish heritage clearly displayed in his dark eyes, black hair, and hawkish nose.

His expression now made her hesitate to question him

further, but suddenly she remembered her promise to her dying mother that she'd watch out for him. She could only do that if she knew what he was up to. "What matters?" she demanded boldly.

"Just leave me alone, won't you, Elina? I need to think," Alex bit out.

She started to retort, then stopped. It wouldn't do any good and would cause them both more pain. Still, she wished he'd realize that with Mama dead they needed to work together now more than ever.

Elina could scarcely believe that Kathleen Vannier's lungs had finally collapsed after all her years of illness, and she felt the pain of losing her mother rip through her once again. Oh, what were they to do without Mama's calming presence?

The carriage lurched toward their horse farm as she stared blankly at the fields sprinkled with pink wildflowers, seeing only her mama's body draped in pink silk. With a terrible aching, she remembered the rigid form that was like a sculpture of her mother and not her real mama at all.

After a while, Alex's voice broke into her thoughts. "Now that . . . that Mama has been put to rest, we must make plans."

"What sort of plans?"

"We should go to New Orleans and find Papa. There's a steamboat that leaves St. Louis tomorrow."

"What?" she asked, surprised. She looked at him, but he refused to meet her eyes.

"We must tell Papa that Mama's dead," he insisted. "We must find him."

"But why so soon? His last letter said he'd return shortly. What would he say if he returned to find us gone?"

"That letter was dated three months ago, Elina. Three months! Papa may neglect us at times, but it's not like him to extend one of his damn buying trips without sending word."

Alex's criticism of Papa instantly raised Elina's ire. She

10

retorted with sarcasm, "Perhaps you should remember that those 'damn buying' trips finance your wild nights at the gaming halls."

"Yes," Alex agreed, although his tone showed how little her comment bothered him. "But if he'd been home or if we'd known where he was, Mama's attack wouldn't have been so bad this time."

Elina didn't answer right away, unwilling to admit she'd thought much the same thing. She didn't want to blame Papa. His trips to seek out high-quality horses for wealthy men supported the family. Despite her deep-seated fear of horses, she could understand his choice of livelihood. It gave him the adventure and excitement he craved. Yet, it was true that Mama's worrying over his uncharacteristic silence had proven too great a strain for the delicate woman, and Papa was at fault for that.

She thrust those uncomfortable thoughts from her mind. "We should give him a few more weeks before we go anywhere. There's enough money in the household account to support us for a while, and I can always give drawing lessons if we need more."

"But Papa's never been gone this long," Alex protested. "He could be lying dead in some godforsaken wilderness town!"

"Don't say that!" Elina burst out. "I can't believe it! Thinking such terrible things is what drove Mama to her grave, and I won't have you talking about them!"

Her shoulders shook from the effort of holding back her tears. How could he assume the worst? She could barely contemplate such a possibility!

Alex lay one hand over hers. "Listen, Puss," he said, using her childhood nickname. A new note of urgency was in his voice. "I can't just idly wait for Papa to return. I must know what's happened to him. Don't you want to know, too?"

She swallowed a sob. Of course she wanted to know. But she feared he wouldn't be that easy to find.

"Why go to New Orleans?" she asked. "He could be anywhere."

"His last letter was from there. And remember . . ."

"Yes?"

"Well, I mean, our grandparents do live there."

She turned then, scornfully regarding her brother. "Ha! As if they'd be any help. They won't even acknowledge us, their poor little half-American grandchildren. Papa himself doesn't talk to them or about them. For all we know, they're dead."

Alex shrugged. "I doubt that. He'd have told us. And if they're alive, I can't imagine their being completely unaware of their own son's whereabouts. If they're dead, well, there must be other Vanniers to help us." His voice held a thread of pleading in it. "Come now, Elina, someone must know something."

Her eyes were green chips of ice as she glared at Alex. "You're just interested in the Vannier money. You hope our wealthy Creole grandparents will open their loving arms to us when they hear Mama's dead, even though they've never even sent us a letter."

It hurt her to think about *Grandpère* and *Grandmère* who hated Kathleen Wallace Vannier for being American and for stealing their son. Just because they were descended from kings, they had ignored their own grandchildren.

And Alex wanted to go to them! "You'll have to go alone, Alex," she said with pride. "*You* go seek the fortune you think is due you. *I* shall wait here for Papa."

"You damn well will not!" he shouted. "I won't have—" He broke off.

In confusion, she looked at him, then followed his gaze to the horizon. Her blood ran cold as she spotted thick clouds of black smoke rising above the trees a short distance ahead of them.

He whipped the horses as she clutched the sides of the carriage.

"It can't be . . . It can't be the farm," she told him, leaning forward in her seat. She felt as if she were having a horrid nightmare that continued despite her will for it to end.

"I'm afraid it can," Alexandre muttered under his breath, but not softly enough to prevent her from hearing his words.

She clutched his arm as they neared the farm and the smoke moved closer and closer. "Alex, what's going on? Has something happened you haven't told me about?"

He ignored her questions and merely used the whip to urge the horses forward.

"Alex!" she insisted.

At that point, they rounded a bend a few yards from the house. Alex threw himself from the carriage, and Elina gasped.

Rising alone amidst a vast expanse of charred timbers and rubble was the chimney to what once had been their home. Nothing else remained, not even Papa's precious stables. The ground was black, the air thick with smoke, and gray ash seemed scattered as far as she could see.

She climbed down slowly and went to stand beside her brother. "Who did this?" she whispered in disbelief. She turned to him and saw the color drain from his face. Her voice rose. "Who did this, Alex? Tell me! You know who did it, don't you?"

He nodded slowly, his eyes fixed on the grisly sight.

"Does this have anything to do with why you went to that dreadful place?" she demanded.

He spoke as if in a trance. "He . . . he said he'd show me he meant business. My God, I didn't think he'd go this far." He turned toward her, his expression tortured. "I swear it, Puss. If—if I had known—"

"Who? Who did it?" she cut him off.

Alex slumped as he answered, a deadly weariness in his voice. "Wyatt. You wouldn't know him. He . . . he owns several gambling dens in St. Louis."

"I suppose you owe him money," she said woodenly, but she knew the answer. Of course Alex owed him money.

Alex owed money to every saloon owner within a hundred miles.

He put his arm around her shoulders, but she thrust him away.

"How much do you owe that he'd do this . . . *this* . . . to us for it?" she asked.

Alex swallowed and looked away. "More than I could ever pay. He wants his money now. But I can't pay him. I—I tried. I emptied my account and most of the household account—"

"What!"

"—but it wasn't enough. And we can't touch Papa's account. The banker told me so. He claimed Papa told him not to give us money because we had plenty in our own accounts." Alex clenched his fist. "Damn them all! Wyatt isn't going to stop here, you know." Alex swept his arm around to include the destruction before them. "All this is just a warning."

"We should go to the sheriff."

Alex's harsh laugh grated. "Wyatt has the sheriff in his pocket. How do you think his men could ride out here and burn the place to the ground without even being challenged?"

She stood in desolate silence. They had nothing. Nothing! Not without Papa.

"I've put Wyatt off too long. He says he won't wait another day. And he has a reputation to uphold," he said sarcastically. "He has to show everyone he won't tolerate being ignored. Next time it won't be the house his men destroy." He paused and leveled his gaze on her. "Next time it could be you."

Her blood raced in fear. "Surely they wouldn't—"

"If they think hurting you will accomplish what they want, they'll do it," he assured her.

She paled, horrified by the idea that Wyatt and his men might strike at Alex through her.

"Now you understand why I wanted to leave?" he cried

as he watched his words take effect. "We must find Papa! Papa must take care of it! Because if I don't pay, they'll destroy us!"

Elina stared at the black rubble. *Destroy us?* she thought. Wyatt's men were already well on their way to doing that. Her home was gone, and even Papa couldn't bring it back. But he could seek vengeance, and she'd make certain he did.

"Very well then, we'll find Papa," she whispered. Then her voice rose as she turned to her brother. "We'll find Papa if we have to search all of New Orleans!"

Chapter One

When all other sins are old, avarice is still young.
—French Proverb

To Elina's relief, the *Belvedere*'s steam engines had ceased running, so she no longer had to endure their noisy hum. As she stood on deck, the city of New Orleans lay spread before her, its sights so various and colorful she wished she had her sketchpad to capture them on paper. Men toiled at the docks, hoisting cargo from the steamboat deck to waiting carts. Other men drove the richly laden carts up and over the levee.

Beyond the levee, a cathedral's majestic steeple rose over a square flanked by maples. The levee obstructed her view somewhat, but she could see enough to realize that the buildings of New Orleans with their wrought-iron balconies and odd roofs were unlike any she'd ever seen in Missouri.

A breeze played over her long slender neck. Thank heavens she and Alex had arrived during late April instead

16

of summer. The other steamboat passengers had told her horrible tales of New Orleans' summers. As it was, the slight breeze vanished in an instant, and once again the late-afternoon sun beat down on her. Apparently, even in April New Orleans was hot.

"Miss Wallace?" a voice spoke behind her.

Vaguely, she wondered who was being called.

"Miss Wallace?" the voice repeated.

She started guiltily. Of course the man was calling her. Alex, fearful that Wyatt would track them down, had insisted they use assumed names. So she'd been Miss Wallace the entire trip, although she still wasn't accustomed to being called by her mother's maiden name.

Now she turned to find the steward hovering over their bags.

"Your brother said to have your luggage brought to the hotel," he said. "Is this all of it?"

She nodded. He started to turn away, but she stopped him. "Is Mr. Wallace still in the men's cabin playing cards?"

The steward looked down at his feet. "Uh, yes, ma'am, I believe so. But I'm sure he'll be here shortly."

"Of course," she murmured, unconvinced as she glanced up at the roundhouse that was the men's cabin.

The steward quickly took his leave, and she again turned her gaze to the city before her. What would she and Alex find there? Could it be any worse than what they'd left behind? Everything had happened so quickly— Mama's death, the destruction of the farm, their hurried flight from Creve Coeur— that she'd had no time to consider what New Orleans might be like.

She'd never traveled anywhere before without one of her parents. And she and Alex had so little money. If they didn't find Papa, what would they do? She shuddered, praying they'd find him soon.

Once they found Papa, she thought, he'd take control. She longed desperately to see him, to know he was safe. She'd sustained herself through the trip by inventing reasons he hadn't come home or sent word. Perhaps his letters had been lost. That often happened. Mail service between Creve Coeur and the rest of the country left much to be desired. Or perhaps he'd found himself cut off in a small town where the coach came through only occasionally. Only one possibility did she refuse to accept—that he might be wounded or dead.

Facing Mama's death had been wrenching enough. She'd tried to be strong for Alex's sake, but there were times. . . .

Oh, Mama, she thought, *I miss you so. How could you have left us?*

Without Mama's gentle nurturing presence, the strange city terrified her. Tears filled her eyes, reducing the panorama of New Orleans to a blurry nightmarish scene. Her hands balled into fists as she fought to clear her vision. She wouldn't torment herself like this! She mustn't!

She glared at the stairway leading to the men's cabin, willing Alex to saunter down it. But there was no sign of him. Obviously, the fact that they'd docked hadn't affected his enjoyment. Well, she wasn't going to stand out on deck waiting for him to remember why they were in New Orleans in the first place. With grim resolve, she strode toward the stairway.

When she reached the door to the men's cabin, she hesitated. Women were only allowed in at meals. But did those rules apply once the boat docked? She shrugged. If they did, she'd just ignore them. She and Alex needed to begin searching for Papa.

Summoning her courage, she knocked, relieved when a male voice bade her enter. The roundhouse was deserted except for some men sitting at the center table. As she approached them, she heard Alex say, "I'm surprised you play poker so well, Bonnange. I didn't think Creole gentlemen favored it."

"Not all Creole gentlemen are alike," an unfamiliar voice answered, its rich tones holding only a trace of a French accent.

As she walked toward the table, she picked out the man who'd spoken, noting that she hadn't seen him before. Had he boarded when the boat had made its last plantation stop? Intrigued by his resonant voice, she paused to observe him. On the surface, he resembled the men in her family. He had the same Creole night-black hair and olive complexion.

Suddenly he placed a bet, and she realized she'd been staring at this complete stranger.

He is not my concern, she reminded herself sternly as she focused her attention on her difficult brother.

No one had noticed her enter. But once she approached her brother, the two men who'd played cards with Alex most of the trip looked up and grinned. She gave them a brief smile, pleased that Alex had chosen to play with these decent older businessmen instead of the more dissolute professional gamblers.

Alex didn't smile, however, but flashed her an angry glance.

She ignored it, leaning down to whisper in his ear, "We've docked now. Don't you think it's time we go to the hotel?"

His face mirrored his displeasure at being summoned by his sister in front of the other men. Then he shook his head and gave the men a look of annoyance. "Women. Always impatient, aren't they?" He turned his attention back to her. "Can't sit still, can you, Puss?"

She cringed at his use of her nickname.

"We don't have to be off yet," he continued. "The pilot said we could stay aboard until this evening, so sit down and watch awhile. You might learn something."

Elina reddened in anger, but she knew arguing with him was futile. If she insisted he leave, his embarrassment at being upbraided by his sister in front of the older men would know no bounds. Then he'd become stubborn, and she might not get him to leave for hours. With reluctance, she acknowledged she had no choice but to stay and hope she could convince him to leave soon.

One of the gentlemen sitting next to Alex pulled a chair up for her, and she sat down uneasily.

"Now that we have your friend situated, do you think we could continue, Wallace?" said the man called Bonnange.

This time Elina looked more closely at Bonnange. Unbidden, the thought came to her that she'd enjoy sketching his sharply sculpted features with their intriguing lines and shadows. Then there was his chin, so strong and determined, and his lips full of promise. Still, something about him frightened her. He reminded her of her papa's few wild stallions who appeared to be tame and gentle until the constraints of civilization were placed on them, making them bolt.

The man returned her gaze, his compelling brown eyes assessing first her face and then her form. She blushed, particularly when she realized belatedly that her brother hadn't bothered to correct the man's mistaken impression that she was Alex's "friend."

"Please excuse the interruption," she said with a glance at Alex. "I'm afraid my *brother* and I have some rather important business to attend to. I'd hoped he might be ready to abandon his gambling and leave."

If she'd thought to shame Alex into heeding her request, she was unsuccessful. He merely ignored her.

Bonnange, however, arched his thick dark brows and smiled in a way that told her he was pleased to hear Alex was her brother. "As you can see," he said in silky tones, "your brother insists on remaining."

One of the other men added, "Now don't you worry about his gambling, little lady. You're in New Orleans now. Gambling's a way of life here. The gentlemen gamble on cards and dice while everyone else gambles on surviving the mosquitoes, the heat, the yellow fever, and the ne'er-do-wells."

"Don't forget the duels!" another player said. "We get too many of them in New Orleans. Yes, ma'am, I'd say just living in New Orleans is a gamble."

Elina paled. What kind of rough city had they come to? Creve Coeur had been far enough away from St. Louis to be a quiet country town. And even St. Louis, which they'd visited occasionally, had been fairly respectable.

Alex saw the alarm in her face and recognized what she must be feeling. "Don't listen to them, Puss. It can't be as bad as all that."

He flashed the other men a warning glance.

One of them shrugged. "Sorry, ma'am. I guess we shouldn't tell you such things. But you and your brother ought to be prepared for what's at hand. He's gonna want to watch out for you. You're a lovely girl, and, beggin' your pardon, men in New Orleans tend to take what they want."

That comment elicited a broad smile from Bonnange. She colored and avoided his eyes.

But she couldn't help feeling warmed by the other card player's compliment. She'd never considered herself pretty. Granted, Alex always joked about what he termed her "siren's eyes." He said she'd catch a rich husband with those vivid jade eyes someday, but she'd dismissed his words as simple teasing. Her few female friends in Creve Coeur had pitied her for having green eyes and red hair, an unusual coloring that they'd believed would make it difficult for her to find suitors.

Alex seemed annoyed by the direction the conversation was heading, and the familiar way the men were treating her. "I can take care of my sister," he said firmly. "So stop filling her head with these stupid ideas, and let's get on with the game."

But the men's comments had renewed Elina's determination to convince Alex to leave. "Perhaps this is a good time to call an end to it," she murmured in Alex's ear. She used a new ploy. "These men with all their talk about New Orleans are scaring me—"

"We're not leaving!" he hissed back.

"Now, now, Miss Wallace, let him stay a bit longer," one of the men put in. "He's taken a beatin' today from Mr. Bonnange here. He needs to win some of his money back."

For the first time, Elina noticed the pile of gold coins spread on the table before the stranger and the pitiful number in front of her brother. She turned to Alex, a stricken expression on her face.

Alex avoided her eyes. "Don't worry, Puss. My luck will change in a bit. It always does."

Elina tensed as a quick jolt of anger passed through her. Why couldn't he have left well enough alone? He'd won nearly two hundred dollars during the course of the trip. Now she could tell he had only a quarter of that amount left. The devil take him!

As she fumed, Bonnange began to deal, and the men fell silent. She watched the game anxiously, so upset about Alex's losses that she didn't bother to hide her chagrin.

After a while she sensed eyes watching her. She lifted her head to find Bonnange staring at her with interest. Defiantly, she met his gaze, unaccountably angry at him for winning her brother's money. They stared at each other for several seconds. Then his lips curved in a faint smile before he turned to his hand, leaving her breathless.

No one had ever smiled at her like that before, as if they offered her something she wished to take, but shouldn't. She didn't know what to think of the glint in his eye, except she knew it made her feel intensely warm. Confused, she ignored him and tried her best to concentrate on the card game.

Normally she would have taken pleasure in watching the men play. She too enjoyed playing cards, for that had been one of few activities she, Alex, and Papa had participated in together.

But these days, she worried whenever Alex approached a card table. The plain and simple fact was she didn't trust him. Alex was notoriously unprincipled and irresponsible

22

when it came to money. He'd always taken the easy road in trying to acquire it.

At twenty-two years old, he continued to live off Papa's money, gambling it away in some ridiculous hope that he'd amass a fortune in one night. He'd never cared what his gambling did to Mama or even to Papa. Ever since Papa had refused to let Alex accompany him on his trips, Alex had lived a dissolute life as a way of tormenting him.

Sometimes she felt exasperated with them both—with Papa for insisting that Alex stay home and take care of the family and with Alex for resenting it so. Papa had seemed exasperated, too, but he'd never stopped Alex's gambling. Papa had seemed to understand, even accept, Alex's frustration.

She twisted her hands together as she watched her brother deftly deal. Alex's irresponsible streak often extended to his behavior at the card tables. Now she had to wonder if Alex had really been as lucky this trip as he'd claimed. Or was he cheating? She'd learned early on how adept he was at palming cards and dealing from the bottom.

Still, after the last time angry players had caught and nearly beaten him to death, he'd sworn he wouldn't cheat anymore. Mama had believed him. So had she.

Surely, she thought, *he won't do something so foolish again*. Yet her uneasy suspicions continued to plague her. She knew his tricks and watched for them now, relieved when it became apparent he was playing fairly.

But it also became apparent after a few hands that Alex was no match for the Creole. Bonnange was too experienced, and it showed in his playing. For every hand Alex or the other men won, Bonnange always won two or three. To make matters worse, Alex was becoming quite agitated by his repeated failures. His hands wavered noticeably each time he picked up his cards.

The game seemed to last an eternity. Although every window in the cabin was open, the sun beating down on the roof right above them counteracted any breeze that wafted through the room. Elina drew out her handkerchief and wiped it across her face and neck, but before long she felt hot and sticky again. The room dimmed as the sun started its slow descent.

Then suddenly it happened when she least expected it. Alex was dealing. His hands moved quickly, but she saw the way he held the cards, with his index finger at the top, and knew he was dealing from the bottom.

Her first impulse was to glance at the others to see if they'd noticed, but she resisted it. She kept the same blank expression her brother wore, while inside she despaired. Didn't he realize how foolish such an action was? If he were caught, it would, at the very least, cause them great embarrassment, and more likely endanger them.

She mustn't let his action be detected. Swiftly, she rose to her feet and paced the room impatiently in a manner she hoped was distracting. She wasn't experienced at attempting to draw men's eyes, but she put all her effort into it now.

A curt command from Bonnange to "stop that irritating motion" made her return to her chair, but at least the dealing was over and no one had spoken. She determined to let a hand or two pass. Then she would insist they leave, before Alex mustered up the nerve to cheat again.

He won that hand, of course, and the next one as well. She relaxed slightly in her chair, hopeful that the fickle finger of Lady Luck had now settled on her brother and he wouldn't be tempted to cheat anymore. But that hope soon vanished as her brother began to lose again.

"Look here, Bonnange," Alex said just as she was about to suggest they leave, "I'm feeling lucky at present. Why don't we raise the stakes?"

Elina nearly screamed, for she could guess her brother's intentions. Had he completely taken leave of his senses? Didn't he realize what a chance he'd be taking if he continued to cheat? She held her breath, praying desperately that Bonnange wouldn't agree to raise the stakes, but the man looked her squarely in the eye as he stated his approval.

The other two men seemed unhappy with the idea, but they agreed as well, presumably because they too hoped to win some of their money back in one hand.

She glanced at the Creole, expecting to see triumph on his face, for surely he realized that the others were no match for his skill or his luck. But he was coolly watching Alex as he dealt the cards. When at last he lifted his eyes to her face, they were filled with icy suspicion. She shivered involuntarily as he brought his attention back to the table. Was it possible he too knew what Alex was about? A premonition of danger made her stiffen. Urgently, she whispered to Alex that they really must leave.

"Not yet, Puss," Alex whispered back. "But you could make yourself useful. Why don't you pour me a glass of whiskey? The decanter's over there. Then I'll play a few more hands and we'll leave, I promise."

She started to protest, to refuse to leave his side, but he didn't give her the chance.

"Anyone else need a whiskey?" he asked, and when one of the men answered affirmatively, Alex looked at her expectantly. She dared not make an issue of it. She didn't want the others to know why she balked. So she rose stiffly and walked across the room.

She heard the hand begin, the men making their calls in turn. Then suddenly all was silent. Her back was to the card table when the voice of the Creole broke the silence.

"I wouldn't move another inch, Wallace, if I were you," he stated, and she whirled to find him leveling a gun at Alex.

She froze in fear. It had happened. Alex had been caught.

"What's the meaning of this, Bonnange?" her brother replied indignantly. His right hand, which lay on his left arm, moved slightly.

"If you try to slide that hand another inch, you'll regret it," Bonnange replied. "I want to see what's under it. Now!"

"What are you insinuating, sir?" her brother asked, his face suddenly flushed. She could see his legs stiffen under the table. A thick queasiness assailed her. *Not again*, she thought despairingly. *Oh, Alex, why must you do these things?*

"I'm not insinuating anything," Bonnange replied coldly. "I'll make it clearer for you. I chose to overlook it when you dealt from the bottom while your companion distracted us all with her delectable pacing. But I refuse to be taken for a fool more than once. Show me what's under your hand. Unless, that is, you want to find out what life is like without fingers."

Alex jerked his hand over, and Elina's heart leapt into her throat as the king and queen of spades tumbled onto the table.

"I don't do this normally, Bonnange, I swear it," Alex sputtered. "I was desperate and went a little crazy. I don't even know how to deal from the bottom. Really I don't."

"For someone who doesn't know what he's doing, you did a fine job of dealing yourself three aces that hand," Bonnange responded harshly.

Alex looked startled, as if he hadn't realized Bonnange was paying such close attention. Then his eyes narrowed. "I only took such measures in defense. I was certain you were cheating, too. After all, how else could you have won so easily?"

Elina groaned aloud. Taunting Bonnange could only worsen matters. She knew the Creole hadn't cheated. Watching Alex and her papa play had taught her to recognize the signs that gave away such activities. And Bonnange had certainly not shown any of them.

The other men glanced uneasily from Alex to Bonnange, confusion and uncertainty clearly written on their faces.

"Stop acting the fool, Wallace," Bonnange bit out. "We both know the only card cheat in this room is you. But you can tell your story to the magistrate. I'm sure he'll be amused."

The magistrate! Elina thought. *We can't go to the magistrate! He'll jail Alex for certain!*

Her knees trembled as she approached the table. "Please, *Monsieur* Bonnange, don't take him to the magistrate," Elina pleaded, her voice nearly failing her in her fear. "Just let us go. We don't want the money." She flashed a scathing glance her brother's way. "And I assure you my brother won't be so foolish in the future!"

Bonnange's eyes left Alex and bore into her, glittering with a fury that set her heart racing in terror. The planes of his face seemed suddenly much harsher and grimmer than before.

"Making sweet eyes at me will not aid you, *ma petite*. Surely you can see the game is up. I don't like card cheats, especially those who rely on a woman's pretty face to cover their inexpert abilities."

Elina's face flushed with humiliation as she realized that he thought she and Alex had planned to cheat him.

"It's not what you think—" she began.

"Oh? Was it a trick of the light that made those cards appear under your brother's hand? Sorry, sweet eyes, but you're fighting a lost cause. Your friends in Missouri may allow such behavior, but in New Orleans, cheating isn't regarded lightly."

She flashed the other men a silent plea, at a loss for what to say that might convince Bonnange not to prosecute her brother. But they looked uncomfortable and stared down at the table without meeting her gaze. Of course, she thought bitterly, they were older businessmen on holiday. They wouldn't involve themselves in such a confrontation. She turned her eyes back to Bonnange, but his gaze was fixed on her brother.

"Stay out of this," Alex urged his sister with forced bravado. "*Monsieur* Bonnange and I will settle it between ourselves."

"Of course," Bonnange responded. "But the settling will take place in the magistrate's chambers."

27

Her brother leaned forward then, a wild light in his eyes. "Why not keep it between us? You've accused me of cheating and I've accused you. Why not fight to settle our differences? Tomorrow. Yes, tomorrow we'll meet to duel."

Elina gasped aloud, her fingers digging into her palms. How stupid could Alex be? As if Bonnange wouldn't see through Alex's flimsy attempt to escape retribution!

Bonnange's humorless smile chilled Elina to the bone. "Dueling with you would be beneath me." The Creole's voice taunted Alex, the rich tones now sharp and cruel. "The duel is for honorable men, not criminals and cheats. You cheated not once, but twice, which signifies that you earn your living this way. It's time you faced the consequences of your actions."

Elina's heart sank as Bonnange rose from the table, the gun still fixed on her brother.

"You're afraid to fight me!" Alex shouted hysterically. "You—you know I'd win!" Then he jumped to his feet and drew his own gun. With shaking hands, he held it on Bonnange. "Don't—don't come any closer! I'll shoot you! I will!"

Elina despaired, any hope that she might convince Bonnange to release her brother dissolving. She could see rage course through the man. His entire body stiffened, and his mouth became a rigid line of pure fury.

"Please—" she said mindlessly, a sob escaping her lips.

Her words distracted Bonnange for a moment. Slowly, he turned his eyes to Elina's frightened face.

"Your brother's a fool, *mademoiselle*. I hope you'll impress this on him later when he's in his cell. Even if somehow either of you escaped this room, I promise you wouldn't escape me for long. I would find you both, if I had to comb every gambling den in the city to do it. But you won't be leaving here."

Elina knew Alex hadn't the courage to shoot Bonnange. Evidently, Bonnange knew it as well, for he advanced upon her brother and wrenched the gun away before Alex could even react. He then emptied the bullets onto the floor and threw the weapon scornfully down on the table as Alex stared at him, a dazed expression on his face.

Then Bonnange grasped Alex's arm forcefully and pulled him around the side of the table. "You and I have a visit to pay," he ground out.

For a second, time stood still for Elina. She could see Alex locked in jail while she, penniless and friendless, searched for Papa, who might not even be in the city. And her grandparents, who already despised her and Alex, what would they think when they learned their grandson had been jailed?

She couldn't let it happen! She mustn't! As the Creole pushed Alex past her toward the door, she glanced frantically about her. Then her eyes fell on the whiskey bottle. Without taking another moment to think, she clasped the bottle and darted behind the man. Before anyone in the room could even protest, she brought the bottle crashing down on Bonnange's head. He slumped to the floor as the other men stared in shock.

"Run, Alex, run!" she shouted, half-afraid Bonnange would rise from the floor any minute to wreak vengeance on her.

"Now see here—" one of the men began.

But Alex had lost his surprise at seeing Bonnange lying senseless on the floor and was already wresting Bonnange's gun from his hand. Alex then turned the gun on the men at the table.

"Come on, Alex!" Elina urged, pulling on his arm. "We've got to get out of here!"

Oblivious to her hand on his arm, Alex continued to stand there, staring at the gold on the table. She glanced fearfully down at Bonnange's face. A trickle of blood trailed down his cheek from where she'd hit him, and she felt an inexplicable stab of remorse.

"He's not . . ." she began, and then swallowed. "He's not dead, do you think?"

"Of course not," her brother replied sharply.

She forced herself not to look at the blood, to be strong. "Then he'll be up and after our necks in a moment if we don't leave!" she said, becoming frantic when Alex continued to hold the men at gunpoint.

"Yes," he replied mindlessly, and she realized he had no idea what he was saying. Then she watched in shock as Alex lowered the gun and scooped the money off the table. Hurriedly, he crammed the coins in his emptied purse.

"You can't do that, Wallace!" one of the men protested.

"He stole my money, I tell you," Alex insisted. "You saw how easily he won nearly every hand."

"You were the only one caught palming cards," the man stated angrily. "And you've done your share of winning this trip. Besides, some of that money is ours—" The man fell silent as he noticed that Alex had once again lifted the gun, only this time he leveled it at the man who was speaking.

"Alex!" Elina cried. "You mustn't! This is robbery!"

"I know what I'm doing. We have to have money!"

"Not this way!" she protested, reaching for his purse.

Alex pushed her hands away, and when she wouldn't stop, his face went purple with rage. "Stop it!" he cried, and then slapped her with such force she stumbled back. In numbed shock, she rubbed her cheek and stared at him, scarcely able to believe he'd done such an awful thing.

For a moment, he seemed to regret what he'd done. Then his face hardened, and he whirled to face the men again.

"My sister and I are leaving, do you understand? And you'd best not follow us."

Clamping his hand on Elina's arm, he propelled her roughly down the long hall toward the door. Still reeling from having seen her brother's violent side, Elina allowed him to push her along. But when they reached the exit, she made one last attempt.

"If you leave the money . . ." she muttered.

"It would make no difference. They'd still bring me to

jail. Besides, we need the money. We can't survive without it."

She knew that much was true. But stealing! Oh, why couldn't she think of some way out of the mess Alex had gotten them into?

He thrust her through the doorway so hard she nearly fell down the stairs. She stared at the dark silent deck, her feelings in turmoil while Alex closed the door and slid the bolt in place so no one could follow them.

"Well, are you coming with me?" he whispered to Elina as she gazed at the cabin door with regret.

"Yes," she said, a lump rising in her throat to choke her. It was out of her hands now. Bonnange would be coming out of his stupor soon and tracking them in a city they were unfamiliar with. There was no time to fight with Alex over the money.

She'd promised Mama to look out for foolhardy Alex, and now she'd have to live with that promise. "Yes," she said more firmly.

And without a backward glance, they both fled the boat into the New Orleans twilight.

Chapter Two

To a hoarding father succeeds an extravagant son.
—*Spanish Proverb*

René Bonnange groaned as the room came into focus. Why on earth did his head feel like splintered lumber? Slowly, he realized he lay on one of the beds in the steamboat cabin.

"He's come to!" a voice shouted near him, making him growl as the sound echoed in his head.

The face of the boat's pilot, Captain Martin, loomed over him. "Sorry about your head, Mr. Bonnange."

"What the hell happened?" René ground out.

"Miss Wallace hit you over the head with a whiskey bottle," one of the men he'd played with said uneasily.

"Damn her! So where is the little witch?" René grumbled as he began to remember the rest of the afternoon's events.

"She and Wallace left the boat. Took all the money and fled. Wallace locked us in, too. We couldn't get out until

Captain Martin came along and heard us shouting."

René struggled to sit up. "I'll find those two if it's the last thing I do," he swore.

"Now, Mr. Bonnange, don't get so upset." Captain Martin attempted to press him back down onto the bunk, but when René flashed him a dark quelling glance, he dropped his hands to his sides. René eased himself into a sitting position and swung his legs over the side of the bed.

"We've already sent someone to the authorities," Captain Martin added. "They'll find them both and haul them off to jail."

A grim smile crossed René's face. "I'm sure the *gendarmes* have better things to do than search for one lone cardsharp and his companion. Don't worry. I'll track them down myself."

"Right now, you should see a doctor," the steward put in. "She hit your head pretty hard. I tried to clean and bind it, but a surgeon ought to look at it."

"I appreciate your concern," René said to the steward. Then he fixed his eyes on the man he'd been playing cards with. "It's more than others have shown."

The man knew what he was being accused of. "Now see here, Bonnange, I didn't see no reason to interfere while you had a gun on him. Then before we could move, the girl acted. Wouldn't have expected either of them to do such things. He'd been a right congenial player until yesterday. Claimed you'd been stealing from him. Who was I supposed to believe?"

The pilot flashed the man a look of mingled disgust and pity. "Considering that Mr. Wallace took all your money, I would think it's clear whom you should have trusted. The Bonnanges are one of the finest and oldest families in New Orleans. Surely you aren't suggesting Mr. Bonnange would do anything criminal?"

The man's eyes widened. "N–no, of course not," he stammered. "But they seemed such a nice pair—brother and sister and all."

"I'm beginning to wonder if they're really related," René said dryly.

"Come to think of it, he didn't behave too brotherly. He slapped her pretty hard while you were knocked out. She seemed to disapprove of the way he handled things."

"The *mademoiselle* probably wanted him to finish me off after she'd maimed me," René muttered, rubbing his aching skull. Yet for some reason the thought of Wallace striking the girl angered him. He shook off the feeling. "It doesn't matter anyway. The two have escaped for now. But his type never leaves the gambling dens for long. No doubt he'll appear again in town."

He rose to his feet. When he straightened, his fellow card player, who was considerably shorter, fidgeted nervously. "If you find them and want me to testify, I'll be more than happy to—"

René didn't let him finish. "Thank you. I'll keep your kind offer in mind," he said with sarcasm.

"Shall I see you to your lodgings, Mr. Bonnange?" the pilot asked.

"There's no need. My man awaits me at the docks. I'm staying in town tonight, so send the *gendarmes* to my *pied-à-terre* if they arrive and wish to talk to me."

None of the men moved as René then strode stiffly from the cabin. Outwardly, he was composed, but inwardly, he seethed. How could he have allowed the incident to occur? He should have been more cautious in exposing Wallace's cheating. Yet he would never have expected the girl to act so unwisely. To take such chances with a man holding a gun, she must have been desperate to keep her companion out of jail. *Mon Dieu*, she had really crowned him, he thought in fury as he rubbed his sore head.

Of course, she must have felt she had no choice. Wallace had begun blundering the moment René caught him cheating. Until then, Wallace had been fairly smooth. He hadn't cheated early in the game, but had waited until cheating became a necessity. Then he'd used his lovely companion to cover his actions. The man was obviously experienced at what he did. The girl, too, with her pacing the floor, knew what she was about.

And he'd thought she was really the man's poor beleaguered sister! Anger surged within him again, remembering how her look of innocence had fooled him when she'd pleaded with him to release her brother. Yet despite his anger, he couldn't put her face out of his mind. Such a lovely face, too, all softness and purity with no trace of her underlying deviousness. She'd no doubt used that look of wounded virtue on many a stupid card player. The minx! Did she think he was *un enfant*, that he didn't realize she was part of her companion's scheme? He knew too well what lurked behind those emerald eyes.

"We shall meet again, sweet eyes," he whispered to the lingering image of her. Momentarily, he remembered her seductive walk and the way her full breasts had strained against the material of her tight bodice.

Then he lifted his hand to his throbbing head. "*Mon Dieu!*" he hissed aloud again as pain stabbed him afresh.

If he'd known he'd have such a distasteful return, he wouldn't have gone to his friend's plantation to look at that horse. His trip had been fruitless anyway. None of the horses had been worth buying. No, trying to start a stud farm in New Orleans to breed racehorses wasn't going to be easy, particularly if he encountered thieves and cheats everywhere he went.

In any case, he'd find the two particular cheats who'd made a fool of him this evening. And when he did, they'd both wish they hadn't crossed him.

"You're truly a madman!" Elina shouted at Alex, finally able to vent her anger now that they were alone in the hotel room. "What has happened to you?" She touched her bruised cheek tenderly, and her eyes flashed sparks. "I can't believe you hit me. You should have listened to me instead."

"If I'd listened to you, we'd be penniless now," Alex muttered.

"But we wouldn't have the *gendarmes* after us, would we? It's not enough for you that we've lost our home because of your card playing or that we've been forced to flee because of Wyatt. Now you have to put us in even more trouble. Didn't you learn anything from what Wyatt did to us? No, of course not. You never do. You cheat from a man who clearly knows what he's doing. Then you threaten him with a gun and steal his money. Did you once stop to consider the foolishness of such behavior?"

Alex's mouth twisted angrily. "What else was I to do? He had all our money!"

"Which you stupidly gave him by playing with him in the first place!" She stamped her foot in frustration. "Don't you see, Alex? This man is a Creole. He might know our relatives. Now you've infuriated him. If he doesn't have us arrested—which he'll no doubt attempt to do—he'll at least blacken our names in this city forever!"

"I'll duel with him to uphold my honor," Alex said stiffly. "I meant what I said when I offered to do so tonight. And if he crosses me again, we will duel, I assure you!"

Elina sighed in exasperation. "Yes, yes, duel with him. As if you could best a Creole who probably duels at the snap of a finger. Besides, what honor have you to uphold? You cheated and stole from him."

"He was cheating too," Alex whined.

"No, Alex. I know you too well to believe that. You always blame someone else for your mistakes. You were cheating. You've done it before." She dropped onto the bed, pulling the pins from her hair so it came down in a cascade of rich auburn curls. "Tomorrow we may have to meet Papa's family. What will they say when they discover what a criminal you are? They'll be ashamed. *I* am ashamed."

Her brother's face softened as he saw the anger smoldering in her eyes. He sat on the bed beside her and tried to pull her close, but she resisted, holding herself stiffly away from him.

"You didn't exactly sit there and do nothing yourself, you know," he reminded her, smothering a grin. "You cracked him pretty good on the head. You pulled me out of a tight spot, Puss, and I won't forget it."

Her face whitened in abject shame at his reminder of her actions. "I hated to hit him. It was wicked to do so. Now he probably believes we're both criminals."

"Come, Puss," he wheedled. "Don't let it vex you. It'll be all right. You'll see. This man is probably a card cheat himself. He won't speak for fear he, too, might be caught."

"He threatened to take you to the magistrate," she said matter-of-factly, wholly unconvinced by her brother's optimism. "That doesn't sound to me like a man afraid of being caught."

Alex frowned.

"You see, Alex? You don't think. You simply act and then everyone must cover up your actions for you. Just like with Wyatt."

"You won't tell Papa about tonight, will you?" he pleaded. "Coming on top of everything else, it will infuriate him. You know Papa. He'll restrict my funds again. So if he doesn't discover it on his own, you won't tell him?"

She gazed at him, astonished that he seemed to think he would suffer no ill effects from his actions. In a voice decidedly even, she asked, "If we find Papa, will you seek this Bonnange out and return his winnings to him?"

Alex's face mirrored his shocked disbelief. "Surely you jest! Seek the man out? Risk his anger to return money that was mine in the first place? What kind of silly idea is that?"

Elina turned her face away from him as an unpleasant realization hit her. "What he said, about your using me to help you cheat. I covered for you the first time because I didn't want you to get caught. But did you deliberately use me the second time? Was that why you asked me to get the whiskey?"

Deborah Martin

The uncomfortable silence that filled the room caused her to dart a glance at her brother. He was staring at the door with a petulant expression which he always affected whenever he felt trapped.

He shrugged. "And if I did, so what? Don't be naive. Sometimes a man must act unpleasantly to provide for his family."

"Provide for his family?" she bit out. "You shan't blame this on me! We had enough money to survive when we left Creve Coeur. But not enough for you, oh no. You must have more."

Alex jumped to his feet angrily. "Yes, more. I had to have more. What if Papa's dead?"

His harsh words struck her like a cold gust of wind. "He can't be," she said with conviction. "Something clearly happened to keep him from writing us. I refuse to believe he's dead."

"But you'll admit it's possible. And if he's dead, then we're left to our dear grandparents. What if they won't help us? Then what will we do? We've lost everything. We can't live without the farm, without money!"

She faced him bravely, though her voice faltered. "Then—then we'll find work, as other people do."

Alex snorted. "Hah! And do what? Will you become a famous artist and have them all clamoring for your sketches? I think not. What do you know about finding work? Of course, I could always find you some rich suitor, I suppose." At her look of dismay, he went on cruelly. "I'm not Papa. I wouldn't refuse your suitors as he did. God only knows why he didn't choose one. You're already twenty-two, for God's sake! You should have been married long ago to one of the rich men who offered for you."

Though she knew Alex was seeing how far he could push her, she couldn't keep her dismay from showing. The subject was a sore one. Her papa's seeming reluctance to see her married had always hurt her. That one area never failed to make her resent the father whom she otherwise adored. She'd never understood why he'd refused all suitors without a word of explanation.

What purpose could Papa have in keeping her from marrying and having children? His refusal even to discuss the matter always wounded her. Not that she'd been very interested in her suitors. Still, one or two had been acceptable, and none had been so awful as to justify Papa's strange behavior.

Her eyes flashing, she asked, "Surely you wouldn't sell me to the highest bidder, would you, Alex?"

"Probably not. But I don't intend to spend my days as a clerk in a stuffy office, either."

Elina gritted her teeth, trying to calm her rising rage. "There's plenty *I* could do. I could give drawing lessons as I did in Creve Coeur," she said, ticking the items off on her fingers as she spoke. "I could be a governess. I could even be a seamstress or laundress if necessary. You see, I don't fear hard work as you do."

"I don't fear it," Alex answered coolly. "I simply find such drudgery beneath me. Papa brought me up to be a gentleman, not a servant."

"I see," she said with equal coldness. "So cheating at cards makes you a gentleman? Then I want no part of such gentlemanly behavior. It smacks too much of the criminal to me."

He raised his hand as if to strike her.

"Go on," she said softly, but her voice held clear defiance. "Hit me again. Now that you've begun the habit of striking your sister, you might as well continue."

With a curse, he lowered his hand and whirled on his heels, heading for the door.

"Where are you going?" she demanded.

"Out!"

How could he even think of leaving her alone after what had happened? She leapt from the bed and ran to clasp his arm. "You can't go out now, Alex! Suppose Bonnange sends the authorities after us? Suppose they come here?"

Her brother read the worry in her eyes, and some of the anger left his face. "Bonnange won't look for us tonight. His head will hurt him too much for that. And if I find Papa tonight, he'll use his influence to make certain Bonnange never bothers us again."

She stared at her brother suspiciously and continued to hold his arm, unwilling to let him leave. "Let me go with you. We can both ask questions."

"Don't be silly," he said with irritation. "New Orleans is no place for a woman at night. I promise you I won't gamble. I'll only ask a few questions at the hotel where Papa's letter came from. Then I'll come back."

Elina searched his face for some sign that he was lying, but he seemed to mean what he said.

"You've made promises before that you haven't kept."

He shrugged, acknowledging the truth of that statement.

"Swear to me, Alex. Swear you won't gamble tonight."

He sighed and took her hands. "All right, Puss, if it will make you feel better, I swear on Mama's grave that I won't gamble tonight. Will that satisfy you?"

She nodded, although she still had misgivings.

"I'll be back before you even realize I'm gone," he added.

She sighed. "All right. But leave the papers with me."

They had carried with them their parents' certificate of marriage and their own birth certificates, so the Vanniers could confirm their identities. After all, their papa's relatives had never laid eyes on them.

"I can't leave them," he protested. "Suppose Bonnange does find me? I'd need to prove I'm from an influential family, wouldn't I, to keep him from having me tossed in jail."

Elina knew he was right, but still she hesitated. A sudden fear had gripped her that she simply couldn't shake. "Wait until tomorrow," she urged. "Then we can go together."

"Oh, stop it, Elina!" Alex told her, impatient to be away. "Don't be such a child. I'm going now, so just calm down and release me, all right? It's late. Go to bed and get some sleep. You'll need to be rested for tomorrow."

Elina turned away then as she realized that more objections on her part would only increase his stubbornness. "Go," she muttered, half to herself. "Go then."

But when he'd gone, she threw herself across the bed and cried, the events of the day having overwhelmed her. "Don't be such a child," he'd said. Couldn't Alex see how awful it would be if he were taken away from her, too? He might be irresponsible and completely lacking in moral fiber, but he was still her brother. Until they found Papa, she had no one else.

Longingly, she thought of Papa. He'd been away from home sporadically for much of her life, but when he'd been there, life had been happy. His stern manner softened around her and her mother. He sometimes did seem overly harsh with Alex, but only because he wanted Alex to grow into a strong man.

With her, Papa had always been kind. She could remember his praising her paintings and encouraging her to learn as much as she could about her art. And although he sometimes withdrew into himself, preoccupied by some sorrow he never seemed able to explain, most of the time he seemed to enjoy his family.

She wiped her eyes on the sleeve of her gown. She wanted Papa with her at that very moment, so she could bury her face in his neck and cry out her sorrows. He wouldn't make light of her fears as Alex had. He would listen to her, and he would share her grief for Mama in a way Alex didn't seem capable of doing.

She lay there a long time, remembering her parents together. Things would never be the same. No more family walks in the fields. No more celebration dinners held to herald Papa's return from one of his trips. No more. . . .

A sob caught in her throat, and she shook her head, trying to force the bittersweet memories from her mind. Slowly, she sat up and dried her eyes. She refused to let her grief overwhelm her. For Alex's sake, she had to be strong.

She rose from the bed and began to undress as a dreadful weariness stole over her. Alex was right. She did need rest. Grateful, she slipped between the clean sheets of the small, but adequate, bed.

Yet she couldn't sleep, not at first. Her mind began to replay the afternoon's events. Once again she saw Bonnange's gun leveled at Alex. Once again she felt panic surge through her as it had when Bonnange had thrust Alex toward the door. She put her memories out of her mind determinedly, but she couldn't forget one thing. Bonnange's eyes. That look of icy suspicion after Alex had cheated the first time.

Shame once again washed over her at the thought that she'd been a party to her brother's actions, albeit unwillingly. With a groan, she buried her face in the pillow. She should have made him see that what he was doing was wrong. In fact, she should never have let him gamble on the riverboat at all.

But what could she have done? He never listened to her, and things had worsened between them every day. But he had never before lifted a hand to her. The older he got, it seemed the more he changed, the more obsessed he became with making money the easiest way possible. Nothing stood in the way of that desire—not honor, not pride, not family.

And what if they couldn't find Papa? What if they had no one? Alex would never engage himself in legitimate work and might refuse to let her do so as well.

Softly, she chided herself for becoming alarmed over something that might never happen. Tomorrow everything would look much brighter, she told herself. They'd find Papa and all would be well.

Yes, it would all turn out in the end.

But the nagging memory of Bonnange's threat to comb the city for them tormented her. When at last she fell asleep, it was to the sound of his deep menacing voice echoing in her mind.

Creole Nights

* * *

Alex strode nonchalantly into the hotel where their papa's last letter had come from. With but a glance at the clerk's desk, he went straight into the hotel saloon. Sitting down at an empty table, he quickly ordered a glass of wine. When it came, he gulped it, trying to put out of his mind the scene with Elina. Nervously, his eyes traveled over the room. It wouldn't do to be discovered by Bonnange. But the room held no one of any consequence, so he relaxed.

Already he regretted the way he'd treated his sister. He knew she had good reason to worry. The whole incident on the boat had been a fiasco from the beginning. But what had she wanted him to do? Watch that arrogant bastard take away all the money he'd worked so hard to accumulate? Bonnange didn't need the money. Alex had immediately realized from the cut of the man's clothes and the way he held himself that he was an aristocrat. To him, two hundred dollars probably seemed like so much dust.

But Alex needed that money. Unlike Elina, he had no doubt Papa was dead. Only death would keep Papa from returning home, of that Alex was certain. And now he and Elina were to be left to the mercies of a family who had never wanted them. He couldn't afford to lose any of the money that would make them independent.

Not that he wasn't going to make sure the Vanniers gave them their rightful estate, Papa's holdings. He'd take the Vanniers to the highest court in the land if they refused him and Elina what was lawfully theirs. He told himself he was doing it all for Elina, so she wouldn't have to marry a rich man if she didn't wish to. But he knew that wasn't the whole truth.

At any rate, his first duty was to find news of Papa. He had to be discreet, though. If Papa weren't in New Orleans, Alex didn't want to leave a trail for Wyatt and his bloodthirsty henchmen in St. Louis to follow. Wyatt would find some way to track them, but Alex could make it as difficult as possible.

Quickly, he called the waiter over to his table.

"More wine, *monsieur*?" the waiter asked politely.

"No, not just yet. But perhaps you can give me some information." Alex leaned forward and fingered the glass in front of him. "I just arrived in New Orleans today. I'm here on business, but my . . . er . . . papa asked me to look up an old friend of his while I was in town. The man was staying here at this hotel. Do you think you might know if he's still here?"

"*Un moment*," he replied. "I will fetch the owner."

When the owner appeared, Alex repeated his question. The man scratched his head. "I do not know, *monsieur*. Perhaps. I remember many of my guests, if they stay here often."

"This man's a Creole. His name's Vannier. Philippe Vannier. I was hoping to find out where he might have gone if he's left the hotel already." Alex said. He struggled to keep his eagerness to hear something of his papa from showing, but despite his control, his hands began to tremble.

The man looked both puzzled and uncomfortable for a moment. "*Monsieur* Vannier? Ye–es, I know of him. But . . . ah . . . he has not stayed here. He comes to the hotel to drink, but not to stay. Perhaps you should talk to his son. Yes, yes, his son could help you. I know him quite well. He comes here often after a night at the tables."

Alex's face turned a sickly yellow as he stared at the hotel owner. He couldn't have heard correctly. What in God's name was the man talking about? "His son?" he asked, confusion making his voice waver.

"*Oui*. Francois. Your papa did not tell you Philippe Vannier had a son?"

Alex's fingers closed around the wineglass so tightly he nearly crushed it. "No," he said, his voice laced with bitterness as a few realizations began to hit him. "No, Papa didn't tell me about this Francois." Then his face brightened. The man was confused, of course. He was talking about another

44

Vannier. "Are you certain you have the right Vannier? The man I seek has no son named Francois. He doesn't live in New Orleans. He merely visits occasionally."

The owner frowned as he concentrated a moment. "I'm sorry, *monsieur*. If there was . . . is another Philippe Vannier, I do not know him. The only Philippe Vannier I know is the man who sells the racehorses."

Alex's jaw tightened. No, there'd been no mistake.

"You should talk to Francois or *Madame* Vannier, Philippe's wife," the owner continued, oblivious to Alex's distress. "Perhaps they know this other Philippe. Francois spends most of his time at Orleans Hall, *Monsieur* Davis's new gambling palace. I can direct you there if you wish."

Alex stared at the owner for a moment, incapable of speech. It couldn't be possible! Papa wouldn't do such a thing! Other men had mistresses, other men had secret lives, but . . .

A knot grew in the pit of his stomach. Was it possible Papa's trips had masked something as unbelievable as another family?

Yes, he told himself in anger, remembering the strange look that had always crossed Papa's face whenever Alex and Elina had asked about his travels. His answers had been sketchy at best. They'd thought nothing of it, since Papa wasn't very talkative. And mentioning the older Vanniers had always angered Philippe.

No wonder Papa hadn't wanted his son to accompany him on his trips, Alex thought bitterly. Alex's hand balled into a fist. All those years of thinking he wasn't good enough for Papa when in reality, Papa was simply a lying son of a bitch! Alex couldn't wait to face him with his new knowledge. The man was probably even now with his other wife, while his real wife lay dead and his own son and daughter struggled to find him.

Another son. Papa has another son, Alex thought resentfully, pain choking him. *I'll see this other son and find out the truth for myself.*

"*Monsieur*?" the owner asked gingerly. "Do you wish me to tell you where to find Francois or no?"

Alex nodded and forced himself to relax, pasting a pleasant smile on his face. "Please do. I should very much like to meet Francois Vannier." *Yes*, he thought with a mixture of dread and disbelief. *I think it's time my "brother" knew about Papa's little secret family.*

Chapter Three

It is a question with many young men whether they will practice law, medicine, or deception.—Creole Proverb

Francois Vannier dealt the cards quickly in his eagerness to continue the game, the rings on his thin long-fingered hands flashing. The lamplight cast dark shadows on his already swarthy face. Any passerby would have thought he looked the very picture of the dashing Creole gentleman. But the cruel slant of his mouth and the bitterness that made his dark eyes so often glitter belied that image to those who knew him well.

Now, however, his eyes were bright with anticipation. Tonight he was winning heavily. He'd only recently mastered poker, the game the Americans had introduced to New Orleans, but he found he had a liking for it. Uncle René would be pleased to know he'd come so far. That thought gave him a bittersweet pleasure, however. His uncle was entirely too willing to embrace the ways of the stupid Americans. Francois himself only played the game because it amused him and not to socialize with the Americans, as his uncle did.

"Damn Americans!" he muttered half to himself.

"Damn Yankees," responded Etienne Pannetrat, Francois's closest friend. Unlike Francois, Etienne was blond. His coloring, though unusual for a Creole, perfectly suited his boyish good looks.

"My uncle says we must learn to live with the Americans if New Orleans is to prosper," Francois continued.

"And I say we should drive them from the city," Etienne's brother, Alcide, put in. Alcide's dark looks and oily charm had given him a reputation for being the Creole ladies' darling.

"Even the Spanish were preferable to the Americans," Etienne insisted. "These Yankees have no polish, no manners. Their only interest is money. Who are they to come in and bleed us dry?"

The men fell silent. Their complaint came up often, like a cadence, in their discussions. When conversation lagged, one of them instantly began their favorite theme and the others automatically joined in. Without the Americans to complain about, their card games would have been dull indeed.

"Mr. Vannier?" a voice suddenly asked in English from the doorway.

Francois looked up to see a stranger who stood uncertainly gazing at them. His accent was Midwestern, and he was clothed rather poorly, though his bearing seemed that of a gentleman.

Probably an American, Francois thought, although the man was darker than most Americans.

"Yes?" he asked curtly, irritated that a representative of the very people he'd been disparaging deigned to interrupt his game. He and his friends had purposely chosen a secluded room far from the noisy crowds of the rest of Orleans Hall so they wouldn't be disturbed. Why was this man bothering them after everyone else had left the private rooms?

"I wish to to speak to you alone, if I may?"

The young man looked about twenty-two, a bit older than Francois. And he stared at Francois with an unnerving intensity.

"Perhaps later, when we're finished," Francois responded, having no desire at the moment to talk to a Yankee.

The young man's eyes narrowed. "It's about your papa," he said with an unexpected iciness. "I assume what I've been told is correct. Philippe Vannier is your papa?"

Francois shrugged. "Of course. Everyone knows that."

"Do you know any other Philippe Vannier who might have come from New Orleans? You see, he was a . . . a . . . ah . . . friend of my family's, and I didn't know he had a son. I wish to make sure it's the same man."

Francois studied the stranger and didn't like what he saw. The man was hiding something, he felt certain, but what? "We are the only Vanniers in New Orleans and my papa the only Philippe. To be truthful, now there's no Philippe at all."

"What do you mean?"

Francois watched the man carefully for his reaction as he said, "He passed away nearly three months ago."

Unexpectedly, the young man's face drained of color, and he leaned against the door frame. Francois became alarmed.

After a short pause, the man spoke again, "We had feared as much. Yet it's a blow to hear it."

"Who are you?" Francois demanded, acutely wary of the man.

"My name is Alexandre . . . ah . . . Wallace." He glanced at the other men as he spoke. "We must speak privately."

Something in the man's urgent manner convinced Francois that he'd best meet this Alexandre's request.

"As you wish," he said. Turning to his friends, he nodded toward the door. "Why don't you both go get us more wine? This bottle is nearly empty."

They exited, passing Alexandre with a suspicious air.

"Well?" Francois asked, his fingers drumming nervously on the table top as Alexandre closed and locked the door.

"Did . . . did your papa spend a great deal of time out of town?" Alexandre turned from the door to ask.

"His business took him away a good bit, yes. Why?"

Alexandre's face grew even paler. "And there are no other Philippe Vanniers from New Orleans," he stated flatly.

"As I said, none that I am aware of." Francois was becoming impatient. He didn't like the air of this American and the fact that he'd locked the door. "I have no time to waste with—"

"I should give you my real name. Alexandre Vannier. Philippe was my papa as well."

The statement fell between them like a challenge. At first Francois could only stare at him in disbelief. Then he relaxed, his face lapsing into a slow grin. "So I have a bastard brother, is that it? And an American at that! How very amusing!"

Alexandre bristled. "I am not a bastard! So *you* must be the bastard!"

Francois bestowed his coldest stare on the American. "Papa married *Maman* in the sight of many witnesses. If you doubt this, I can bring you to the parish priest who performed the ceremony. Can you do the same?"

Alexandre's eyes widened. "Married? They were married?"

"Yes, so don't think you can claim any part of his fortune. In Louisiana, a bastard receives nothing."

"I told you," Alexandre said with exaggerated dignity. "I am no bastard. My papa—Philippe—married my mother as well. Here, see for yourself." He withdrew some papers from beneath his waistcoat and thrust them at Francois.

Slowly, Francois grasped the papers and leafed through them. A marriage certificate, showing that Kathleen Wallace and Philippe Vannier had been married in Creve Coeur, Missouri, on June 16, 1805, was the first thing he saw. Then followed two birth certificates—one for Alexandre

Vannier and one for Elina Vannier—both dated May 2, 1806. All bore a signature that was most assuredly his papa's.

He dropped into the nearest chair in shock, the papers clutched in his hands. He didn't speak for several long minutes.

Alexandre's anxious request finally broke the silence, "Please return the papers to me."

Francois, incapable of speech, at last forced himself to stare at his half brother, a cursed American. No, not wholly American, but worse. A half-breed. No doubt the man's *maman* was a servant wench who'd seduced Papa and forced him to marry her. Why else hadn't Papa brought her to New Orleans? Whey else had he married *Maman*, knowing he already had a wife?

For indeed, if the papers were to be believed, his papa had married this Kathleen Wallace a year before he'd married Julia Bonnange. The documents looked authentic enough. Francois stared more closely at Alexandre. Yes, he could see some family resemblance. And certainly it explained a great deal. Why Papa had disappeared for weeks at a time on those trips to buy horses when he could have sent Francois instead. Why he'd insisted on having Francois handle only the plantation affairs.

"How old are you?" Alexandre asked as Francois remained silent.

"It is none of your concern, Yankee," Francois said with a tightness in his throat as he rose to his feet.

"You're younger than I am. I'm sure of it. Have you any older brothers? Has Papa more children, or are you the only one?"

"You mongrel American, you can't be my brother! I won't allow it!" How could he have an older brother? And an older sister as well! It was an impossible situation! If everything was as he feared, *Maman* was not Papa's legitimate wife and Francois's claim on his inheritance was about to be nullified by these new siblings.

"You have no choice," Alexandre said threateningly. "Mama died, so I came in search of Papa, hoping my grandparents would help us." Suddenly he paled. "I suppose the grandparents who Papa said refused to acknowledge us don't really exist," he remarked, half to himself. Then he laughed bitterly. "And if they do, I doubt they've ever heard of us."

"Papa's parents died a few years ago. His only other relatives are now dead. Only I and *Maman* remain. But you're mad if you think I'll ever claim you and this Elina as my family. The Vanniers and Bonnanges are of pure French and Spanish blood. No strain of impurity mars the Creole line. And I, yes, *I*, will carry on that line—not you! So go back where you came from."

Alexandre stepped forward, reaching for the papers that Francois held, but with the agility of a man accustomed to fencing, Francois sidled away and put the table between them.

"Give them to me! You have no right to them!"

"And you have no right to Papa's money," Francois shot back.

Before Alexandre's disbelieving gaze, he snatched the lamp chimney off the nearby lamp and lit the papers.

"Damn you!" Alexandre exclaimed, throwing himself across the table at Francois's throat. Francois fell backward, Alexandre's fingers still gripping his neck. He dropped the papers and fought to push Alexandre off. He struggled to draw breath, struggled to break his half brother's stranglehold. His hands groped frantically for a weapon until they found the pearl handle of his pistol, which lay in a holster at his side. Without thinking, he withdrew the pistol and fired into Alexandre.

Alexandre released Francois's throat with a cry of pain, and Francois thrust him away. Francois stumbled to his feet, gasping for air as his half brother lay on the floor. Alexandre rose to a sitting position and pressed his hand tightly over his waist in shock, blood spewing from between his fingers.

A pounding at the door signified that Etienne and Alcide had returned. They shouted to be allowed in, but Francois wouldn't at first respond. He could hardly think. This was awful. Not only had he a half brother, but he'd wounded the man. Even if he said that Alexandre's claims were groundless, who would believe Francois when they saw the hole in Alexandre's side? Besides, even if the papers were destroyed, his half brother surely had other ways of proving his claims. It was not to be endured. He wouldn't permit this Yankee to steal his inheritance!

With deliberate intent, Francois lifted his pistol and aimed at his half brother's heart.

"You can't do this," Alexandre whispered, his face suffused with horror. "I am your brother."

"You should never have come here," Francois whispered back, and with deadly accuracy, fired.

Alexandre shuddered, his eyes widening in disbelief. Then he fell back onto the floor.

"Francois!" the voices shouted in alarm from beyond the locked door.

"I'm here, safe!" he called out. Swiftly, he stuffed the half-burned papers in his waistcoat. Then he searched Alexandre's pockets for any other revealing documents. He found a letter written by his papa and crumpled it, shoving it in his pockets. He grimaced when he found a heavy purse, undoubtedly filled with his papa's money, but he left it where he'd found it.

When he found the pistol in Alexandre's pocket, he smiled grimly and lay the gun in Alexandre's lifeless hand. Then after a cursory glance about the room, he opened the door. Alcide and Etienne burst in, halting abruptly when they saw the body.

"He attacked me," Francois said in a voice hoarse from having Alexandre's hands around his neck. Lies came forth easily from his lips. "He was a madman. Stupid Yankee fancied that Papa was his enemy and chose to revenge himself on me instead. I had to shoot him before he killed me."

"The magistrate will have your head for this!" Etienne said. "Remember what he told you the last time you dueled?"

"I know, I know," Francois replied. "But we could dump the body in the river." Then he cursed in frustration. "No, we'd never be able to move it without being noticed."

"Perhaps if you convinced the magistrate you were merely defending yourself," Alcide put in. "Tell him the man came to rob us at gun point and you were forced to shoot him. We'd support your story, Francois."

There was never any question of that. Francois knew much about his friends' lives, about Alcide's affair with his sister and Etienne's tendency to beat whores and leave them for dead. Francois had made it a point to know enough to keep them loyal, so they wouldn't balk at the unsavory tasks he sometimes gave them. He knew he could count on their silence.

"The magistrate wouldn't believe any story you gave him," Etienne countered. "He hates you. He's never believed you killed his son in a fair duel, even with all the witnesses. And he won't let this rest, either. He'll have you in the *calaboso* before the night's over, and once you're there, he'll make certain you hang, regardless of the circumstances."

Francois silently considered what Etienne was saying. It was true. Juan Oliveira would have him hanged if he could.

"Then we have no choice. We must slip out without being seen. No one could possibly have heard the shots with all the noise in Orleans Hall. But we'd best work fast before someone happens upon us. Etienne, tuck a couple of cards up the man's sleeve to make it look like someone killed him for cheating. He's a stranger. No one will care about his murder, especially if they think he's a cardsharp. His purse is full, so perhaps the *gendarmes* will assume he was killed by an honorable man, perhaps even in a duel, and they'll not investigate further."

"It isn't right to leave a man like this," Alcide whispered, gazing down at the body. "What if he comes back to haunt us?"

"Would you rather I hang?" Francois asked.

"Of course not," Etienne said, nudging his brother. "We'd best go, though, before someone finds us here."

"Yes," Francois said, his eyes on Alcide.

"Yes," Alcide agreed as he caught his brother's warning eye.

"No one's in the next room," Etienne said. "Let's pull him in there. That will give us some protection."

While his friends dragged the body, Francois stripped off his jacket and tried to sop up the blood that seemed to be everywhere. That proved pointless, for the blood stained the hardwood floors. Quickly, he took the remainder of the red wine they'd been drinking and poured it over the stains. *Perhaps the wine will mask the smell,* he thought. Then he laid the empty bottle on the floor beside the stains. He strode around the room, carefully arranging the chairs to cover up signs of his and Alexandre's struggle. Finally he followed his friends into the other room and threw Alexandre's pistol, which had fallen when they'd moved the body, down beside the dead man.

"Ready?" he asked.

They nodded. For a long moment he looked at the corpse with a slight twinge of regret. It might have been interesting to discover how Papa had managed to hide his other family for so long. But other than that, he didn't wish he'd been able to know his half brother better.

Suddenly something alarming occurred to him. The girl! What about this Elina, Alexandre's twin? For a moment he panicked. Then he told himself he had no reason to believe Alexandre had brought his sister to New Orleans. Surely she would have remained at home with some relative. And once she heard no news from Alexandre, she would probably give up the hope of hearing from him. Or would she come to New Orleans herself? Well, he'd deal with that when the time came. He could certainly handle a girl, if he were able to handle her brother.

His brother. He cringed at the thought. Then he turned his back on the body and left the room. He'd done the right thing, that was certain. But no one must ever know the truth. No one at all, he decided.

A very weary René strode through Orleans Hall, his head throbbing. He was beginning to regret he'd embarked on this wild-goose chase. He'd been to several gambling dens searching for Wallace, but no one had seen or heard of the man and his companion. René didn't expect to find Wallace in a luxurious gambling hall like this one, but who knew?

As he passed through the lavishly appointed gaming rooms and scanned the crowds, he spotted several familiar faces and regretted he hadn't come to Orleans Hall more often. When he'd left New Orleans at eighteen, nearly fifteen years before, Orleans Hall hadn't existed. René and his friends had gambled in private homes for the most part, leaving the public gaming rooms to the new Americans.

Strange how things had changed, René thought. Some of his old Creole friends still avoided any place where Americans were gathered, but many were realizing they needed the Americans to conduct business.

Bernard de Marigny, for example, had recognized the Americans' importance and had come far in his relations with them. Still, Bernard was one of few. Most of the Creoles were suspicious of anyone not of their society. They regarded even René warily, awed by his wealth and good name, but uncertain how to deal with his "foreignness."

The feeling was almost mutual, for although René had been back in New Orleans for four months, he found he had the same distaste for some aspects of Creole life that he'd had before he'd left. If René hadn't been visiting when Philippe had fallen ill, and if his sister, Julia, hadn't begged him to stay after Philippe died to help her control Francois, René might be back in England breeding and racing thoroughbreds and enjoying the life of a country gentleman.

He sighed. He couldn't blame his sister for wanting him to stay or for worrying about her son. Everything René had seen of Francois had proven that his nephew had no sense of responsibility whatsoever. At least René had been able to salvage his own ravaged sugar plantation, the one he'd sold to Philippe before he'd left for Europe as a young man. Francois had jumped at the chance to sell the plantation back to René and make some ready money, so he could waste it all on gambling and drinking.

Owning the plantation again, René could pursue the same dream his brother-in-law had pursued. Philippe had bartered in horses, scanning the new states in America for stock that might enhance a rich man's stables. René's own interest in horses had been kindled by Philippe after René had gone to live with his sister and brother-in-law. René had followed Philippe in and out of the stables daily.

But René wanted to go a step further than Philippe and breed his own superior stock. Only the plantation itself posed a stumbling block. It had been René's legacy to his sister, and she'd managed it as best she could while he was gone. He knew she wouldn't want it destroyed to make way for his stud farm. So René would have to keep the sugar crop for a while.

But with a workable division of the land, he could learn to live as he had in England. For Julia's sake, he must. He was now the only person who cared enough about her welfare to ensure she was provided for, since Philippe had died intestate.

René's thoughts so engrossed him that he scarcely noticed he'd been through every noisy room in the place until he reached a long secluded hall. Clearly, he'd come upon the private rooms used only by the wealthy. Wallace might be in one of these, he thought. After all, the man was out to fleece the rich amateur, and these rooms would provide plenty of rich targets.

One look and he'd be finished, René told himself. Then he'd forget the whole damn thing and let them keep the money. Still, it hurt his pride to allow the two thieves the satisfaction of having bested him.

After finding the first five rooms empty, he glanced in the sixth. At first it, too, seemed deserted until he noticed a man lying facedown in the farthest corner of the dimly lit room. From where René stood, the man didn't appear to be moving. René drew nearer. Then he noticed the man's blood-soaked clothes.

"*Mon Dieu!*" René said with a low whistle as he knelt to examine the body. He placed his fingers against the man's neck, unconcerned about the blood soaking his gloves. He could feel no pulse. Swearing softly, he removed his gloves and stuffed them in his trousers pocket. Once again he felt for a pulse. The body was warm, but there was no heartbeat. The man was dead. Then René turned the body over.

He rocked back on his heels in astonishment. How ironic that it should be Wallace! "So you met someone else who didn't take kindly to your cheating, eh, cardsharp?" he muttered softly once he'd adjusted to the shock.

Then he stood abruptly to his feet and left the body to search out the owner of Orleans Hall, John Davis.

When they returned, Davis paled at the sight of the bloody corpse. "Goddamn it, Bonnange!" he exclaimed as he mopped his forehead with his sleeve. "This is just what I need to destroy my reputation for running a clean house."

"He was a card cheat," René said matter-of-factly. "Most of your customers would feel he deserved to die."

"You know him?"

"You might say that. His name's Alexandre Wallace. He and a companion robbed me this morning."

"So you killed him," Davis remarked blandly.

René faced him with annoyance. "No, I didn't kill him."

"Then who did?"

"I have no idea. I found him like this."

Davis scratched his head. "The culprits caught him in the act, I suppose, and shot without thinking. Then they ran."

René's eyes narrowed. "Perhaps."

Davis leaned down and gingerly reached inside the man's waistcoat. "He's got a heavy purse here. At least we know it wasn't robbery." As he drew his hand away, something fell out of the man's sleeve. Two cards.

René frowned. How could Wallace have been so foolish as to try the same trick twice in one day?

Something a foot away from the body caught Davis's eye. He picked it up, and René saw it was his own pistol.

"That's mine," René said. "He stole it from me earlier today."

"Well," Davis said, his face expressionless as he straightened, "looks like he tried to cheat and somebody caught him. Maybe he even pulled . . . ah . . . your gun. Who knows? But whoever it was moved too fast for him."

All the evidence pointed to that being the case, but the patness of it bothered René. If the killer had been defending himself, why had he fled? Then René told himself he was being overly concerned about something that clearly was bound to happen to the card cheat sooner or later. Wallace had been on the road to destruction long before René had ever met him.

"Guess I'd better send for the *gendarmes*," Davis said. "Not that they'll be able to do much. You'd best stay here. They'll want to talk to you."

René settled into a chair and stared at the body. With interest, he picked up the gun to see if Wallace had managed to fire off a shot this time. But, no, of course not. The chambers were still filled with bullets.

Poor cowardly bastard. René could almost feel sorry for him. Wallace's inept cheating had certainly caught up with him. In New Orleans plenty of hotheaded Creoles and Americans alike wouldn't hesitate to shoot a man for cheating. Nor would they have invoked the *Code Duello* for a dishonorable man. When faced with such a scoundrel, René preferred to go to the authorities, but others weren't so circumspect with cheaters. No, Wallace hadn't had a chance.

Not that he deserved one, using a woman to cover his devious tricks, thought René. Then he sat up abruptly as he remembered the girl. Where was she? What part had she played in this?

Questions spun through his head as he waited for the *gendarmes*. Had Wallace's girl helped him cheat tonight? If so, why hadn't she tried to protect him again? Perhaps she hadn't been here. Maybe Wallace had abandoned her after what had happened on the riverboat. In any case, René wondered what her response to her protector's death would be.

Just remembering her whispered "please" made his loins grow warm. He didn't understand his reaction at the very thought of her. She was a cheat and a liar and God knew what else, but something about those sparkling emerald eyes made every inch of his body ache with wanting. He tried to thrust her image from his brain. Yet her sweet, low-voiced plea to let Wallace go still thrummed through his mind, despite his attempts to convince himself her pleas were carefully contrived.

"So you found the cheat and killed him, eh, *Monsieur* Bonnange?" a voice came from behind him as four men burst into the room accompanied by Davis. The voice belonged to the *gendarmes'* robust sergeant. "Oliveira will find this interesting. You've saved him the trouble of jailing the villain."

"I didn't kill him," René growled. "He was dead when I found him."

The sergeant gave him a sly wink. "The *Belvedere* pilot reported the incident involving you and *Monsieur* Wallace earlier this evening. You had every right to satisfy your honor. I'm only surprised the coward agreed to duel with you."

René cast the sergeant a look of controlled anger. "I didn't kill the man. There was no duel."

The sergeant's face clouded over at the insistent note in René's voice. "Then who killed him?"

"I don't know," René said firmly.

Davis hastened to tell the sergeant his own theory, pointing out the various pieces of evidence. The sergeant glanced at René again. Then with a shrug, he agreed with Davis that the killer or killers were probably local men who had reacted hastily and hadn't wanted to be questioned by the law.

René watched both men cautiously. He had to admit they had the right to assume he'd killed Wallace. But he certainly didn't relish being seen as a man who'd murder for something so petty as cheating at cards.

"I realize that the gun and the money are really yours, but I'm afraid I shall have to take them with me, *monsieur*," the sergeant told René after he'd searched the body. "We will need them as evidence."

"You'll return them later, of course," René asked, wondering if this was the *gendarme's* subtle way of asking for a bribe.

The *gendarme* seemed to guess what he was thinking. He stiffened. "Of course," he repeated coldly as if to impress upon René that he didn't take bribes.

Their eyes locked as both men assessed each other.

Satisfied by the expression of civic pride René saw on the sergeant's face, he was content that the sergeant would be fair in his dealings. "Do whatever you must to investigate this fully."

The sergeant nodded and relaxed. "What about the companion, the one who hit you over the head?"

Davis looked questioningly at René.

"A girl distracted us while Wallace was double-dealing," René explained. "They claimed to be brother and sister, but I doubt they were."

"Why?" Davis asked.

René shrugged. "First of all, they looked nothing alike. Her hair was reddish, and her skin pale as magnolia blossoms. She was a beauty," he said, his tone of voice softening for an instant as he remembered her face with startling clarity. Then he recalled the men saying that Wallace had slapped her, and his voice unconsciously grew steely. "No man would allow his lovely sister to sit with gamblers and help him fleece his victims, even if he needed money. All he'd have to do is find her a rich husband."

"Perhaps the *mademoiselle* was not . . . ah . . . pure and so could not find a husband," the sergeant interjected.

A smile rose to René's lips unbidden. "Pure? I daresay the *mademoiselle* was most likely far from pure. But I assure you that wouldn't have stopped many a rich man from marrying her. One look at those vivid green—" He broke off as he saw John Davis smirk. "Besides," he continued gruffly, "the other men said he struck her while I was unconscious. Few men strike their sisters. But far more strike their recalcitrant mistresses. No, I'm sure of it. He was her protector." He glanced coldly at the body. "Not a very good one, either."

The sergeant grinned in a way that annoyed René.

"May I go now, Sergeant?" René asked stiffly.

The sergeant's grin faded. "Certainly, but . . ."

"Yes?"

"Will you come tomorrow to repeat your story to Oliveira?"

"If I must."

The sergeant hastened to add, "Of course, nothing will come of it. The magistrate respects you and wouldn't wish to offend you without cause."

"You mean, even if I were guilty, he would hesitate to arrest me."

"*Oui . . . non . . .* I mean, he wouldn't doubt your word."

"And you do?"

"*Non, non, monsieur,*" the sergeant said anxiously as he could see he was bungling everything. "But you must admit it looks suspicious. Your gun is here. And in New Orleans, the duel is a common thing, *non?*"

René knew what the sergeant was getting at. In New Orleans, committing murder under the auspices of a duel almost ensured the killer wouldn't be prosecuted. Duels were, in a sense, considered respectable. "If I'd dueled honorably with the man, Sergeant, I'd have been more than willing to tell you about it."

"That is so. But I want everything handled properly, so no one can accuse me of failing to do my duty."

"Fine," René said. "But as you see, only the presence of my gun implicates me, and I have witnesses who will confirm that Wallace stole it. There is no other evidence against me."

"True. Except for, of course, the blood on your gloves."

"What?" René asked, and looked down in surprise. Damn! His bloodied gloves were hanging out of his trousers pocket. "That can be explained."

"Of course. It is a petty thing anyway. We would not arrest you, even with more evidence—"

"Enough," René stated, suddenly disgusted with the conversation. "I didn't kill the man. I wasn't that desperate for revenge. And send those who say otherwise to me!"

"And we will see you tomorrow at the magistrate's office?"

"Oui!" René said impatiently. "You will see me."

"I will send someone from John Bonnot's Undertaking Parlor to carry away the body," the sergeant said. He turned to the two men who'd come with him. "We have finished here," he told them, and they started to leave.

Suddenly he stopped. "What of this companion? Do you think we should find her?"

"If you can," René stated, his anger shifting to another target as he recalled the girl. He wouldn't mind doing his own looking.

"And her name?" the sergeant asked.

René's anger abated as he realized he didn't have the faintest idea. "Wallace called her Puss and other men called her Miss Wallace. I guess you'd better look for a Puss Wallace."

The unexpected droll comment broke the tension in the tiny room. The men laughed easily, and René found himself joining in.

So when the sergeant and the *gendarmes* left, it was with appreciation for the congenial *Monsieur* Bonnange who'd had the good grace to kill a villain in an honorable duel and the wisdom not to take credit for it.

Chapter Four

If there were no sighing in the world, the world would stifle.—Creole Proverb

Elina woke shortly after dawn and glanced around the room, hoping Alex had returned since the last time she'd awakened during her restless night.

The room was still empty, and she felt a sinking sensation in the pit of her stomach. He couldn't be gambling again, could he? she thought. He'd vowed not to, and she couldn't believe he'd break such a vow.

So what was taking him so long? Had he decided not to come back until he'd actually spoken to Papa? Was it possible Alex had found Papa, and they were so busy discussing what had happened that they'd forgotten about her?

Her mind feverishly produced reason after reason for his lateness, trying to avoid the one possibility that frightened her most—that Bonnange had found him. She didn't want to think about it, but unbidden a vision of Alex sitting in a cell crept into her mind.

"No!" she shouted aloud, wanting to block out the picture. At the same time she remembered Bonnange saying, "Your brother is a fool, *mademoiselle*. I hope you will impress this upon him later when he's in his cell."

Her thoughts became more tortured as she remembered tales Papa had told of criminals being pilloried in New Orleans. She'd never seen a pillory, but it sounded awful. She imagined Alex, his hands and feet trapped in the wooden contraption, wearing a placard around his neck and sitting in the Place d'Armes for all to mock and spit upon. How horrible that would be!

Trying to thrust the terrible images from her mind, she forced herself to leave the bed. Then she slowly drew her best dress from her bag and shook it out. Before fleeing Creve Coeur, she'd found a dress shop owned by a friend who was willing to give her the jade-green gown in exchange for her new mourning dress. She hated not being able to wear black for her mother, but it had been out of the question. Alex's enemies would have found them instantly if they'd appeared at the St. Louis docks dressed in mourning.

Unfortunately, the jade dress and the poor gown she'd worn the day before were all she had now. With the farm gone, they'd had only the money left in their pockets after paying for their passage to spend on their wardrobes.

Now she clothed herself with care, determined that Papa would see her at her best, despite her inability to dress appropriately to show respect for her dead mother. She lifted her thick heavy hair, coiling and pinning it atop her head in a simple chignon. After donning the dress's matching bonnet, she was forced once again to face the fact that Alex hadn't returned. Where was he, for heaven's sake?

Her stomach growled, reminding her she hadn't eaten in some time. *I'll fetch some breakfast for us both*, she thought, *and by then he'll surely be back.*

Taking the few coins she had, she left the hotel and found a vendor selling *estomac mulâtre*—a kind of ginger cake—and another selling strawberries. After buying some of both, she scanned the streets for any sign of Alex. The city literally hummed with activity, even though the sun was barely up. Vendors' cries mingled with the noise of squeaky wagon wheels and steamboat whistles, creating a cacophony of sound that Elina would have found interesting if she hadn't been so worried.

The many intriguing faces made her fingers itch for a pencil. She saw coffee-colored women with bright scarves tied around their hair, half-naked Indians, lean Spaniards, plump Americans, and even a scraggly child or two.

But there was no sign of Alex.

Slowly, she paced up and down, wondering what she should do. She felt terribly uneasy in these congested streets. In the country, she hadn't had to deal with such crowds. And the horses! There were entirely too many horses around, she thought with a grimace as the beasts passed around and in front of her, increasing her nervousness.

One passed a little too closely in front of her, and she jumped back. When she noticed people staring at her, she chastised herself for letting her childhood fear make her behave so oddly. At home, it had been a curse not to be able to watch Papa work his animals without remembering the time as a five-year-old when she'd been locked in the stable and nearly trampled by a frightened stallion. She never could erase from her memory the fear she'd felt lying in the hay sobbing for what seemed like hours until someone found her.

Fortunately, Papa had understood her blind fear and had indulged it. He'd never forced her to ride and had endured her insistence on travelling only in a cart or a carriage. Although even a horse-drawn carriage made her anxious, she felt safer with something between her and the horse. Papa had seemed to appreciate that.

But the horse's passing directly in front of her was like a bad omen, a black cat crossing her path. With a pounding heart, she hurried back to the hotel. She stopped in the lobby to look for the desk clerk, hoping he might have seen Alex. But the clerk had disappeared. Then, hearing voices drifting from one of the rooms adjoining the lobby, she moved toward them. She had almost reached the half-open door, when the bits of conversation reaching her ears stopped her short.

"Was he a professional gambler, Sergeant?" asked a voice she thought belonged to the desk clerk.

The other man answered with a tone of authority that filled Elina with dread. "*Non, non.* The captain doesn't think so. More likely he was some foolish Kaintuck who didn't know what he was doing. No professional gambler would be so stupid."

"What a fool!" said the clerk. "To cross *Monsieur* Bonnange once is unwise, but to cross him twice is downright dangerous!"

Elina sucked in her breath sharply and then inched closer. She struggled to hold her emotions in check. Surely they weren't referring to Alex?

"The *monsieur* says he had nothing to do with the whole affair."

The clerk laughed. "Bah! What do you expect? Dueling is still illegal, even if no one's ever arrested for it. But you know as well as I that *Monsieur* Bonnange took his chance to rid the city of a public menace."

"In any case, *monsieur*," the sergeant replied, "we wish to question his sister, this Miss Wallace."

Elina began to shake. So they *were* discussing Alex. But how could he have done something so idiotic as to duel with *Monsieur* Bonnange? She shivered involuntarily, wondering if Alex even now languished in a prison infirmary. And did they intend to take her to prison as well?

"Sister?" the clerk said. "I thought she was his wife. He told us so."

The sergeant chuckled softly. "Ah, yes. Doubtless she's neither, if you understand my meaning."

The two men laughed together as Elina blushed. She'd forgotten. Alex had told the clerk they were husband and wife so they could share a room and save expenses without raising suspicions. "After all," he'd explained to her beforehand, "the clerk's sure to think it odd if I want to share a room with my sister. He might not even believe you *are* my sister."

She hadn't liked the lying. She hadn't even wanted to continue using the name Wallace, but Alex had said he didn't feel safe using Vannier until they'd found Papa or were certain Wyatt wasn't following them.

Now all the deceptions Alex had concocted, deceptions she'd unthinkingly agreed to, were coming back to haunt her.

"If you will bring me to her room, I will speak with her," the sergeant said with a note of finality that sent Elina into a panic. Quickly, she moved back from the doorway.

"She left the hotel not long ago. But she hasn't checked out yet, so I'm sure she'll return. Would you like to wait?"

Elina glanced around uncertainly. What was she to do? If she stayed there, she'd be arrested for certain. Her first impulse was to leave the hotel that moment and not come back. Yet what good would that do? She had no money and nowhere to go—not yet anyway.

The sergeant chatted amiably with the desk clerk about other matters while she stayed hidden from their view, motionless in indecision. She had to know what had happened to Alex. He might be dead, lying in a ditch somewhere! *No,* she told herself firmly. *Not Alex. He can't be dead. He mustn't be!*

Oh, what to do? she thought, wavering between fleeing and staying. She could search for Papa herself, and he could find Alex. If Alex were in jail, Papa would know what to do. Yes, that was what she'd do, she determined as she started toward the hotel entrance. But she paused as she neared it.

What if she couldn't find Papa and had to go to her grandparents, whom she'd never even met? How could she tell them her brother might be in jail? Wouldn't it be better to know for certain what had happened to Alex before approaching Papa's family for help?

With a sense of impending doom, she turned back as she realized that the best way to determine if Alex had been wounded or even jailed was to approach the sergeant herself. Her hands began to tremble. He might choose to jail her, she thought, if Bonnange had reported the incident on the riverboat. Yet she couldn't just sit and wait.

Thrusting her unpleasant thoughts aside, she stood silently in the lobby, waiting for the sergeant to enter from the other room. When minutes later, he and the desk clerk walked in together, she forced herself to face them calmly. The desk clerk stopped in his tracks, while the sergeant glanced at her with raised eyebrows. She swallowed, all ability to speak having momentarily left her when she saw the sergeant's official uniform.

"May I help you, *mademoiselle?*" the stalwart Frenchman asked as he watched her stand there in confusion.

"This is Miss Wallace," the desk clerk interjected.

"I see." The sergeant's voice was noncommital. He regarded her cautiously, as if uncertain what to do with her now that he'd found her. "You came to New Orleans by riverboat yesterday?"

Her heart began to pound. So Bonnange *had* related the incident to the authorities. "Yes," she said, somehow finding the courage to speak.

"And you were *Monsieur* Wallace's companion?"

"I am his sister," she asserted, though her voice trembled. "I had hoped . . . you might tell me what has happened to him."

She waited breathlessly for his answer, her pulse quickening as she noticed he wouldn't meet her eyes.

At last he said quietly, "He is at the undertaking parlor."

"I beg your pardon?" she asked, her heart thudding so loudly in her ears she was certain she hadn't heard correctly.

The Frenchman's face filled with pity. "I'm sorry, but *Monsieur* Wallace was killed last night at Orleans Hall."

The wrenching cry that escaped her affected the sergeant immediately. He glanced back at the clerk, uncertain what to do.

Elina stared at him with unseeing eyes, her face a mask of misery as his words echoed in her head. Her brother, dead. It couldn't be true! Yet these men said it was. The conversation between the sergeant and the desk clerk came back to her, and she shuddered. Bonnange and her brother had dueled, but Alex hadn't simply been wounded. He'd been killed! She grew faint. Her dear impossible brother— dead! She swayed unsteadily, and the sergeant rushed to support her.

The sergeant had the good grace to look alarmed and guilty at the same time. "Forgive me, *mademoiselle*, for telling you so baldly. You took me by surprise. I didn't expect a . . . a woman like yourself. I mean, after what happened yesterday on the boat and then with what *Monsieur* Bonnange said—"

"*Monsieur* Bonnange?" she asked, her voice sounding faraway as cold pain washed over her. "He killed Alex, didn't he?"

"*Non, non, mademoiselle*. We do not know who killed *Monsieur* Wallace. *Monsieur* Bonnange found his body in a gaming room at Orleans Hall. We think perhaps that *Monsieur* Wallace was caught cheating and tried to shoot his way out of it."

"No," she whispered, tears suddenly starting from her eyes. "No, I don't believe it. Alex promised he wouldn't' gamble last night. He swore it!"

"I'm sorry, *mademoiselle*. We found cards in his sleeve," the sergeant said quietly.

Faced with that irrefutable evidence, she still couldn't believe it. She clutched the sergeant's arm. "You don't understand. He didn't go out last night to gamble! And he wouldn't have drawn his gun again, not after yesterday! It can't be! I don't believe it!"

"But you admit that you and *Monsieur* Wallace stole *Monsieur* Bonnange's money yesterday?"

"Yes, yes," she said in her frantic haste to make him understand. "But don't you see? That's why *Monsieur* Bonnange did it. He hunted my brother down and killed him because he was angry about what had happened. Then he . . . he concocted this tale about finding Alex's body. Don't you see? *Monsieur* Bonnange murdered him for revenge!"

The sergeant's face became very grim. "You accuse a man from one of the foremost families in the city, *mademoiselle*. Men in our city, men of honor like *Monsieur* Bonnange, do not hunt men down, even criminals. That is why *Monsieur* Bonnange reported the incident yesterday. Why report it if he wished to kill *Monsieur* Wallace himself?"

She knew what he said made sense, but Bonnange's words of vengeance also rang in her ears. She dropped the sergeant's arm and glanced at the desk clerk, noting the hostile glare he gave her. "You must listen to me!" she pleaded. "I don't know why *Monsieur* Bonnange chose to report the incident on the boat. But I know he killed my brother, and it wasn't as you say. Alex acted unwisely at times, but he wasn't a complete fool! He wouldn't have made the same mistake twice. You can't just let his murder pass!"

The sergeant steered her firmly toward a chair. "Calm yourself, *mademoiselle*. You do not know what you're saying."

She twisted away from him. "I know exactly what I'm saying! *Monsieur* Bonnange murdered my brother in cold blood, and now you're going to let him escape punishment!

Is he rich? Is that it? Does he pay you to cover up his crimes?"

Belatedly, she realized she'd gone too far in her anger.

The sergeant's face became a mottled red. "You dare to say such things about the *gendarmes*!" he exploded. "You, a whore of the worst kind, who uses her talents to help a man cheat others!"

She paled, horrified by his accusations.

"You have admitted that you and this Alex stole money," he said, gesticulating furiously. "Yet you accuse us of hiding a crime and then claim that a resident of this city has done the wrong. I see you are not only a criminal, but a foolish one!"

"I am no criminal!" she cried with growing panic. "My brother stole the money. I wanted no part of his scheme!"

The sergeant regarded her with an expression he might have reserved for a nasty insect. "*Monsieur* Bonnange says otherwise. Witnesses as well can testify that you hit the *monsieur* to ensure your companion's escape. I ought to jail you for that alone and rid the city of another criminal . . ."

Terror filled her, momentarily blotting out her righteous indignation against her brother's killer. Papa, her relatives—what would they say to such a thing?

"You mustn't!" she cried. "Papa's family lives here and they'd be terribly disgraced. Please—"

The sergeant softened visibly, his anger somewhat mollified by her pleas and her stricken expression. "I only said I *ought* to jail you, not that I would. Under the circumstances, I won't arrest you. Perhaps your companion's death will show you the error of your ways. You seem unaccustomed to such criminal acts. This Wallace, he led you astray, *non?*"

No! she wanted to shout. *He led himself astray. I just followed him blindly into the abyss.*

"May I see him?" she asked suddenly, no longer caring if she were arrested or not. She swallowed. "May I see my brother's . . . his body?"

The tense lines of the sergeant's face slackened. "Yes, of course," he murmured. "But you must promise to forget these fruitless attacks against one of our citizens. If I should hear you have been maligning people publicly, I shall—"

"I only wish to see justice done, Sergeant," she couldn't resist saying.

He drew himself up stiffly. "The *gendarmes* are already investigating *Monsieur* Wallace's death. We questioned *Monsieur* Bonnange this morning and will question others as well. If you had not been so hasty, *mademoiselle,* I would have told you that. But I understand. You are distracted with grief."

"Yes," she answered numbly. "And thank you for telling me of the investigation. You're right. I shouldn't have been so hasty."

"You must leave these things to the law," he told her with less harshness. He ran his fingers through his hair absentmindedly as he saw the misery on her face. When the desk clerk snorted behind him, he stiffened and became the stern guardsman once again. "But remember you remain free only because I have no firm proof that you intended to participate in your brother's actions. And the men on the boat, including *Monsieur* Bonnange, said nothing about pressing charges against you."

Of course, Bonnange didn't, she thought. He was guilty of a larger crime.

"But if I find new evidence against you," he continued, "I will search for you. You understand."

"Yes," she said meekly, her common sense besting her desire to lash out at the sergeant.

"Come now, I will escort you to the undertaker's."

Outwardly, she appeared resigned to the situation, having realized nearly too late that she could accomplish nothing on her own. But inwardly she seethed. *I will find Papa,* she thought. *He'll help me. Then these men will see that Alex, too, has someone of importance on his side. And justice will be served. Yes, justice will be done at last,* Monsieur

74

Bonnange, even if I alone have to mete it out. Then she followed the sergeant out of the hotel, a grim expression on her face.

René stood by the mantel in the parlor of his sister's house, smoking a cheroot as he waited for Julia to finish dressing for lunch. Francois entered the room and drew his attention.

"*Nonc* René!" Francois said with his usual oily smile. "What a pleasure it is to see you."

René greeted his nephew without enthusiasm. He always felt uncomfortable with the boy, even though the boy was really a man now. He preferred to think of Francois as the six-year-old child he'd been when René had left New Orleans. The grown man had proven a great disappointment. René wondered if he shouldn't remind Francois of his position as head of the Vannier family.

"Thank you for agreeing to accompany *Maman* this afternoon," Francois said genially. "I so hate these affairs. I don't think I could sit still listening to the ladies chattering after the delightful night I spent with Etienne, Alcide, and three charming . . . ah . . . women." He gave his uncle a sly wink. "The six of us began our wild night at dinner and didn't stop until dawn. We never left Etienne's townhouse, but we managed to enjoy ourselves. Anyway, I appreciate your looking out for *Maman*."

René surveyed his nephew with irritation, idly wondering why Francois always preferred to boast of his sexual pursuits than to discuss anything of import.

René chose his response carefully. When he spoke, his voice smooth and even, he nonetheless managed to convey that his words were not to be taken lightly. "The best way to thank me is to spend more time with your mother yourself and less time gambling, dueling, and whoring. She needs your support now more than ever. Her mind is entirely too occupied with grieving for Philippe as it is. She doesn't need to be worrying about you."

"I can take care of *Maman*," Francois said, visibly bristling at the admonition. Then he added with a certain peevishness in his voice, "But you do your own share of gambling, dueling, and whoring, no? What Creole gentleman doesn't?"

"The successful Creole gentleman," René said with unusual sternness. "I do gamble on occasion, and I've been forced to defend my honor once or twice. Certainly I'm no stranger to women. But I don't make a profession of such reckless living, as you and your friends do."

A cunning smile crossed Francois's face. "Ah, but rumor has it that you dueled only last night, *Nonc* René. Someone who was at John Davis's told me you killed a card cheat. The man considered you some sort of hero for murdering the vermin."

René's eyes glittered in cold fury as he stared at his nephew. "You should have learned by now that New Orleans reeks with rumors that, upon closer examination, prove to be rubbish. As I recall, you killed the magistrate's son in a duel last year. Are the rumors that claim you killed him in cold blood also true? It might explain the magistrate's hatred of you."

Francois flushed and fidgeted under his uncle's discerning gaze. "It was a fair duel."

"Perhaps. But I've been watching you since I returned to New Orleans. I've also spoken to your father's solicitor."

Francois seemed resentful, but he wisely said nothing.

"I realize you're only twenty-one and think the whole world is yours for the asking. But if you don't take some responsibility, your father's estate will be sadly diminished in a short time. The plantation needs more attention than you give it. Even the townhouse needs work. You will look into it, won't you?"

Francois's eyes gleamed as if he wanted to argue with his uncle. But he seemed to control his urge after a few moments and at last choked out the words, "Yes, Uncle."

Then they both heard Julia at the top of the stairs calling for one of her maids.

René stepped closer to his nephew. "And, Francois," he hissed under his breath, "Julia will worry if she thinks I've done something that could cause my arrest. If the rumors about that man's murder ever reach your mother, I'll personally throttle you. Do I make myself clear?"

Francois nodded, a hint of wariness in his eyes.

"Good," René said. He turned to stub out his cheroot, then gave Francois a smile. "Relax. As long as you remember that your first duty is to your mother, we'll deal quite well together, don't you agree?"

Francois managed a nod before abruptly taking his leave.

René watched him go with a niggling sense of apprehension he couldn't explain. It irked him that Francois of all people had heard about Wallace's death. Yet René could do nothing about it. Once rumors flooded New Orleans, they couldn't be dammed, and denying them only worsened matters. His best course of action was to ignore them, continuing to protest his innocence to the people that mattered—the *gendarmes*. Everyone else was welcome to their damnable speculations.

Except Julia, of course. And one other person whom he'd rather have kept in the dark. A woman with sea-green eyes and sweetly tempting lips. He chided himself harshly. The woman was probably miles away from New Orleans by now, on her way to finding a new protector. And remembering her face wouldn't do him a bit of good. None at all.

Without the real flesh behind it, her image was like Da Vinci's *Mona Lisa*—all mystery and no life. It would fade in time, he told himself, just as so many other images had. But some small remote part of him admitted it would be a long time before he forgot *that* face. A very long time.

Chapter Five

To whom you tell your secrets, to him you resign your liberty.—Spanish Proverb

Only a green wooden door stood between Elina and her papa's family. She stared at the building that she'd been told was the Vannier townhouse.

Please let them help me find Papa, she prayed silently. Although she'd gone to the hotel where Papa's last letter had come from, the owner had refused to answer her questions once he'd heard her name. He too had heard about the death of *Monsieur* Wallace. Since he'd sent Alex to Orleans Hall, but for what he wouldn't say, he didn't wish to be further involved. Fortunately, the Vannier name was well known, and she'd had little trouble finding someone willing to direct her to the Vannier house.

Was this the place? she wondered now, although the address matched the one she'd been given. With trembling fingers, she used the heavy knocker. Several minutes passed before the door opened, revealing a towering black butler dressed in full livery. He surveyed her, noting her dress and coloring.

"May I help you?" he asked in heavily accented English.

She answered in French, thankful that Papa had insisted they all learn to speak French fluently, as he did.

"I'm looking for Philippe Vannier," she stated, her head erect in what she hoped was an air of confidence. "I was hoping someone here might help me find him."

For a moment, the butler looked nonplussed. "Philippe Vannier?"

"Yes," she said a little less assuredly. "This is his parents' house, isn't it?"

He regarded her with suspicion. "And you are . . ."

"Elina. Just tell them Elina." If she said more, they might not see her, feeling as they did about her father.

The man coughed nervously. "I will find the master. You come in, please."

She followed him through the doorway and down a wide brick-paved passageway. When they emerged into a court-yard, she gazed about her in awe.

"Wait here," the man said.

She mumbled her thanks, unable to do more as she stared at her surroundings in rapt amazement. She'd never seen such a courtyard, filled with tropical plants she'd never even known existed. A fountain ornamented with laughing cher-ubs dominated the center, its trickling streams inviting.

Then Elina turned her attention to the three-story brick structure surrounding the courtyard. Wide arched windows faced the patio, their sills covered with pots of herbs. She sniffed the strong scent of rosemary and sighed. *Such a beautiful house*, she thought, knowing she'd want to sketch it one day. She'd known her grandparents were wealthy, but hadn't been prepared for the physical evidence of that wealth. Ashamed of herself for being so awed by it, she nonetheless couldn't help gazing about in wonder.

At one side of the courtyard stood a beautifully appoint-ed and very fashionable carriage, and beyond it a winding cypress staircase led to the house's upper apartments. Above her, wide painted balconies overlooked the courtyard. It was clearly time for spring cleaning as thick rugs in rich designs hung over those balconies, drying in the sun.

Suddenly her clothes seemed not so grand to her, and she began to feel terribly out of place. She shouldn't have come, she thought. Papa's family would be ashamed of her. And what if Papa weren't here? She'd be forced to deal with them alone.

Without Papa, the Vanniers might not believe her when she told them who she was. Why should they? Her clothing marked her as being beneath them. That wasn't her fault, she thought stubbornly. She couldn't help it that all had been lost in the fire. Her clothing was respectable, but by no means grandiose. Still, surely they'd understand when she explained.

But there were other problems, too. She didn't resemble Papa, so why should they accept her as his daughter? Before, she'd had the papers to fall back on, but when the undertaker had given her Alex's effects, the documents hadn't been among them. She'd asked about them, but he hadn't seen them. Why would anyone have stolen those papers? she wondered. And who had done it? The *gendarmes*? Bonnange?

Without the papers, she felt less than confident. If Papa weren't here, how would she convince them of her identity? She clung to the slim chance that he was with his family. Since Mama's death, she'd missed him terribly and all she wanted was to throw herself into his arms.

What would he say when she told him about Mama and Alex? The news about the farm would pale beside the news of the deaths of his wife and his only son. How would he endure it? She could scarcely endure it herself. She fought back tears as she remembered her mother being lowered into the grave, and then her brother, lying in a cold parlor in bloodstained clothing.

Mama's death hadn't come so unexpectedly. She'd always

been of delicate health. And there'd been money to give her a respectable funeral. But Alex! No matter what he'd done, his death was unjust! She couldn't even bury him properly. Until she found Papa, she only had enough money to have Alex put in the poorest of graves.

She knew Papa would share her feeling of outrage over Alex's death. He would obtain justice for Alex; he'd make that horrible sergeant listen even though she couldn't.

"You wished to speak to Philippe?" an oddly familiar voice asked in English, startling her out of her thoughts.

She whirled to find the owner of the voice staring at her in amazement. She stepped back instinctively as she recognized the one man she hated and feared more than any—Bonnange. What on earth was he doing here?

His thoughts were clearly the same. "What possessed you to come here, you thief? And how did you find me?"

His questions momentarily stunned her into silence. What was this wretched man doing in her grandparents' house? Did he know them? Dare she tell him who her papa was? She mustn't, not yet. He'd guess what she was there for and might do something to keep her from telling her story.

His eyes trailed over her with contempt. His head now sported a bandage, reminding her that he had good reason to suspect and dislike her. She thrust that thought aside. Her brother had paid dearly for Bonnange's hatred, and she refused to feel any sympathy for his killer.

He seemed to realize exactly when her surprise turned to hatred. "I see you've heard about Wallace," he stated.

His casually spoken words helped her find her voice.

"You murderer!" she whispered. "You monster!"

The virulence of her accusations seemed to stun him, but not for long. Oblivious to the presence of the butler, he crossed the courtyard and gripped her shoulders.

"I didn't kill Wallace, regardless of what you've heard. But we can't have this conversation here," he said, propelling her toward the passageway as the butler followed.

His denial of his crime infuriated her. "Let me go, you—

you fiend!" she protested as she struggled futilely to escape his grip. "I came here to find Philippe Vannier, and you won't stop me from seeing him!"

Bonnange smiled grimly, his hands jerking her closer so he could see her face better. "Philippe? So Pierre didn't get the message wrong. You really *aren't* here to see me. What do you want with Philippe?"

"It's none of your affair," she retorted, meeting his searching glance steadily, although inside she quaked.

They were already in the passageway when a lilting voice wafted from one of the balconies. Bonnange started. "Who is it, René?" the woman's voice repeated in French.

Abruptly, he jerked Elina up against him so he could clamp his hand over her mouth as his other arm slid around her midriff. "No one you'd know, dear," he called out evenly. "Go on in and finish dressing."

Elina's heart thudded as she fought to free herself, but struggling was useless, for his arm held her as tightly as an iron chain. She'd never been pressed against a man's chest before like this, and it infuriated her.

How dare he restrain her! She kicked backwards, her boot heel contacting with his shin instantly. With satisfaction, she heard his grunt of pain, but he didn't release her.

"We're still going to the Charbonnets, aren't we?" the woman on the balcony asked.

Bonnange let out an exasperated sigh. "Hold her here until I return," he murmured, and thrust her at the butler, who quite easily adopted the same hold on her. He was even more oblivious to her struggles than Bonnange had been.

Terror began to build within her. Why wouldn't Bonnange let her see Papa or even this woman, who, for all Elina knew, was a member of Papa's family—perhaps her *grandmère*? Did Bonnange somehow know that Vannier was her real name and wish to prevent her from telling Papa what had really happened? Worse yet, she thought with a sudden chill, did he plan to have his vengeance on her in the same manner he had on Alex?

Her confusion and fear mounting, she listened to the conversation he carried on with the woman. What she heard surprised her. Gone was the menacing voice speaking threats, replaced by a tone of tender solicitousness. He explained to the woman that he'd have to forgo their outing and apologized courteously. But what he said only terrified Elina more, for she was certain his plans for the afternoon involved her in a way that could only be sinister. All too soon she heard a door close and steps return. She would have bolted if the butler hadn't prevented her.

"Thank you, Pierre. That will be all," Bonnange said curtly as he rounded the corner.

Then Elina nearly collapsed as Pierre suddenly released her and left them.

Bonnange's hands lifted to steady her, but she regained her balance without his help and backed away, her eyes wide with fright.

"You stay away from me!" she warned. "You have no reason to keep me from *Monsieur* Vannier, unless you mean to kill me as you did my brother! And I promise you, if that's the case, I'll scream the house down if you so much as touch me again!"

Bonnange's first reaction to her speech was to arch his brows. "I'll admit the two of you gave me such a nasty time the other night that vengeance had crossed my mind. But killing you wasn't my intention. So if you'll just calm down, we'll go somewhere and talk things over sensibly."

"We've nothing to say to each other. You murdered Alex in cold blood. I'm not going anywhere with you." Warily, she continued to retreat, her eyes moving constantly in search of a weapon. When she spotted a riding crop hanging on the brick wall, she grasped it and brandished it before her, woefully aware that it was at best a puny weapon.

"Stay away from me, *Monsieur* Bonnange!" she threatened.

The amused grin that crossed his face infuriated her. "Ah,

chérie," he said softly. "Wasn't that crack on the head you gave me enough for you?"

"No, not nearly enough!" she said with venom.

His grin faded. "Listen to me, little spitfire. I told you already. I didn't murder Wallace."

She glared at him suspiciously. "Then who did?"

"Who knows? Any number of people could have. Undoubtedly, whoever shot him had good reason, since I found him with my gun beside him and two cards up his sleeve. You, of all people, should know he's fond of threatening people with guns when they object to his cheating."

She lifted the crop above her head, looking for all the world like an angel of vengeance. "He wasn't like that! It couldn't have happened as you say, you liar! Alex wouldn't have been such a fool! No, I know what happened, *Monsieur* Bonnange. You tracked him down and killed him for revenge. Then you no doubt told your *gendarme* friends it was an honorable duel. But I'll see that you pay, you beast. I'll find someone in this wretched city who won't be afraid to arrest the high-and-mighty *Monsieur* Bonnange!"

His eyes gleamed with an oddly chilling intensity. "Is that why you wish to see Philippe? Do you have reason to believe he would help you in your absurd fight for vengeance? Perhaps you were his mistress before you were Wallace's."

The absurdity of that statement struck her suddenly, despite her fear of Bonnange. Bubbles of hysterical laughter welled in her throat, and only with an effort could she contain them.

"*Monsieur* Vannier will tell you who I am, don't worry," she responded. "Now, let me see him if he's here."

"You can't."

"If you think to keep me from him, I'll scream—"

"He's dead."

The words dropped between them like a cold stone.

She stared at him in disbelief. "What?"

"Philippe Vannier died some time ago of typhoid."

Something broke inside her then. She gave a pitiful cry of distress, her arm dropping to her side as she gazed at Bonnange with pain and uncertainty written on her face. Her mind was a jumble of confused thoughts. Dead? Could Papa really be dead? She didn't know what to believe. Had Bonnange known Papa? Could he be telling the truth?

All along Alex had tried to prepare her for the possibility of Papa's death, but she'd refused to accept it. Now, faced with Bonnange's words, she felt numb, incapable of enduring any more pain. An image of Papa's face twisted and racked by pain flashed before her, forcing a sob from her lips.

Bonnange watched her, perplexity making his expression less guarded. When she caught him staring at her, she steeled herself to hold back the tears. Suppose this was all a lie? Bonnange's perverse way of wreaking vengeance on her? Why should she believe him, of all people?

"You're lying. Let me see his family. I won't believe it until they say it is so," she stated baldly. She didn't want to tell him who she was until she knew what he was doing in the Vannier house. If he was a friend of her grandparents, she would have to rethink her plans to have them help her get him arrested. But she had to find someone who wouldn't lie to her, who would confirm that Papa was indeed dead.

"Your meeting his family wouldn't be wise," Bonnange told her, his face grim. "They've suffered enough without having his mistress flaunted before them."

Her desire to keep her identity secret was forced from her mind as his insults struck her. With surprising agility, she swung the crop at him, narrowly missing his head.

"Mistress! Mistress?" she repeated, pure rage lacing the words with venom. "I'm his daughter, you animal! Are you so wicked that the only relationships you accept are illicit ones? You beastly scoundrel! Alexandre and I are brother and sister, and our papa is Philippe Vannier. I'll speak to my grandparents, regardless of your efforts to stop me. And I don't know what you're doing in his house, but I demand you leave at once!"

Deborah Martin

His jaw dropped as her words registered. "Your father? Grandparents? You must be absolutely insane! Daughter? His daughter, you say? Perhaps an illegitimate one, but even that I doubt. You have no place here. So we'll follow my earlier suggestion and continue this conversation elsewhere, before anyone else hears your ridiculous assertions!"

"I'm not leaving!" she cried, but he ignored her, taking the few steps between them in one large stride. Easily, he tore the crop from her hand and threw it aside. His hand closed over her mouth as it had before, gripping it so tightly she couldn't even bite him. She fought him every inch, but he had her arms pinned at her sides and her body squeezed so close against him that struggle was fruitless. In a voice of authority he called for the groom to saddle his horse.

"If I hear so much as a whisper from you before we leave here," he hissed, "I promise I'll bring you to the *gendarmes* immediately and insist they jail you. You know quite well they would. Now I'll remove my hand from your mouth, and you will not say a word. Understand?"

She wanted desperately to shake her head no but she feared being jailed almost as much as she feared him. So despite her anger, she moved her head forward the fraction of an inch his grip would allow. He dropped his hand from her mouth then and thrust her roughly ahead of him. Before she could protest, his well-knit arms lifted her onto a saddled horse. Then he mounted behind her, one arm girdling her waist.

Motionless in utter horror, she stared down at the tossing head and golden mane of the beast she straddled. *Oh, God, not a horse*, she thought in helpless despair. Senseless terror washed over her, a soft cry escaping her lips. For a moment, she was transported to that time seventeen years before— to that musty smell of horses and manure. Dimly, she remembered again the sound of horses whinnying, moving restlessly around her.

Then Bonnange clicked his tongue and muttered "*Alleé, Sauvage.*" Elina despaired as she heard the horse's name,

Savage, and felt him respond to the call, straining against
the reins and walking toward the open gates as if he'd like
nothing better than to dash through them. She wasn't certain
whom to fear more—the terrifying man behind her or his
wild beast.

She clung to the pommel for dear life, panic keeping
her immobile and speechless. Her skirt and petticoats hiked
up to display the lacy edges of her drawers and a goodly
portion of her calves, but she didn't care.

"Damn bonnet," René muttered as they began to move
along the street. His hand went to her chin and pulled at
the bow. Then her bonnet went flying. At her low moan of
distress, he murmured, "I'll buy you a new one if you wish.
But I refuse to have that monstrous thing poking me in the
face the entire way to Cour de Cyprés."

Cour de Cyprés? Where on earth was he taking her? She
only had a moment to wonder, before the horse moved into
a trot, and she stiffened in the saddle, bracing herself for a
fall. In her fear, she didn't notice where they were going,
didn't even care when the horse moved into a wide muddy
thoroughfare where carts emptied of produce were heading
in the same direction she and Bonnange traveled. They
passed fewer and fewer houses, and somewhere in the
haziness of her paralyzing terror, she realized they were
leaving the city. They rode for miles in silence, her knees
quivering every time the horse stepped into a pothole.

She must do something to escape Bonnange! But her
stubborn body refused to move as long as she was on horseback. Her limbs already ached with the effort of bracing
herself for a fall.

Bonnange, however, seemed perfectly comfortable astride
the horse. Slowly, she became aware of how closely he
grasped her against him. Her rigid thighs were molded
against his supple ones. She could feel the strength in
his powerful legs as they easily guided the horse that now
moved at a steady gait. Ironically, only the pressure of his
thighs against hers kept her from panicking completely.

Somehow being held by him worked to calm her fear of the horse. But she hated herself for not resisting his intimate hold, especially since his arm pressed up under her breasts, making her blush.

As her awareness of him grew, however, other fears asserted themselves. What did he plan for her? She shivered despite the hot midafternoon sun. He could do unspeakable things to her and no one would stop him.

"I won't hurt you, *chérie*," he muttered softly against her ear, as if he could read her thoughts. "I'd be a fool to harm such a lovely creature. But I couldn't let you stay there. You left me no choice."

Why? she wanted to ask, but the word stuck in her fear-choked throat. Instead, she continued to allow him to hold her, forcing herself to notice where they were going.

They passed fewer and fewer people as they rode down the sycamore-lined road until at last they were alone. "Now we can talk," he said, relaxing in the saddle somewhat.

She remained stiff as a board, her hands still gripping the pommel.

His voice sounded softer when he spoke again. "You mustn't sit so rigidly, *ma petite*, or you'll be sore tomorrow. Relax and let the horse know you don't fear him."

She *did* fear him, she wanted to protest, but couldn't. At her silence, Bonnange settled her more closely against him. That simply heightened her fears. Only when they turned into a drive that wound between a gallery of towering, moss-hung cypress, and he murmured, "We're here," did she relax ever so slightly.

Then he spurred the horse into a gallop, and she nearly fainted. If not for his muscular arm gripping her waist, she would have fallen apart. Fortunately, they galloped only a short distance before reining in directly before a house she could only describe as a mansion. She stared at it in silence, awed by the imposing edifice in front of her. Surely this wasn't his, she thought. She'd never seen such a magnificent house. What justice was there when a wicked man like Bonnange could own such a beautiful mansion?

He dismounted, then lifted his hands to her waist, and swung her down. She resisted the urge to fall to the ground and kiss it. Besides, the beast was still too close for comfort. She wouldn't feel entirely safe until she was well away from the animal.

Thankfully, a groom scurried to lead the horse to the stables. Once the animal was gone, however, her thoughts turned to the more lethal danger before her—Bonnange.

"Why have you brought me here?" she asked, her voice trembling.

Bonnange's eyes played over her face, as if searching for some clue to her identity. "So we can talk. I told you that."

She glanced at the huge white two-storied house that rose behind them, wide galleries encircling each floor. "This— this is your house?"

"Yes. We won't be disturbed here."

Those words held an ominous ring to her. Did he plan to murder her in his secluded mansion? Trying to control her fear, she dropped her eyes to the ground so he wouldn't see just how much he intimidated her.

Bonnange quietly surveyed her. "Odd. You don't look like Philippe," he said at last.

The skepticism in his voice effectively banished some of her fear. Swinging her gaze back to him, she drew herself up with pride. "I resemble Mama. Alex looks . . . looked more like Papa than I do."

"I hadn't noticed, but then you counted on that, I suppose," he said with a hard edge to his voice. "And, of course, you had a very good reason for using the name Wallace instead of Vannier."

She refused to explain her reasons to him. Her relationship with the Vanniers was none of his affair.

"This mother of yours," he continued, "why isn't she here to state her case?"

"She died a few weeks ago," Elina said softly. "That's why we came. To find Papa."

She thought she glimpsed sympathy in his face, but then it was gone so fast she doubted it had ever been there at all. Instead, his expression hardened into one of undiluted suspicion.

"Was that the only reason you showed up in New Orleans yesterday? Or did you already know Philippe was dead and hope to get your hands on some of his money?"

The fact that his accusation was somewhat true in Alex's case didn't prevent Elina from being insulted.

"None of this concerns you, *monsieur*," she said, tossing her head back in indignant defiance. "I wish to speak with Papa's parents. They can decide if I have reason to be here. They can tell me to leave, if they so wish."

There was no mistaking the blind anger in his face. "Philippe's parents, his aunts and uncles have been dead for some time. I don't know quite what to make of you, but I suspect you know precisely why this concerns me. It involves my sister and nephew, for whom I promised Philippe I would take responsibility in the event of his death."

"And what does your sister have to do with it?" she asked, something within her dreading his answer.

"My sister," he bit out, "is Philippe's widow, and my nephew is his son. So you'll forgive me if I'm not too congenial to someone claiming to be Philippe's daughter."

At first she simply stared at him, her face frozen in disbelief. Papa had another wife? But that wasn't possible! She'd seen her parents' certificate of marriage. It was authentic. No, Papa couldn't have had another wife. A million fears and doubts from her childhood filled her mind, whispering that Bonnange spoke the truth, but she ignored them. Papa couldn't have been a bigamist. He just couldn't have!

"I don't know what possesses you to tell such lies," she said, her shoulders shaking with pent-up rage. "But I'm not the fool you believe me to be. For some reason, you wish to keep me from . . . from Papa's family, but you shan't, not unless you kill me. And if that's what you intend, please get it over with. Yes, kill me just as you killed Alex!"

Bonnange scanned her face warily. "Is that what this is all about? Have you struck upon this strange way of wreaking vengeance on me for supposedly killing your companion? By destroying my family with claims that can't be proven? I promise it won't work. No one will believe your ridiculous tale."

"I *am* Elina Vannier, Philippe's daughter!" she cried. Her voice cracked a bit as she sobbed out, "Mama is dead, you say Papa is dead, and now you've killed Alex. All of them were Vanniers. Do you hear me? It's the truth, every word! Stop trying to twist everything I say to mean something else!"

"As you wish. Since you claim that your mother was Philippe's mistress—"

"Wife! My mother was his wife!"

"Oh, yes . . . wife. And I claim that my sister is his wife, how do you propose to prove your claims?"

She gazed at him in despair. "I don't need to prove anything to you."

His hands gripped her shoulders. "You have no proof, do you, little liar?"

"My parents were married in Creve Coeur, Missouri. Anyone there will tell you that!"

"And I suppose if I went there, I'd find a house filled with lots of evidence—Philippe's personal effects and business papers, for example."

She blanched. "N–no. Our farm burned to the ground." She added more eagerly, "That's why we left, Alex and I! We had to tell him about the destruction of our home."

His smug smile made her despair. "How convenient for you that all your evidence should go up in smoke."

"You must believe me," she whispered. But his implacable expression told her she'd have to give him something more. She could tell him about the documents, even though she wasn't certain where they were. "I—I have papers—my parents' marriage certificate among them."

His hands relaxed on her shoulders. She could tell by his skeptical expression he didn't believe her. She wished she could say something to make him take her claims seriously.

"All right then. Show me these papers."

Oh, no, she thought. *Now what shall I tell him?* She decided to brazen it out. "I'll show them only to a Vannier, and you're not a Vannier."

She hoped she sounded convincing, but lying wasn't something she did often, and she couldn't look him in the face as she said the words.

"I suppose you have these papers with you?" he asked.

She refused to answer as she lifted her head and tried hard to look proud and defiant. But she felt certain he could feel her body shaking.

"If you won't show them to me," he continued, his hand dropping from her shoulder to clasp her waist, "then I could always look for them myself. I wonder where on her person would a woman such as yourself hide important documents?"

His derisive words had the effect he'd intended. Her eyes widened in alarm as she felt his hand creep around to her back. Surely he wouldn't do such a thing. He was supposed to be a gentleman!

His fingers slid up to the buttons at the top of her dress.

"No!" she cried. "Stop it! I don't have them with me!"

His hand remained where it was. "Where are they?"

She swallowed. "I—I'm not sure," she whispered in a small voice.

He grinned broadly, his hands dropping to his sides. "I see. It appears you have misplaced your important documents."

She stared at him, her face paling. Of course, she thought, that explained why the documents had been stolen.

"You! You stole them, didn't you?" she accused. "It must have been you! You killed my brother and then took the only proof we had that we were Vanniers!"

"You'll have to do better than that." His brows drew together in a warning grimace. "This charade of yours is so inept it's beginning to annoy me."

"But why would you do such a thing?" she continued, ignoring his comment. "Why would anyone be so heartless?" Then her eyes widened in horror. "Perhaps you expected to inherit from Papa. Once we arrived, you realized you'd lose it all. That's why you killed Alex and—" She stopped short as she realized she'd said too much. The eyes she lifted to him were filled with fear. "—why you must kill me," she finished in a whisper.

Bonnange's face took on a deadly expression that gave Elina pause. She remembered suddenly that even if he didn't plan to murder her, he could do other things to her, unmentionable things, that might be even worse. Oh, why had she said so much? What would he do to her now?

"I have no intention of killing you," he bit out. "I will say it only once more. I didn't murder your companion. As for who is truly Philippe's wife, you may not have proof, but I do."

Without another word, he grabbed her hand and dragged her roughly toward the house. She stumbled after him, fear and suspicion mingling within her. Was this just a ruse to get her away from all eyes so he could take his revenge? She tried to fight him, but he only jerked her along faster, forcing her to run to match his stride.

Too concerned about keeping her balance to notice the house, she was conscious only of his tight grip on her hand and the reckless pace with which he pulled her down a long hallway.

They finally stopped in a study. Only then did he release her. She stood warily beside him, wondering whether to run as he rummaged through papers on the desk. At last he pivoted to face her, a sheet of paper in his hand.

"You see!" he said, thrusting it at her. "Any other man wouldn't humor your foolish claims like this, *ma petite.*

Consider yourself fortunate that I'm taking the time to show you that your scheme won't work."

Elina scanned the obituary notice in disbelief, centering on the words that said: "*Monsieur* Vannier is survived by Julia Bonnange Vannier, his wife of twenty-two years, and Francois Beauregard Vannier, his son."

For a few moments, she simply stared unseeingly at the paper. Then the letters melted into each other as her eyes filled with tears. The obituary notice was real, even if the whole morning's events seemed but a nightmare. Papa had indeed been married, had died still married, to another woman.

She read again the date of death and then the words, "his wife of twenty-two years." The tears streamed unchecked down her face. Papa had married Julia Bonnange *after* he married Mama. His supposed love for Mama hadn't even prevented him from marrying another woman within only a year after his first marriage! How could he do such a despicable thing, with no concern for anyone but himself?

She wanted to believe there'd been some mistake, that there had to be another Philippe Vannier. But the possibility that Papa had been a bigamist was too strong to ignore, for it explained so much about their lives. No wonder he'd been secretive about his family in New Orleans! No wonder he'd refused to allow Alex to travel with him!

Then she sobbed as another painful thought struck her. No wonder he wouldn't accept any of her suitors. A suitor would need to know about her family background. A suitor would ask questions.

Pain ripped through her. Had Papa planned that she never marry? That she die an old maid, with no one to care for, no one to care for her?

With sudden wrath, she tore the notice into bits, not caring any longer what Bonnange would think. All she could see was Papa. All she could think of was his treachery. She didn't know his reasons. She didn't *want* to know, though she suspected they had something to do with the

Vanniers and his infernal inheritance. But she knew she'd never forgive him for what he'd done, for treating her and Alex and Mama as if they'd been only appendages to his life. If it hadn't been for his secrets, Mama would be alive and so would Alex.

"What kind of man would do such a thing?" she whispered aloud, crumpling the bits of paper in her fists. Then she dissolved into tears that wracked her entire body.

Until that moment, René had been convinced that Elina's claims were simply a way of revenging herself on him for Wallace's death. She'd tried unsuccessfully to have him arrested. He knew that because she'd told him. And she'd made it clear she wanted revenge. What better way to have it than by destroying his family? After all, it did seem strangely coincidental that she should appear at the Vannier *pied-à-terre* only after her brother's death. If she and Wallace had come to New Orleans in search of Philippe, why hadn't they gone to the Vannier house immediately? And why hadn't they known of Philippe's death?

René had convinced himself she'd gone to the *pied-à-terre* in an attempt to reach the Vannier family with her stories before he could defend himself. He'd told himself he was going to enjoy putting holes in her nicely woven scheme.

But faced with her alarming and believable distress, he began to wonder if he'd been wrong. Perhaps she hadn't been lying—not about being Philippe's daughter anyway. A second marriage was absurd, but Philippe could have had a mistress, and this girl could be his love child. Perhaps he'd even told her he and her mother were married.

Her quiet sobs proved too much for him. Determined to comfort her, he drew her to him. She seemed willing to accept any comfort at that moment, for she curled against him as innocently as a child and let him hold her.

Some minutes passed before she stopped crying. He stared at her head cradled against his shoulder and wondered how on earth such a lovely girl had become embroiled with a man like Wallace. She seemed too innocent for Wallace's maneuverings, too ignorant of the world to be his companion. Yet she'd helped Wallace cheat and steal, René reminded himself, perturbed by the direction his thoughts were taking him.

When she lifted her head, he was unprepared for the look of frightened hesitation he saw in her face.

"You aren't going to murder me, too, are you?" she asked him, her voice so plaintively sweet he cringed at the fear she displayed.

Her question should have angered him, but it was so earnestly spoken that he felt nothing but an instant desire to disabuse her of her crazy ideas concerning him.

"I wouldn't kill you, *chérie*, no matter what you've done. I promise you that," he muttered, his fingers brushing one lone tear from her cold cheek. "And I didn't murder Wallace, either."

Her luminous eyes filled with bewilderment as she stared up at him, clearly wanting to believe him, but still afraid. Suddenly he couldn't bear to have her stare at him that way, as if weighing whether he was a scoundrel.

For lack of any other way to reassure her, he did what he'd wanted to do since he'd first seen her on the riverboat. He kissed her.

She seemed startled by his action, yet she didn't move away. His lips pressed hers gently, insistently, until her lips softened and trembled beneath his mouth. Her cheeks wet with tears dampened his skin. She tasted incredibly sweet, like honeysuckle nectar. Only with the greatest restraint could he keep himself from deepening the kiss.

"That's the only revenge I intend to take against you, sweet eyes," he murmured as he lifted his lips from hers.

And to his satisfaction, her look of fear had vanished.

Chapter Six

Let the needle but pass, the thread will follow.
—*Creole Proverb*

Elina lifted two fingers to her lips in speechless shock after Bonnange's kiss. She'd been kissed before, polite little pecks by the occasional suitor, but no kiss had ever surprised her like this one. Swiftly, she dropped her hand, her color rising in her embarrassment. What must he think of her that he'd do such a thing? Worse yet, what kind of hussy was she to allow her brother's murderer to kiss her?

But he didn't look like a murderer, she thought as she stared up at his finely molded features and warm, probing eyes. His bemused expression told her his behavior had surprised him as much as it had her. Two strong hands still encircled her waist, but they held her gently, as if she need only remonstrate against their presence to have them removed.

For the first time she wondered if Bonnange had told the truth about her brother's death. Alex had been angry when he'd left the hotel. He'd also been behaving abominably. That slap he'd given her on the boat had shown her he could be wicked when he wished. But wicked enough to break his vow, to cheat and then pull a gun yet again on someone? She wasn't sure.

Then she brought herself up sharply. Alex wouldn't have done such a thing so soon after her argument with him. She couldn't believe it. How could she make excuses for Bonnange? He might comfort her, but he'd also called her a liar and carried her against her will to his house. *No*, she thought, *I must be on my guard against these Creole gentlemen with their smooth charm. They're all like Papa and Alex—deceivers to the core.*

Slowly, she drew away from him. "You've proven that Papa married your sister," she said with more composure than she felt, "so there's nothing else for us to say to each other." She drew in a shuddering breath and then added, "Will you . . . will you please return me to town?"

Her words broke the spell that had engulfed them both.

His jaw tightened slightly as his hands dropped away from her waist. "And what would you do there, *mademoiselle*?"

His question stopped her. What *would* she do, with no money and no home? "I'll—I'll find work of some sort, I suppose."

"You have money?"

She fixed him with an accusing glare. "You know I don't. Alex carried our money with him, and it was taken by . . . by whomever killed him, I suppose."

Whatever little warmth for her lingered on his face now faded. "Indeed, *chérie*," he said in a voice that dripped with irony. "I assume you mean my money, the money you and your companion stole from me."

That much was true, she acknowledged to herself with a sinking feeling in her stomach.

His voice softened at her look of despair. "The *gendarmes* took that money as evidence, so it's lost to both of us for now. Was that all you had? What about your home and family? Can't you write to them for funds?"

"My family is dead," she stated in challenge. "All of them. The farm was burned to the ground, and we took everything out of my account when we left. Papa had money in the bank, of course, but he wouldn't let us draw on his account."

"I can see why," René bit out, clearly angry that she was sticking to her story.

"I can't get any more funds without having some proof of Papa's death to show the banker in Creve Coeur."

His eyes narrowed. "Of course. And you expect me to send this proof, I suppose. But by sending the proof, I will in a sense acknowledge that you are who you say you are. I wonder what a lawyer would make of that."

"No more than he would make of your claims that you had nothing to do with Alex's death!"

"We're back to that, are we? I assure you that my claims can be proven. Yours clearly cannot."

She couldn't help pleading with him. "You could inquire from the banker about me and my brother."

He laughed harshly. "I suppose the banker is a . . . ah . . . particular friend of yours?"

She went rigid and refused to reply to that nasty insinuation.

"So you have no money," he stated when she kept silent.

"What do you care? Throw me out in the street. It makes no difference to me. I can make my way alone."

"I can't do that, *mademoiselle*," he said after a moment's hesitation.

Her eyes darted to his face in alarm. "Why not?"

"If this story of yours were to become known, it would seriously damage my brother-in-law's reputation. Surely you see how that would affect my sister and nephew? Before I allow such a thing to happen, I must attempt to discover if there's any support for your claims. If Philippe did have such a relationship, someone in New Orleans must have known of it. His solicitor perhaps?

"Besides," he continued coolly, "I haven't forgotten your quest for revenge. You've already said you'll find someone in this city who'll have the ethical fortitude to hang me. I don't want to set you loose in New Orleans to tell lies about me. As it is, I'll have difficulty keeping the rumors from Julia."

She felt trapped. What was she to do? She must escape and find someone in authority who'd straighten the tangled mess Bonnange had placed her in, before he'd covered up his crime so completely no one would ever guess the truth. She didn't doubt for a minute that Bonnange had no intention of really investigating her claims. Why should he?

Yet it angered her that after all Papa's deceptions, she should also be deprived of everything he'd left behind. She had no name, no home, no money. And all because of Papa—and Bonnange.

"What do you intend to do with me?" she asked, her voice taut with worry.

He glanced away from her, his expression rigidly controlled. "You'll stay here, at least until I've been to town."

Her face mirrored her dismay as his words sank in. Such a proposal only proved he intended her harm. She couldn't stay unchaperoned with him, and he knew it!

She flashed him a mutinous glare. "And what about my reputation in New Orleans, *monsieur*?"

The brown eyes she'd thought so warm only moments before darkened with treacherous quickness as they met her gaze. "At the moment, Julia's reputation concerns me most. After all, you and Wallace have already rather effectively destroyed yours. So I'm afraid you give me no choice for the present but to keep you here, sweet eyes."

"Don't call me that!" she hissed. "I won't have you speaking so intimately to me, as if I were some . . . some soiled dove! I was as gently bred as your sister, and I won't tolerate your ungentlemanly behavior!"

His harsh laugh wounded her. "Gently bred? I sincerely

doubt it, unless your lady's education included methods of cheating and stealing from gentlemen. You almost convinced me a few moments ago with your tears and sighs. But I'm suddenly reminded of where and how we met. Your behavior wasn't the behavior I'd expect of Philippe's daughter, illegitimate or not. Still, I'll give you the benefit of the doubt while I make inquiries. You'll have to be satisfied with that for now."

She stared at him in open-mouthed astonishment. "You unprincipled wretch! You've probably known all along who I am! You probably found those papers on Alex and killed him just to protect your dear sister's inheritance!"

"That's enough!" he commanded, stepping toward her.

She backed away, her arm raised to cover her face. "Would you hit a woman?" she asked, the memory of her brother's slap fresh in her mind.

Angrily, he jerked her arm down. "Only your friend, Alex, would do such a thing! Although I can see how he was tempted. It would give me great pleasure to beat some sense into you!"

"Then do it!" she told him, her voice shaking with anger.

He gazed at the stubborn tilt of her head and the flashing green eyes. Then his eyes turned a golden chocolate-brown with some indefinable emotion. "I'd rather do this," he murmured, his hands moving to frame her face firmly before she even knew what was happening.

Then his mouth was on hers, moving insolently on her lips, forcing them apart to allow his questing tongue to enter. Fear tinged with something else she didn't understand kept her motionless, but only for a moment. Then she pushed at his chest, trying to escape the punishing thoroughness of his mouth. But one of his hands dropped to clutch her waist, yanking her up against him while his other hand tightened on her uptilted chin.

She beat against his chest, but he wouldn't release her. She couldn't think of what to do as an earthy masculine smell of horses and leather permeated her senses. Her lips tingled from the pressure of his mouth against hers. His lips felt so hard, so demanding . . . so persuasive. She closed her eyes to blot out his face, but that only made her more aware of his intimate possession of her mouth.

As his tongue swept over and around hers, her body became suffused with warmth. Sweetness, like a flood of honey, seemed to seep through her every pore. It lulled her even while it enticed her resistance away. Her hands at his chest no longer pressed against him. She felt his hand slacken its grip on her chin, but still she stood immobile, even when his fingers crept to her nape and loosened her hair from its pins so it tumbled down her back.

Abruptly, his kiss gentled as he explored her mouth and then slid his lips to caress the exposed skin of her neck, startling a trembling joy within her. Her hands clutched his shirt when he once again claimed her mouth. She opened to him, scarcely knowing what she was doing and no longer caring. Never before had anyone done such an intimate thing to her, yet she took pleasure in it, enjoying the way he possessed her. It was several long minutes before he lifted his mouth from hers.

"Gently bred or no," he whispered huskily between brief kisses, "you could play the soiled dove to perfection, sweet eyes."

His words stemmed the tide of longing coursing through her as nothing else could have. Her eyes widened in horror as she saw herself the way he must see her now, as a wanton woman eager for his advances.

Her hands balled into fists at his chest as she pressed against him with a small cry. "You . . . you . . ." No words would come that could properly express her dismay.

He ignored her sudden distress, attempting to pull her closer. "Let's not stop now," he said in a seductive voice.

That comment drove her over the edge. How dare he think she was some lightskirt? In a burst of strength fueled by anger, she shoved him away from her. Looking around in desperation, she spotted a heavy book. She lifted it and hurled it at him, but he merely grinned and ducked as it went sailing harmlessly by.

"*Bon, chérie, bon!*" he cried, clapping his hands as she glared at him. "I've never seen one woman play the innocent so well. On the boat and then here . . . Why, you're quite convincing. But before you take to throwing something more breakable, I'd best leave."

Horror gripped her as she saw he intended to continue with his plans. "You can't really mean to imprison me on your plantation!" she exclaimed in dismay as he strode for the door, leaving her standing in the middle of the room.

His only answer was to call out into the hallway for someone named Louis.

The call was answered not by a slave as she'd expected, but by a wiry old Frenchman. "*Monsieur?*" the man asked, clearly not surprised to find his master alone in the study with a woman.

"I'm afraid you'll have to put aside your other duties for the day," Bonnange said in French. "This young lady needs company until I return. She's not to leave the plantation under any circumstances."

"*Oui,*" Louis answered, his eyes twinkling.

"I don't need company," Elina told the smiling servant in flawless French. "This man is holding me here against my will, and I demand that you help me!"

Louis flashed his master a look of sympathy, but Bonnange only laughed. "So you speak French, do you?" Bonnange said. "I suppose Philippe is purported to have taught you."

"*Oui, monsieur,*" she said icily. "*Et tu es un chenapan et un diable—*"

"Enough, enough," he cried, his tone sarcastic. "Louis already knows I'm a scoundrel and a devil, so you won't change his mind any. He may even think of some stories to tell you about my scandalous adventures. And don't think you can use those green eyes of yours to mesmerize him into helping you. He'll keep you here as I ask because he

103

knows me well enough to know I don't act without provocation. And you, *mademoiselle*, have given me enough provocation to excuse my behavior for a lifetime!"

With those words, he turned on his heels and left, slamming the door behind him. Louis had the good grace not to laugh, but his tightly pursed, quivering lips told her that he found the entire incident amusing.

She gave Louis a look of undisguised animosity. "Men are all wretched creatures!" she stated, sinking into the nearest chair in exasperation. "Eve may have tempted Adam with the apple, but his contemptible behavior surely drove her to it!"

Louis regarded her thoughtfully. "You are upset, *non*?" he asked. "But you should not worry, *mademoiselle*. *Monsieur* Bonnange will not leave you here alone for long. He is kind to all his mistresses. You will have as much of his attention as he can spare."

Louis had chosen to say the one thing that would *not* mollify Elina. She had no doubts about what he meant, though her knowledge of such women was decidedly vague. But she knew, from things Alex had told her, that men often kept mistresses for the purpose of "having their pleasure with them." Unfortunately, Alex hadn't ever told her the details of such doings, but she knew something wicked was involved. And to be taken for such a woman three times in one day was more than she could bear.

She rose to face Louis in indignation. "His mistresses! I'm not his mistress, I'll have you know. How many hordes of women does this man keep, anyway? And where are they hiding?" she asked, one sweep of her hand indicating the entire house. "I suppose I'll have to share a room with one or two of them!"

Her anger renewed, she stalked the room like a caged lioness, her hair tossing wildly about her shoulders.

"You do not wish to be *monsieur's* companion?" Louis asked in amazement.

"Certainly not! Especially if he makes a practice of keeping women imprisoned in his house!"

"*Non, mademoiselle,*" Louis hastened to tell her. "You are the first. Most women, they find the *monsieur* very attractive. They would stay of their own desire, if he would let them. He does not usually keep a mistress in his residence. But he never lacks for the women."

His knowing grin infuriated Elina, because unfortunately she, too, found the *monsieur* extremely attractive. It irked her to acknowledge it, even to herself. Her lips tingled and her blood quickened as she recalled René's kiss. She rubbed the back of her hand across her lips unconsciously, as if she might erase the memory of his mouth on hers.

"Why does the *monsieur* wish you to stay, if you do not desire his company?" Louis asked.

Elina chewed on her lower lip, wondering if she should tell him the whole story. She wanted someone on her side, but she wasn't certain she could trust any servant of Bonnange's. Besides, if she told Louis the truth, it would simply convince Bonnange she couldn't be trusted to be discreet. Then he'd never release her.

With a sigh, she decided to give Louis only part of the story. "Your dear *monsieur* and I have had a difference of opinion about a relative of ours—*Monsieur* Philippe Vannier. And until we resolve it, he insists on keeping me here."

Louis winked and laughed. "So that is his excuse for keeping his lovely lady here, is it? His sister's family?"

His laugh bewildered Elina. "Are you saying he isn't concerned about his sister's family?"

"But, of course, he is," Louis protested. "He adores his sister. He was quite fond of her late husband as well. But a disagreement over a distant relative is such a paltry thing for which to keep a woman prisoner."

Louis's second wink irritated her extremely. His implication that she and Bonnange were merely having a lover's spat over some invented disagreement annoyed her. But she knew she mustn't set him straight, not when she could

Deborah Martin

use his erroneous perception to find out about her father's second family.

"I wouldn't have thought that *Monsieur* Bonnange and *Monsieur* Vannier would deal well together," she said, hoping Louis was really the talkative man he appeared to be.

He was. "Oh, *mademoiselle*, *Monsieur* Bonnange has always had great respect for his sister's husband. *Monsieur* Vannier was *très genereux* to my master when he was but a *garçon*. You see, *Monsieur* Bonnange's parents died when he was only twelve. *Madame* convinced her new husband to care for *Monsieur* Bonnange until he could manage his parent's plantation alone. *Monsieur* Bonnange has always been grateful to his brother-in-law and sister for their kindness to him. He would do anything for his sister if she but asked."

Even kill to protect his sister's inheritance, thought Elina, forcing her anger down with an effort. She made herself continue her casual questioning, determined to discover enough about Bonnange to prove her claims. She must find out as much as she could while Louis was in a discursive mood.

"So *Monsieur* Bonnange lived with his sister until he reached his majority?" she asked, her tone carefully nonchalant.

Louis shook his head. "Not so long as that, *mademoiselle*. When he was sixteen, he sold this plantation to *Monsieur* Vannier and left New Orleans to go abroad."

"Why?"

"I do not know. He never speaks of why he left."

The merest chill of fear struck her. What mysterious crimes had Bonnange committed in the past to make him leave New Orleans?

"But he preferred England to New Orleans," Louis continued. "Did he tell you he owned a horse-breeding farm there?"

"He has told me nothing of any substance," she mur-

106

mured. Then her expression turned curious. "Why did he return here?"

Louis's face darkened. "It was not really his choice. In the past he had occasionally returned to visit his sister, but had never wished to stay, although *madame* begged him to. But during his last visit, *Monsieur* Vannier became ill. And then once *Monsieur* Vannier died, *Monsieur* Bonnange felt it his duty to stay and help *madame*, so he brought Cour de Cyprés back from his nephew. But I know he would rather be in England."

Elina didn't know how to interpret such information. This refusal to stay with his family and estate disturbed her. "And you? Have you worked for him all your life?"

"Except for his first few years abroad," Louis said, his expression one of fondness. "I began serving him when he was a boy. He was a wild one, that one. Such a trickster. But he is a good man. Deep inside he is good."

Good! she nearly cried aloud. Didn't Louis realize his master was a murderer? She scrutinized the old man's face and sighed. Yes, she thought sadly, he probably did. She was beginning to think that New Orleans citizens were so familiar with death—from yellow fever, typhoid, and yes, from thieves and murderers—that they wouldn't blink twice to find another murderer in their midst. In fact, they seemed to have made a hero out of Bonnange for having killed her brother.

Suddenly she wondered if she could use that to her advantage. "Louis, do you know if your master has fought any duels recently?" she asked, hoping the question sounded innocent.

Evidently it didn't, for he narrowed his eyes in suspicion. "Why do you ask?"

She smiled with feigned timidity. "Oh, I was just curious. I heard the most remarkable story today about a duel he fought last night. He sounded so brave and fearless, quite unlike what I would have expected. I just wondered if it were true."

Louis's weathered old face reflected his uncertainty. She knew he was wondering whether to keep silent or to try to convince this skittish woman, whom his master seemed to desire, that his master was a courageous man. His matchmaking instincts apparently prevailed.

"The master is an expert duelist, a brave and indomitable foe," he stated with initial reluctance. Then he drew himself up proudly in spite of himself as he went on, "He never misses his man."

"And last night?" she prompted.

He shrugged. "Last night? I have not heard him say, but his gloves were bloodied when he came home, so it is possible. With what man did he duel?"

Her lips tightening were the only evidence she gave of the effect his words had on her. "No one of importance, I think," she said with bitter irony.

Louis glanced at her. "The *mademoiselle* seems unwell," he said, a look of concern on his face.

"No, no, I'm fine," she told him, turning her back to him so he couldn't glimpse the turmoil that gripped her.

"Is *mademoiselle* hungry perhaps?" he inquired.

His question brought her out of her troubling thoughts and reminded her that she'd eaten nothing since noon the day before except for her meager breakfast. But she was too upset to eat.

"I have no appetite," she muttered.

"Nonetheless, I shall bring you a light *déjeuner*," Louis said with kindness as he turned to leave.

She whirled around at his words. "You're going to leave me here? I—I thought your master said you were to be my companion at all times."

He winked. "I'm sure he meant me only to make certain you do not leave. I don't think *monsieur* would wish me to be your shadow. And I think it would be *très difficile* for you to saddle a horse and ride away before I could return with nourishment. Don't you agree?"

She couldn't help but smile at his matter-of-fact approach

to her escaping. "I suppose you're right," she told him, wondering how much more freedom he'd give her if he knew there was absolutely no chance of her willingly saddling a horse for any reason, much less riding away on it. The only way she'd consider escaping was on foot and at the moment, it seemed unlikely such an escape could succeed.

"I will find something to tempt the *mademoiselle's* appetite so she will not wish to leave. *D'accord*?"

She gave a small shrug. Nonetheless he left the room with a confident look.

When he was gone, she surveyed her surroundings. In addition to the desk, the study contained ceiling-to-floor shelves lined with books. Most of the volumes dealt with planting and growing sugar, but she also saw several books on politics. And tucked away on a shelf near the floor were slim volumes of poetry by Percy Bysshe Shelley as well as novels by James Fenimore Cooper, Alexandre Dumas, and a number of other authors. A few thick volumes of Shakespeare also graced the shelves.

For a murderer, Bonnange was certainly well read, she thought. But that didn't excuse his behavior. Even if he hadn't been lying, even if someone else had killed Alex, he had no right to hold her prisoner. But what Louis had told her convinced her Bonnange was lying.

She paced the room, wondering how she could prove Bonnange was a villain beyond a shadow of a doubt. With the right evidence, she might convince the magistrate that Bonnange had deliberately murdered Alex to protect his sister's inheritance. The more she thought about it, the more furious she became. No doubt he, too, wanted a piece of that inheritance! After all, it must take a great deal of money to maintain a plantation like Cour de Cyprés.

Her eyes turned to the desk. Perhaps his plantation books would reveal his need for money. Yes, she should glance through his ledgers for evidence. But first she must get Louis out of her hair while she searched.

Deborah Martin

When Louis returned with his *déjeuner*, she was sitting in an armchair, calmly reading a passage from Shelley. He greeted her with warmth, clearly pleased to see her amusing herself.

The sight and smell of so much food—sliced cold meats, chicken, a loaf of crusty bread, apples, and strawberries—brought back some of her appetite. She told herself she'd only nibble a bit, but after the first bite, hunger took over and she found herself eating more and more of the "light *déjeuner*" as Louis looked on approvingly. When she stopped at last, she was dismayed to see how much she'd eaten, a feeling only heightened by his joking comment that "the *mademoiselle* managed to find her appetite."

"The *mademoiselle* eats like a bird," Louis added with delight. "Three times her weight."

Frowning, she set her fork down. "Are you always this complimentary to *monsieur's* mistresses, Louis?" she asked petulantly. "If so, it's no wonder he doesn't keep them here with him."

Louis laughed. "You are right, *mademoiselle*. I am as much a wretched creature as *monsieur*. But at least I feed you well, *non*?"

"That you do," she admitted, wiping the last crumbs from her mouth. Then she gave an exaggerated yawn. "But I fear you've fed me too well. All that food has made me tired."

"Oh, of course," he said, jumping to his feet. "You should rest. I will show you to your room."

"No! I mean . . . if *monsieur* returns to find me in bed, he might get the wrong idea."

Louis looked at her in perplexity. "You will have to sleep eventually."

"Yes . . . Well, right now I think I prefer to stretch out on that settee there. It looks quite comfortable. If *monsieur* returns before I wake up, he . . . he won't be tempted to do things he shouldn't. *N'est-ce pas*? And when I awaken, I can read a book."

110

Louis shrugged. "As *mademoiselle* wishes." Then he left the room with the tray of dishes, shaking his head and muttering about the strange whims of ladies.

As soon as he was out of sight, Elina darted to the desk. It took her only moments to find the plantation ledgers. She settled into the chair to peruse them, thankful that handling the household accounts had been one of her duties at home. Some time passed, however, before she could decipher Bonnange's system well enough to read the books knowledgeably.

But once she had, she found some astounding information. René Bonnange was no fortune hunter, that was certain. Although the estate had clearly been in a deplorable condition when Bonnange had bought it back, he'd managed in only three months to put it on its feet again. He must have had income from somewhere else that he poured into the plantation. He also had other investments that seemed to bring him large dividends.

She leafed through the books with increasing perplexity. He owned no slaves, only hired workmen, yet he'd already made substantial improvements on the estate. And it was evident that he'd spent most, if not all, of his past months in New Orleans at the plantation, expending all his effort there. She knew from Papa's stories that many of the wealthiest Creole planters spent little time at their plantations. They left overseers to do the work. In the winter, these planters lived in *pied-à-terres* in New Orleans. They summered outside the city, but only to escape the merciless heat and mosquitoes that plagued New Orleans from April to September.

Yet Bonnange clearly didn't subscribe to that common practice. This bit of information annoyed her, for it implied he was far more responsible than she wanted to believe. She refused to accept that, so she renewed her search, but could find nothing to support her belief that Bonnange had killed her brother to secure an inheritance for his sister and gain money for himself.

She thrust the papers and ledger aside in exasperation. Why did this man always destroy her expectations? Was he angel or devil? Her thoughts drifted to the touch of his warm hand on her cheek as he had brushed a tear away. From there, her mind wandered to other, more intimate memories, and she blushed as she recalled his comment about soiled doves.

That remark resolved her on the matter. He'd only treated her with kindness because he'd thought she would welcome his attentions. What arrogance! Well, she'd not let him off lightly for having kidnapped and insulted her. She'd make him regret trying to keep her at Cour de Cyprés against her will!

Now thoroughly irate at his treatment of her, she scanned the room for something she could destroy, something that would make him see he'd have a fight on his hands if he continued on his present course. But the only items of any value were the papers on his desk.

A smile crept over her face as she stared at the neat and orderly stacks of documents. Bonnange was clearly a meticulous person when it came to his business affairs. That was about to change, she thought as she swept all the papers to the floor. Then she began opening drawers and dumping out their contents. Receipts for produce and horses, daily records, and gambling vouchers all floated to the floor. When the desk was finally empty, she stared at the pile of papers with satisfaction.

But she couldn't just leave them there. Louis might notice them and straighten them before Bonnange had a chance to witness her destructiveness. She wanted Bonnange to sit down at his desk, reach for something—hopefully something important—and discover it wasn't where he'd put it. With determination, she mixed the papers thoroughly before placing them back in the desk drawers and on the desk in neat piles. A frown crossed her face as she wondered what he'd do when he discovered that nothing was as he'd placed it. But she refused to worry about it, choosing to dwell instead on the image of him surrounded by mounds of papers as he attempted to organize them.

With a grin of complete pleasure, she surveyed her handiwork one last time. Then she curled up on the settee with *Ivanhoe*, looking for all the world like a contented cat as she settled down to wait.

Julia Bonnange Vannier, a dark Creole woman with a fading but distinct beauty, gave her usual gentle smile when the youngest Charbonnet girl complimented her on her coiffure. But her mind was on other things. Her brother held most of her thoughts. Why had he departed her house so abruptly, leaving her to attend the *soirée* at the Charbonnets alone? It wasn't like René to be so thoughtless. He knew how difficult these social occasions were for her since Philippe's death.

A knot formed in her throat as she thought of her departed husband. She'd loved him with a passion bordering on madness. That was what made his perfidy even more painful. She glanced around the room, wishing she could confide in just one among her friends. But to tell them of her sorrow, she'd have to reveal what Philippe had done, and that she refused to do. Not even to René.

She lowered the demitasse cup with dainty exactness, Philippe's final confession playing over and over inside her head. Lately, she couldn't escape the words, couldn't find relief from them.

It's because I have a guilty conscience, she told herself, and knew it was true.

Her husband's dying words echoed in her mind. "I have done a terrible thing, Julia. A terrible thing. If the priest arrives in time, I'll confess to him, but I must tell you first. I can't die with the knowledge of it weighing on my soul. You must listen. I have another wife—another family—in Missouri. They don't know of you, either. In my locked chest you'll find my will. It provides for all of you. Give it to my solicitor. He has never seen it, but he's an honest, discreet man. He'll take care of everything once he adjusts to the shock. Promise me, Julia, that you'll do as I ask. Promise!"

She had promised, and therein lay her dilemma. She hadn't kept her promise and had kept the will. Not that she hadn't thought about it night and day. In her mind, she met the other woman—she always thought of her as "the temptress"—and threw the will in her face. It would be a pleasure to see her endure the pain Julia suffered. But even the thought of that pleasure wasn't enough for her to contact this woman.

Once again, she prayed to God to understand. *It's right what I'm doing, isn't it? The temptress—surely he did not marry her in the church? She's probably one of those cursed Americans with their Protestant religion, so the marriage is invalid in Your eyes, isn't it? Of course, it is.*

The pain washed over her again. Some other woman had stolen her Philippe's love. Some other woman had even borne him children! She tried to tell herself that the woman was a witch, that the woman had entrapped him and enticed him away from his first true wife, but the documents were against her. He hadn't told her, but the will gave the date of his marriage to the other woman. This Kathleen had married Philippe one year before Julia had. Julia silently choked back a sob. Kathleen and not Julia had been his first choice!

She'd known her husband didn't love her when he married her, but whose husband did? She'd even known he'd wanted to break the betrothal, that his mother had said she'd disinherit and destroy him if he did. That had disturbed Julia when she'd learned of it, but she'd been convinced she could make Philippe love her.

What did she care if he married her only because of his inheritance? Many marriages began with only fortunes to tie them together, but it mattered not. The men always came to love their wives. Or so her *maman* had told her. She and Philippe had been betrothed since childhood. The

Bonnanges and the Vanniers—it had always been intended that the two families unite. Their property adjoined each other's. Each was considered *bon famille*. Of course Julia would marry Philippe! And she'd make him glad he hadn't broken the betrothal.

But Julia had made the mistake of falling deeply in love with her handsome husband. Even when he left on his long buying trips, even when he neglected their son, she loved him. And all the while he'd been going to visit *her*, the temptress! Julia struggled to contain herself, suddenly aware that everyone was noticing how quiet she'd become.

She made some comment about the weather, and the conversation went on, blessedly passing her by. Oh, why couldn't René have come with her today? she thought. He alone made her forget her dilemma. He alone brought laughter to her lips. But now everyone would say, "Poor Julia, she suffers so for Philippe. They were so devoted, two lovebirds. He died so young. What a pity!" She wanted to throw their words back in their faces, to tell them she hated her husband, yes, hated him for tearing her heart into little pieces! She was glad he was gone!

"And how is dear Francois these days?" *Madame* Charbonnet asked politely.

The question drew Julia from her terrible thoughts. Had anyone noticed she wasn't paying attention?

"He is well," she murmured. A few moments of polite talk passed during which they talked of their children. Then the conversation was once more dominated by the younger Charbonnets.

Francois, poor Francois, Julia thought. He was one reason she hadn't kept her promise. What would he say if he learned his papa had dishonored them so? And the money . . . She nearly sighed aloud. Francois would be angry to find he must split his inheritance with three new members of the family. No, she couldn't tell him. He would hold it against her for not being firm with his papa. "You are too meek, *maman!*" he would say as he had always said. He used to tell her, "You should tell Papa to stay at home." Or worse yet, "Tell Papa I need more money. He must give me a larger allowance."

Madame Charbonnet made some witticism, and Julia smiled mechanically. *No*, she thought. *Let this other woman find her own way. Let her suffer instead of me for a change.*

And the children? She tried not to think about that. The will had said Philippe had twins—a girl and a boy. The boy she cared nothing about. She'd always been proud she'd given Philippe a son, and she hated the temptress for having given him one, too—the first one, in fact. But the girl was another matter. Elina. Such a pretty name. Julia had always wanted a daughter.

She was being silly. This girl was the temptress's daughter, probably as wicked as her mother. *Let her suffer, too*, she thought in anger. *Let her learn as I did that men aren't to be trusted.*

Except for René, of course. The one bright spot in her life. She'd like to unburden her heart to him, but she dared not. He'd insist she do the right thing. And she refused to let the temptress win again. This Kathleen would wait and wait for her husband to return, as Julia had waited. She would worry and worry, as Julia had worried. *Let her suffer, too*, Julia thought.

And all the while Philippe's confession played in her mind like a tedious orchestra: "I have done a terrible thing, Julia . . ."

Chapter Seven

*Never lie in bed and think that the cat who is howling
in the backyard will grow weary and go away.*
—*Creole Proverb*

René sat casually on the bed while Louis, the man who'd
been more like his older brother than his servant, helped
him remove his muddied boots. Despite his fifty-five years,
Louis was spry and witty and always happy to serve René.
In the first years of René's sojourn abroad, Louis had
worked for Francois. But as the boy had grown older, Louis
had come to detest him. During one of René's visits home,
Louis had asked to be taken into René's service and René
had agreed readily. Francois's loss had been René's gain.

"I have made the necessary arrangements for *mademoiselle's* stay," Louis told René with a twinkle in his eye.

"Where did you put her?"

"In the next room, of course."

"Of course," René murmured, perturbed to discover that
every inch of his body tensed at the thought of her being

117

so near. "What did she think of that?"

"She pretended to be angry with me. This *mademoiselle,* she is very strange. But I like her. She is not like other women."

René's sharp laugh was bittersweet. "I suppose she told you her silly tale about being Philippe's daughter. What a way to revenge herself on me!"

Louis's eyes widened in shock. "She says she is *Monsieur* Vannier's daughter?"

"She didn't tell you?" René's face looked incredulous. Then his expression grew cynical. "No, of course not. She'd rather defame me by perpetuating those rumors that I killed her companion. She's so eager to believe the worst of me. And not only her, damn it! I find the poor man lying dead in Orleans Hall, and everyone brands me as his murderer. I'll admit I wanted revenge last night, but I wouldn't have killed him. I only wanted him jailed."

When Louis went suddenly still, René glanced up. The older man had an expression of pure guilt on his face.

"She *did* pass on the rumor to you, didn't she?" René asked.

Louis began to polish the boots silently with the cloth.

René clasped the man's arm to stay his nervous actions. "Didn't she tell you?"

"The *mademoiselle* would not say anything except that you disagreed about a relative of yours—*Monsieur* Vannier. If I had known she believed these peculiar things, I—I wouldn't have told her anything."

René frowned. "Anything? What exactly did you tell her?"

"I told her about your family."

"And?"

The older man's hands began working even more furiously on the boots. "And I may have happened to mention . . . er . . . that you may have . . . perhaps . . . fought a duel last night."

"What?" René exclaimed, jumping to his feet. "My God,

Louis, why did you tell her that?"

Louis's worried eyes turned to his master. "You had blood on your gloves, *monsieur*, and she told me you had fought a duel, and I just assumed . . ."

René gritted his teeth. "That little baggage!"

"*Non, non, monsieur,* you should not say such things," Louis said, dropping the boots as he stood to face his master. "She is confused, but that does not mean—"

"She is not confused," René stated firmly. "She's trying to destroy me and my family for something I didn't do. I'm growing weary of her absurd claims."

"You said she also claims to be *Monsieur* Vannier's daughter?"

René's smile was grim. "Yes. But I know she's lying. She says she's Philippe's daughter by a second marriage in Missouri."

Louis looked astounded. "Another marriage?"

"Yes. According to her, Philippe was a bigamist. Of course, the entire idea is ridiculous. Nonetheless, I spent the better part of the afternoon checking out her story with those who would know—Philippe's solicitor and his friends. None of them had ever heard that Philippe kept a mistress, and certainly not in a remote place like Missouri."

"As I recall, *Monsieur* Vannier had business investments in Missouri," Louis put in helpfully.

René nodded. "Several. And in Ohio and Mississippi and God knows where else. That proves nothing except he had many investments. Not that there's anything to prove. My brother-in-law was far too concerned about his station in New Orleans society to have shamed Julia in such a way." The barest hint of cynicism lay in his words. "The solicitor agreed. He assured me Philippe would never have done such a scandalous thing."

"What else would the solicitor tell her brother?" Louis pointed out.

René gripped the back of the armchair. "Perhaps. But there were other holes in the sweet *mademoiselle's* story."

119

Deborah Martin

"Yes?" Louis asked with interest, turning away from his master to pick up the boots.

"The *mademoiselle*'s been lying since she got here. She told me she had papers to prove her claims. But she didn't have them with her and insisted they were stolen from her companion's body. John Davis and I searched the gaming rooms. We found no papers."

René didn't tell Louis that he'd half hoped to find those damn documents of hers. Something in him wanted her to be truly as innocent as she appeared.

"Maybe she's right about the papers," Louis said, attempting to be fair. "Maybe whoever killed her companion took them."

"You're getting soft in your old age, my friend," René said dryly. "But, yes, I considered the possibility. Not for long, however. Think about it. She says I stole them to prevent her from claiming her inheritance. Since I didn't kill the man, that claim is absurd. And who else would want to? Who would care about the documents of a card cheat?"

"Then why did she mention them?"

René sighed. "Don't you see? It's just one more way to make her claims seem legitimate. You should have seen how she acted when I pressed her for more details about them. She was jumpy as a catfish on a line."

"Poor *mademoiselle*."

"I wouldn't feel sorry for her if I were you. I offered to travel to her home to find some other proof for her claims. You know what she said?"

Louis remained silent.

"She told me her home had burned to the ground, so no proof existed there, except for the word of some banker. No doubt the man's an admirer of hers. She had an answer for everything, but it all came back to the same truth. She has no tangible evidence. Nothing! Even with my doubts, I did everything I could to prove the woman right, but I met lies at every turn. The clerk at her hotel said she and Wallace

120

had registered as husband and wife. Yet she'd told me and the sergeant that Wallace was her brother."

"But such a small lie—"

René sighed and shook his head. "I searched their belongings and found nothing to support her story. For example, she'd told me their mother died and that's why they'd come here, but neither of them owned mourning clothes. In fact, the few clothes she did have were very poor. That dress she's wearing is the best she's got. Now do you really think Philippe would allow his children to live like that, even his illegitimate children?"

Louis shrugged. "I suppose not."

"No, certainly he wouldn't," René corrected. "And don't forget the way we met. She's the one who hit me over the head last night while her partner stole my money."

"*Non!*" Louis exclaimed.

"Yes," René assured him as uncertainty filled Louis's face. "I tell you, Elina is a practiced deceiver. But I'll not let her play her games with me!"

As Louis began tidying the room, René sat down to put on his dress shoes.

Elina and her patently absurd stories. Anyone else would have simply dismissed them as the ravings of a desperate woman and thrown her out. How was it she could make him go to such trouble? *Nom de Dieu*, but she knew how to manipulate a man! Those tear-filled eyes, that innocent sweet mouth . . . No wonder the sergeant hadn't arrested her when he'd found her. René found it nearly as difficult to resist her. He felt a stirring in his loins just thinking about her mouth moving sensuously on his.

He clenched one fist in frustration. She'd not use that attractiveness to twist him around to her way of thinking. He wouldn't let her.

He couldn't deny, however, that he'd like nothing more than to have her in his bed. That alabaster skin, so cool to the touch. He'd love to bring its hidden heat to the surface. He'd love to have those tapered fingers roam his body, love to feel them clutch his arms in blatant need.

He tensed, wondering how he could let his desires so blind him to the problems she presented. Her stories might be lies, but plenty of people in New Orleans were willing to believe lies, particularly juicy, scandalous ones. She could easily tell her tale a few times and have the Bonnange and Vannier names forever ruined—all because she wanted money.

And vengeance. An angry woman with a quick tongue and soft eyes was always dangerous when her emotions guided her. Judging from the very real sorrow and anger she felt over Wallace's death, it was possible he'd been her first lover, and that would only intensify her thirst for revenge.

He rose from the bed. If he simply threw her out, she'd stir up trouble. He easily dismissed her claims that she wished to do honest work. If she'd wanted such a thing, why would she have helped Wallace cheat? No, René could tell from her smooth-skinned hands she'd never done any heavy work. Her pretty body and intelligence had clearly made her way for her in the past. And now her quick mind had fixed on a scheme to gain a dead man's money.

If money was all it took . . . His mind began to race. That was the obvious choice: pay her to leave town. It galled him to consider it. Not because of the money. He could afford to make her rich enough to buy her silence. But he hated allowing her to best him in this way.

Yet it seemed the only easy solution. Even if her story about Philippe couldn't be proved, even if no one believed it, the trouble she could stir up with her accusations about Wallace's death could be just as damaging to Julia as rumors about Philippe. Having her arrested, even if he'd wanted to do so, couldn't stop her mouth.

No, he had little choice. He'd have to give her enough money to satisfy her grasping hands and be rid of her.

"Where's the *mademoiselle* now?" René asked, suddenly anxious to settle the distasteful matter.

"She is eating dinner downstairs," Louis told him. Then he fought back a smile. "You must admit the *mademoiselle* has spirit. I had to endure her rage this afternoon. She is very angry with you."

"She won't stay that way," René told his servant with confidence as a grim expression crossed his face. "Not when she hears what I have to offer."

He had no doubt that the *mademoiselle* would change her story readily when he offered her enough gold. No doubt at all.

Elina toyed with the food on her plate. She felt odd sitting at one end of the huge table in Bonnange's dining room. Louis had insisted she eat her late dinner there, treating her like a welcome guest instead of a prisoner. But she couldn't forget she was there against her will. Any minute her jailer would return to torment her.

She touched the damask napkin to her lips, her hand then freezing in midair. The soft cloth on her mouth reminded her of . . . No, she wouldn't think about it, she told herself. Clearly Bonnange was trying to make her lose her resolve to fight him. He wanted her to forget who she was and what he'd done. But she wouldn't forget, she vowed, crumpling the napkin in her hand.

He kept twisting everything so it appeared she wanted only Papa's money. The truth was she cared about her possible inheritance only because she needed the money to survive. Otherwise, it meant little to her. Papa's betrayal had wounded her and the words of the death notice were branded on her mind so that she couldn't think about him without seeing them. How could he have done so despicable a thing? She would never forgive him! Never!

Nor would she forgive Bonnange for his insults. Even if he found out on his visit to town that she'd been telling the truth, even if he apologized, she would refuse to accept his apology.

As if she'd conjured him up, René suddenly entered the

room, causing her to start. Her jailer had returned. Nervously, she bit her lip, wondering what she should say to him.

"Did you miss me?" he asked with an insolent grin.

"Hello, *monsieur*."

He scowled. "Don't you think it might be more pleasant if you called me René instead of *monsieur*? It sounds like an insult each time you speak the word."

"It's meant as an insult," she replied with quiet dignity. "I wish to be reminded that you consider yourself above me and above the law as well."

"I see you're still angry with me," he remarked, sitting down at the other end of the long table as servants scurried to bring him dinner.

"Of course." Her words were icy, even though his presence in the room was already making her feel decidedly warm.

She tried to mask her eagerness to hear what he'd discovered in town. Had Papa told anyone in New Orleans about his other family? And did Bonnange's affability mean he'd found out she was really telling the truth?

"You didn't let your anger keep you from eating my food, I noticed."

"Louis insisted," she responded, suddenly wishing she'd gone hungry instead.

"Louis can be persistent at times," Bonnange said, lifting a newly filled glass of wine to his lips. With the glass in midair, he paused to add, "As can I."

Ignoring that vaguely threatening statement, Elina summoned up her courage. "Was your persistence rewarded in town?"

He chuckled. "What do you consider a reward? If it's concrete proof that you're Philippe's daughter, you should realize I found no such thing."

She gazed down unseeingly at her plate, struggling not to give him the satisfaction of seeing how much his news upset her. What had she expected? That he'd tell her all was well? She knew she shouldn't have expected much. Yet anything would have been better than his casual words, "I found no such thing."

He was curiously silent. When at last she could bear to look at him, the smile he'd worn before was gone, and he watched her with a guarded expression.

"What *did* you find?" she asked.

"No one's ever heard of you. The solicitor knows nothing of your existence, Philippe's friends say he had no mistress in Missouri, and there are no papers anywhere. Not at Orleans Hall and not at your hotel."

Anger surged through her. "You searched my room? How dare you! What right have you?"

He quirked one eyebrow. "The same right you had to force your way into my sister's house claiming to be Philippe's long-lost daughter. Incidentally, I found it *très intéressant* to discover that your 'brother' told the hotel clerk he was your husband. You and your companion should have kept to the same story."

She twisted her napkin in her lap. She'd forgotten all about Alex's little subterfuge. Choking back the bitter replies she wanted to hurl at Bonnange, she said evenly, "As I've said before, I owe you no explanations."

"Of course not." His dark eyes mocked her.

She suddenly wished she could box his ears. He was so maddeningly sure of himself. "And even though you murdered my brother, I suppose you think you owe me no explanations, either."

He leaned forward, his clenched fists resting on the table.

She continued, blithely ignoring his suddenly angry expression, "In any case, I can see why you refuse to believe me. If you accept my story, you'll have two problems on your hands. One is that I'm Philippe's legitimate heir and your sister and nephew clearly are not. You see, Papa married Mama before he married your sister."

"How clever of you to think of that," he bit out.

She ignored the implication in his words. "And two is that if Alex is a Vannier and not some faceless nonentity, the magistrate won't take his death quite so casually. In either case, it isn't to your advantage to believe me, so it matters not what you uncover, does it? Because even if you discover I'm telling the truth, you'll certainly suppress that knowledge."

"*Mon Dieu*, but you're intelligent, aren't you?" His voice dripped with sarcasm. "You're right, of course, on both counts. It wouldn't be to my advantage to discover you speak the truth. But you've failed to consider that I'm an honorable man, regardless of what you might believe. I wouldn't willingly cast aside any child of Philippe's, legitimate or illegitimate, no matter what the consequences to myself or my family."

"You already have!"

He ignored her outburst. "Nor did I kill your Alex."

Her hands gripped the table in rage. "Why deny it? It's not as if you'll be prosecuted. The entire city seems to know you killed him in a duel, and not a soul has yet said you should be punished." Her voice held a note of disgust. "Everyone considers you a hero for it."

A muscle worked in his jaw. "Without any evidence to prove I murdered your dear lover, you still persist in believing the innuendoes and rumors that say I did."

"No evidence? You said you'd find my brother, that he couldn't escape. Of course you killed him. Who else desired his death?" Her eyes narrowed. "Besides, your gloves were bloody the night of his murder."

"Blood that soaked my gloves when I felt for his pulse," he spat out, his eyebrows drawing together in warning. "But let's not allow the facts to overrule your assumptions."

"Why should I believe you?"

"Perhaps because I'm telling the truth. Even though I haven't lifted a hand to harm you since I brought you here, you believe I killed Wallace in cold blood, simply because he stole my money." He shook his head and raised his hands in a gesture of helplessness. "Believe what you wish then. I refuse to defend myself to a liar like you. Furthermore," he said with ominous firmness as he rose to his feet, "I think it's time you considered this situation from my point of view instead of your own vastly distorted one." He left the table to pace the room, gesturing adamantly as he spoke. "Two complete strangers conspire to cheat and steal from me—"

"But—"

"Silence!" he thundered. "Later one of them returns to do the same to someone else and is killed. After I, *le pauvre idiot* that I am, find his body and report his death, his companion appears at my sister's *pied-à-terre* demanding revenge. By some ironic twist of fate, she also claims to be the legitimate daughter of my sister's dead husband. She has no proof of any kind. She hasn't been using his name and doesn't even resemble my brother-in-law. Yet on the strength of her word, which she's proven to be worthless, she wishes me to believe my brother-in-law was a bigamist. And just think! This man, who supposedly has supported her and her 'brother' for years, died without a will that provided for this family and without even mentioning to anyone that this other family existed!"

He whirled on her, his eyes dark with accusation. "Yet you ask me to believe what you say. Is it so hard to accept that I can't?"

His last statement about the lack of a will left her speechless. Why *had* there been no will? Had Papa cared so little he hadn't even bothered to ensure they were taken care of? Yet surely if there'd been a will, someone in authority would have notified Mama of Papa's death. So Bonnange could be speaking the truth about the will. If that were possible, Bonnange had good reason not to believe her. Who would in such a case?

Her eyes filled with tears as she stared at his harsh face. "It appears we are at an impasse," she managed to get out, too aware of the validity of his statements to refute them.

Her strained voice and troubled expression brought him up short as he paced the room. Slowly, he turned, his eyes searching her face. For a moment, he seemed to soften. Then he grew stiff again. "Perhaps not."

He strode to the table and sat down in the chair at her right. When he took her hands, she started to pull them away, but he refused to relinquish them. "Listen, *chérie*, I know why you created this story. And I understand. You depended on Wallace, no? The two of you must have been together a long time. Once he died, you wanted to strike out at the person who you thought had taken away the source of your companionship and your livelihood."

Her eyes widened in outrage as she realized what he implied.

"I do want to make up for that," he continued, oblivious to the way his words incensed her. "I won't have you prosecuted for your part in the cheating incident."

"And in return I'm expected to forget that you murdered my brother and want to deny me my birthright? Is that it? I'm sorry, *Monsieur* Bonnange, but I'll never do such a thing."

His hands dropped hers abruptly as he stood to his feet. He leaned on the table so that he towered over her, resembling an eagle about to swoop down on its prey.

"For one who has few choices, you are surprisingly stubborn, sweet eyes. And greedy, too, no doubt." He sighed. "I suppose that's to be expected. But you have me in a quandary. With that innocent smile of yours, you just might be able to stir up a great deal of trouble for my family in New Orleans. And I simply won't allow that."

"Is this where you tell me you must kill me?" she taunted.

He pounded the table. "No, damn you!" He paused, as if to rein in his anger. "I'd like to offer you a . . . ah . . . business arrangement. I give you enough funds to keep you in fripperies and gowns for a good long while. In return, you leave New Orleans and abandon your foolish tales."

She stared at him in amazement. "You—you can't mean what I think you mean?"

"Don't play the innocent with me, Elina. I'm offering

to compensate you for the loss of your protector, now that he's gone."

"Dead!" she spat out. "Not gone! Dead!" Then she enunciated carefully as if she were talking to a child. "He was not my 'protector'—at least not in the sense you mean it. He was my brother." She ignored the way his eyes began to glitter with devilish fury. "And you're not offering to 'compensate' me. You're offering to buy my silence about your wretched crimes!"

"Yes," he stated with deceptive softness. "I'm offering to buy your silence. Surely taking my gold is a better alternative than risking your life helping a gambler cheat or—"

"Or languishing in jail, where you'd be certain to put me. I have the choice of taking your money and keeping silent or being jailed. Do I understand you correctly?"

"No, damn it!" he exploded, grasping her arms and jerking her out of the chair. "I'm not bringing you to the magistrate. I never intended to. But I can't believe you'd prefer starving in the streets or making your living on your back in a city like New Orleans to taking my money!"

She paled at the crudity of his words, but met his gaze staunchly. "I don't care what you believe. I am refusing your 'generous' offer. I will *not* keep silent about the truth."

The tips of his fingers dug painfully into her upper arms as his face smoldered with anger. "Be aware, *chérie*, of what you're saying. You think I'll allow you to return to New Orleans and spread your lies? Certainly not. So you'll stay here until I can make you see how foolish your precious scheme is."

"Bring me to the magistrate," she begged. "I'd rather be jailed by a proper jailer than by you."

"Would you now?" he responded, his hands dropping to her waist. The tone of his voice had somehow changed to one more frightening than before. He spoke as if against his will while his eyes fixed on her mouth. "Do you fear me? It wasn't fear I sensed in you earlier. Or was that a conscious mimicking of desire you showed in my study?"

"You pompous, arrogant scoundrel! I couldn't possibly desire my brother's murderer!" she cried, but her skin quivered when, heedless of her words, he lifted one hand to run his thumb over her lips.

Furious at the way her body betrayed her, she drove both of her fists forward into his stomach. But the muscles that met her hands didn't crumple. They were stone-hard and bruised her knuckles.

"Don't tempt me to have you tossed in the *calaboso*! You wouldn't like it there, I assure you," he said as he clasped her wrists and twisted her hands around behind her, bringing her up against his body roughly. His calloused fingers felt cold against her slender wrists.

"If the magistrate heard my story, he wouldn't jail me. I know he wouldn't!"

"Are you so sure?" he hissed.

"I'll take my chances with him either way."

"No, you won't. Not yet anyway. I trust Oliveira to be discreet, but I'm not so sure about his men. They'd just as soon believe your rumors as believe the truth." His eyes narrowed. "If you really were Philippe's daughter, you wouldn't want his name dragged through the mud."

What he said was true, she grudgingly acknowledged. She was hurt and angry with Papa for what he'd done, yet she didn't wish to see him publicly villified. She kept hoping that somewhere there was evidence that he'd cared, that he'd regretted his actions.

No, she didn't really want to see Papa's good name destroyed. Unfortunately, anyone she told about the situation could reveal the truth, even the magistrate's men.

But did Bonnange really believe the magistrate's men would be so indiscreet? She scrutinized Bonnange, cursing his unusually long lashes that shadowed his eyes so she couldn't tell what he was thinking. Matters were becoming increasingly complicated, she thought. What was she to do?

"You'll consider my offer, won't you?" he asked as he noted her confusion.

She didn't know what options remained to her, but that certainly wasn't one of them. "I won't take your money," she said in defiance.

"Fine. I suppose you think you can raise the price by holding out awhile longer. You're welcome to try, but . . ." he paused, then lowered his voice to a threatening whisper, " . . . in the meantime, you'll be my guest. And you may find I'm not a pleasant person to live with when forced to endure the company of someone trying to steal my family's fortune and good name."

She spoke with a clear conscience. "I only want what I have the right to expect. I want justice."

"If I gave you what you have the right to expect, *mademoiselle*, you'd be in the *calaboso*! So be very careful about demanding what you deserve!"

With that sally, he thrust her away from him and strode from the room. She stood for several moments, her heart pounding. What an awful situation! He seemed determined to keep her prisoner unless she agreed to let him buy her silence. He clearly thought very little of her if he could assume she'd take his money despite what he'd done.

Worse yet, he thought other awful things about her. That was clear from the way he touched her. He truly did regard her as a soiled dove. For a fleeting instant, she remembered her brazen behavior when he'd kissed her earlier in the day. She had to admit he'd had some reason to think her a hussy. Why, she'd practically swooned in his arms!

She must guard against the insidious feelings he seemed to arouse in her against her will. It bothered her that she couldn't control the way her body leapt to meet his touch. Perhaps she'd simply been too tired to fight it, she rationalized.

Well, tonight she'd prepare herself for the ongoing struggle as best she could. In the morning, she'd be fresh and ready to think clearly. In the morning perhaps he, too, would be more willing to listen to what she had to say.

Tomorrow, she determined, *will be different. I will make him see I'm telling the truth and he can't keep me here. But I won't let him too close to me. That's the only way I'll be safe.*

She only hoped she could stick to her resolution.

Chapter Eight

Don't try to fly before you have wings.—French Proverb

Elina awoke to a blessedly cool morning. Staring up at the canopy, she rubbed her weary eyes. Although the bed was soft and covered with fine linens, she'd slept badly. She'd been unable to keep from thinking about her past and her future. What would she do without her family, without the farm at Creve Coeur? Where could she go? She'd told Alex, and later Bonnange, that she could take care of herself. But inside, she wasn't so sure. She'd never had to fend for herself. Never had she felt so alone, so abandoned. She missed her parents and she missed Alex. Without them she felt numb, even while she ached from the pain of their loss.

Yet she couldn't let her grief and fears keep her from finding some way to support herself. If Bonnange wasn't lying, Papa clearly hadn't provided for them, which left her few choices. Either prove her identity or manage alone.

She might have considered abandoning any attempt to prove who she was, even if it meant working in the meanest hovel, because of Bonnange's threats and her own reluctance to slander her papa. But more was at stake than her inheritance. It went against her pride to give up her claim to what was rightfully hers. She'd lose her identity and her heritage as well, and she didn't want to give them up.

What's more, the desire for revenge against Bonnange for her brother's death burned strong within her. She knew it was possible Bonnange hadn't killed Alex for the diabolical reasons she'd accused him of. After all, if Bonnange's motive for murdering her brother had been to keep Papa's secret quiet, surely he would have murdered her, too.

No, although he most assuredly had killed her brother, he'd probably done so only in anger. Yet regardless of Bonnange's reasons, she couldn't let him go unpunished for her brother's death. She had to see justice done.

She stifled a sob as she thought of Alex lying on the cold marble. Poor dear Alex. He'd often given her nothing but grief, but now she felt most of his actions were justified. He'd been right all along to resent Papa for refusing to take him on buying trips. Perhaps Alex had sensed Papa's split loyalties. She had reacted by finding excuses for Papa's absences, but Alex had just struck out blindly. Now she wished she'd done some of that herself.

She licked her lips and realized from the salty wetness that she was now crying noiselessly, the tears flooding her cheeks. Turning her face into the pillow, she let the tears flow a moment longer. Then she beat the pillow in futile rage. She would make certain that Alex's frustrated attempts to be heard weren't in vain. Somehow she'd find someone to listen to her story who would help her avenge her brother's death. Only then could she learn to live her life without her family.

She gazed around the room in despair as she sat up. At the moment she didn't even seem to have any choices, kept a prisoner as she was. She crept out of bed and went to the window. Disappointment and anxiety filled her when she saw the plantation spread out before her. Bonnange had carried her several miles from the city, of that she was certain. How on earth could she escape when she couldn't even mount a horse? Meaning to peek through the door onto the gallery, she tried the handle only to discover it locked. Then she remembered Louis's apologizing for having to lock her in the night before.

She froze at the door, suddenly remembering something else Louis had told her. Bonnange's room adjoined hers.

With a sharp cry of distress, she scurried to dress herself. But she'd scarcely had time to remove her nightdress and pull on her drawers and chemise before the door burst open to reveal a fully clothed Bonnange. Dark eyes flashing, he ignored her protests, and she cringed when she saw the sheaf of papers he held in one fist.

"Since Louis tells me you spent yesterday afternoon in my study 'resting,' I suppose I have you to thank for the chaos in my desk."

She didn't know whether to be pleased her little revenge had worked so well, or frightened by the ominous glare he now bestowed on her.

"Chaos?" she asked with as much innocence in her voice as she could muster.

"I'm not in the mood for the guileless virgin this morning, Elina, so if you'd tell me what purpose you could possibly have had in such petty destruction—"

"I merely wished to find out more about you," she said with an air of feigned unconcern. She shrugged. "Then I didn't remember what order I'd found everything in, so I put the papers back in the best order I could."

With exaggerated nonchalance, she turned to find something to cover her thinly clad body. But before she could grasp anything, he'd yanked her back around to face him.

"Don't give me any more lies!" he warned, his hands gripping her shoulders. "Do you have any idea how many hours of work it will take to straighten out the mess you created? Do you?"

135

By this time she realized he was far angrier than she'd at first noticed.

"Let me go!" she said, but her words came out as only a hoarse whisper.

"You are undeniably the most trouble I've ever come across in my entire lifetime—" he began.

She tried to push his hands away from her shoulders, but succeeded only in making them slide downward, one of them taking the sleeve of her chemise with it.

She stood still as a statue, her eyes fixed in horror on her naked shoulder. His gaze followed hers until he was staring at her bared skin as if he couldn't tear his gaze away. Slowly, he dropped his hands and began to really see her. His eyes still glittered with unspent fury, but something else shone in them as well as he took in the state of her undress.

She slid the sleeve back in place, her skin beginning to glow rosily in her embarrassment. He watched entranced as the color spread down her neck to the tops of her creamy breasts that showed above the scooped neckline of the chemise.

He lifted his eyes to her face, but when their eyes met, she gave a belated gasp and fled toward the bed. With total chagrin, she snatched the sheets up and twisted them around her.

For a moment he paused, staring at her as if contemplating some wicked action.

"Get dressed!" he then commanded as he pivoted on his heels. "I want to see you downstairs in five minutes!"

She didn't hesitate to obey him, afraid that he might decide to come back if she didn't. In frantic haste she dressed, her skin still tingling and warm from the shame of it all. Never had she been accosted by a man while she was so . . . so undressed! She could hardly contain her outrage and embarrassment.

But running through that outrage was a sincere fear of how her jailer might punish her for her action. For the first time, she regretted she'd chosen her particular method of showing her anger the day before.

As soon as she'd hastily pinned her hair in a soft coil at the back of her neck, she raced down the wide marble stairway, past the inquisitive maid who eyed her with blatant curiosity. Elina stopped short on the last step as she glimpsed Louis and Bonnange.

Bonnange stood silhouetted in the front doorway with his back to her as he gave Louis some instructions. She'd been too concerned earlier with what he was saying to notice how he looked, but now she couldn't help but be aware of it. He stood there so wickedly handsome in his riding coat of black superfine, his emerald pantaloon trousers, and his shining Hessians that she was taken aback. The bandage he'd worn the day before was missing, revealing dark thick hair cropped at medium length so the waves could be swept back from his face. She stared at his broad back and cursed him for being so attractive. Oh, why did she always have to be so aware of her physical attraction to him? What sort of demon had taken hold of her?

Slowly, she realized he was dressed for going out. Was he taking her somewhere? she wondered, a sinking sensation making her stomach queasy. She crept closer, wanting to catch sight of how he intended her to travel. Just as she glimpsed the two horses, one with a sidesaddle on it, he whirled and saw her.

"I'm not going with you," she whispered, her eyes widening in fright as she backed away. He wouldn't get her back on a horse, not if she could help it.

"You most certainly are," he replied evenly. "We are going to tour the place you showed so much disdain for yesterday when you ravaged my desk. I want you to see how many people's lives and livelihoods your petty destruction affected." He darted forward and grabbed her hand, pulling her along beside him onto the front gallery.

A desire to show him she felt no remorse for her actions warred with her fear of being on horseback. She couldn't get on a horse alone. She just couldn't! But she couldn't let him see her weakness, either, she told herself, certain that he'd take advantage of her fear if he knew.

"The *mademoiselle* knows how to ride?" Louis asked with concern as he noticed her staring at the horse in thinly masked terror while Bonnange spoke with the groom.

"Of—of course," she said shakily.

If she didn't ride, she knew Bonnange would never believe she was Philippe's daughter, so she forced herself to stand up straighter. She wouldn't let him use this against her. Surely she could conquer this silly fear of hers once and for all!

They were both silent as Bonnange helped her into the sidesaddle. Fleetingly, she wondered how women ever stayed in such contraptions, but Bonnange gave her little time to think about it. In seconds, he was astride and heading off down a worn path. She followed uncertainly, trying to remember the few rudiments of riding she'd learned as a child. Alex had attempted to give her riding lessons, but much of what he'd tried to teach her she'd been too frightened to assimilate. Fighting down the waves of distress already threatening to engulf her, she gripped the pommel with one hand while with the other she halfheartedly tried to use the reins.

Fortunately, the horse, a quiet mare, seemed only concerned with following her companion. The mare trotted along complacently behind Bonnange's stallion while Elina tried to stay clam. Terror built within her, but she determinedly ignored it. She blotted out as best she could the images of the dark stable that assailed her.

But when they reached an open lane through the fields, Bonnange spurred Savage into a gallop, and her horse began to gallop as well. In seconds the sudden speed brought her panic to the fore. She jerked hard on the reins, wanting only to make the horse stop so she could dismount, but the horse reared, panicked by her strange behavior.

She screamed. Then she dropped the reins to cling to the pommel as the horse took off, frightened by the unpredictable, crazy rider on its back. Elina couldn't think, couldn't move as the horse barrelled off to the right across the cane fields. All she could do was clutch the saddle and whisper fervent pleas that God would spare her. In her mind's eye, the brilliant sunlit morning faded into a dark stable. Horses milled around her, neighing softly and bumping against their stalls in confusion. Their smell filled the air. She felt closed in and abandoned.

"Please, God, don't let me die," she whispered now as she had then.

Bonnange didn't at first notice she wasn't behind him, so caught up was he in nursing his anger at her over what she'd done. But when he heard her scream and saw her racing off, he cursed himself for not keeping a closer watch on her. Apparently, she was trying to escape, he thought irrationally. But the foolish girl was destroying his cane crop in the process!

His anger renewed, he spurred his horse after her. Then as he closed the gap between them, his eyes took in the dragging reins, and he realized she wasn't in control. In seconds he was beside her, leaning forward for the reins. When his hands closed around them, he drew both horses in slowly, a task made easier by the fact that Elina's mare was fast tiring, being unused to such strenuous exercise.

As soon as both horses halted, Elina threw herself from the saddle, lifted her skirts, and ran sobbing through the cane fields, oblivious to the short stalks that caught at her clothes. Bonnange gazed after her in blank astonishment for only a moment before leaping down to follow her. But before he could reach her, she stopped, collapsing on the ground in a shaking heap.

When he leaned down to touch her, she started away from him and lifted terror-filled eyes to his face. "Please don't make me get back on that beast!" Her hands clutched his in supplication. "I'll do anything you ask, just don't make me mount that horse!"

Quickly, he knelt beside her, drawing her close to him so her head lay against his chest. "*Sacre bleu, chérie!*

What happened?" he asked as she continued to tremble in his arms.

"It started to move so fast, so very fast . . . I pulled back . . . It jumped up . . . I—I let go . . ." she said incoherently.

"Haven't you ridden before?" he asked as he tried to piece together what had occurred.

But he needed no answer to that question. Not only had she clearly not ridden, she also seemed terrified by the very thought of riding.

She attempted to calm her rapid breathing. "Alex tried to teach me," she said between great gasps of breath, "but I just couldn't learn, not after . . ." She stopped.

"Yes?" he asked, his hands stroking her back.

"You'll think me silly if I tell you," she whispered, her green eyes luminous and wild in their fright. He stared at the dewy lashes and felt something twist inside him.

"No, I won't, sweet eyes." He moved one hand to clasp hers and squeezed it reassuringly. "Now, tell me what happened. Not today. What happened before to make you so frightened?"

She rubbed the tears from her eyes with her free hand. "I—I'm all right now, really I am. But if you don't mind, I'd rather walk to wherever it is you're taking me."

"I'll put you back on that horse if you don't tell me why it frightens you so," he said sternly. Instantly, he regretted the threat as her face went ashen.

"I—I'll tell you," she hastened to say. Then she took a deep breath and stared at her hands for a while before continuing. "It happened when I was five years old. I followed Papa when he went to the stables. It was near dusk, so he didn't see me. I kept out of sight because I knew I wasn't supposed to be there, but I got to see Papa so seldom . . ."

She paused, her eyes filling with pain for a moment. "Anyway, I saw a kitten in the stables, so I began to play with it in the hay. No one noticed me, I suppose, and I didn't see Papa leave. So while I was on the ground searching in the hay for the kitten, the stableboy closed the doors for the night."

Her eyes lifted to his in an earnest plea for understanding. "At first I was only a little frightened. I started calling for Papa, but, of course, he didn't hear me. My unfamiliar presence made the horses uneasy in their stalls, and they began to get restless. I'd never really been around horses much, so the noise they were making scared me. I started crying, they became even more fidgety, and when no one came I began to panic. I—I groped my way around the stalls, hoping to find the door and open it myself. But I got confused in the darkness and opened the latch to a stallion's stall instead."

She began to shudder and he pulled her closer to him. "He . . . he pushed his way out of the stall past me. I could feel his coat as it rubbed along my cheek. I knew he was loose in there with me, and it terrified me. I should have just huddled in a corner somewhere until someone discovered me missing and found me, but instead I kept looking for the door. Evidently, I came up behind him. I'm not certain. All I remember is touching a rounded part of him. The next thing I knew I was flying through the air.

"Fortunately, he didn't hurt me too badly when he kicked me, but it did frighten me something awful. I lay there for what seemed like hours, wondering when he'd come to kill me and convinced that he'd trample me to death." She gave a shaky laugh. "The poor thing was probably as frightened of me as I was of him, but I didn't see it that way. At any rate, it was a long time before they found me. I— I couldn't even talk about it for days. And ever since, I . . . I just haven't been able to get near a horse without panicking."

He started to point out that she'd ridden with him to Cour de Cyprés. Then he remembered the way she'd sat rigidly in the saddle, clutching the pommel for dear life, refusing to relax. She must have been immobilized by fear.

His anger over her willful destruction of his desk temporarily faded. Unconsciously, he began to stroke her hair soothingly, as one does to someone who's had a bad dream.

"You should have told me," he said, brushing the hair back from her face.

She glanced up at him startled, as if it had suddenly occurred to her she'd been pouring out her soul to the enemy. Her lips tightened, and she stared off at a piece of cane she'd trampled in her flight.

"Why didn't you tell me?" he persisted.

She gave a small frown. "And what would you have said? 'No daughter of Philippe's would be afraid to ride.' It would have given you some other imaginary proof to use against me."

Against his will, he smiled at the stern face she'd made as she mimicked him. She really did see their struggle as a battle and him as the evil tyrant.

"In the end you were forced to ride anyway, so what difference would it have made?" he said, his smile widening.

Her face became even stonier. "I have some pride, you know." Then she added, so softly he had to strain to hear her, "Besides, I'd hoped I could control it. The fear, that is."

"Fears like that don't disappear solely because you will them away," he told her, cupping her face in his hands. "You have to coax them out into the open and fight them, just like you fight anything else. And sometimes it's hard to know what weapons to use."

"I don't want to fight it," she whispered as she stared up at him. "I don't ever want to go near a horse again."

"I'm afraid that's not possible, *chérie*. We'll have to ride to get back to the house."

"I'll walk!" she said in a rush, her breath starting to quicken just at the thought of riding the horse.

He looked down at her anxious face and sighed. "It's too far to walk dressed as you are. By the time you crossed the cane fields, your dress would be nothing but rags. And you'd probably run into all the mice and snakes in the fields. Besides, the day is sure to come when you'll have to ride. It's time you began learning to overcome your fear."

He could see her struggling with her emotions, part of her terrified of riding and the other part still determined to show him she could master it. In the end, her pride won out. Stiffly, she stood to her feet and smoothed her skirts with dainty movements, as if her appearance was of the utmost importance in the battle to come. He rose to stand beside her.

"You'll ride with me," he said, pleased when a flash of relief passed over her face. "But first, I think you and the horse should become acquainted." He took her hand and led her back to where Savage stood nuzzling the mare.

Instinctively, she hesitated as they neared the horses. He released her and approached the mare who eyed Elina suspiciously. He spoke some soothing words to the horse and then beckoned Elina to approach. He could see her stiffen, but she did as he said, attempting to mask the fear on her face with a forced smile.

"First of all," he said as she came up beside him, "you need to see horses as individuals. Your fear of them comes partly from lack of knowledge and partly from the assumption that all horses are alike. Horses are just like people. Some are pleasant and easy to work with while others are vicious and hard to manage. For example, consider Monique here . . ."

"Monique?" Some of the fear in her eyes abated.

"Yes," he said with a laugh. "Louis named her after one of his childhood sweethearts."

He took Elina's hand and pressed it to the horse's mane. Monique allowed Elina to stroke her. "As you can see, she's meek as a lamb. And because she's a gentle horse, you must treat her gently. A slight tug on the reins and she will do as you wish."

"So when I jerked them back . . ." she murmured with some remorse.

143

"Yes, you hurt and frightened her. She's unaccustomed to such treatment." Without a word he released Elina's hand. He noted with pleasure that she continued to stroke the mare. But when Monique turned to nuzzle her hand, Elina jumped away.

"Easy," he murmured as he slid his arm around Elina's waist. "She won't bite you. That I can promise."

"I know my fear isn't rational," she told him. "But I can't help it. I can no more be calm around a horse than I could be around a snake."

It was a good thing she couldn't see his face at that moment, he thought, because if she could, she'd realize he was enjoying his role as comforter. She hadn't even protested when he'd clasped her waist. Wryly, he thought to himself he ought to make her ride every day just so he could have the pleasure of comforting her after it was over.

"It will take time," he told her as he led her to his horse. "But the more you see the horse as you'd see a person, the easier it will be for you, *chérie*."

At his use of the endearment, she looked down at the hand resting familiarly on her waist. "There are people I fear as well," she said as she moved his hand away.

"Perhaps with time, you won't fear them either," he said in a husky voice, delighted as she blushed at his words.

Then he hoisted her onto the back of his horse before she could even protest. In seconds, he was behind her in the saddle. He could feel her body growing stiff, could almost smell her mounting terror. Deliberately, he swept her hair aside and pressed a kiss on her neck. He felt the change in her immediately as her fear turned to anger at his action.

"Shall we go?" she asked shakily, but with a certain amount of imperiousness in her voice.

He smiled to himself. "Whatever you wish." Then he took up the reins and gently started the horse walking.

But once they began to move, she didn't relax. Her back was so rigid it didn't even touch him. He frowned and cast about for something to say to distract her from her fear. He began describing for her the workings of the plantation. Before he knew it, he was dredging up long-forgotten memories from his childhood. And when at last some tale of his elicited a hesitant giggle from her, he deliberately elaborated the story until he could feel her lean back against him.

Within a short period of time, they'd come within sight of the house. He felt her back grow ramrod straight again. "I thought you were going to show me your vast plantation," she said suspiciously.

"You've seen enough for today, sweet eyes. I don't relish chasing you through the cane fields again."

She didn't reply, but her body relaxed against his, and they rode on in a companionable silence until they reached the house. After he'd dismounted and lifted her down, he stood there with his hands on her waist, reluctant to release her. She stared at him, started to open her mouth to say something, and then faltered.

At last she began again. "You didn't have to do that. I mean, help me with the horse. I suppose I should thank you for being so understanding."

"It was my pleasure." Yes, it certainly was, he thought.

She stood twisting her hands for a moment before adding, "And I'm sorry for disturbing the contents of your desk."

The smile faded from his face. "Don't think I've forgotten—or forgiven—that. I'll still have to find some suitable way of punishing you for such an irresponsible action." He hadn't meant to sound quite so harsh, but his anger at finding his papers in shambles still smoldered.

She gazed at him, her own anger returning. "If you wouldn't keep women imprisoned in your house, they wouldn't take such 'irresponsible actions.'"

"There'd be no need to imprison you if you'd tell the truth."

"Or the lies you'd pay me to say."

He impaled her with his fierce gaze. "My offer still stands."

Eyes cold and green as the sea stared at him with undisguised animosity as she stepped back, pushing away the hands that had rested on her waist. "If I weren't still terrified of riding, you know I'd get back on that mare the moment your back was turned and ride straight to the magistrate's office."

"To ruin your father's reputation forever."

She swallowed. "Yes, if that's what I had to do to get justice and escape you."

He wondered if she really would. Gazing into that stubborn, angry face, he decided she just might. "You wouldn't get very far. I'd find you before you could even reach the city."

She shrugged. "It doesn't matter anyway. As you well know, I'm not riding anywhere. But I'm not going to do as you wish, *monsieur*, no matter how you torment me." She crossed her arms and lifted her chin in defiance. "And I most certainly will not take your money to ignore your crimes and my identity."

He wanted to shake her, but knew he wouldn't. Why was he treating her with such gentleness when he knew what she was? The answer to that was clear, he realized. He couldn't forget the way her soft lips had clung to his the day before, or the way she'd turned to him for comfort when she was frightened.

Yet he must. There was nothing to be gained in letting her under his skin. If he could just endure the situation for a time, she'd change her mind. Of that he was certain. She'd change her mind when she realized he wouldn't allow her to tell her story to anyone else and thus accepting his offer was to her advantage. Right now her pride still smarted, and her anger over the death of her companion was fiercely alive. But in time she'd come to her senses. In the meantime, he'd simply have to wait her out.

"Since you seem determined to be stubborn, sweet eyes, I'll have to find some way to amuse you during your stay."

"You could begin by calling me by my name instead of by that—that nickname you use," she bit out. "I am *Mademoiselle* Vannier, not sweet eyes."

"Indeed. I would have thought you'd prefer my nickname for you to your dear Alex's. Would you prefer I called you Puss?" At her mixed expression of outrage and pain, he instantly felt contrite. But he resisted the impulse to pity her for her grief, unreasonably jealous that she could show such emotion for that cowardly gambler.

More cruelly than he'd meant, he added, "So if you don't like Puss, it will have to be sweet eyes, won't it?"

He ignored the gasp of indignation that escaped her lips. With exaggerated courtesy, he offered her his arm. She didn't take it, but whirled away from him to stalk in fury toward the house.

He followed her. "As I was saying, amusements are in order. We can begin by sorting out my papers." He sighed. "A pity there's not much you can do to help since you've conveniently forgotten the order my papers were in, but you can keep me company." When she stepped onto the gallery and crossed it in stony silence, he added, "And since it's so warm in my study, you may wipe the perspiration from my brow with a handkerchief or feed me tidbits when my hands are full. I'll need the occasional sip of wine, of course."

She flashed him an angry glance, her mouth open to retort until she saw the grin on his face. Her mouth snapped shut again as she entered the house, her back rigid with the effort of controlling her anger.

"I'm afraid it will be very dull for you," she retorted once they were inside. "I'm fairly immune to the charms of devious Creole gentlemen. You won't find me quite such good company as those ladies Louis told me about who find you attractive."

"You'd prefer I sought out those other ladies?" he asked, taking her arm and guiding her toward his study.

"As long as you leave me alone, I really don't care."

147

"Ah, but, *chérie*, there's small chance of my leaving you alone. I'm looking forward to our little *tête-à-têtes* a great deal. Why should I seek companionship elsewhere when such a lovely dove roosts at home? I still remember our delicious kiss and anticipate future ones."

"There won't be any future ones! And don't call me a dove!" she burst out, trying to jerk her arm away from him as the color flooded her face.

He said nothing when they entered his study, but he thought to himself, *There will be many future kisses, sweet eyes, I can assure you.* Then, a confident smile lingering on his face, he closed the door behind them.

Chapter Nine

Necessity knows no laws.—Spanish Proverb

Elina watched as René separated his papers into neat piles — household receipts in one stack, letters in another, personal documents in another, and so on, as he'd been doing for three hours. He worked silently while she simply sat in the hot, close room, becoming more irritated by the minute. He wouldn't let her read, wouldn't let her work, wouldn't let her do anything but watch him meticulously read pieces of paper and sort them. He even refused to converse with her, and the silence was driving her to insanity.

Even though he'd refused her help twice before, she asked again if she could do something to speed the process.

He didn't answer immediately, merely turning his chair around so he faced her. While rubbing his stiff neck, he surveyed her. Satisfaction flickered in his eyes as he took in the way she fidgeted in the chair he'd confined her to.

"Are you finding it tedious to watch me?" he asked at last. "Believe me, doing the work is far more tedious."

"Then let me help you," she said, eager to do something other than just sit there. "You'd finish much faster if I did. You've made your point quite well, so there's no reason to continue in this way." Her voice began to grow the tiniest bit sarcastic. "At any rate, I'm certain I could stack papers as well as you can."

His eyes flashed to her hands. "We wouldn't want to risk dirtying your precious white hands with something so mundane as household accounts. I think you should save your energies for other things."

His meaningful glance caused her to blush.

"Despite what you may think," she said coldly to cover her embarrassment, "my experience is not in the area of 'other things.' I'm capable of a great deal more. I used to handle the accounts for Mama, so I know about running a household. Why not let me help you, so we can get out of this horrible room?"

She didn't say it, but part of her reason for wanting to escape the study was the air of sensuality that seemed to linger there from when he'd kissed her the day before. The occasional piercing looks he'd given her while he worked hadn't improved matters. His eyes traveled over her as if trying to fathom what lay under her clothes. Every time he turned that gaze on her, she found herself feeling desperately uncomfortable.

And the heat didn't help. The tendrils of hair that had escaped her coil during her mad ride through the fields clung damply to her forehead and neck. She felt sticky and warm, her body growing warmer each time he looked at her. His stares only served to remind her of the way she'd responded to his kiss.

Now he was smiling, and she knew he realized the direction her thoughts were taking.

"I don't need your help with the papers, sweet eyes," he murmured. "You've done enough damage as it is, and I certainly don't wish you to do any more." He paused. "But there is something you could do."

"Yes?"

"Rub my neck for me."

She crossed her arms over her chest and glared at him. "I don't know how."

His lips curled up. "I could teach you."

His assumption that she'd willingly cater to his needs rankled. "I'd rather do something else," she told him. Then she added perversely, "I wouldn't want to make you more comfortable than you already are."

That statement elicited a laugh from him. "*Touché.* Yes, I suppose you'd consider that entirely out of the question."

She raised her head, her chin set stubbornly. "Entirely."

"I see." His eyes danced with amusement. "In that case, perhaps I *could* use your help in sorting my papers after all. If you'd just come sit here on my lap—"

She started out of the chair. "You are . . . are . . ." She searched for a word that would completely silence him. "You are a lecher!" she said at last, recalling that her brother had once characterized one of their neighbors that way. "I would rather be the lowliest slave in the most wretched hovel in New Orleans than be imprisoned here with you!"

The smile faded from his eyes. "I wouldn't be so certain of that if I were you. If you were a slave, you wouldn't be sitting down taking your ease. You'd be scurrying to do your master's bidding. Slaves don't have choices. You do. Only your monumental greed for my late brother-in-law's money keeps you from taking the obvious choice—my offer to buy your silence."

"If I took your offer, I'd truly be a slave," she avowed, "for I'd no longer be able to speak the truth. I'd be a slave to the lie you'd have me live, and I won't be that—not for you, not for anyone."

He leaned back, his fingertips pressed together as he scrutinized her. She could tell from her expression that he didn't know quite what to make of her speech. At last he sighed and moved his chair back to his desk. "Here," he said curtly, turning his face away from her as he handed her a drawer's worth of papers. "You wanted to help. Now you have your chance."

"I've changed my mind," she said with a sniff, pleased by the small victory she'd gained. "I think I'll just sit here and watch you after all."

He turned to fix her with threatening eyes. "Don't press me, or you'll find yourself far more of a prisoner than you are now. I'll confine you to your bedroom if you don't behave."

She swallowed, her resolve wavering. Then she took the papers, although her hands trembled from the urge to throw them in his face. At least she'd gotten him to stop his suggestive teasing. Perhaps now she wouldn't feel quite so . . . so tormented.

His face still stormy, he explained how she was to sort the documents. She paid careful attention, even asking the occasional question in her determination to show him she wasn't some lightskirt who hadn't a clue about household management.

They worked for some time in silence until Elina came across something she hadn't noticed when she'd rifled his desk the first time. It was a rough sketch of a woman. The sweet, smiling face was framed by curls, and her eyes held a hint of laughter. Elina couldn't help but wonder who she was. Was this René's sister? Or was it one of those mistresses Louis had referred to?

For the first time, Elina wondered about the women in René's life. No one—neither Louis nor René—had mentioned a wife, so Elina could only assume René had none, at least not at the moment. He seemed to be in his thirties, so perhaps he'd had a wife in the past who had died. No, that seemed unlikely, for surely Louis would have said something.

Had Bonnange had no one except a string of mistresses? That seemed plausible. She felt certain a rakish gambler like him, could toy with the affections of any woman he wanted. But was there some Creole woman he intended to marry, some woman he was betrothed to? And was she the woman in the picture or even the woman at the *pied-à-terre*?

She looked up to find René staring at her, his eyes faintly curious.

"I see you've found the only example of my poor drawing ability."

She glanced at the sketch again. It was indeed the work of an amateur, though it captured surprisingly well some of the love of life that must have been in its subject. "Who is she?"

"Julia, my sister. I drew it shortly before I left New Orleans the first time."

Elina examined the picture for signs of resemblance. Except for the coloring and perhaps the eyes, Julia hardly resembled her brother. Elina stared in fascination at the image of her mama's rival. She wanted to hate the woman, just as she wanted to hate René, but both Bonnanges seemed to have this ability to make her like their images against her will.

"She's very pretty," Elina said, a trace of wistfulness in her voice.

"She is, isn't she? But I'm afraid my sketch doesn't do her justice. I drew it only because one of my tutors forced me to. There's a much better portrait of her upstairs in my bedroom."

But Elina scarcely heard him as she stared at the drawing with longing. She wished she had her materials so she could at least occupy her time with sketching. Her drawing materials had perished in the fire, along with everything else. If only she had them now, she could sketch Mama, and Papa, even Alex, before their faces completely faded from her mind. Then she'd have something of them besides just her memories.

Suddenly her hands began to tremble as an idea struck her. Of course, why hadn't she thought of it before? She could sketch Papa for René! Then he'd have to believe she was Philippe's daughter, for how else would she know what Philippe looked like?

"I, too, can draw," she told René, handing him the sketch of his sister. "I also paint. I used to give lessons."

"Really?" he said, disbelief evident in his tone of voice. "Was that before or after you embarked on your life of crime?"

Her lips tightened. "Oh, after, of course." She held her hands clenched in her lap, belying her casual tone. "After I left the boat and before I went to your *pied-à-terre*, I gave lessons to three distinguished children I met in the street. Then I abandoned my lucrative endeavors in order to find Alex so that we could rob a few banks. Now aren't I the clever one?"

"You are indeed," he said, his eyes twinkling, although he didn't smile. "But not clever enough to recognize when you've met your match. You're not going to convince me, sweet eyes, that the two of you hadn't planned your little game on the ship and hadn't played it many times before."

"Perhaps I will and perhaps I won't. But I can at least prove I know how to paint. All you need do is provide me with materials, and I'll demonstrate my skill, *Monsieur Sceptique*."

He flashed her a mocking grin. "If it hadn't been for my skeptical view of life, *ma petite*, I would long ago have lost my money to one of the many charlatans in Europe who wished me to invest in his ventures. One must be careful if one is to succeed, you understand."

"So you won't take my challenge and give me materials?" she said, giving him her own mocking smile.

His eyebrows quirked upward at her taunt. "I hadn't realized it was a challenge. But, yes, I'll humor you and let you show me your abilities. It will keep you occupied at something less damaging than searching my desk." He leaned back in his chair with a self-satisfied smile. "Of course, you'll have to repay me for my generosity."

Of course, she thought bitterly. "I have no money, as you well know, so I suppose you want something illicit," she said, her chin tilting up.

His eyes grew cold. "Don't be so hasty to assume things. I don't need to use such petty bribery to have you in my arms, *chérie.* You know that as well as I."

With the smooth grace of a stalking beast of prey, he rose to his feet and rounded her chair to stand behind her. His warm fingers grazed the soft hairs at her nape before they began insolently to toy with a stray curl.

Suddenly feeling like a trapped deer, she sprang to her feet and put the chair between them.

"No, you don't need bribery," she spat out as she stood glaring at him. "You have brute force at your disposal."

"Nor do I need force," he replied, although he pushed the chair aside with such strength it slid across the floor. He advanced on her, his eyes compelling her to stand motionless. One hand grasped her waist. Then he captured her chin with the other, forcing her head up so her mouth was so close to his she could feel his warm breath when he spoke. "You're like the cotton plants in the fields —all prickly and proud on the outside, but on the inside soft as silk. When I ignore the barbs and reach deeper to find the real woman, I find more willingness than the woman will admit to feeling."

She struggled to keep from trembling under his touch, but in vain. The moment his lips brushed hers in a feathery caress, she knew he could sense the way her body shook under the gentle onslaught. Her eyes closed involuntarily as his mouth pressed teasing kisses along the warm skin of her chin and cheeks, and his fingers snaked around to stroke her nape. She felt his other hand slip down to cup her hips, and her eyes flew open. In that moment, she caught a glimpse of his confident smile, and that gave her the strength to resist him.

Her pride wounded, she slapped him, delighting in the fact that her action was sufficient to wipe the smile from his face. He released her, one hand rubbing his cheek as his eyes flared with anger.

"One day you'll tire of having the barbs prick you," she told him. "And it won't matter if there's a softness inside. I hope and pray the day comes soon, so I can be free of this house and of you." She whirled, ready to flee, but his hand caught her arm and twisted her back to face him.

His gaze trailed over her from head to toe as she tried to force her blood to stop racing. With some effort, she maintained a cool composure, although his eyes strove to pierce it.

"I'm a very patient man, sweet eyes," he said at last, his steely even tone hinting at the determination behind his words. "I can wait for you to acknowledge defeat. Perhaps you'll even offer me your sweetness one day, when you discover that your chance for having greater riches is but a foolish dream. When that day comes, you may find I, too, have barbs. You may even discover that they left their mark on your hard heart long before you realized it."

"I'll die before I let you win," she whispered as she strained against the arm that held her.

"We shall see," he murmured.

Then he let her go, and she ran from the room, anxious to escape the eyes that promised he wouldn't relent until he'd gotten what he wanted.

It was nearly dusk when Elina crept down the stairs, hoping she'd been right and that she'd actually seen a carriage in front of the house. Perhaps if it had carried visitors, she could prevail upon them to take her back to the city. René was gone. He'd left shortly after their last confrontation. She'd seen him ride off on Savage, leaving several hours ago already. She only prayed that he'd stay gone long enough for her to slip away.

Her gloved hand clutched the three silver dollars she'd found at the bottom of her only reticule. Thank heavens

René hadn't searched it the way he'd searched her meager belongings at the hotel.

The house seemed deserted, although the wind had grown strong during the afternoon and now shook the shutters and blew the curtains at the open windows. The servants worked in the kitchen outside preparing dinner, so they were occupied. As for Louis, Elina hadn't seen him since shortly before René had left.

Stealthily, she tiptoed to the front door, keeping her eyes open for the slightest movement in the rooms she passed. She pecked out the window and smiled to herself when she saw the carriage and a brawny man dozing as he sat on the driver's seat. She slipped out the door, but the wind caught it, slamming it shut behind her. The driver awakened, startled.

"Lord have mercy, what was that?" he cried. Then he grinned broadly as he noticed Elina standing there. "You lookin' for someone, missy?"

She swallowed. "Yes, I suppose I am. I was hoping your employer might give me a ride into town."

"Wal, I suppose he would if he was here," the driver said, scratching his head. "But he's in town this very moment. I don't believe he's meanin' to go back into town again today. I mean, you should 'a just rode with him when he left this mornin'."

A dreadful sense of hopelessness began to steal over her. "Who's your employer?" she asked sharply.

"Why, Mr. Bonnange, of course." He drew himself up with pride. "I'm the coachman he hired just last month for his house in town. He sent me in from the city a lil' while ago. Came in on his horse, did some shoppin', and asked me to bring his purchases back here while he stayed in town a bit." His curious gaze traveled over her. "Don't believe I seen you here before."

"I'm only visiting," she hastened to tell him. Then she flashed him a winning smile. "I really need a ride into town. I wonder if you might take me?"

Deborah Martin

He thought about that a moment. "I s'pose I could. Course, I have to wait for Mr. Bonnange to come back afore I can leave."

She fought the urge to rail at him. Instead, she held out two of her precious silver dollars. "I can't wait until he decides to return. I need to go now. If I give you this, will you take me?"

Her heart pounded in anticipation as his eyes widened. "I'd sure like to, missy, but Mr. Bonnange told me to come here with this stuff and wait for him. He should be along any minute now, so if you just wait—"

She pulled out another dollar. "Please . . ." She drew in a deep breath and thought quickly. "Please," she began with more firmness. "My brother died in town the day before yesterday, and I haven't yet arranged for his burial. I simply must do so. You understand, of course." She held the three dollars up to him, her face pleading.

She wasn't sure if he believed her, for his eyes seemed to take in her lack of mourning clothing.

Then he shrugged. He climbed down and took her three dollars. With a grin, he tucked them into his breast pocket. "I s'pose I can't ignore a pretty missy like you when she needs some help. All right. But I have to unload the stuff Mr. Bonnange sent back with me first."

"Fine. I'll help you."

But she wasn't prepared for the large number of boxes packed inside the carriage. She didn't bother to wonder what was in them, so eager was she to get the carriage unloaded. Paying no attention to the driver's remonstrations, she pulled out boxes, heavy or light, and carried them onto the front gallery.

"I think we should bring them inside, missy," the driver said, but she insisted they had no time to do so.

She'd just lifted another box when the sound of hoofbeats made her freeze.

"Why, hello, Mr. Bonnange," she heard the driver call out cheerfully. "Glad you got back before we left after all."

158

"Left?" the cool voice responded.

She continued moving forward as if in a daze. Too late! She was always too late to escape, curse him! Forcing herself to behave calmly, she set the box down and turned to face her jailer.

René's eyes were on her. She steeled herself to meet his gaze. His eyes stayed on her while the driver was talking, but they weren't smiling, and she shivered at the frigid smile pasted on his face.

"The missy told me she needed to get into town to arrange for her brother's funeral," the driver was saying. "I told her I should wait till you got back, but she kept insistin' she wanted to go right away."

René's gaze grew even colder. "The 'missy' was unaware, perhaps, that I've just arranged for her brother's burial. In fact, I was returning to accompany her to town for it."

She stared at him in shock. Was he telling the truth, or just trying to keep his coachman from feeling sympathetic toward her? Why would he arrange for Alex's burial? And if he'd truly done it, what kind of burial had he planned, given the way he felt about Alex?

"I think I should remind, you, Halsey, that I'm your employer, not *Mademoiselle* Wallace," René continued. "I'd already given you an order, one that shouldn't have been countermanded—even by a guest. In future, you should remember that. Now finish unloading the carriage, and take it back to the stables."

The driver glanced at Elina, who wouldn't look at him. Then he drew her three dollars out of his breast pocket.

"To be honest, sir, the missy gave me three dollars to take her into town or I wouldn't have considered leavin'. It seemed to me that anyone who'd give that much money must be kinda desperate. I'll just give it back to her now, if you don't mind." He started up the steps toward Elina, but René's voice stopped him.

"Keep the three dollars, Halsey. *Mademoiselle* Wallace won't be needing them. Consider it payment for unloading the carriage, which I'd planned to have Louis do. And next time someone offers you money to go against my wishes, remember that I alone have the power to dismiss you. Is that understood?"

"Yessir," Halsey mumbled as he quickly dropped the three dollars back into his breast pocket.

"Good."

As Halsey carried the last few boxes past where Elina was standing, René swung down from Savage with sleek agility and hitched his mount to a post. Halsey passed him and then drove the carriage out of sight around the side of the house as René strode onto the gallery.

Elina faced René, her face flushed with anger. "How dare you give him *my* money! You had no right!"

Her distress didn't seem to bother him at all. "And you, *mademoiselle*, had no right to coerce my coachman into doing your bidding. Couldn't you at least wait to see if I'd meet your request?" René remarked casually as he stood in front of her.

"Request?" she asked, his words throwing her off guard.

He waved his hands at the boxes stacked around them. "I hasten to the city to purchase your drawing materials and return to find you hauling them up the steps like so many sacks of seed before bribing my own coachman to help you run away. Such lack of appreciation," he said, shaking his head in stern disapproval. "I'll have to work faster next time."

She gazed around the gallery, for the first time noticing the thin rectangular objects wrapped in paper and string that were undoubtedly canvases. A murmur of dismay escaped her lips as she noticed the haphazard way the canvases were stacked.

"But you said . . . I mean, I thought—" she began confusedly, trying to remember if he'd finally agreed to provide her with materials or not. Her pulse quickened as she recalled that he'd told her she'd have to repay his generosity.

She shook her head. "No, I can't use them. I won't do wicked things for the sake of having a few pencils."

"A few pencils!" he cried in mock reproach. "I beg your pardon, *mademoiselle*, but there are more than a few pencils here." He strode over to one of the boxes and undid the string. Then he opened the box and carried it back to her to show it was filled with pots of paint in assorted colors.

"The other boxes contain more of those," he told her. "Along with charcoal, brushes, sketchbooks . . . whatever your little artist's heart desires."

He watched her as she scanned the gallery, her face glowing with the wonder of having such a hoard at her disposal. So much new paper to transform into sketches for paintings! So many colors to paint with! Think what she could do with it all! She opened the next box he held out to her in one hand and discovered it held an artist's palette, new and untouched. She reached inside to touch it, and he clasped her wrist with his free hand.

"First, you must agree to my proposal."

Her head came up with a snap as she remembered that the drawing materials carried a price. Sternly, she reminded herself this was his bribe, his way of making her do what he wanted—to tempt her with the things she loved.

"It's not what you think," he continued as she stiffened. "None of those wicked things you abhor are involved. If indeed you have some small ability to produce reasonable reproductions, then I wish you to paint a portrait. That's all."

Surely he wasn't serious, she thought as she looked at him in bewilderment. Of course she'd paint a portrait! She'd paint the devil himself if he'd give her the materials needed to show she really was a Vannier.

"Who—whom will I paint?"

"Me."

She couldn't have been more astonished if he'd suggested she paint the mayor of New Orleans.

Deborah Martin

"Why would you want me to paint your portrait?" She eyed him with suspicion. "You don't know my abilities. You didn't even believe I *could* paint. What new trick is this?"

He carefully set the box holding the palette down on the floor. "No trick," he said as he straightened. "My sister has been begging me to have my portrait done for her. If the portrait you produce is adequate, I'll give it to her. If it's wretched, I'll have had other compensations."

For some reason, that statement made her uncomfortable, particularly when he was standing so close to her she could scarcely move without touching him. She bit her lower lip in thought. His eyes seemed to focus on that slight gesture, and she stepped back out of his reach, nearly falling over a box.

"What . . . what other compensations?"

"Let's just say it will give us the opportunity to learn more about one another. I'll have to sit for you for hours at a time. Perhaps when you've come to know me, you'll realize I couldn't have killed your brother. In itself, that would be a step forward in our relations." He grinned. "Who knows? The constant sight of me might soften you toward me, sweet eyes."

His use of that nickname helped her regain her composure.

"You're insufferable, *monsieur*," she responded haughtily. "I'll never see you as anything but a monster."

"Ah, but how many monsters would buy you such lovely toys?" he said with a laugh. Then he sobered. "Relax, *chérie*, and accept my offer. That is, if you do indeed know how to paint."

"I do," she assured him. "And I'm not afraid of you. But don't think this means you can take liberties with me."

"Sweet eyes, you know me better than that. I only take liberties when it's clear they are allowed to me."

She blushed scarlet, remembering the kiss she'd responded to so wantonly.

"But if you wish," he continued, "you may consider yourself my resident artist. Would that lessen your objections to being my . . . ah . . . visitor? Not that you have any choice, of course."

She took one long look at the boxes around her. If she could only draw a reasonable likeness of her papa to show René she wasn't lying, then he'd be forced to accept she was who she said she was. None of the rest would matter. Besides, why not paint René's portrait? She'd depict him as she liked—as the murderer he was. Then he wouldn't be so self-satisfied. She had nothing to lose and everything to gain by agreeing to his proposal.

"I'd be quite happy to paint your portrait," she announced. Then she thought of her plan to sketch her papa. "But I'll need some time to work on another endeavor that's important to me."

"Oh?"

She avoided the scrutinizing gaze trained on her. "Yes, something I've wanted to sketch since I came here. It won't take long, just a day or two. But if you won't give me the time—"

His throaty chuckle made her stare at him in surprise. Had he guessed what she wished to do?

"Always bargaining, aren't you?" He stepped closer and her fingers tightened on the folds of her dress. "Why so nervous? Does my nearness upset you?" He snatched her right hand without warning and pulled back the worn kid gloves to expose her wrist. When he placed his lips against the sensitive skin on the inside of her wrist, she felt her pulse quicken under his disquieting, though brief, caress. "I see that it does. *Bon*." He drew the glove slowly off her hand, his eyes locked on hers.

She felt powerless to stop him as he lifted her hand briefly to his lips. "You may have your day or two to finish your endeavor, sweet eyes. I'll be delighted to have you occupied with something other than rearranging my desk and bribing my coachman."

Deborah Martin

His statement brought her back to his earlier words about Alex. She went very still, though her hand suddenly clenched his.

"Did you really arrange for Alex's burial?" she asked. "Or was that just a tale to fool the coachman?"

"I arranged it."

"And you're taking me to town for it."

"Not to town. He'll be buried in a cemetery near here, so we've no need to go to town and risk your trying to spread your lies to everyone you see."

She stifled a sob and looked away from him. "I—I suppose it's a pauper's grave, since we had no money except what we stole from you."

He tensed. "It will be a marked tomb. You needn't fear your lover will be buried less than properly."

She ignored his sarcasm, staring at him with blank surprise. She didn't know what to think. What kind of man would do such a thing?

"Why have you arranged for him to have a proper burial? He was your enemy. You owed him nothing. Why do this kindness?"

He released her hand, turning to stare out over the grounds. "To be honest, I don't know. I suppose I felt someone should."

"If you think such an act absolves you of guilt—"

He whirled on her, his mouth tense with fury. "I have no guilt. I didn't kill him, honorably or otherwise. And if you weren't so intent on finding a way to use his death for your own gain, you'd accept the truth!"

Her hands itched with the desire to claw his face, but she knew she wouldn't be able to get near him. So she merely replied, "I've asked for nothing from you but a few drawing materials. You, however, have bought me much more than I requested and are going to a great deal of trouble and expense to keep me here. I say only a guilty man would feel the need to shower a man's bereaved sister with gifts while keeping her a prisoner."

"The only thing I'm guilty of," he said, his fists clenched at his sides, "is allowing myself to become intrigued by a conniving schemer like you. Believe me, that's something I'm truly beginning to regret."

And with those words, he stormed into the house, leaving her to stare blindly around at the boxes of materials while tears slowly streamed down her face.

Chapter Ten

Life is like an onion, which one peels crying.
—*French Proverb*

The face was familiar, but still not familiar enough, Elina thought as she stared at her sketch of her papa. It sufficiently depicted her papa's features, his hawkish nose and deep-set eyes, but it didn't really capture his soul. Not yet, anyway. Abstractedly, she unbuttoned the sleeves of her nightdress and pushed them up above her elbows. Then she licked the tip of her pencil and renewed her efforts.

Sunlight streamed through the open windows, but she scarcely noticed there was no longer any need for the candle that burned at her bedside. She'd awakened before dawn and hadn't been able to go back to sleep. How could she sleep in air so hot and damp? After tossing fruitlessly underneath the mosquito netting, she'd finally risen and decided to continue working on Papa's sketch.

Attending Alex's quiet burial the day before had only strengthened her determination to prove her identity to

René. Alex's gravestone had carried his assumed name, not his real name, because René had refused to have "Alexandre Vannier" carved on the stone of an impostor. The sight of it had nearly broken her, for she could hardly bear the fact that her brother would now be buried for all time with the wrong name. She'd hold René accountable for that, she had told herself, along with all the other wrongs he'd committed against her.

After their return from the burial, he'd disappeared, and she'd returned to her room and the drawing materials, her mind fixed on only one thing—proving her identity. She'd even skipped supper in her eagerness to sketch her papa. Yet now she didn't even feel hungry. As always, being absorbed in her work drove away all other physical considerations.

A tap at the door that led to René's bedroom startled her, making her drop her pencil. She stared at the door uneasily, thankful she'd chosen to use René's and Louis's absence the day before to sneak into Louis's room and steal his keys. It had taken her awhile to discover which key fit the lock to her room, but it had been worth all her trouble to find out. At least now she was protected from any surprise visits by René. And she couldn't believe Louis would begrudge her that once he found the key missing.

Another tap sharper than the last made her start. "Yes?" she asked, trying to put some imperviousness into her tone.

"It's time for breakfast, Elina," René answered.

His voice, husky and deep in the early morning, sent an uncontrollable thrill through her that she attempted to ignore. "I'm busy. I'll eat later."

She heard him try the door and then mutter a low curse.

"Open the door so we can talk about this," he commanded.

She had to suppress a giggle. The high-and-mighty René Bonnange couldn't get to her. How delightful to be able to thwart his desires for a change.

167

Her knowledge that he couldn't get in emboldened her, although she knew he'd make her regret her little rebellion later. "I'll open the door when I'm quite ready. Now go away and leave me alone!"

When she heard no response from him, she gave a satisfied sigh. With a grin on her face, she groped for the pencil she'd dropped among the bedclothes. Then she heard a key rattle in the door that led to the gallery, and she looked up to see René opening the glass door. In dismay, she realized she hadn't thought to steal the key to the gallery.

As René entered the room, his eyes flickered over her, dark with barely controlled anger. Instantly, she slid off the bed, putting it between them. "Am I to have no privacy at all?" she cried as she clutched her nightdress closed at the neck.

"None. Not when you use your privacy to starve yourself. What did you intend to do—faint away with hunger so I'd be forced to call a physician?"

She stared at him incredulously. He'd been worried she might starve herself on purpose? What an absurd idea! Her sense of humor overcame her at the thought of her doing such a thing. It reminded her too much of tragic heroines in plays. Starve herself indeed!

At her expression of surprise, he became agitated. "Answer me, Elina! Were you refusing to eat for a reason? Or do you have another bizarre explanation for your behavior?"

His words reminded her of what she'd been working on before he came in. She glanced at the bed, suddenly aware she'd left the sketch in plain view. His gaze followed hers. His expression softened, and she held her breath, hoping he'd had his answer and would leave her alone. Instead, he strode forward and snatched up the sketch before she could react. Rounding the bed in alarm, Elina forgot all about the way she was dressed, forgot about everything except getting the sketch away from him.

He still hadn't looked at it, intent on watching her.

Oblivious to the fact that her hair loosely tumbled about her shoulders and her nightdress gaped, Elina darted forward and tried to wrest the sketch away from him.

"Let me have it!" she said in frustration as he held the sketch out of her reach. "It's not finished! You may not see it yet!" As she pulled at his arm furiously, she didn't care that her body pressed up against his, that only a thin piece of linen covered her.

"Is this what has kept you so occupied you won't even eat?" he asked in amusement, his thickly muscled arm easily resisting her tugging. "*Mon Dieu*, sweet eyes, this endeavor of yours must be fascinating. Now stop hanging on me, so I can see what you've been up to."

"No! You can't see it until it's finished!"

Heedless of her protests, he tossed the sketchbook onto the bed, but when she pivoted toward it, his arm went around her waist, lifting her and trapping her against his body.

"Release me this instant!" she cried. She kicked backward at his shins. Barefooted, she could do little damage.

With ease he carried her to the gallery door, then thrust her outside on the gallery, and locked her out. She beat on the glass, livid with helpless rage as she saw him stride toward the bed and pick up the sketchbook. How dare he ruin her plans this way! she thought as she dashed to the nearest open window. In minutes, she had clambered over the sill and into the room, but it was too late. René was studying the sketch, his brow furrowed.

She stopped in her tracks, a sense of frustration overwhelming her as she waited breathlessly for him to speak. Surely even in the state it was, he could recognize her papa. She knew the drawing was far enough along for that.

And if he did recognize Philippe? Then he'd be forced to admit she was telling the truth.

Slowly, he lifted his head to fix her with a gaze of undiluted suspicion. "What is the purpose of this?" he asked harshly.

Her startled eyes met his. "It's Papa," she stated, confused by his reaction. She nervously twisted the material of her nightdress in one hand.

"You mean it's Philippe. I know that. I'm not blind, and you're indeed quite talented. But that doesn't answer my question."

And why not? she thought. Couldn't he understand what she intended to show him?

"I wanted to prove Philippe was my papa," she explained, "so I sketched him as I remembered him. Now that you've seen it, you can't deny I must have known him before he died, long before I ever met you. If the sketch doesn't prove it, I don't know what else you require."

He stared at her for a moment, his expression showing his astonishment. Gradually, his astonishment was replaced by a fierce anger that flamed in his eyes, making her back up a step. "You really think you've got me hoodwinked, don't you? That I'm so enamored of you I can't think straight anymore."

"What are you saying?" she whispered as she met his glare. How could he ignore the proof she'd given him? He said he recognized Philippe. So what did he find objectionable?

He tossed the sketch on the bed in disgust. "You're not only talented, you're clever, *chérie*, but I'm every bit as clever as you. I suppose this was to be the proof that forced me to release you, to bring you to Philippe's solicitor and arrange for you to obtain your inheritance?"

"Of—of course." Surely he couldn't ignore the evidence staring him in the face!

"Did you think I'd conveniently forget that a portrait of all three Vanniers, including Philippe, is prominently displayed in my own bedroom? Somehow that was to have escaped my notice?"

"What?" she asked in bewilderment, backing away from him as he advanced on her.

He closed the gap between them in moments, his hands clutching her shoulders. "Don't use that expression of surprise on me, Elina. It worked once, but I've grown used to your deceptions. You know quite well what I'm talking about."

She shook her head mindlessly. "No, no, you're just saying these things so you won't have to believe the truth! I don't know what on earth you could mean!"

His hand closed on her arm, and he dragged her out onto the gallery and then through the door into his room. They stopped in front of his dresser. At first she didn't see the portrait, so chagrined was she at being in his bedroom. Then she noticed it. The sight of Papa standing behind his seated wife and young son sent a sharp pang through her. He looked so happy, so comfortable. It was difficult to accept that this was his family, too—these smiling strangers. She stood staring numbly at the portrait with its excellent likeness of Papa.

"What do you have to say for yourself now?" René's harsh voice grated from where he stood at her elbow, his hand still gripping her arm. His question brought her out of her thoughts. Suddenly she realized what he was implying: that she'd seen the portrait before and copied it.

"Until this very moment, I hadn't seen this picture," she told him, turning to gaze up into his anger-darkened face. "Tell me, when, to your knowledge, have I even been in this room?"

"To my knowledge?" he asked, his voice rising. "What has my knowledge got to do with anything? You rearranged the contents of my desk without my knowledge, you tried to bribe my coachman without my knowledge, and you copied that portrait without my knowledge. It seems to me, *mademoiselle*, you're very adept at doing things behind my back. You've had plenty of opportunity in the last two days to observe and to copy the portrait." His eyes narrowed.

171

"And plenty of time before that to plan your strategy to ask me for your materials."

She looked at him in exasperation, her green eyes alight with her own fury. "Why should I even think to enter your room, *monsieur*, when I've spent all my time avoiding it? I didn't come in here, I tell you!"

"So you completely ignored my mentioning yesterday that there was a portrait of my sister in my room."

"Yes, I did," she said firmly, becoming more and more irritated by his refusal to see the truth. "I don't remember your saying such a thing. You're making it up."

"I don't make things up, Elina. I'm afraid I don't possess your incredibly active imagination nor your ability to play a role to perfection."

He was still angry, but something else was beginning to encroach on his anger, making his fingers loosen perceptibly on her arm.

But she scarcely noticed, for now her dander was up. She stamped her foot in frustration. "You just won't listen to me, will you? You're determined to paint me as some sort of fortune hunter!"

He gestured to the portrait hanging above his dresser. "I think the evidence of that is there before you."

Her fists clenched helplessly at her sides, she decided to try another tack. "You must admit the two pictures aren't the same!"

He smiled grimly. "Both are pictures of Philippe. That's all that matters. An imaginative artist is quite capable of changing the expression or posture of a character in a painting, as you well know."

She wrenched her arm from his grasp and started toward the gallery door. Then she stopped and whirled to face him before she reached it. "You think to cow me with your tricks and evasions, *monsieur*, but I'll find a way to beat you yet. Then you'll regret you didn't treat me more honorably."

He advanced toward her in even strides. "Is it honorable in your eyes for me to condemn my sister's husband as a bigamist on the strength of one girl's word?"

"I'm telling the truth!" she shouted. "An honorable man wouldn't doubt me. Nor would he bring me to his bedroom against my will!"

He was beside her in a flash, his hand restraining her. "An honorable woman wouldn't prance about in her bare feet with her nightdress half undone and expect to be left alone," he said, his iron-hard eyes raking over her.

With an effort, she kept from showing how his words had mortified her. He was taunting her on purpose and she knew it. Still, her free hand flew to clutch her nightdress at the neck. "It was hot. Besides, I was in my bedroom. I certainly didn't expect to be disturbed."

She tried to escape his grasp, but instead of releasing her, his other hand captured her waist. His eyes warmed as they lingered on the neck of her nightdress. "You should always expect to be disturbed when I'm around, sweet eyes," he murmured. His gaze traveled over her wild and unbound hair, rose-tinted cheeks, and delicate nose, before they stopped at her mouth, which parted slightly as she sought to catch the breath he seemed to suck from her without even trying.

She wanted to look away from the naked hunger that shone in his eyes and had replaced his earlier anger. But the promise his gaze offered held her entranced. She'd never felt the siren call of desire before, not with any of the men who'd courted her. Even the ones who'd stolen kisses had never made her feel anything but impatience. But now she wanted this man to kiss her, to slake the thirst for his lips that grew moment by moment within her.

He smiled, a low lingering smile of awareness that stripped her, laying bare her every private feeling. She forced her face away from him, wanting to escape that smile so she could escape her own yearnings, but he ignored her slight gesture of resistance and planted a soft kiss on the delicate skin beneath her ear. At the touch of his wind-roughened lips on her skin, she jerked away, but he pulled her up against his body, his muscular arms crushing her against him.

"I don't mind your being dishonorable, *chérie*," he murmured, his sweet breath warming her cheek an instant before his mouth moved sideways to meet hers. As his words registered, she clenched her teeth, determined not to let him enter her mouth as he had before. But his mouth played insistently over hers, the tip of his tongue sliding along the crevice of her lips until she felt weak and hot.

"Open your mouth to me, Elina," he whispered.

"I—I mustn't," she said, scarcely realizing she'd spoken the words aloud, but he smothered any other protests with his lips and slipped his tongue inside her mouth.

It was as if her whole body sighed with the pleasure of having him kiss her so intimately. She knew she shouldn't revel in it, but she did.

He explored her velvety mouth at his leisure, his hands stroking downward to the small of her back and then upward. She could feel the warmth of his hands through the thin cloth, a warmth conducted instantly from his hands to the nether reaches of her body. The place below her belly tightened. She'd never felt so tight and aching there before.

Oh, what was he doing to her? she thought hazily as his lips pressed kiss after kiss on the corners of her lips, the swell of her cheeks, the tip of her nose. The protective shield she'd erected against him was melting away from her like wax, leaving her soft and exposed to his invasion.

Her fingers, which had clutched her nightdress so tightly moments before, fell limp from the neck of the garment, and her arms twined around his powerful waist. He groaned and grasped her closer, his mouth devouring hers with increased fervor as she responded mindlessly.

His lips left her face to touch her neck, her ear, the hollow of her throat, making her skin tingle wherever they lighted. One of his hands slid up to the collar of her nightdress and slipped under the material to fondle her naked shoulder. His touch sent shivers through her, temporarily jolting her back to reality. But before she could even protest, he pressed yet another drugging kiss upon her, driving every thought of resistance from her mind.

Then his hand descended to cup her breast with warm intimacy, his fingers lightly teasing the aching nipple. She could feel the rough skin of his hand against her own tender skin, but it played so expertly on her that all she seemed able to do was clasp him more tightly as a low moan escaped her. His lips moved to replace his fingers, closing over the tip of her breast in hungry ardor. With passion-glazed eyes, she looked down to see his dark head against her pale skin and the sight of it at last shocked her into reacting.

She pressed against his shoulders, weakly at first as the feel of his tongue swirling over her nipple made her incapable of movement. "Please don't!" she whispered frantically, her fingers digging into his shoulders with insistence.

His head left her breast, but before she could even think, he'd lifted her in his arms and was carrying her toward his bed.

"Surely you realize you tempt me beyond endurance, sweet eyes," he told her with a searing gaze that sought to reach her very soul. For a moment, she was motionless in his arms, scarcely daring to believe what he meant. But when he lay her on the coverlet and she felt the mattress beneath her, she realized with a shock that he intended to have her.

He lowered himself to the bed beside her, his eyes never leaving her face. With a cry of distress, she struggled to sit up, but his arm pinned her waist as he threw his leg over one of hers. Despite her fear, she found a certain bitter pleasure in the intimate way his body was now pressed along the full length of hers as he lay half on top of her. With weakening resolve, she struggled, but he was too consumed by desire to pay attention to her feeble attempts at resisting him. His eyes devoured her, while his hand stroked languidly down along her hip to her thighs. She turned a flaming red, painfully conscious that she wore nothing under her nightdress. Wherever his eyes fell, the material seemed to grow even thinner before her very eyes.

"Don't do this, René," she murmured as he lowered his head to nuzzle her neck, but her voice sounded seductively inviting, even to her own ears.

He lifted his head, and she could tell by the way his eyes turned a warm chocolate that he was thoroughly aroused. "You're not going to show me your prickly side again, are you?" he asked in a silky voice as his hand glided from her hip to rest on her flat abdomen. She could feel the heat of his touch even through the linen. She watched in helpless fascination as his long fingers slid into the open collar of her nightdress. He pushed the material aside to bare her breast to his gaze.

For the first time in her life, she felt a sensation there that made the deep pink tip harden even before his fingers could touch it. Horrified by the visible evidence of her own weakness, she pressed her hand against his as he moved to caress the soft mound. His eyes locked with hers, a hint of frustration in their depths.

"If you could only know what it's like to see you here as I've imagined you so many times in the past few days, you wouldn't deny me." His eyes trailed with burning thoroughness over her trembling form. "If I were as talented with a paintbrush as you are with that pencil of yours, I'd strive to capture you on canvas, just as you are now. But no one would ever be allowed to see that painting . . . no one but me. I wouldn't share such a masterpiece with anyone."

His fingers trailed blazingly over her breast, but they didn't find the response he'd anticipated. His reference to paintings reminded her of why she'd entered his room in the first place, giving her the resolve she'd otherwise seemed to lack. This time when her hand gripped his wrist, it was firm as she pushed his hand away.

"My talent seems to have done me no good and neither would yours, for I'd never allow you to paint me in such a state," she vowed. Once again her fingers flew to the neck of her nightdress and pulled the gaping ends together.

He released an exasperated sigh. His hands moved to grip her wrists. Then he pressed her hands back against the bedcovers, his body still half hovering over hers. He stared down at her coldly glittering eyes.

"Listen, *chérie*. We may not have chosen to feel this desire for each other, but we seem to have lost the will to fight it. So why not succumb to what's natural?"

It stung her that he easily recognized her desire for him. He thought to use her weakness against her, did he? She wasn't the fool he took her for. She'd recovered her wits enough to remember how little René could be trusted.

"It isn't natural to succumb to an unnatural man—a murderer like you—and I shall never do it," she hissed, her fingers tingling with a sudden longing to scratch his eyes out.

She writhed beneath him in blind fury, wanting to escape before he managed to turn her desires against her yet again. Her anger was fueled by the realization that she'd encouraged his advances, that even while she told herself she hated him, she regretted that he'd stopped caressing her.

His eyes traveled over her wriggling body, longing tinged with regret showing in his face. Then he released her abruptly. A low curse escaped his lips. He left her on the bed and stalked across the room to the dresser. Silently, he picked up her sketchbook. She buttoned her nightdress in haste and then flung herself from the bed toward him. He didn't resist as she snatched the book from his hand.

"Your sketch proves nothing, as I hope you realize by now," he told her.

Although his back was to her, she could see his face in the mirror. Both seemed as stiff and unyielding as carved oak.

"You refuse to see the truth because it would ruin your life to admit it!" she accused him. As his face became even bleaker and grimmer, she lashed out, wanting to hurt him for viewing her and her life so callously. "Perhaps I was right after all. Perhaps you *have* known all along who I am! Maybe you killed Alex because of that knowledge. Does it give you pleasure to humiliate Philippe's daughter? Did you have something against him that you're not saying?"

He whirled to face her. His eyes were those of a fiercely proud stallion, and she had to fight to keep from showing how vulnerable she suddenly felt in the wake of his anger.

"You wanted to see the magistrate, didn't you?"

The cold question startled her.

"Didn't you?" he demanded through gritted teeth.

"I did," she responded, hope already stirring within her at his words.

"Then you will see him. Let him listen to your insane accusations and wearying half-truths. I refuse to endure either anymore."

"You'd take me to see him?" she asked, suddenly afraid this was his way of telling her he intended to have her jailed.

"No," he bit out, turning toward the door. "I'll bring him here. If he takes your collection of lies for the truth, then I'll concede defeat and release you."

"And if not?" she asked in a trembling voice, scarcely daring to believe he was at last giving her a chance to be heard.

"If not . . ." he paused, then turned to fix her with eyes as dark as oiled wood. "If not, the choice is yours. Take my money to keep your lies to yourself, or stay here and paint my portrait until you admit you can't best me, *mademoiselle*."

She squared her shoulders, crossing her arms over her chest protectively. "The magistrate will believe me. You'll see."

"Aren't you just a bit afraid he might cart you off to jail, *chérie*?" he asked in a voice deceptively soft.

She paled. Could he read her mind? Did he know her fears even as she felt them?

"Would you let him?"

Time seemed to wait on his answer as her desperate words hung in the air between them. His eyes met hers and froze for a moment, his face filled with bleak turmoil.

"You know the answer to that, sweet eyes," he responded in a voice tinged with rancor.

She did know. In the depths of her being, she knew he wouldn't do such a thing.

He turned to leave the room again, but paused when he reached the doorway. "Breakfast will be served as soon as you show yourself at the table, so I expect you dressed and downstairs in five minutes, or I'll come up for you." Then he added casually, "And how did you manage to lock yourself in? I don't recall giving you any keys."

She hesitated to answer. Should she tell him the truth, or would that result in her losing what little freedom she had? He half-turned toward her, his expression clearly stating that he'd find the truth out one way or another.

"I—I took them from Louis's room," she admitted.

"I see. Funny how you had no qualms about entering his bedroom, but refused to enter mine under any circumstances." The look of triumph he flashed her made her instantly regret telling him the truth.

He left the room then, but Elina couldn't resist hurling what was in her hand at the closed door. As soon as it bounced to the floor, she saw she'd thrown the sketchbook with the portrait of her papa.

Her tears half-blinding her, she crouched on the floor beside the book to stare at the face of the man who'd betrayed her, Alex, and Mama. If it hadn't been for him and his treachery, she wouldn't be here in this house, at the mercy of an unfeeling brute who nonetheless had magic in his touch.

"Damn you, Papa!" she murmured as she took one last look at the smiling face. Then silently she tore the picture into tiny bits and left them on René's bedroom floor.

Chapter Eleven

When we come close to a giant, he often turns out to be only a common man on stilts.—Creole Proverb

Juan Oliveira leaned back casually in his chair with his fingers pressed together. René watched the older man's face, wondering what had made their longtime friendship endure despite Juan's hatred for Francois. René and Juan had little in common. Although both were *bon famille*, accepted in every household in Creole society, the resemblance ended there. René had no interest in holding his prominent position in Creole society, but Juan loved the little powers his position as magistrate afforded him. He enjoyed the inane *soirée* conversation that René so hated. And his easygoing nature made him more apt to be out hunting with friends than in his chambers.

Yet beneath the jovial smile ran a thread of intelligence that made him a good judge despite his easy air. He wasn't easily fooled, a fact that had surprised many a Yankee gambler. It had also made René extend him a grudging respect, and their mutual respect was no doubt what kept them on congenial terms.

René felt certain the man would see the truth despite Elina's pretenses and blatant lies. Juan was very discerning. That was why René had told him nothing more about his purpose for bringing him to Cour de Cyprès than that he wished him to meet someone. René didn't want Elina to be able to accuse him of poisoning the man's perceptions before Juan had heard her side.

What René hated to admit was that part of his reason for bringing the magistrate out to meet Elina was to have another more objective opinion of the situation. The deeper René found himself involved with her, the less he seemed able to see her for what she was. His mind told him she was a practiced deceiver. His heart . . . No, his body protested otherwise. His heart wasn't part of it, he told himself. Surely he wouldn't feel anything but this cursed desire for her kind of woman.

"So where is this visitor you wish me to meet?" Juan asked, drawing René away from his uncomfortable thoughts.

"Louis has gone to fetch her. She's rather perturbed with me at the moment. This morning I managed to . . . ah . . . wound her feelings."

Juan chuckled. "I imagine you're quite capable of dealing with such matters, my friend. One look at that devilish face of yours and the women swoon. Why, my wife thinks you're extremely dashing. Of course, if I ever thought she had a reason for saying it other than to make me jealous, we'd be dueling before the day was out."

"Of course," René said with a smile. "But you needn't worry. As you say, Lisette is only trying to make you jealous. Besides, once women come to know me well, they discover I'm not nearly so dashing as they thought. It's the fact that I breed and race horses that attracts them. They don't realize it's a tedious business most of the time."

"And your visitor? What does she think?"

A quiet voice answered from the doorway. "She quite agrees that *monsieur* is not as dashing as one might think."

Both men stood abruptly as Elina swept into the room, wearing the same dress she'd worn for three days. Even though it wasn't in the height of fashion, René couldn't help but feel a surge of desire every time he saw her in it. The sea-green gros de Naples became her, highlighting the red of her hair and her startling green eyes. Still, he couldn't help wondering what she'd look like dressed in rich silks and satins that would make her creamy skin glow.

Annoyed with that wayward thought, René introduced her to Juan, but only as Elina. He immediately sensed her fear of the magistrate, though she masked it well with a dignified nod.

"*Monsieur* Bonnange tells me you wish my help," Juan said as the three of them sat down. "He wouldn't explain what he meant, but I assure you I'll do anything in my power to aid such a lovely friend of René's."

René fought back a smile at Juan's effusive language. *Always the Creole gentleman,* he thought, noting with a twinge of jealousy the way Elina seemed to relax at the magistrate's words. Still, she did cast an inquiring glance René's way.

"*Monsieur* Oliveira doesn't know anything about you," René explained. "I haven't yet told him who you are. I left that to you. I trust you'll tell him the entire story, including the . . . ah . . . unsavory parts. Otherwise, I'll be forced to interject my own version."

She glanced from René to Juan, her face reflecting her nervousness. Then she squared her shoulders in a gesture that was becoming all too familiar to René, as if she were preparing for battle. Yet she still said nothing, her brow furrowed.

Juan seemed to sense she wasn't sure how to begin. "How did you and *Monsieur* Bonnange meet?" he asked with a polite tone in a clear attempt to put her at ease. ·

René's eyebrows arched as Elina grew even stiffer in her chair. How ironic that Juan had chosen the one subject certain to unnerve Elina.

"We . . . we met on the *Belvedere*," she said with a stout defensiveness that René recognized as typical. "My brother, Alex, and *Monsieur* Bonnange played cards together."

Juan frowned as if trying to remember something he'd dismissed. René knew the exact moment when Juan realized who Elina must be, for although the magistrate's smile remained, his eyes became those of the suspicious interrogator.

"I believe I've heard something of that meeting," he said with a coolness calculated to make criminals feel guilty.

Elina turned accusing eyes on René.

"I didn't tell him, *chérie*," René said. "But I reported the incident, after all. You can hardly expect that the magistrate wouldn't have heard of it."

"I'm here to listen to your side of it, is that it?" Juan asked, his eyes growing thoughtful as he observed the way Elina and René looked at each other.

"Not just that," René said, his gaze still on Elina. "But perhaps we should begin there."

"All right then," Juan replied. He settled his portly frame more comfortably in his chair, his eyes fixed on Elina. "What happened on the *Belvedere, mademoiselle*?"

Ignoring René entirely, Elina described for Juan the card game and why she'd been present in the men's cabin. But when she came to the part about Alex's cheating, she faltered.

"What's wrong?" René taunted. "Don't you want to tell the magistrate about your part in your companion's deceptions?"

"I . . . I didn't wish to be part of it," she said.

"Indeed," René remarked, now oblivious to Juan's presence in the room. "Your pacing wasn't designed to cover Wallace's double-dealing?"

"No!" she cried. Her eyes darted from René to the magistrate. "At least, not the way you mean. I didn't want to help him. I just didn't want him to be caught."

"Ah, I see," René responded with triumph.

Elina flushed as she realized her words hadn't really helped her case.

René continued, mindful that he had the upper hand. "How unusual for a respectable woman such as yourself to know when someone is cheating. None of the other men noticed it. I'm surprised you did."

Elina twisted her hands in frustration. "You don't understand. I'd played with Alex myself. I knew what tricks he used when he was desperate."

"And you wished to protect your brother?" Juan interjected, casting a glance of annoyance René's way.

Elina turned to the magistrate as if to someone who understood. "Yes. I couldn't let him be caught. He is . . ." she paused to throw René a look filled with bitterness " . . . *was* my brother."

"Why didn't you simply insist that the two of you leave?" Juan asked.

"I did! But he wouldn't. Alex could be stubborn at times."

René ground his teeth together as he noticed the flash of sympathy Juan gave Elina. He couldn't blame the man for being taken in, but he knew Elina was showing her actions in the best possible light.

"Why don't you remind *Monsieur* Oliveira just how you chose to keep me from carting Wallace off to jail?" René said.

Elina paled as Juan turned his inquiring gaze on her. Then she drew a deep sigh. "I hit *Monsieur* Bonnange over the head with a whiskey bottle," she said in a voice that was scarcely more than a whisper.

To René's surprise, Juan guffawed. "Ah, yes," he said after a moment. "I'd forgotten the part about the whiskey bottle. You must admit, René, it was most resourceful of her. I'm certain quite a few women would have enjoyed hitting you over the head with a whiskey bottle when you were difficult."

René smiled grimly. "Most of them wouldn't have then stolen my money, however."

"I didn't steal it!" Elina protested as Juan's face sobered. "Alex did. I tried to stop him, truly I did!"

"Is that why he slapped you, *chérie*?" René queried, determined to drive his point home. "Or does your brother always hit you when he's angry?"

"Alex wasn't himself," Elina said with a sigh. "He'd never done such a thing before."

"Before what?" René persisted. Without waiting for her answer, he turned to the magistrate. "Tell me, Juan. How many respectable men do you know who hit their sisters, particularly after their sisters have just saved their hides?"

Juan said nothing, silently regarding Elina with pity.

She half-turned in her chair toward René, a look of protest on her face. "Leave Alexandre out of this. Isn't it enough that you murdered him? My past relationship with him has nothing to do with you."

René's eyes flashed as he saw that Juan waited for some rebuttal to that. "It has everything to do with me, particularly when you claim that the two of you are Philippe's children!" René said, his anger growing as he realized that Juan was softening toward Elina with every word she spoke.

But René's words had the effect he'd intended.

Juan was known for his self-control in the courtroom, but René's outburst made even his jaw drop. "What?" he asked as Elina's face reddened.

She leaned forward in her chair, her hands gripping the sides of it in fury as she faced René. "You said I could state my case! You said you'd say nothing unless I left something out! You lied, just like you always do! You're a murderer and a liar and this whole investigation is a farce, isn't it?"

"What's going on here?" Juan demanded as Elina glared at René, her entire body shaking with anger.

But René was too wrapped up in his own fury to pay Juan any heed. "You tell the stories too well," René told Elina. "How can anyone keep their wits about them when you turn those pleading eyes their way? *I* will tell the story now, and *you* may interrupt if I leave something out."

"No!" Juan commanded. "I wish to hear the *mademoiselle*. It's what you brought me here for, and I want to hear her tale from her lips, not yours."

René glared at them both for a moment. Then regaining his self-control, he bit out, "All right then. Do as you wish."

Juan turned to Elina and took her trembling hands, a certain gentleness in his expression. "What is all this about your being Philippe's child and René's being a murderer?"

She darted a quick glance at René, but he refused to mask his fury with her for her benefit. Let her believe he'd kill her on the spot if she voiced her accusations. He didn't care.

"My papa was Philippe Vannier," Elina said quietly as she leaned back in her chair and withdrew her hands from Juan's. "My brother and I came here to find him after Mama died. Papa hadn't returned from his latest trip when he was supposed to, and we were worried about him. We were alone. We needed him. So we came here. I never dreamed—" She broke off.

"Are you saying your mother was Philippe's . . . ah . . . *paramour*?" Juan asked in a futile attempt to couch his question in delicate terms.

"No!" Elina shouted. Then her voice softened. "No. They were married."

"Have you proof of this?" Juan asked, his face reflecting his skepticism.

"I . . . I—"

René's short hollow laugh made Elina flush. "Elina is trying to tell you she had a copy of her parents' marriage certificate, but it mysteriously vanished when Wallace was killed."

"It was stolen!" she insisted, her eyes flashing to René's for an instant in accusation.

Juan's eyes narrowed as he turned his gaze to René.

René explained, "Elina's story is that I murdered her supposed brother and then stole the papers to protect Julia's and Francois's inheritance, or even to give myself a share in the inheritance. You see how plausible her story is."

Juan stared down at the floor at the blatant sarcasm in René's voice. Then he glanced at René, his eyebrows raised as if to say, "Poor misguided girl." René knew Juan was thinking that René would never do such a thing. He didn't need to. He had money enough to support himself and his sister for years to come. As for Francois . . . Well, René was certainly not going to commit a crime to aid his irresponsible nephew.

Elina's face turned so ashen as she saw the unspoken exchange between the two men that for a moment René tensed in alarm. In a voice low but bitter, she said, "I know all of this seems impossible to believe. When *Monsieur* Bonnange first told me that Papa . . . that Papa had another wife, I didn't believe him, either. Papa was a good man, or so I thought. I couldn't bear to think otherwise." She sighed deeply. "But I was wrong. Somehow he managed to fool us all, to keep up the farce for the past twenty-three years without anyone suspecting."

"The only farce here is yours, Elina, and you know it," René said with quiet confidence.

Elina's eyes grew a brighter emerald-green in her anger. "So you'd like to believe. But the truth is that Papa wronged us all, and I am paying for his crimes. Is that fair? I don't see why I must suffer for his and my brother's misdeeds."

Juan turned eyes sharp with cynicism on her. "I see. You think you should be given your due—your portion of his estate."

She stared at him in confusion. "Yes! No! I mean, part of it belongs to me. That's only fair. But it's more than that. Now I have nothing, no money, no family, not even my name." She gestured to René. "This monster keeps it all from me. I—I have nowhere to go but here, yet here I can't be who I am. *Monsieur* Bonnange won't even let me leave his house unless I take his money to deny who I am and betray my brother."

Her answer made Juan glance questioningly at René.

René clenched one fist. "Betray your brother? You won't be avenging your Alex, *chérie*, if I hang for his murder as you wish me to do."

"I don't want you to hang!" she blurted out. When René looked at her askance, she pulled her gaze away from him. "But . . . but I want justice. And everyone except the authorities seems to know you killed him. It isn't fair that my brother's murderer should go free." She faltered, her shoulders shaking with the force of her emotion as she whispered, "It isn't right that Alex should be killed, then buried with a false name only because Papa was a foolish man."

Her earnest statement affected René more deeply than anything she'd said to him before. Despite all he knew about her, it had the ring of truth. Was it possible she told the truth about who she was? Was there someone besides René who wouldn't want the truth to come out?

Francois. He was certainly capable of murdering a man. Yet Francois had said he'd been at Etienne's house that night, and that was a claim easily proven. Besides, how would Wallace have found his half brother so quickly when he didn't even know he had a half brother? And how could Philippe have hidden this other family for so many years?

René stared at Elina intently, wishing he could see into her mind and know the truth. He knew she couldn't be Philippe's daughter; he just knew it! He must force himself to accept what was obvious—that she was a liar and a cheat. Furiously, he reminded himself of how he'd met her and what she'd been doing.

Elina's sincerity also affected Juan, but clearly not so much he didn't notice the incongruities in her statements. "What is this about the false name?" he asked calmly. "Why did the report state your names as Alexandre and Elina Wallace, not Vannier?"

The question seemed to throw Elina completely off guard. Her hands became very still in her lap, and she dropped her eyes.

"And something else, *mademoiselle*," Juan continued, his voice a tiny bit more sharp. "Why did you accompany your brother to New Orleans? If you didn't know your father was dead, why didn't your brother go searching and have you remain at home?"

Her face pinkened as she bit her lip anxiously. "We—we both had to leave," she stammered.

"Why?" the magistrate asked.

"Our home burned down," she whispered in a far-off voice.

"You didn't have anyone there you could stay with while your brother sought your father?" Juan persisted.

"No."

"No one? You had no friends?"

She seemed on the verge of tears. "We—we kept to ourselves. We lived in the country."

"Couldn't your brother have left you with enough funds to keep you taken care of in a lodging house until he returned?"

"No," she whispered.

"Why not?" Juan asked with force.

She looked down at her hands, clearly agitated.

"Yes, why not?" René asked, leaning forward as he saw she wouldn't, or couldn't, answer the magistrate's questions. "Why did you have to leave, Elina? And why would any daughter of Philippe's travel in such poor clothing? Where were the mourning gowns you would have worn for your mother's death?"

That last question seemed to undo her completely.

"S–Some men . . . one man really . . . was after Alex for his gambling debts," she stammered as if the words were wrung from her. "It was they who burned down our house and everything with it. Alex said they would kill him. We had to travel unnoticed, so they wouldn't follow us and . . . and hurt us."

René leaned forward. "That's a rather pat explanation, don't you think? Is it the entire truth? Was Alex running from debtors or was he running from men he'd cheated? I suspect it was the latter."

"No!" she cried, and turned to him, her voice pleading. "Alex wasn't like that!"

Then realizing the absurdity of what she said, she turned her head to stare out the window, and René saw a soft silent tear escape. That lone tear tore at his insides. He suddenly wished he'd never brought the magistrate at all.

It took her a moment to regain her composure. Then she answered him in a voice laced with implied accusation. "I knew you'd turn it into something sordid. I knew if I told you everything, it would only make matters worse," she said, her voice quavering from the effort not to cry. She turned her face back to them. René could still glimpse the tiny wet trail on her cheek. "So I suppose my only recourse is to say just this. I am Elina Vannier. Nothing you believe or think about me will change that. I have no concrete proof, I have no money, and I have no mourning clothes. But I am Elina Vannier all the same."

Then she rose with a regal air that astounded René, for he knew she'd seen her plans sadly battered in the past hour. She gave them both the slightest of curtsies. "Good day, *Monsieur* Oliveira, *Monsieur* Bonnange," she said in that soft courteous voice René had often heard his sister use. Then with erect carriage and only a hint of trembling, she walked from the room, leaving the two men to marvel at her apparent calm.

Little did they realize that Elina scarcely made it into the hall before she crumbled, her stiff back going limp as she shoved her fist to her mouth to hold back the sobs threatening to erupt.

Never had she felt such humiliation! Even when Alex had placed her in the position of covering his cheating, she'd not felt like the lowest worm as she felt now. Why had she let Bonnange do this to her? The moment he'd mentioned Mama and the mourning clothes, Elina had virtually collapsed. But she hadn't been able to help it! René's insinuations and accusing looks had so unnerved her she could hardly think straight. Throughout the interview, she'd been forced constantly to remind herself she wasn't guilty. Otherwise, she'd have burst into tears and confessed to every crime known to mankind. Oh, how could one man be so heartless!

She leaned back helplessly against the wall, reliving the last few minutes. René had been right, she thought with bitterness. No one in authority would believe her story, not under the circumstances. She'd been foolish to think otherwise, to think the magistrate would know she was telling the truth.

With a weary sense of defeat, she started to climb the stairs to the second floor and her room. But the voices drifting into the hallway from the drawing room made her pause on the first step.

"Perhaps she's insane," Oliveira remarked in French. "I've heard of such things before. Maybe this is some peculiar delusion of hers—to believe her father is a man of wealth."

"She's not crazy," René asserted. "She knows just what she's doing."

"But the girl's not your average schemer, René. Surely you see that."

At least the magistrate wasn't entirely convinced by René's perception of her tale, Elina thought.

"Oh, yes, I do see that. Elina is certainly not average."

"She holds herself like a well-bred lady, despite her poor clothing."

"Indeed she does. But I suspect Wallace taught her how to maintain that facade for his own purposes."

Elina clenched the bannister in frustration. How dare he say such things! How dare he!

"What about her own purpose in all this?" the magistrate asked. "She says you offered her money. Knowing you, it must have been a large sum. If money is all that concerns her, why doesn't she just take yours and leave? Surely she realizes her flimsy story will never get her more than that."

There was a long pause during which Elina waited with indrawn breath for René's answer.

She heard him sigh loudly. "She doesn't care how flimsy her story is. She knows someone will believe it. And that's all she needs to get what seems most important to her—revenge for Wallace's death. With her half-baked lies, she can strike at the one thing I treasure—my family."

"Have you tried to see how much she knows about Philippe in order to test her?"

"She'd pass any test well, I assure you. She thinks on her feet. Clearly, she took time the morning after Wallace's death to ask questions about me, to find out the situation with my family. I'll admit she seems to have talked to the wrong people. She arrived at Julia's *pied-à-terre* believing that Philippe had parents whom she could convince to take her in. But once she saw her way clear, she performed impressively. No, as you say, Elina is anything but average. As for the money, surely she'd rather have an inheritance than whatever sum I'd give her. She hopes to force me to give it to her rather than risk her spreading her lies."

Elina gritted her teeth. René had a talent for twisting every situation to suit his purposes. And his purpose now was to make certain she never told the truth to anyone.

"Her story is wildly improbable, of course," Oliveira said, "but not impossible. Philippe was gone a great deal. And other men have managed to maintain two families for years undetected."

Elina felt a tiny stirring of hope within her. Perhaps the magistrate was perceptive enough at least to guess at the truth.

"I've already checked anyone who might know something of this," René said. "No one knows anything. Philippe left no will. Surely he would have provided for his family. If her home had indeed burned down, there would still have been someone to turn to for money . . . a solicitor perhaps. She mentioned a banker, yet this banker apparently wouldn't give her enough money even to buy mourning clothes. Her story is full of such incongruities."

"Still, she has an air about her—"

"Yes," René said sharply. "She does."

There was silence for a moment, during which Elina choked back the protests she wanted to make anew.

Then Juan spoke, "What will you do with her?"

"I can't let her run loose in New Orleans. You must appreciate that."

"Of course. So you intend to keep her here? For how long?"

"As long as it takes to make her see sense," René bit out.

"You want to make her your mistress, don't you?" Oliveira said quietly.

Even as Elina bristled at Oliveira's words, René exploded. "My mistress? For God's sake, Juan, she's a liar and a cheat. Why would I want such a mistress?"

"Because she's beautiful. Because she dared to resist you. There's no more powerful combination when it comes to desire. Besides, if you seduced her, perhaps she'd be less eager to punish you for her brother's death."

"At this point, I'm not sure anything would convince her to give up her plans of revenge."

A long silence ensued.

"You know I didn't kill her brother," René added.

"No, of course not. I know you too well for that. The Code Duello forbids dueling with those beneath one's class.

No Creole would ever forsake those rules."

A dishonorable Creole would! Elina thought in protest.

"You must convince her of that somehow," Juan continued.

"I don't care what Elina thinks of me. I suspect her revenge will dissipate if I offer her enough money. As for seduction—"

"It's a two-edged sword," Juan said dryly. "Of course, if anyone can handle that sword, it's you."

Both men laughed, and Elina got the impression she'd missed something.

"There's another alternative," Juan remarked. "I could just jail her for a few days to put the fear of God and man into her."

Elina sucked in her breath.

René's response was swift and stronger than Elina would have expected. "Absolutely not! There's no need for that. I can deal with Elina, I assure you."

"As you wish. Then I'll take my leave, if you don't mind. I have another appointment later this afternoon."

Elina had heard enough. Swiftly, she began mounting the stairs again, hoping to reach her room before the men left the drawing room and spotted her, but she wasn't swift enough. Halfway up the stairs, she heard René's boot heels on the wooden floors of the hallway and knew he and the magistrate stood below and behind her. With careful steps, she continued up the stairs.

René's voice stopped her. "Elina, one moment! I wish a word with you."

She remained still, angry that he'd caught her listening to their conversation. She was tempted to ignore his command and flee to her room while he saw the magistrate out, but she knew that would do her no good, for he could enter her room whenever he wished.

So with growing impatience she waited, steeling herself for whatever he might say. She wished she could force herself just to take his money and leave. But it wasn't in her to do it, not when she knew she had every right to remain. She had nowhere to go anyway. Anywhere she went, she'd be haunted by the pain of knowing what Papa had done, yet never knowing why. Why had he married two women? Why hadn't he provided for her and Alex? She couldn't leave until she'd learned the whole truth about him.

Nor could she leave the city with Alex unavenged and her identity unproven. Suddenly it had become a matter of pride to make René admit she was truly Philippe Vannier's daughter and not some scheming gambler's woman.

Her only chance was to escape and find her own proof. Otherwise, she'd never be free of her past. So when she heard him mounting the stairs behind her and felt him clasp her arm, she knew she'd never take his money. She just couldn't.

"You heard us, I suppose," he murmured casually as he took her arm and began to lead her up the stairs.

"Of course I heard," she said in an affected air of nonchalance. "You hardly bothered to keep your voices down."

"I had thought you'd be upstairs in your room, pouting over today's disappointment. But I can see I underestimated your resilience. Did you learn anything of interest?"

Although his words angered her, the presence of his hand at her elbow disturbed her more. Why was it that the merest pressure of his hand made the blood rush to her head? She kept her body stiff, her manner aloof, but her insides felt consumed by white heat. Somehow she feared he knew it, too.

"Well? What did your little eavesdropping reveal to you?" he asked again, his voice deeper and huskier.

"I learned that you plan to continue holding me prisoner. But that didn't surprise me. I should have known the magistrate was a grand friend of yours who would do as you asked."

"He won't hang me on the basis of some story told by a gambler's companion, if that's what you mean. But he's a fair man. If he'd thought you were telling the truth, he would have insisted I release you. I'd say he gave you a fair chance to make your case. And you might have convinced him if you'd thought out your story more carefully."

She knew he was referring to what she'd said about why she and Alex had left Missouri. But explaining that to him had done her no good. The magistrate hadn't believed her, and now René had a new reason for disbelieving her himself. She had no choice but to find some other way out of her predicament than the magistrate who clearly wouldn't help her.

By this time they'd reached the top of the stairs. She tried to pull herself free, but he turned her around to face him, his hands sliding up her arms to hold her shoulders captive.

"My original offer still stands, you know," he said, his eyes cunning and cold. "Why not admit you lied? The magistrate doesn't believe you, so you have no reason to persist in your story. But I promise I can make you wealthy enough to make it worth your while to give up your tale."

She lifted her head proudly. "I won't take your bribes. No amount of money will change my mind about who I am."

Suddenly she remembered one of the other alternatives *Monsieur* Oliveira had proposed—that René seduce her into doing his bidding.

From René's altered expression, she could tell he remembered it, too. Her breath quickened as his eyes became like those of a predatory bird, sure and confident in its ability to prevail. In them she read the truth. Escaping his desire for her or her own desire for him was impossible. Neither of them seemed able to avoid it. They could stall it for a while, but if they stayed in the same house much longer, she feared what might happen.

Angry with herself for even thinking such thoughts, she lashed out at him. "*Nothing* you can do will change my mind," she vowed, determined to make it clear to him that Oliveira's suggestion of seduction wouldn't work with her, either.

For a moment he was silent, his eyes taking in her flushed cheeks and parted lips. "Nothing?" he then asked, his hand sliding to her neck. He pressed his finger under the collar of her dress and along her smooth skin until he felt the spot where her pulse throbbed, felt her heart's pace quicken even as he touched her. "Are you certain about that?"

"Nothing," she whispered, trying to force some note of confidence into her voice. "N–nothing at all."

"One never knows what might tempt a schemer, sweet eyes," he murmured.

The low chuckle that followed his words drove her wisp of confidence away, for it told her what she feared—that he knew how flimsy her defenses against him were when he touched her. He knew and basked in that knowledge.

His fingers pressed her cheek in a lingering caress. Then he was gone, leaving her to stand there shaking, wondering how on earth she would ever prove him wrong.

Chapter Twelve

Truth and oil always come to the surface.
—Spanish Proverb

A scowl on her face, Elina attacked the canvas vigorously with her charcoal. Just when she'd begun to believe René could be bearable, even likable when he wished, he had once again proven himself a complete and total cad!

After the magistrate's visit, she hadn't known what to expect. Except for her confrontation with René at the top of the stairs, he'd kept his distance for the past few days. True, he'd been gone or busy most of that time, taking trips to town, spending hours closeted in his study with horse dealers and bankers, and riding out to deal with the workmen in the fields.

Still, she'd gotten the distinct impression that he was trying to make some sort of amends by giving her time to adjust to her situation. He'd made no more indecent advances. She'd remained aloof since that horrible meeting with the magistrate, but he'd worked hard to lessen her anger toward him. Their morning and evening meals he'd spent telling her about New Orleans and its customs as he tried to coax her to talk. And sometimes she'd even forgotten who—and what—he was as she listened to the picture he drew for her of a fascinating, but strange social structure.

What's more, she'd been surprised to discover that René could be witty and pleasant when he wished to be. That discovery had caused turmoil within her. How could a man who was so ruthless with her brother be so utterly different with her? At times she even wondered if she'd misjudged him. If it hadn't been for the fact that everyone in New Orleans seemed to believe he'd killed Alex, she might have listened to her doubts.

As it was, treating him as she should treat her brother's murderer was rapidly becoming difficult. She found herself participating in conversation when she should keep him at arm's length, asking him questions when she should ignore him.

But René wasn't the kind of man one could ignore.

Occasionally, she'd caught him staring at her, his brow furrowed in thought even while his eyes seemed aflame. At those times, she'd felt as if he were tying to entice her closer by the utter power of his gaze. Like a wild animal that stands fixed at the sight of a sudden flame, she'd seemed momentarily incapable of looking away. Only sheer force of will had enabled her to wrench her eyes from him at such times. And long afterwards, his low bitter laugh had haunted her.

Yet except for the unspoken words that passed between them in those few moments, he'd not offered her money again. So four days had passed in a sort of truce, though an uneasy one. He'd attended to his business, and she'd whiled away her time sketching her parents and Alex from memory.

Until today.

She peered over the canvas at René, who was now forcing her to hold to her promise to paint his portrait. That morning when he'd announced they could begin, she'd been upset. Looking at him for hours, watching him watch her was not her idea of a relaxed way to spend her days. And after her first tumultuous and grievous days in New Orleans, she needed some time to regain her strength for the struggle ahead.

No, painting René wouldn't be easy, she thought, squirming restlessly on the hard wooden stool as she gave the canvas her full attention. Every time she looked up to see those faintly smiling lips, she remembered the way they'd danced over her naked skin. And his hands! She blushed now just to think of where his hands had been a mere five days before.

She kept trying to imbue his likeness with some of the cruelty she knew had to be lurking inside him. Only a cruel man would murder a stranger for a few hundred dollars and then hold his sister captive. But even with the portrait in its beginning stages, she couldn't seem to sketch him as harshly as she would have liked.

"I hope those vicious strokes aren't indicative of the way you're depicting me," René said now in a lazy voice. "If I can find time to sit for you, the least you can do is portray me in a good light."

"I'd rather not portray you at all, as you well know." The words were bitten out as she concentrated on her canvas. "If you're so busy, I'm more than happy to do this some other time . . . or abandon the endeavor altogether."

She glanced up, piqued to see he'd once more relaxed his stance so he was leaning against instead of standing in front of the wall.

He flashed her an insolent smile. "Don't you think I make a good subject? Or is there some other reason you don't wish to paint me?"

She slashed again at the canvas with her charcoal. "I don't enjoy sketching criminals, if you must know."

The smile faded from his eyes, though not from his face. "Ah, so we're back to that, are we? Yet once again, you lie about what you do and do not enjoy. You sketch Wallace, and if ever there was a criminal, it was he."

She fought back her bitter retort. For once she'd keep her head about her. He'd caught her sketching Alex after breakfast, and she knew that had prompted his sudden renewal of interest in the portrait. So the quickest way out of painting his portrait would be to make him forget about her brother.

"Nothing to say, sweet eyes? Aren't you going to protest Wallace's innocence and tell me yet again that the man was your brother?"

She lifted her head from the canvas to fix him with a haughty stare. "No. You don't believe me anyway, so why waste my breath? A man of your undeniably bad manners simply doesn't listen to anyone but himself."

His soft chuckle made her even angrier. "You know, *ma pétite*, your affronted lady act affords me endless amusement. Every time you lecture me about my poor behavior, I'm reminded of your amazing ability to use a whiskey bottle as a club. Tell me, is that a skill you learned in the polite parlors of St. Louis?"

"Creve Coeur," she said, returning her attention to the canvas. "I lived in Creve Coeur with Papa, Mama, and Alex, my *brother*. Not that you care."

"Ah, but I do. I'd like to know all about what you learned growing up. And since you won't tell me the truth, your fabrications will suffice at the moment. I think the artist should always entertain her subject—to keep him alert, so to speak. So entertain me. Tell me just what you think gently bred ladies spend their time doing."

She glared at him, but he raised his eyebrows innocently and she realized this was his peculiar way of challenging her. Well, she'd not disappoint him. She'd take his challenge.

"Gently bred ladies in Creve Coeur," she said with icy dignity, "spend their time sewing, doing needlepoint, and being schooled in drawing, music, and dancing. Sometimes they go for long walks in the woods—"

"With suitors?" he interrupted.

She felt her throat tighten as painful memories assailed her. "Actually, no," she said acidly. "Not with suitors. Papas who don't wish their crimes to be found out by enterprising sons-in-law don't accept suitors."

He gazed at her in silence for a moment. "I see you've used these four days well in thinking out your story," he said at last. "That twist is something even I wouldn't have thought of."

With rising irritation, she went on, "Sometimes gently bred ladies spend their time wondering when their papas are going to return from those long buying trips. And sometimes they just sit with their mamas while their mamas worry that their loving husbands are cold or lonely away from home."

"That's enough, Elina," René said with sudden iciness. "I can see where this is leading."

She quirked one eyebrow up. "Can you? I hadn't thought you would. So far you haven't shown yourself to be a man of much sensitivity. I suppose that comes of being ill-bred."

When he answered her, his voice was flippant, but she thought it masked a stronger emotion. "It's a good thing my mother isn't alive to hear you say that. She took great pains to make me into a gentleman. And my sister worked hard at it after my mother died."

Elina shrugged. "Obviously, your boorishness is too ingrained to be rooted out easily. Is that why you left New Orleans? Did you tire of being a gentleman all the time? Is that why you abandoned your sister and your estate, even though she begged you not to? Was it because you wanted to be free in Europe to live a lawless life?"

She'd struck a nerve, she could tell, for he pushed himself away from the wall and stood there tensely as if preparing for a fight.

"My reasons for leaving New Orleans are irrelevant. And I assure you they have nothing to do with my family. So leave Julia out of your nasty speculations."

She continued, ignoring his suddenly stormy face, "Perhaps you left because of some other duel. Did you make a mistake the first time and kill someone whose family was too rich to ignore? Someone who wasn't penniless?"

"Penniless? Your Wallace had at least two hundred dollars on him when I found him dead!"

He'd got her there, but that wouldn't stop her. "Yes, but that was all he had, and you knew it. Perhaps it was another such as he whom you killed the first time, those many years ago."

She knew she was wildly grasping at straws, for she really had no idea why René had left New Orleans. But he hadn't told anyone and he'd left abruptly, which led her to believe his reason was something sinister. Now that she had him angry, she was hoping he'd reveal something, anything, that she could use against him.

His chiseled jaw became even stonier as he advanced on her. She drew back instinctively, suddenly wishing there were something more than a flimsy piece of canvas between them.

"So you want to know why I left New Orleans, do you? Well, it wasn't because of something as simple and clean as a duel." He whirled and paced to the tall glass doors that opened onto the gallery. "No, not nearly that simple."

The charcoal dropped unheeded into her lap as she watched him. He leaned against the doorjamb in a gesture of pretended casualness, but underneath his air of unconcern, she sensed his tension. Unwillingly, her eyes were drawn to his powerful limbs, wrapped so close in his trousers of buff moleskin that she could see every muscle move as he shifted position. She forced her gaze from the sight, determined that she'd be alert if he should slip and say something he shouldn't.

After several long moments, he spoke, his voice a finely strung thread of steel. "I left New Orleans because I couldn't stomach a good many things anymore. You wouldn't believe that, as eager as you are to believe the worst of me, but it's true."

"So I was right about your not enjoying the life your sister made you lead," she murmured unthinkingly.

He half-turned toward her, and his piercing glance forced a shudder from her even in the sunny warmth of the room.

"No," he enunciated. "No, you were quite wrong."

He turned his attention to the outdoors. Outside she could hear the shouts of laboring men and the laughing chatter of children.

"Julia and Philippe took very good care of me after my family died," he continued. "I suppose Louis told you all about that. The cursed man has an inveterate case of loose lips. He's also a Creole through and through, which is why I've never told him my reasons for leaving New Orleans. He wouldn't understand. No Creole would. I doubt you would, either."

"You're right," she said, determined to find out what he was hiding. "I don't understand why a man would abandon his family and his estate for the sake of a little adventure. All of you men do it, because you'd rather escape your responsibilities whenever possible. My father did, Alex did . . . you did."

His entire body stiffened as he struggled to control his rage. "Some things make you rethink your responsibilities, indeed make you rethink your entire upbringing."

"I suppose," she said casually, but the contempt in her voice was clear.

He muttered a low curse, then whirled to face her. "You're right," he ground out. "I abandoned my sister. But she had her own family. She didn't need me."

"Still, you must not have cared much for her."

His eyes narrowed. "Julia was, and still is, the finest Creole woman I know."

Deborah Martin

She turned back to her canvas and calmly picked up the charcoal again. "So you left her."

"No. I left New Orleans," he emphasized.

When Elina continued sketching with a superior air, he went on, "I was raised in a family that wasn't typical. My father was a sugar planter, but he ran our plantation casually. We had slaves, of course, to run the plantation and the two households, but they were never mistreated, never beaten for any offense. My father didn't believe in it."

His face held a trace of wistfulness. "So I grew up believing the whole society was one big family. The slaves were our children, whom we treated with benevolent largesse." She could hear the sarcasm lacing his words. "When I turned sixteen, my brother-in-law decided to introduce me to Bernard de Marigny, one of his friends. Bernard was much older than I, but we took to each other immediately. He began to invite me to his lavish dinner parties and balls."

"The Marignys!" she whispered in awe, her fingers pausing in midair. Her father had told her once about the Marignys of New Orleans and of all the gold Bernard's father had spent entertaining Louis Philippe, Duc de Chartres. It frightened her to be reminded of how powerful René must be to have such friends.

René continued, unaware she'd made any sound at all. "Bernard was married to his first wife when I knew him then, to Mary Anne. She was an attractive woman. I was a little enamored of her as were many of us. I took her to be a gentle, mild Creole woman, much like my sister, even though she was really only half Creole. Then one day I went to Bernard's *pied à terre,* intending to invite him to a card game. And there I found, in the courtyard, the dear sweet *Madame* de Marigny directing a man with a whip. Before her was a naked slave woman tied to a ladder, whom the man had apparently been beating for some time. The poor slave had passed out, but *madame* wanted her revived to endure more."

Elina's mouth fell open in horror, but he plunged blindly on, his tone harshening with each word. "I had only heard of such things, but never seen them. And I'd been told that Creole women were crueler about beating their slaves than were Americans. I'd simply refused to believe that, for wasn't my Creole sister the very image of human kindness? But when I found the reality staring me in the face, I couldn't stomach it. I turned around without a word and left. And when I learned, through my own slaves, that the slave woman had died as a result, I was angered beyond belief. I couldn't even associate with Bernard anymore, the entire incident horrified me that much."

Elina couldn't speak, so overcome by emotion was she. Slavery was something she'd taken for granted, particularly since she'd never examined the institution closely. Mama had refused to have them, insisting on hiring servants, but Elina had never heard it discussed and had always sensed that Papa only indulged Mama's wish because he could afford to. Hearing René's story made her glad now that they'd had no slaves. No one deserved such barbaric treatment—no one!

"I've always wished I could relive that afternoon," he said, his voice thick with self-reproach. "I've always regretted that I did nothing to stop it—absolutely nothing. But I know I couldn't have stopped it. The slave woman was *madame's* property, to do with as she wished. My interference would have changed nothing. Yet I still see that scene with startling clarity, every time I think about my early days in New Orleans."

She had imagined several reasons for his making his home elsewhere, all of them equally despicable. But this? No, such a thing had never crossed her mind. That he could be so concerned about someone he would consider beneath him . . . Well, she just wouldn't have expected it.

She couldn't keep the incredulity out of her voice. "And that incident made you leave your family, your home?"

He looked up surprised, as if he'd forgotten she was there. "Not at first, no. I stayed a few more months in the city. But each time I went to a dinner or a ball, I saw those mild, languid Creole women with their charming smiles and imagined that every one of them held a whip in her hand."

He paused to fix her with tormented eyes. "I told myself they weren't all like that, that my sister wasn't like that. I reminded myself that a few good people among my peers were working to eradicate slavery and its abuses. Yet I couldn't escape the disgust I felt each time I witnessed a slave auction or heard another story about slaves being mistreated. I decided there had to be a better way to make a living than to feed on the misery of other human beings."

"So you went to England."

"First to France to study," he told her grimly. "But I ended up in England. And, of course, England had its own set of problems. Thinking back on it, I don't know that I solved anything by escaping to Europe. In fact, this time when I came back, I think I was half considering making New Orleans my home again. I knew it was time for me to do something other than run away from the problems that existed here."

Suddenly she remembered the things she'd discovered going through his desk. "Is that why you have no slaves?"

His eyes searched hers thoughtfully, the golden lights in them becoming more pronounced. "How did you know I had no slaves?"

When she looked uncomfortable, he nodded slightly. "Ah, yes, the papers in my desk. I suppose you examined them. Did you discover much that might help you in your scheme?"

She ignored his attempt to change the subject. "Well? Is that why you have no slaves?" she persisted.

The expression of careful nonchalance he suddenly assumed didn't hide the keen interest in his eyes as he faced her. "Since you think you know my character so well, why don't you answer that question? I can almost guess what you're thinking. Perhaps he simply uses hired men because he can afford to do so and because it soothes his conscience. Perhaps if he weren't so rich, he'd be just like the other planters, beating his slaves when it suited him, wringing every ounce of work out of them—"

"No," she whispered to make him stop saying such dreadful things. "No, you wouldn't."

His lips turned up very slightly in a smile. "I wouldn't?"

She dropped her eyes from his. "I—I don't *think* you would," she amended lamely.

She felt rather than saw him approach her. "But you were so ready to believe I'm a cold-blooded murderer who hunted Wallace down and fought him over mere money. Surely such a man as you think I am would be a cruel master to his slaves, don't you think?"

She toyed with the charcoal, then clenched it in her hand. He confused her so. She no longer knew what to believe. "I—I don't know."

Now he rounded the canvas. His hand clasped her chin lightly, turning her face up to his. "What don't you know?" he asked, his eyes a rich velvet brown.

"I don't know what to think of you," she stated, an earnest expression on her face.

He smiled. "I don't know what to think of you, either."

"Yes, you do," she said in despair, trying to pull away from his hand. "You think I'm like one of those women in the ballroom—mild and beautiful on the outside . . . terribly wicked and ugly on the inside."

His thumb stroked the delicate bones of her chin, refusing to let her go. "Not exactly. Beautiful, yes. Mild? I think not. And certainly not wicked. Not like those others are wicked."

Her chin quivered in his hand.

"Though I don't trust you any more than I would trust them," he added softly. "That's why I dare not let you leave here."

She made some weak protest that neither of them really heard. She couldn't tear her eyes away from his mouth. He lowered his head and she waited breathlessly, powerlessly, for the first touch of those pensive lips.

Then they both heard the door open and someone cough in embarrassment. Elina jerked back from René so quickly she nearly lost her perch atop the stool.

"What is it?" René demanded as he reached to steady Elina.

Elina studied the canvas while her face turned scarlet.

"The woman is here, *monsieur*," she heard Louis say from the doorway. "You told me to let you know when she arrived."

"Yes, of course," René said, a slow smile replacing the frown on his face. "Send her in."

Elina twisted around to watch as René strode to the door. Before he'd even reached it, Louis had returned, a matronly woman with sharp gray eyes in tow.

"Thank you for coming, *Madame* Laplante," René said in greeting. "I trust you're here for the fitting."

"Yes," the woman responded as she scrutinized Elina. "This is the girl?"

René nodded. The woman's intense perusal suddenly made Elina aware of the charcoal smudges on her hands and the fact that her hair wasn't as nicely coiled as she might have wished.

"It wasn't easy making up the gowns from the measurements your servant gave me, but we managed," *Madame* Laplante continued with a smile.

"Gowns?" Elina asked in confusion.

"I'm sure you'll be delighted with the finished designs, *mademoiselle*," the woman said as she clapped her hands. Two men entered, carrying a large trunk.

Elina leapt from the stool and whirled to face René with accusing eyes. "What is *Madame* Laplante talking about?" she demanded. "Who are the gowns for?"

The smug expression on René's face told her all she needed to know.

"There's been some mistake," Elina told *Madame* Laplante. "I didn't order any new gowns."

"Yes, yes, dear," she said impatiently, rolling her eyes in René's direction. "The *monsieur* has told me all about it."

"He has?" Elina asked, glancing again to René. How much of the truth had he told this woman?

"And he's right, you know," the woman continued as she began to draw gowns from the trunk and drape them across the chairs in the room. "A girl as lovely as yourself requires the means for displaying her charms to their best advantage. I know you'd rather he chose to show his regard with something other than clothing but—"

Elina's eyes went round in horror as she opened her mouth to protest.

René cut her off. "As your patron, dear, I felt that you really must be dressed properly. It's not as if you need any more paints and such. But when we begin showing your work to potential buyers, you'll need to be more concerned with dress. That's why I had *Madame* Laplante come while you were here sketching me. I knew the two of us together might convince you, since you won't listen to me."

Elina glanced around her, feeling more and more caged in by the minute. How dare he pass himself off as her patron to cover the fact that he was keeping her a prisoner in his house!

"This man is not my patron, *madame*. I'm not even here by choice!"

She'd expected that statement to be accepted with more seriousness than it was. *Madame* Laplante merely cast a glance toward the easel and paints and then winked at René. "Yes, of course," she said, as if she shared a secret with René.

"You must believe me!" Elina urged. "This man is keeping me prisoner here!"

Deborah Martin

To Elina's surprise, the woman laughed and turned to René. "You're right, *monsieur*. She does have an active imagination. Ah, these *artistes*, they are so droll."

Elina turned accusing eyes on René. The look of superior pleasure in his face, as if he knew he'd outsmarted her, infuriated her.

"I warned the *madame* you might say anything to keep from being fitted," he explained, as if she were his troublesome ward. "She understood perfectly when I explained that you're one of those artists who prefers to dress *au naturel* and thinks that the trappings of civilization shouldn't be allowed to hinder your work."

Elina wanted to throw the charcoal at him that was still clasped in her hand. He'd prepared well, she could see. And apparently he fully intended to place her under obligation to him by buying her clothing regardless of her wishes.

She glanced at *Madame* Laplante, who stood patiently with a lush forest-green walking dress in her hands, waiting to help Elina try it on.

One thing René hadn't prepared for, Elina thought with a sudden smugness. "I'm afraid you've come out here for nothing, *madame*," Elina said. "I won't try them on, so there's really no point in your staying."

Madame Laplante's face fell as she looked helplessly at René.

"Then *madame* will leave them here," René said, his voice holding a subtle threat, "and you'll just have to wear them as is, whether they fit you poorly or not."

"Fine," Elina said, turning back to her easel as she called his bluff. She knew he didn't want her to wear the clothes half-finished. His point in having them made in the first place was so that he could dress her up for his pleasure like some brainless, smiling doll.

"Please, *monsieur* . . ." *Madame* Laplante protested.

Elina smiled to herself. The dressmaker wasn't about to risk her reputation by leaving poorly fitting gowns to be worn by some crazy artist.

"If you'll excuse us one moment, *madame*," René said in hard tones. Then he forcibly led Elina through a door into an adjoining room.

"I won't take your gowns, René," she told him when they cleared the door. Futilely, she tried to escape the iron grip he held on her elbow. "Everyone will think I'm your . . . your mistress or something, and I won't have it! You can't force me to take them!"

His penetrating stare gave her pause, even while her anger still smoldered.

"I don't understand you," he said in a voice whose quietness didn't belie the fact that he was very, very angry. "Any other woman would be glad to receive such elaborate gifts. When I made up that story for *Madame* Laplante, I really didn't expect to have to use it. I felt certain you'd be pleased and delighted to wear something other than that worn dress of yours."

The slight hurt she thought she heard in his voice made her feel a bit guilty. "I'm sorry. But I can't take such gifts from you."

"You didn't like them?"

She hesitated before answering. "I find them lovely, every one." That wasn't a lie. No woman could have helped noticing such exquisitely designed gowns. But that made it all the worse, for it meant they were expensive.

"Then there's no reason for you not to take them. You may consider them payment for the portrait, if you wish."

She knew better than to think her portrait was worth the price of such lavish clothing. Nonetheless, she found still another reason to refuse. "I should be wearing mourning. It wouldn't be right to wear such glorious colors under the circumstances."

When his face immediately clouded over, she realized she'd blundered. His jaw set with determination, he jerked her around so her back was to him. One arm crossed her waist, pulling her up against him as he began methodically to unbutton her dress with his other hand. She gasped in horror and tried to wriggle out of his grasp.

"So that's it," he hissed. "You're still mourning Wallace. And I suppose your story requires that you also mourn your parents. Well, my little actress, I won't help you dress the part for that, but I'll make certain you look like the beguiling woman you are and not the downtrodden miss you pretend to be. Once you're reminded of what my money can buy for you, you might be more inclined to take it and leave town! So you're going to be fitted for those dresses, if I have to undress you myself!"

Vainly, she strove to free herself from the hold he had on her. The thought of being undressed by him outraged and terrified her. She knew what conjuring tricks he could perform on her body, on her feelings. And if she were naked. . . .

"You wouldn't humiliate me so in front of that woman, would you?" she asked in desperation.

His fingers paused a third of the way down her dress. "If need be, I'll strip you naked while both Louis and the *madame* watch."

"Louis wouldn't let you do that," she said, a very small measure of confidence in her voice. "He's a gentleman."

"Don't be too sure, *ma petite*. Your 'gentleman' has seen more ladies naked than either you or I could dream of. Don't let his age fool you. If I told him to stand there and watch, he would, take my word for it, and he just might enjoy it."

She drew in a deep breath, wondering if what René said about Louis were true. She didn't think so, but she wasn't certain she wished to chance being wrong. The renewed movement of René's fingers at her buttons decided her.

"I'll put your wretched dresses on," she hastily told him.

"You'll try on every stitch of clothing that woman has brought and stand still while she fits you?" he asked, his voice like flint.

"Yes. But I won't like it."

"You don't have to like it," he told her as he released her. "As long as you do it."

Then he led her from the room back to *Madame* Laplante and her cursed dresses.

Chapter Thirteen

Love, pain, and money cannot be kept secret. They soon betray themselves.—Spanish Proverb

René glanced up the stairway impatiently as he waited for Elina to come down. Someone entered the room, but he didn't bother to turn his head.

"So, *monsieur*, what did you say to the *mademoiselle*? She's as skittish around me as a doe."

At the sound of Louis's voice, René turned to face his old friend and servant. Louis stood there, unsmiling but his eyes twinkled.

"What do you mean?" René asked, his gaze moving back toward the stairs.

"The *mademoiselle* behaves as if I am not quite trustworthy. She did not do so before," Louis persisted. "Ever since the dressmaker came, she has been almost wary of me. And then today, she tripped, and I reached out to steady her. You should have seen the look she gave me! Pah! You would not believe she could look so murderous and uncertain at the same time."

"I would believe anything you told me about that woman," René said with a sigh.

"Then believe this. The *mademoiselle* seems convinced that I, too, am a villain. Now tell me, *monsieur*. What ridiculous tale did you tell her to make her behave so oddly?"

René stared at Louis. Then he suddenly remembered what he'd told Elina and found himself more annoyed than he should be by Louis's words about Elina's behavior.

"The *mademoiselle*," he said, "has been laboring under the misconception that she can trust you to take her side. I thought it important to disabuse her of that absurd notion before she began playing on your sympathies in the hope that she could convince you to help her escape."

"But, *monsieur*," Louis retorted in mock anger, "surely you did not tarnish my good name. What did you say to the *mademoiselle* to 'disabuse' her of such an 'absurd notion'?"

René shrugged. At the moment, he found Louis's questions extremely irritating. "I'm afraid I led her to believe that you . . . ah . . . found her attractive and were a bit of a rake. If anything will squelch her overtures to you, that will."

Louis drew himself up with an air of pained nobility. "So you *did* tarnish my good name," he said haughtily, though the twinkle hadn't left his eye.

"Damn it, Louis, it wasn't entirely an untruth. For a man of fifty-five, you attract a goodly share of the ladies."

"So you are worried about me? You think I might forsake my old friend and master?"

"No," René clipped out. "Your loyalty isn't in question. But you do have a soft heart. I can't afford to have her loose in New Orleans spreading her lies because you choose to watch her less carefully than you should. It's particularly important that you keep an eye on her now that I'm teaching her to ride."

The twinkle left Louis's eye as he looked at René in horror. "Teach her to ride? But, *monsieur*! She fears the horses; you said so yourself! You would not force her to ride, surely!"

René's jaw tightened. "She *requested* I teach her. She wishes to overcome her fears, undoubtedly so she can ride off in the dead of night when she has gained enough courage to do so."

"You know this and yet you teach her? Why?"

René paused. The question was a good one. Why *was* he going to give her one more means to escape him, so she could go into New Orleans and spread her tales?

One reason was he hated the imprisonment he was imposing on her. He wanted her to have part of the day when she could be in the open, her body as free as her spirit seemed to be. Then perhaps she'd resent him less and be more willing to abandon her charade.

Yet there was another, more basic reason for teaching her to ride!

"Because I hate to see her afraid," he said, surprised to realize it was true.

"But it does not bother you to make her afraid of me," Louis said softly. "Is it possible you are concerned she will use her wiles on *me* instead of you, so she can escape? Is it possible you are a bit jealous?"

"No!" René said through clenched teeth. One look at Louis's knowing grin made him relax the tense muscles of his face. "I just don't want her turning to you behind my back."

"I will admit that the *mademoiselle* has a fetching way about her. It would be hard to refuse any request she made."

"But you will, won't you?" René demanded.

Louis shrugged. "It depends on her request."

"She's bewitched you, too, has she?" René asked with a grating harshness in his voice, ignoring Louis's teasing tone.

Louis's smile softened. "*Non*. I think not. Only the bewitched man would believe such ill things of her as you do."

René swore under his breath. "You really believe she's Philippe's daughter? I suppose you also think I killed her precious lover, Wallace."

"I think you wrong her. That is all. I don't know the truth about her relationship to either *Monsieur* Vannier or this Wallace. But I would stake my life on the belief that she is unfamiliar with the sort of sordid life you think she has led. And I know she truly mourns her *maman* and Wallace."

"Does she?" René murmured, his dark eyes growing even darker with a hint of pain. "I don't know anymore, my friend, I truly don't know."

Then he swung his gaze back to the stairway as Louis digested that statement silently.

It was standing thus that Elina found them a few moments later when she descended the stairs in her new riding habit. She scarcely noticed the peculiar looks both gave her. She was too caught up in her anger with René over the dresses to pay much attention to anything else.

Her skirts swished as she took the last few steps with a jaunty step. With an affected nonchalance that scarcely hid her sarcasm, she announced to René, "Shall we go then? I'm burning with eagerness to break my neck on that horse of yours."

Louis's eyes flew to hers in alarm. "*Mademoiselle*, if you do not wish to ride—"

"Don't be absurd," she assured him, wondering if her fear of horses had been the topic of discussion before she'd come down. "If the *monsieur* is willing to teach me, I'm willing to learn."

"I've been looking forward to the lesson all day," René said, holding out his arm for her.

Elina's eyes darted from Louis's face to René's before she reluctantly took René's arm.

Louis excused himself after speaking a few polite words

and flashing Elina a searching look. Scarcely was he out of the room before she plunged into the subject that had plagued her mind ever since she'd awakened that morning.

"Why did you steal my old dresses?" she asked as she withdrew her hand from René's arm.

"Would you have worn what I bought for you otherwise?"

"Of course not."

"Then the answer to your question should be obvious."

She stopped in her tracks, her hands firmly planted on her hips. "You had no right to take what is mine!"

He studied her. "Agreed. But I saw no way to solve the problem of how to make your inadequate wardrobe adequate. You must admit you needed clothing. If it weren't for the clothes I bought you, I might point out, you wouldn't be dressed appropriately for those riding lessons you so crave."

"That didn't seem to concern you the last time we went riding!" she spat out, her memories of that mad ride through the fields fresh in her mind.

"It concerns me now." At the mutinous glare she flashed him, the hard glint in his eyes softened considerably. "There's no point in arguing about it, *chérie*. I've already given your dresses to the servants. And frankly, I don't regret doing so. If you were honest, you'd admit you're secretly delighted every time you look at your new gowns."

She threw up her hands in exasperation and stalked off toward the door with René following, a smug grin on his face.

"You don't listen to a word I say, do you?" she stated. "Of course I find the clothes beautiful, you infuriating man! But that doesn't matter in the least, for I know why you gave them to me. And I don't appreciate being gowned like some child's doll just to serve your pleasure!"

He caught her arm and pulled her around to face him. With embarrassing thoroughness, his eyes scanned every aspect of her attire—the snug-fitting low-cut bodice made respectable only by the presence of a lace-edged chemisette underneath the jacket that covered Elina from waist to neck, the riding skirt of cotton with its brilliant green print, and her gray leather half boots.

Then before she could protest, he took a goodly portion of her skirt and petticoat in his fingers and lifted the skirt to reveal the silk pantaloons she wore underneath, the ones *Madame* Laplante had said were all the rage in Paris. Elina gasped and jerked her skirts down as a slow blush rose over her face.

René gave a low chuckle. "You look lovely, sweet eyes. But your dressing appropriately doesn't really 'serve my pleasure.' Not in the way you mean." He smiled, his eyes gleaming warmly as they rested on her face. His hand left her elbow to trail down the soft linen-encased arm. "I must admit, however, that I *am* pleased to see you in your new clothing in spite of how angry it makes you to have to wear it."

The contact of his fingers on her bare wrists sent a whispery shiver through her senses.

"I have a right to be angry," she protested, though the words were spoken breathlessly as she tried to fight the unsettling effect his nearness was having on her.

His hand slipped further down to clasp hers. "Shall I try to convince you not to be angry with me?" he asked, his thumb rubbing circles on the top of her hand as his eyes held her gaze captive.

"No," she said weakly, then with more pleading in her voice, "no . . . please."

He lifted her hand to his lips, and to her surprise, began to kiss the tips of her fingers. "I really don't like to have you angry with me."

Somehow she mustered enough will to pull her hand from his. "I—I won't be angry . . ." she stammered, "if you'll just teach me to ride."

He smiled. "Fine. It will be my pleasure."

They walked outside in silence, although Elina was acutely aware of his presence. But her attention shifted once she passed through the door and noticed that only Monique was saddled.

She flashed him a questioning look.

"For this first lesson, I decided we should ride together," he stated. "That way I won't have to worry about having to race after a runaway horse."

Despite her suspicion that his motives for such a decision were other than what he claimed, Elina felt relief surge through her. She'd been dreading this first lesson, dreading being alone atop a horse. The lessons were necessary, she knew, for how could she ever escape René's accursed house without a horse? Still, it had taken two or three days of weighing her options to bring her to the point where she'd asked René to teach her.

Painting his portrait had driven her to it. Every hour she had spent tracing his features had brought her more and more dangerously under his spell. Worse yet, the room he'd provided her as an artist's studio adjoined his bedroom on the other side. As she'd painted, she hadn't been able to thrust from her mind the image of him caressing her as she lay on his bed.

Sometimes she'd even thought he could read her mind, for often she'd caught him smiling when there was nothing to smile about. All of it had brought her to the realization that she had to escape before she succumbed to his unspoken demands.

So she'd made her fateful request, not really certain that he would teach her. To her surprise, he'd been more than willing to do so. His willingness made her a bit uncomfortable. Surely he realized why she wanted to learn? Well, it didn't matter what his reasons were for helping her. She would take what he offered and use it to her advantage.

That is, if she could endure the lessons. She chewed on her lower lip as René demonstrated how to mount the horse.

"Normally, you'd ride sidesaddle, of course," he told her as he dismounted, "so I suggest you sit across the saddle today. It will give you a better feel for what you'll experience later."

She considered saying she'd rather ride astride as he did. It seemed to her it would be far easier to stay on the horse when she could put her legs around the wretched beast instead of perching on its side. But she knew such a request would only reinforce his image of her as something less than a lady.

In silence, René lifted her onto the horse as if she weighed nothing at all. Immediately, she latched onto the pommel. Gently, he pulled her hands from it.

"You must leave your hands free to control the reins," he instructed.

"But I'll fall off!" she wailed.

He chuckled, climbing into the saddle behind her. Then one of his arms snaked around her waist to hold her securely against him. "No, you won't. Trust me."

Her heart pounded as he gave a soft click and Monique began to walk forward. His hands held the reins. Slowly, he transferred them to her.

"Don't let the horse think you're not in complete control. If you handle the reins firmly, being careful to pull rather than jerk them, the horse will follow your lead."

Her hands began to sweat as her fear and nervousness grew. "I—I think you should hold the reins."

"You're doing fine," he murmured into her hair. "Just relax."

Her fingers gripped the reins so tightly her knuckles ached. And he had the nerve to tell her to relax!

"You and the horse must be one," he said, his arm tightening around her waist. "You mustn't act as if the horse is an object stiff and apart from you like a wooden chair. Pretend instead that it's a feather bed, which molds itself to your body and shifts and sways with your movements. You control its motion, so there's never anything to fear. If you treat her right, Monique will no more throw you than your own bed would."

Deborah Martin

Some of the stiffness left Elina's bones, but not much.

He sighed. "Don't concentrate on the act of riding itself. This is no different from when you rode in a carriage. You should control the horse automatically, while your mind is caught up with watching the world around you."

"The world around me can't trample me, so I don't need to watch it," she muttered.

"Forget the horse!" he commanded with irritation. Then his voice softened. "Pretend you're riding in a carriage and someone else is controlling the reins. You and I are just two passengers having a conversation. Look, my dear," he said in imitation of a gentleman making small talk. He lifted one hand to indicate the avenue of cypresses they were slowly meandering down. "Aren't they fascinating trees, *chérie*? What do they remind you of, with their roots above ground?"

For a moment, Elina left off staring at the back of the horse's head and glanced at the trees, though her gaze swiftly flew back to its previous position.

"They don't remind me of anything," she retorted, her hands reaching for the pommel.

He pulled them away, placing them in her lap. "Really? I've always thought they resembled kneeling men. My father named Cour de Cyprès for them. He said they looked just like courtiers dancing attendance on the queen, their knees already bent for her promenade."

With curiosity, she tore her eyes away from the horse to stare at the cypresses again. It was true. They did look almost like a court of trees. Unconsciously, her hands slackened on the reins as she studied the trees.

"Imagine the moss is their finery," René murmured. "They're bedecked in full court costume for the queen's entrance."

A half-smile crossed her face. She *could* almost imagine it.

"And you're their queen," René continued in a whisper, lowering his head to nuzzle her neck. "They're giving you homage as I wish to give you homage." His lips planted a kiss in her hair, sending a delicate tremor through her. Her fingers tightened on the reins, but not in fear.

"You—you're supposed to be teaching me to ride," she said tremulously.

"And so I am. But no one said I couldn't enjoy the lesson as well."

Elina said nothing as he pressed another kiss into her hair. Then his hand lifted to shake her coiled hair loose from its pins.

"That's better," he murmured. "Now you could truly be a queen of the forest, your hair wild and free."

"Free." She pounced on that last word in her struggle to fight his ever-strengthening spell. "I would like to be free, that's true."

"No, *bien-aimée*. You don't wish to be free or you'd take my money and leave. Sometimes I even find myself glad that you refuse it. We are in this trap together, you and I, and I for one am enjoying our enforced confinement. Yet perhaps I would want one small change in our situation."

His breath ruffled her hair, and she instantly knew what change he wished. It was no small one. Then she sucked in her breath suddenly. He had called her "darling."

His arm slid up to clasp her under her breasts, so it brushed their undersides with every step of the horse. Elina fought desperately the delicious languor stealing over her. Her body felt like softened wax, incapable of resisting and devoid of the desire to do so.

Monique continued to plod down the avenue, but Elina's hands no longer reached for the pommel. They rested in her lap as her body began to relax against René's. She felt strangely safe, wrapped in his arms. What was left of her fear of the horse subsided. Her body was too busy responding to René as thirsty flowers respond to water. She drank in his every touch, and each caress left her thirsting for another.

Days of painting his image had reduced her to this, she

thought distantly. She couldn't help but admit he'd been right about what painting him would do to her. It had softened her toward him.

"Shouldn't we move along faster?" she asked in one last desperate attempt to avoid the snare that awaited her in his arms.

"I think not," he said, his warm breath slanting across her cheek. "You might become frightened again."

"No. I feel much less frightened now."

"I don't believe you. Look at me so I can see if you're telling the truth."

Oblivious to the movement of the horse, she twisted her head around to stare at him. She saw the glint of triumph in his eyes only seconds before his lips closed on hers, and she realized her error.

Hastily, she drew back.

"Careful," he murmured. "You wouldn't want to lose your perch."

For a brief moment, she felt the old fear of horses surge through her, and her hands reached to clutch his shirt. Then he wiped her fear out of her mind as he took her lips again. His warm, hard mouth pressed against hers gently at first, but as she clung to his shirt in a mixture of fear and desire, his lips hungrily forced hers apart. With a sigh of satisfaction, he plunged his tongue into her mouth, his hand creeping up to stroke the line of her jaw before it buried itself in her hair.

Their tongues danced in a rhythm that mirrored the slow gait of the horse. The sun beat down on their bare heads, but the warmth Elina felt oozing through her limbs didn't come from the sun. And as he continued to probe her mouth, she found herself wanting to probe his, to raise in him the piercingly sweet desire he raised in her.

Shyly, she licked his lower lip and then slipped her tongue into the forbidden place. His arms tightened on her waist as a moan erupted from his throat. And though she withdrew almost immediately, the subtle change in the way he held her, as if he wished to fold her into himself, told her that he too felt as consumed by longing as did she.

He drew back from her reluctantly, though his eyes held hers. "I think we should return and resume this in more comfortable surroundings."

His words were enough to dampen her desire. What could she have been thinking of, to allow him such liberties?

"I think not," she answered, though she couldn't stop the blush that stained her face. She strove for a light tone. "Remember, you promised to teach me to ride."

For a moment, he looked as if he might protest. Then he smiled like a man who knows he will eventually win the battle. "Of course, I'd forgotten," he said in a husky whisper that sent a thrill of expectation through her.

The next hour was torturous as René mingled instruction and casual caresses until Elina scarcely cared if she ever learned to ride, as long as she could have such lessons.

Then just as he was taking the horse yet again through various gaits, the silence of the avenue was broken by a loud call.

"*Nonc* René!" the voice repeated.

Instantly, René's face stiffened.

Elina's head shot up to see who was greeting them and for a brief moment, her heart caught in her throat. Riding toward them was a man with Papa's face. He was younger, to be sure, but there was no mistaking the resemblance. As he rode closer, she stared at him shamelessly, emotions rioting through her. He had called René uncle so he must be. . . .

"Francois," René breathed as if he'd guessed her thoughts. "Damn the boy!"

The man pulled up beside them, and Elina forced herself to smile. But inside she felt twisted with pain. So this was the half brother she'd only seen in her imagination. He was staring at her with curiosity, his dark eyes flying from her face to René's.

Then he flashed her an oily leering grin that made Elina

dislike him instantly, particularly when he added insult to injury by winking at René.

"So, you've found yourself a mistress in our lovely city, have you, *Nonc* René?"

"What are you doing here?" René demanded in a cool voice that seemed almost hostile.

"Now, my dear uncle," Francois replied, switching to French. "Aren't you going to introduce me to your little American wench?"

Elina's entire body went rigid. "My name is—" she began in perfect French, intending to show him that he was maligning his own sister, but René didn't give her the chance.

"*Mademoiselle* Wallace," René finished for her. "Not that it's any of your concern."

Francois studied her carefully. Did she imagine it or did a hint of something like recognition cross his face?

"Wallace?" he asked. "Such a common name. It doesn't sound French. Are you from here?"

René's fists dug into her stomach in warning, but she ignored him.

"I'm from Missouri," she stated in open defiance. Then she added deliberately, "Although I do have relatives here."

"Indeed," Francois said in a casual tone, but his eyes narrowed. "And friends as well, I see."

Elina straightened her shoulders, fully prepared to give her impudent half brother a thorough dressing down.

René spoke quickly, "Francois, I suggest you go on to the house. I'll follow in a moment, and we can discuss your business inside."

The expression that briefly flickered over Francois's face puzzled Elina. It was as if something had suddenly occurred to him.

He smiled that same unctuous smile, but it took in René as well as Elina. "My business with you won't take long," Francois told René. "I merely wished to ask what you want me to tell Mother about the duel you fought with that vermin card cheat two weeks ago. She's been asking questions."

Elina's heart began to pound, and her body went limp against René's as the import of Francois's words struck her. The duel . . . Of course, it was the one with her brother. She'd pushed it out of her mind, having begun to believe René's protestations of his innocence.

How could she have been so thoroughly stupid? Of course he'd lied. Why had she thought otherwise?

"I fought no duel," René ground out, his entire body tensing.

"Of course not," Francois said as he winked at his uncle. "None of us ever do, do we? Anyway, *Maman* somehow heard the rumors about your . . . ah . . . involvement, and now she's asking me questions. Should I tell her the truth or refuse to tell her anything?"

René's fingers dug into Elina's slender waist as she strained away from him. "Tell Julia the truth, Francois, just as I told you. Explain that the rumors are just rumors and that I certainly didn't duel with anyone, so there's no cause for alarm."

Francois shrugged. "She's not too concerned that you killed a man, so we needn't keep that from her. She's just worried you'll go to jail. Shall I assure her you have everything under control?"

"I—I'd like to return to the house now," Elina broke in before René could answer, her hands pulling at the iron band of his arm that held her against him. "Please don't bother to come back with me. I'll just walk. You and your nephew must have many things to discuss, and you don't need me in your way."

She had to get away from them both. She couldn't stand to hear them speak of her brother so casually, as if he were an inconvenience to be dealt with. She would have cried out against their callousness, but it was clear such an outcry would do no good, for Francois was, if anything, the more callous of the two men. She thought about telling him her story. But she didn't trust him. René's response to her claims had been to keep her prisoner, but his nephew. . . .

She shuddered. His nephew, she felt certain, would do something worse. After all, her very existence was a threat to his inheriting the money he must feel was rightfully his.

"I'll take you back to the house," René insisted.

"No!" Elina responded, her tone of voice higher than usual in her desperation. Then more softly, "There's no need."

"Why, *Nonc*," Francois put in, "one would think you were holding the poor girl prisoner. Surely you're not so enamored of her you can't bear to let her out of your sight for a moment?"

Elina could feel René's thigh tense against her legs. "Ah, but my dear nephew, you've hit it exactly. I'm afraid she's gotten me so thoroughly bewitched I simply must do as she desires. We'll meet you at the house."

Then in one swift motion, he snatched the reins from Elina, turned the horse, and started toward the house at a gallop. Elina clung to the pommel for dear life, her heart thudding madly as fear and anger intermingled within her.

She'd never trust him again, the scoundrel! And if he tried to lay so much as a finger on her, she'd . . . she'd . . . she'd do something! She had to do something. She couldn't just let him continue to seduce her into caring about him. She mustn't! He was her brother's murderer!

As they reined up in front of the house, Elina looked back and noticed that her half brother followed them at a leisurely pace. René dismounted, then pulled her down beside him. His face glowed with pent-up anger, and she shuddered just to look at him. She tried to wrench away from his hands that gripped her at the waist, but he refused to release her.

"Let me go!" she cried. "I can't bear to hear any more about how or why you killed my brother! It's bad enough to hear it from strangers, but to hear it from my own half brother! I can't bear it, do you hear?"

"Francois is a fool . . ." René began as he struggled to restrain her. Her hands struck futilely at his chest, and he grimaced.

"No! I'm the fool!" The words were torn from her. Tears slipped down her cheeks, but she didn't care. "I thought . . . Oh, never mind! I should have known your words were empty, just as Papa's were! I should have known!"

At that moment, Francois rode up. René lifted eyes dark with murderous rage to his nephew, and in that moment, Elina kicked René in the shins as hard as she could with her leather boots. He flinched, but his hands still held her.

"Let me go!" she begged. "Please . . . let me go!"

Without a word, he released her, and she fled into the house, her eyes so blinded with tears she almost tripped on the stairs in her hurry to escape.

René watched her go, a heavy dull thudding in his chest. He fixed his nephew with eyes of black ice. "What purpose could you possibly have had in repeating such lies to Elina?"

Francois sat in the saddle, his hands twitching nervously at the reins.

"I—I thought she would be impressed. Most women shower me with attention when they learn how many duels I've won."

René regarded his nephew coldly, wanting nothing more than to drag Francois from the horse and beat him to a bloody pulp.

"The man you said I killed was her lover, you fool. It has taken me a long time to convince her I didn't kill him, and now you tell her I did."

Francois's eyes widened in surprise. "Her lover?" He was quiet for a moment, then shrugged. "It doesn't matter to women like her. One lover is as good as any other."

This time René couldn't endure his nephew's ignorant barbs. He strode forward and grasped the reins to Francois's horse in one swift movement. Francois struggled to regain control of the reins, but René stood his ground, oblivious to the horse's flashing hoofs only a hairsbreadth away from him. Francois ceased struggling when he saw he couldn't yank the reins away. Gradually, the horse's movements stilled.

"I'll say this to you only once, Francois," René said calmly once man and beast were still. "Elina is not a whore for you to destroy with your petty insinuations. You will not come here again as long as she's here, nor will I allow you to insult her in my presence. I suggest you leave now, while I'm still in control of my temper."

"I didn't mean to ruin things, *Nonc* René—" Francois began.

"Now!" René roared. Then he released the reins and gave the horse a sharp slap on the rear that sent it racing down the avenue. And without another glance he strode into the house.

But as he took the stairs two at a time to Elina's room, his rage began to subside and questions started emerging.

Why had Francois come? And why had he insisted on repeating those rumors to Elina? It was entirely like him to think that repeating them would impress a woman, but he'd never shown any interest before in helping his uncle with anything, and certainly not with women.

René's pace slowed. Was there some other reason Francois might have had for setting Elina off? Perhaps. But what?

René shook his head. It was impossible to fathom the strange byways of his nephew's mind. Sometimes he seemed to act out of pure venom. Perhaps this was one of those times.

Some other doubt lay at the back of René's mind, but he ignored it in his eagerness to resolve matters with Elina. He had to find her and make her accept the truth. He had to!

He wasn't certain why it meant so much to him to erase her image of him as a killer. He only knew that if he couldn't teach her to trust him, she would never be his.

His? For the first time he acknowledged that he wanted

her with a passion he'd never felt before. At that moment, when he'd finally reached her room and opened the door to find the room deserted, he knew only one thing mattered. That he make Elina his, body and soul, so he could rid himself of his obsession with her once and for all. As he stood in the stifling heat of her empty room, he vowed softly into the emptiness, "I'll find you, *chérie*, and slake this thirst before it kills me. Because if I don't . . ."

He cursed, then spun on his heels, and left the room.

Chapter Fourteen

A bed for two isn't a bed for three.—Creole Proverb

Elina stared blindly around, suddenly aware of where she was. What had made her flee to the room she'd been using for her painting? She hadn't run to her bedroom; she'd known René would go there first. And she'd needed room to breathe, to find some way out of this trap.

But why here? She stared at her makeshift artist's room, the painting materials spread haphazardly about. It was her place, the only corner of the house that seemed her own. Perhaps that was why she came there to grieve.

Then she caught sight of the half-finished portrait of René, and she groaned. As usual, he was always encroaching on her world, reminding her of urges within herself that she wished she could deny.

She strode toward the canvas determinedly, intent upon venting her anger on the image of the man who'd wronged her.

"*Mademoiselle*? Perhaps you could tell me where to find the *monsieur*?"

Louis's polite warm voice stopped her. She whirled around to face him where he stood in the doorway leading into the hall.

"*Mademoiselle*!" he cried in alarm as he saw her tear-streaked face.

"Go away! Leave me in peace—if there is such a thing in this cursed house!"

"Surely the *monsieur* has not hurt you," Louis said as he came forward, his expression grim but disbelieving. "I cannot imagine he would lay a hand on you . . ."

She laughed then, the self-mocking laugh of the disillusioned. "No? No. I suppose he wouldn't. Not me. But he killed my brother."

Louis shook his head slowly. "You cannot believe this of him. He told me what happened. He only found the body by chance."

"So he claims," she said through gritted teeth.

"You have been here now for some time. You have seen the way he runs his plantation, the way he treats his servants. Do you honestly think he would kill a man simply for cheating him?"

She rubbed the tears from one eye. "His own nephew said—"

"Francois? He was here?" Louis said, his mouth twisting in his disdain. "Francois is *canaille*, a miserable worm. The only words he speaks are filth."

The force behind his words stunned her. Then her eyes narrowed. "Of course you would defend René," she said, her tone harsh and cold. "He's your master. I certainly can't expect you to say anything bad of him."

Louis's expression softened. "*Ma petite fille*, you must not be so afraid to trust people. Because others have lied to you, must you think everyone lies? Have I ever hidden anything from you? Even that first night? Never. And I tell you the truth now. The *monsieur* did not kill your lov—your brother."

Elina's arms fell limply at her sides. She wanted to believe Louis, but she didn't think she could. "How do you know he wasn't lying to you to make sure you supported his story?"

"The *monsieur* would not do such a thing. I cannot believe he killed your brother."

"I want to believe you but . . ."

The male voice that responded came from behind her. "But you won't because it's safer not to."

Elina turned slowly to face René, who stood in the doorway that led from his bedroom into the studio. He'd peeled off his coat to combat the noonday heat and now stood with it trailing from his hand. She stared at him, perplexed by the flash of relief she glimpsed on his face before his eyes became shadowed. Then in two quick strides he entered the room, and her heart began to pound with dread.

Unknowingly, he stopped beside his portrait. Elina found her eyes drawn to both faces, one an image she'd unconsciously imbued with her own wishes and hopes for the future, the other the flesh and blood she both longed for and feared.

Louis left the room silently while Elina remained standing, her eyes fixed on the dual Renés.

As the silence in the room grew, René dropped his coat and approached her warily.

"Wallace is dead, Elina," René told her, an unmistakable hardness in his voice. "He was a liar and a cheat and now he's dead. He didn't deserve you and certainly doesn't deserve to have you deny your own desires so you can attain some twisted vengeance for him. Particularly when the man you wish to wreak your vengeance on didn't kill him."

His words seemed to empower her to act. With a cry of distress, she pivoted toward the door Louis had left by, intent on fleeing the room before he forced her to listen to any more lies.

But René was upon her in seconds, his hand pulling on her wrist like an iron bit. When her struggles didn't obtain her release, she went limp, refusing to look at him.

"For days now," he continued, his voice growing more biting by the moment, "you've used your companion's death as a bulwark between us. You've lovingly placed on the pile every piece of information you could glean that might add to that protective fortress. And why? Not because you really cared that Wallace was killed, but because you feared if you tore down the fortress, I might destroy you. You've been deceiving yourself if you think Wallace has anything to do with this battle between us."

In shock she wheeled around, her mouth open as she stared at him, reeling from the blows of the words he so callously threw at her.

"I'm not the only one who builds fortresses and lies to himself," she hissed. "You refuse to acknowledge he's my brother, even though you have no evidence to prove he isn't. You simply don't wish to admit I might be what I seem. If I'm telling the truth, then the one thing you found stable and solid—your sister's family—becomes as unstable as the rest of the world. It's easier for you to make me into something I'm not than to admit to what and who I am."

"That's just it," he ground out as he yanked her up against him. "I don't know what or who you are. One minute, I'm lost in those siren's eyes and I would believe that the moon was the sun if you said so. Then I remember that night—"

"Yes, that night," she bit out, her voice low and bitter. "That night when you swore you'd have your vengeance if we left that room. That night when my brother stole your money. That night when—when someone took it upon himself to rid the world of that terrible menace—my brother. No, I shan't forget that night any time soon, either."

She strained against his arms, averting her face from his, but he wouldn't let her go.

"Release me!" she begged, though her eyes refused to meet his. "Neither of us can forget, so why continue to torture each other so?"

One of his hands left her arm to grip her chin, forcing her head back, but still she wouldn't look at him.

"Look at me, damn it!" he commanded.

"No . . ." she murmured, her hands lifting to press against his shoulders.

An exasperated sigh escaped his lips. "Whether brother or lover, Wallace is dead, and I'll make you forget him and that night if it's the last thing I ever do," he vowed as he struggled with her.

At his words, a sound somewhere between a moan and a cry escaped her lips. Then she made the mistake of turning her eyes up to his in a silent plea.

In that moment something happened. His eyes held hers, an unspoken message in its depths making her pause. Was it the warmth of the midday sun streaming through the filmy curtains that caused her to believe for an instant that his was the face of an honest man? Or was it just that she could no longer endure the ravaged lines of raw pain she saw etched in his face?

Whatever it was, as she stared into the questioning dark eyes, the achingly familiar planes of his face, something in her heart told her he couldn't be Alex's killer, that he was incapable of such pointless violence.

His questioning look hardened into one of firm resolve as he saw indecision cloud her face. Her lips parted slightly in an unintentional invitation, and his mouth swooped down, his lips determined but gentle against the uncertain softness of her own. Slowly, his kiss became more fierce, relentless in its attack as it pressed enticingly against her closed lips. She twisted her head away, but his hand swept up to hold it still. As the pressure of his mouth on hers increased and his musky scent filled her nostrils, she felt her control slipping.

Then she found herself opening to him. Somehow all her logical objections faded as the double-edged sword of desire pierced them both with its sweet pain and their bodies strained together in an aching dance of release.

In the deepest recesses of her mind, Elina knew she'd wanted him to touch her, to seal her fate with his mind-numbing kisses. A good part of her mind still feared him, still distrusted him, but her body clung to his, fearless and trusting. As his mouth greedily devoured hers, her soul sighed and she willingly gave in to her longing. All her desire to fight shrank into nothing, leaving only an impatient need to be touched, stroked, desired.

"*Ma chérie, bien-aimée,*" he murmured against her lips as he satisfied that need, his hands roaming freely over the curves of her waist and hips. "You have enslaved me, sweet eyes. But I don't know if I wish to be set free."

"Unfair, oh, unfair . . ." she whispered into his ear as his lips, hot and wet, trailed over her neck and shoulder. "I'm the one who's enslaved. You take what you wish and—"

Her last small protest was smothered as he kissed her again, his tongue gently teasing the delicate recesses of her mouth.

His hands slipped to the buttons of her bodice and began to undo them. In moments, she felt his fingers peeling the Spencer jacket off to expose her stays and a chemisette that scarcely covered her breasts. Then his fingers were spreading over the sleekness of her corseted belly. Slowly, his hands slid up until the thumb and forefinger of each hand formed a half circle beneath her breasts.

A low moan escaped her lips as she felt a yearning to have his hands cover her there. Her body trembled and she feared she'd wither into nothing if he stopped touching her, yet she knew such desires were wrong. What demon had possessed her? How could she allow him to touch her in this shameful manner?

She didn't know the answers, only that she couldn't help wanting him. So when the palms of his hands crept up underneath the chemisette and over her chemise-clad breasts, lightly kneading the spots where she wanted his touch, she allowed it. The unfamiliar sensations his fondling raised in her shook her to her very core. Her entire body

239

tightened as a throbbing pleasure thrummed inside her.

Suddenly alarmed by the strong feelings he aroused, she backed away, but one of his hands left her breast to capture her waist and pull her once more up against the length of his body. She went stiff, whispering "No—o—o—".

But he murmured, "Yes, oh, yes," before he gave her a potent fiery kiss.

Weakened too much to think, she did not protest when his hands loosened the ribbons of her skirt and slid underneath the waistband. With a shiver of both shock and pleasure, she realized that only her thin cotton chemise and even thinner silk pantaloons separated his hands from her skin. She pinkened instantly as he cupped her bottom with his hands, thrusting her up so tightly against him she could feel every inch of his body, of his hardness.

"Please, René, you mustn't!" she cried, pressing her hands against his chest in sudden awareness of just how many liberties she'd allowed him to take.

"Why mustn't I?" he murmured as his fingers reached around her neck to unfasten her starched chemisette. It dropped to the ground as he lowered his head to nuzzle the half-moon of one breast, which peeked above the lacy edge of her corset and low-cut chemise.

"Because—" she began, then gasped as his tongue darted out to lick the sweet-scented hollow between her breasts. "Because it's not right!" she burst out. Her fingers dug into his shoulders as she fought to free herself.

"No, sweet eyes," he told her, lifting a face etched with torment to her. "It isn't right for us to have such yearnings and deny them, to know we have the power to fulfill them and still not do so."

His words sent a thrill of anticipation through her even while she knew she shouldn't listen to him. "But you yearn only for my body," she whispered in protest, determined to make him understand she couldn't be satisfied with having his physical desire alone.

His eyes flickered brightly as he stared at her, a quizzical look on his face. "What would you have me yearn for?" he asked, lifting one hand to cup her chin.

Her eyes fell before that demanding gaze. "Noth–nothing," she stammered, unwilling to let him glimpse the caring she feared shone in her eyes.

"Nothing? Ah, but you lie, *ma chérie*. You want from me the same thing I want from you, and that is more than only your body. If only a body would satisfy me, I could take another body, another woman. No, sweet eyes, I want nothing less than your freely given desire, your complete will."

She stared into his dark, richly warm Creole eyes, any words she might have spoken dying on her lips as she confronted the fierce pleading in his face. It was more than she could bear, this honest voicing of his passion. His lips were poised inches from hers as if silently, almost humbly, waiting for some confirmation that she, too, wanted him, that he hadn't bared his soul to her in vain.

Suddenly she wanted to reassure him, to confess that she ached for him, too, that it didn't matter what he'd done or who she was.

But the words wouldn't come. Instead, her lips made their own promises. Scarcely knowing she did it, she turned her face up to his and pressed a sweet kiss against his mouth.

He released a ragged breath, then returned the kiss, grasping her chin as his lips practiced their silken torment on hers. Then without giving her a chance to protest, he swept her up into his arms and carried her across the threshhold into his room.

It took only seconds for them to cross the room to his bed, but in those seconds, the sensual fog that seemed to surround them both lifted long enough for Elina to consider what she was allowing him to do. How could she willingly permit him to take her innocence? In one last burst of denial, when he lay her on the bed, she rolled to her side, intending to slip off the side opposite him. But he was faster than she and grabbed her before she'd moved more than an inch. Kneeling on the bed, he twisted her wriggling body around so she lay on her back.

"I mustn't," she told him in desperation as she stared up into his now furious face. "I can't do this . . ."

"Because of him?" he demanded as his hands slid from her shoulders to pin her wrists at her sides.

"Him?" she asked. Just lying there before René in her semi-clad state was making her incapable of rational thought. Already she felt a resurgence of her earlier piercing desire. "Him?" she repeated once again, raising her head.

His anger instantly faded. Only then did she realize he'd been referring to Alex. The slow smile of satisfaction that lit his face filled her with a tremor of anticipation. "So that warm glow in your eyes is at last for me," he murmured with deceptive softness.

His eyes demanded an answer, compelling her to tell him nothing but the truth. "It has always been for you," she said in a whisper that was torn from her.

With a groan of triumph, he lowered his head to capture her mouth. His lips moved with excruciating slowness, working their magnificent magic until she dropped back against the pillows in dazed satisfaction. She no longer cared she was about to do something terribly wicked. It didn't feel wicked, this sweetly urgent desire taking over her body. It seemed right, very right, to let him touch her, possess her, as if she belonged only to him.

For she truly wanted to belong to him, she realized. Even as his hands stroked downward over the sensual lines of her body, branding every inch of her, she knew she was his already in her heart.

With infinite care his mouth spread kisses across her shoulder and down to her creamy breasts.

"Damn corsets!" he muttered as he encountered the stiff whalebone that jutted up beneath her breasts. A half-smile sprung to her lips at the pleasurable realization that she could arouse such impatient desire in him.

Then his lips moved to her neck and the delicate skin of her ear, distracting her with tingling sweet kisses, and she moved willingly when he rolled her to her side. He slid down to press against her back, burying his face in her mass of tangled russet hair as his fingers unbuttoned her skirt and then nimbly worked her laces loose.

A loud sigh escaped her lips as the hated corset slipped away from her. He chuckled. "You need never wear it again if you wish, sweet eyes," he murmured into her hair.

Before she could answer, his hands had slid her skirt down and tossed it on the floor.

Freed of her heavy skirt, she felt suddenly light and open and shamefully free. "Wh—what are you doing?" she asked inanely, twisting her head around to look at him.

He lay on his side next to her, resting on one elbow. His gaze lingered over her body, which was now only clad in her chemise and pantaloons. "I'm ridding you of your thorny trappings. I wish to harvest the cotton," he told her earnestly, one hand reaching over to pull the sleeve of her chemise off her shoulder.

"And what of *your* thorny trappings?" she blurted out, then blushed as she realized how shamelessly forward she sounded.

He only smiled, his eyebrows lifting in mock surprise. "Ah, yes, *chérie*, of course, you're right. I must shed my trappings, too," he told her, rising from the bed and immediately beginning to unbutton his shirt.

"I didn't mean—" she began but broke off as his shirt opened to bare a dark, muscled chest sprinkled generously with black curly hair. She knew she should avert her eyes, but she couldn't. The steadily increasing rise and fall of his broad chest held her captivated, for his quickening breathing seemed to mirror her own.

When he pulled off his shirt to reveal well-knit shoulders and a strong, wide neck, Elina suddenly realized she'd been staring. She jerked her eyes down, but that was worse, for now he began unbuttoning his trousers. She gasped and shut her eyes for the rest of the process, though not before glimpsing a part of his anatomy with which she was unfamiliar.

He chuckled. "Don't close your sweet eyes to me," he murmured as he slid onto the bed to lie beside her. "Surely you've seen a man's body before."

Her eyes flew open in outrage. "No, certainly not!" she protested.

He shrugged. "Whatever you say. It matters not."

"It matters to me!"

"Sh, sh," he whispered as his finger flew to touch her lips gently to silence her. His finger then stroked her mouth, tracing the outline of her lips as his expression grew serious.

"Do you realize we've been in this house together for three weeks?" he said, a hint of incredulity in his voice. "And all that time I wanted to have you so badly I ached constantly. Many nights I lay in this bed, forcing myself not to cross into your room and stare at you sleeping, because I knew if I did, I would let my desires rule my good sense . . ." He kissed her forehead. "Then I'd wake you and kiss you senseless until at last you opened to me like a rose . . ."

His words started an ache within her, too, as she remembered the nights she'd lain awake and restless, her body yearning for a nameless something she didn't quite understand. His finger trailed down to catch on the other shoulder of her chemise and began dragging it down her arm.

"And here you are now," he breathed, his eyes riveted on her face. Slowly, his fingers undid the ties at the neck of her chemise.

"I—I shouldn't be."

His hand slid boldly underneath her chemise and pulled it down so he could cup her breast. Then without warning he bent his head to suck at the tender flesh, making Elina's breath quicken suddenly. His tongue swirled expertly over the tiny dusky nub until Elina's short gasps became a barely audible moan.

He lifted his face from her breast to stare into the passion-glazed eyes. "But you will stay, won't you?" he said, and although it was a question, he spoke it as if it could have only one answer.

At that moment, she knew that to stay was her only choice. Her whole body throbbed with a searing thirst she needed quenched and only René seemed capable of quenching it.

"Yes," she murmured, clasping his head as his lips dropped to her breast once again. "I'll stay."

Instantly, she felt the change in him. His mouth moved more urgently over her breast as his hands worked her chemise down to her waist and then past her hips.

Her hands moved to clutch his shoulders as he began to kiss her belly, his fingers stroking her sides as lovingly as a sculptor touches his creation. When he encountered the ties of her pantaloons, he spared only a moment from his labors to undo them. Then he was sliding them down as she, driven by an urge she scarcely acknowledged, arched up mindlessly so he could move them past her hips.

Now he hovered over her and for a brief second, he lifted his eyes to hers. The hunger she saw blazing there made her tremble with a mixture of fear and excitement. Then his gaze swept down the length of her naked body.

Beneath his warm scrutiny, she began feeling a hollow longing between her thighs, and when his fingers strayed over the tangled hair there, the ache grew to unbearable proportions.

"*Chérie*," he whispered almost reverently as his gaze swept back up to drink its fill of every inch of her. "You have outdone my dreams. I thought a nymph had been torturing me these past weeks, but now I find it was a goddess."

Slowly, his fingers began stroking the delicate skin of her inner thighs. Then the tip of his finger traveled over her soft mound to tease the folds of flesh that lay at the very center.

"René!" she protested, her eyes widening in shock as

her hand shot out to grasp his wrist so hard she nearly broke it.

No one had ever touched her there.

He froze and glanced at her face, which was tight with fear. He stared at her for long moments as if some new realization had struck him.

"You really are untouched, aren't you?" he said at last, his tone disbelieving.

She nodded as her body seemed to flame with embarrassment, and her fingers tightened on his wrist.

He lifted his free hand to stroke her hair. "How can this be? You're far too lovely to be unsullied. Wallace must truly have been a fool."

His words tore at her. "I told you," she said tearfully, "he was my brother—never a lover. I—I know nothing of men's ways but what the occasional suitor's kiss taught me. And they didn't kiss like . . . like . . ."

"Like I do?" he said with a smile, then kissed her thoroughly as if to prove it was true. When he had her under his spell again, he murmured, "Your innocence is a gift I didn't expect to receive."

His words reminded her of how drastic a step she was taking. "I—I shouldn't have offered it to you."

He gazed at her, his face reflecting a tumult of emotions. "And as a gentleman I shouldn't accept it." Then his eyes glowed. "But if I don't make you truly mine, you'll soon find some way to escape me." His eyes darkened with desire. "That's something I can't chance, for I don't wish to lose you."

His bold pronouncement reminded her briefly of Oliveira's suggestion that René seduce her to soften her resistance. The thought tormented her, even as she shook her head in wordless denial.

She started to sit up, for his hand at her most secret place was causing her to regret her hasty action in allowing him such freedoms. But he pressed her back against the pillow and swooped down to take her lips with his.

He ignored her fingers biting into his other wrist as he plundered her mouth with a fierce joy that left her dazed. She shuddered and strained against his mouth, her grip on his wrist slackening.

When he felt her weaken, he pressed his advantage, the tip of his finger continuing its brazen teasing movements, forcing from her an equally brazen response as she arched against it. Rivulets of desire turned to torrents within her as he stroked the soft petals. She wanted to scream with the frustration of wanting more, but more of what she wasn't sure.

Then as if in answer to her unspoken longing, his finger plunged abruptly into the slick narrow passage. Her surprised cry was muffled against his mouth.

He kissed her long and hard as his finger began slowly to rub her in the most deliciously satisfying way, moving in a seductive rhythm.

Suddenly his darting movements stopped. "If you're speaking the truth about your virginity, sweet eyes, then I'm about to hurt you," he murmured against her lips, "but I won't ever hurt you again. This I vow, *bien aimée*, and I do not break my vows."

Belatedly, his words registered, and she stared at him perplexed as he lifted his head away from her and slid over her until his legs parted hers.

His finger slid slowly from within her, and she made a soft, nearly unconscious cry of disappointment. But his abandonment didn't last long, for as his mouth again came down on hers, something larger than his finger moved to block the entrance.

Her hands flew to clutch his arms, pushing against them as she felt the alien intrusion. But he ignored her gesture of resistance, devouring her mouth until she scarcely cared he was easing into her. She could feel his arms tremble under her hands as he fought to control his desire.

When he encountered the half-expected barrier, he stopped moving. His head lifted from hers and in his

247

expression, she could see the emotions warring within him. Desire and guilt mingled with another tenderer feeling.

"You didn't lie. Thank you for that." He gave her a light kiss, then murmured, "Now forgive me, sweet eyes, but this is the way it must be."

He entered her, pressing into her with such force that the barrier was broken.

She immediately understood what he'd meant about hurting her. A cry of pain tore from her, and he groaned, his eyes darkening. He stopped all movement.

"My virgin goddess," he whispered achingly against her hair. "I don't wish to hurt you, but you're so small, so tight. I'm sorry, *chérie*."

"It doesn't matter," she said, suddenly wanting to wipe away the remorse in his eyes.

"It does to me. But it will get better if you can relax." He didn't move, but lay still within her, allowing her to adjust to his size.

She forced herself to stop resisting the intrusion.

"That's it. Open to me, sweet eyes," he murmured against her ear, his lips brushing kisses over her tender lobe and then over her hair. "Relax and open to me."

Her hands now clung to him, to the source of her pain and her pleasure as if they knew instinctively what her mind wasn't certain of—that he could be trusted.

"Please . . ." she whispered, not sure what she wished him to give her, but knowing she had an urgent need for it nonetheless.

Hazily, she saw him lift his head and smile. He began to move, slowly at first, then more quickly.

At first all she felt was a soreness, but swiftly that soreness became a piercingly deep craving for more of him inside of her, for a more heightened feeling of joining.

She heard a loud moan and wondered where it came from, then realized seconds later it came from her.

"There are no ghosts between us now, are there?" he asked as he thrust harder and deeper, demanding from her the same impassioned response.

She gave it to him with pleasure, arching into him in blind desire. "No ghosts," she breathed, straining to bind him closer to her, to feel his skin against every inch of hers.

His eyes flashed with triumph, then he drove more fully into her, as if by the very power of his thrusts he could join her to him forever.

"Ah, sweet, sweet dove . . . Elina, Elina . . ." he murmured as his rhythm quickened.

Her body quivered with the intensity of her growing desire. She dug her fingers into his heated skin, her head flung back in sheer wanton pleasure as new sensations wracked her, sending shudder after shudder of nameless joy through her.

Then the distinctions between his body and hers became blurred in her mind as they spun uncontrollably together in a whirling dance of bodies driven by desire.

An aching cry of fulfillment escaped her lips as his final thrust brought his warm sweet seed spilling into her.

"No ghosts," he murmured, the tautness in his face already beginning to slacken as he found his release within her. "You're mine now, *ma petite chérie*. And you must never forget it."

Chapter Fifteen

Nothing is so burdensome as a secret.—French Proverb

Francois toyed with the rosebud standing erect in a nearby vase as he waited with impatience for Etienne to come down. Remembering his afternoon, he groaned aloud. He couldn't believe it! But he had to. His half sister had arrived.

The evidence was incontrovertible. Her professed surname was Wallace, just as Alexandre's was. Her name was Elina, just like the name given on the birth certificate his cursed half brother had shown him. And she'd said she'd come from Missouri. She was most certainly Alexandre Wallace's sister. And that would make her Francois's half sister. No doubt about that. Uncle René might not believe it, but Francois knew more than his uncle did.

The bitch! he thought with venom. She'd ruin all his plans now! Why did she and her meddling brother have to come to New Orleans? They should have remained in Missouri where they belonged.

And how had the girl managed to wheedle her way into Uncle René's good graces? he wondered. Had she told him her story? Was it possible Uncle René had agreed to provide for her in exchange for her keeping quiet? Or was Uncle René keeping her prisoner?

No, that made no sense, for surely Uncle René would have mentioned her claims. Besides, she hadn't acted like a prisoner.

Viciously, he tore off one of the leaves of the rosebud. Was it possible she was his uncle's companion by choice? Could this Elina have willingly gone to Uncle René's bed, perhaps in revenge for Philippe's great deception? Could she even now be trying to deceive his uncle somehow in order to destroy them all?

Willingly or not, he realized, Elina was certainly his uncle's mistress. Never would he forget the way the two of them had been entwined as Francois had come upon them. His uncle's hand had rested intimately on her waist and. . . .

"Whore!" he murmured under his breath, angry that his half sister had become his uncle's mistress. It complicated everything. Even if his uncle knew her story and didn't believe it, he wouldn't be able to resist her for long. It was obvious his uncle was thoroughly infatuated with the little chit.

A sound in the doorway intruded on Francois's unsettling thoughts. "The dinner's not until tonight. I told you that," Etienne said as he entered.

Francois frowned. "I didn't come for dinner, Etienne. I need your help."

Etienne dropped into a chair opposite Francois with a bored expression on his face. "What is it now? A new investment I'm expected to pour my money into?" His eyes lit up. "Or perhaps some whore who's harassing you for more money. I never mind taking care of your women, you know. One night with Etienne, and they always beg to leave town."

"I know. And, yes, this time it is a woman. But you need a more delicate hand for this one. No beating, you understand? I can't risk it."

Etienne looked crestfallen for a moment. "Who is she? Wife of a business partner with whom you don't wish to duel?"

Francois hesitated. No, he mustn't tell Etienne the truth about the girl's identity. Despite his cruel nature, Etienne had peculiar notions about loyalty to family.

"Her name's Elina. She's my uncle's mistress."

"What? You're crazy. You think I want to cross Bonnange? I'd have to be insane! The man's got powerful friends, and he's lethal with a rapier. No, thank you. Do your own dirty work."

Francois cast a quelling glance at his friend. "Before my uncle, her protector was Alexandre Wallace," he bit out.

"So?"

"So that's the man I shot and we abandoned in Orleans Hall a few weeks ago. Remember? Obviously, she's latched onto Uncle René because she's heard the rumors that he killed Wallace. She wants her revenge, I'm sure. But I saw her not two hours ago firmly ensconced in Uncle René's house. Revenge didn't appear to be uppermost in her mind. Do you know what that means?"

"No," Etienne replied in irritation.

"Either she's convinced Uncle René didn't kill Wallace or she soon will be. And Uncle René will be no match for those pretty eyes when she starts begging him to find out who killed her lover."

Etienne began to look uncomfortable. "Come now, Francois, why would he help her find her old lover's murderer?"

"I don't know. But if you'll recall, the rumor-mongers said she claimed to be Wallace's sister. If Uncle René believes that, then who knows how much he might choose to involve himself?"

Etienne sighed in frustration. "Is she pretty?"

Francois drew the rosebud out of the vase and held it to his nose, sniffing meaningfully. "Beautiful. Sparkling green eyes, gorgeous dark red hair. And she has that hint of innocence that you love so much."

Etienne's eyes gleamed. "What do I do to her?"

"Not what you'd like to, I assure you," Francois said sharply. "I don't want Uncle René breathing down my neck in search of her rapist or murderer. I've better ways of getting around this."

"Such as?" Etienne inquired with skepticism.

"I'd try money, except then she might get suspicious and tell Uncle René what happened. No, we must be more discreet. The girl seems attached to Uncle René and nothing ruins a woman's affections more than the knowledge that her lover is engaged to another or has other mistresses. You know the sort of tale I mean. Make up some story to drive her away of her own will. Use your imagination. Tell her he beats his women or he's been unfaithful to her."

Etienne shrugged. "I suppose telling lies to a beauty and watching her squirm could be somewhat entertaining. But I can think of other ways I'd rather use to scare her off."

"No!" Francois insisted. "We'll do this my way. If that doesn't work, then we'll try something else."

"As you wish. But how am I supposed to tell her all these things with your uncle hovering around her?"

Francois frowned. "I don't know. Watch for when he's away from the house, I suppose, and catch her alone."

"You mean you want me to sit and watch his house for the next few days?"

"I can't do it, so you have to!" Francois hissed. "She knows me. She'll be suspicious if I tell her anything. But she doesn't know you. So whatever you do, don't tell her your name or Uncle René can trace it back to me if she happens to tell him about the conversation."

That statement gave Etienne pause. "I don't know about this, Francois. I'm not certain this is wise."

Francois bounded out of his chair to face Etienne with a menacing glare. "Listen, you fool. If I get arrested for that murder, I'll make certain you and Alcide are arrested with me, I assure you. No one will ever believe the two of you weren't involved. So if you want to make sure your neck stays its present length, you'd best do as I say."

Etienne paled, one hand going involuntarily to his neck. "Of course. I'll do what I can."

"Good!" Francois relaxed, though his face still retained its hard malice. "Then do it now, because the longer we wait, the more time we give that slut to work on my uncle's affections!"

Etienne rose quickly to his feet, scurrying to do as Francois asked.

"And, Etienne?" Francois called, stopping Etienne in his tracks. "Don't tell Alcide. We'll have enough trouble keeping him quiet about the other incident as it is. Your brother has a nasty habit of telling all when pressured to do so."

"I won't tell him, don't worry," Etienne said. Then he left the room.

"I won't be denied my fortune," Francois murmured under his breath as he heard Etienne call for the groom. "I'll kill the bitch before I let her have Papa's money."

And to seal the vow, he crushed the rosebud in his hand and let the bruised petals drift to the floor.

Elina awoke slowly, at first conscious only of a strange soreness between her legs. Then a body shifted beside her, and her eyes flew open in alarm. A soft moan of dismay escaped her lips before she could choke it back.

Slowly, she turned on her side to stare at the man whose bed she shared. He slept on, unheeding, his face almost boyish in repose. Her eyes lingered lovingly over the chiseled lines of his jaw, the hard full lips that only hours before were plundering hers. She lifted her hand to stroke his hair, then stopped as she thought better of waking him.

Once he awakened, she'd have to face him, and she wasn't certain she was ready for that yet. She still couldn't believe she'd given herself to a man who thought her a cheat and a liar, who believed her capable of any deception.

But he knows the truth now! she insisted to herself. *He knows Alex was my brother. Now he has to believe me!*

Yet in her heart she feared he wouldn't. He might believe Alex was her brother, but what was to make him believe she and Alex were both Vanniers? None of the circumstances that had painted her black had changed. She'd helped Alex cheat and had lied about her real name. René would never forget that. And could he forget she had hit him over the head and her own brother had stolen his money?

The troubled expression on her face faded as her gaze came to rest on his hands. Those hands had caressed her with tenderness; they'd been gentle even when René had thought her a soiled dove. The second time they'd made love, before they'd both fallen into an exhausted sleep, he'd been passionate but gentle. She couldn't believe he could be so solicitous of her body and not also be solicitous of her feelings.

He stirred and she caught her breath, still reluctant to have him awaken. But he merely turned over in his sleep, presenting her with his back. She sighed, realizing she must stop staring at him in this lascivious manner. As long as she watched him, she'd be unable to think clearly. And just now it was important that she steel herself for what was to come.

She slipped from the bed, noting with chagrin the blood that smeared the sheets. She knew she ought to mourn her lost virginity. But somehow she couldn't. The intense joy she'd found in being his she wouldn't have wanted to miss. After all the losses she'd suffered, it was an unexpected gift.

Being careful not to wake René, she moved to the mirror, suddenly curious to see if her lovemaking had changed her. Except for the blood that streaked her thighs, the woman who stared back at her was the same one she'd seen that morning.

But I'm different nonetheless, she thought sadly as she took a cloth and dipped it into the tepid water of the washbowl that sat on the bureau. Gently, she washed away the stark reminders of just how different she really was now.

Then she walked quietly about the room, gathering her chemise, her pantaloons, and her skirt. Her chemisette lay hopelessly crumpled beneath him and the edge of her corset was pinned underneath his foot, so she left them there. She put on her undergarments and skirt then donned his shirt, hoping it would cover her sufficiently underneath her riding jacket. Then she pulled her jacket and shoes on and left through the open doorway to the studio.

She heard the servants working in the dining room as she descended the stairs. Carefully, she crept to the front door, praying they wouldn't spot her and rouse René. She had to get out of the house, to find a quiet place where she could make some decisions.

Once outside, she breathed a sigh of relief. Thankfully, the lawn was deserted. In moments she was in one of the many secluded gardens René had taken her through.

The day was warm, much too warm for late spring, she thought. Part of the heat, she realized, came from the storm that was building, filling the air with moisture. Still, if this had been Creve Coeur, there would have been a nip in the air instead of the heavy blanketing wetness of the South.

Suddenly she longed for the farm at Creve Coeur. She wished it were still there and Mama and her brother still lived. She wanted back the innocence of her girlhood. She didn't want to know Papa was a bigamist. She didn't want to know her body was capable of betraying her in the most shameful manner.

At that thought, she touched her lips unconsciously, the sweet memory of his kiss still lingering.

No, there was no going back. That thought filled her with an odd sort of regret. But at the same time, she felt deliciously reborn, as if a part of her that had always been hidden had shown its face.

Papa, she thought with a sudden bitter shock, had intended to deny her this glorious pleasure. He hadn't meant for her to know a man, to have a husband, to have children. She fought back the tears that sprang to her eyes. How could he have wanted such a bleak life for his only daughter?

She wandered around the garden in distraction as another thought pierced her heart. What kind of bleak life did René intend for her? Now that she'd given herself to him, would he assume she'd take the role of his mistress, his chattel, whom he kept until she no longer amused him? Was there now to be no husband and family for her, no one to care for?

She might be able to bear even that if she knew René loved her. But in all their lovemaking, no words of love had crossed his lips. Endearments, yes, but no vows, no promises.

In one corner of the garden stood an absurdly out-of-place sculpture of a nymph. It was covered with algae, obviously a long-forgotten treasure of a Bonnange *madame*. Elina stared at the statue, reluctantly reminded of René's words that she wasn't a nymph but a goddess. That was precisely the problem. To him, she was a decorative statuette to be properly displayed, draped with jewels and expensive dresses. She had no say in her fate as far as he was concerned. And when he tired of her, as someday he must, she would be abandoned or, worse yet, tossed out.

No! she told herself. She wouldn't believe he cared so little for her. Surely now that he knew the truth, he would listen to her and give her some say in her future. If he didn't quite believe her, perhaps she could convince him to leave no stone unturned until he found out the truth.

And then? Would he marry her if he knew she were the legitimate daughter of Philippe Vannier? He might, if only to ensure that the family fortune remained in the family. Was that what she wanted, a marriage in which love played no part?

She let out a cry of frustration. It was all too complicated, too much of a coil for her to untangle in one afternoon. And she'd hopelessly entangled it more by falling into his seductive snare.

A sad smile crossed her face. She couldn't have helped it. If she'd had to do it all over again, she would have and she knew it. Somehow he made her whole. Somehow when he took her lips, he took her bitter memories, too, and blotted them out of her mind for the moment, so all she could feel and see was him.

She turned toward the house, suddenly eager to see him. He'd be waking soon, and she wanted to be there when he did. She'd ask him the questions she needed answers to. Perhaps the replies would be better than she expected. In her heart she hoped so.

Then a movement behind her startled her. She whirled, half expecting to find René. Instead, she found a tall, frightening stranger whose eyes played over her with a mixture of lust and contempt.

"I see Bonnange didn't lie. You are indeed a fine piece of work," the blond stranger remarked in heavily accented English, edging closer as she stood frozen.

She backed away, instinctively afraid of the man's predatory bearing and deceptively fine features.

"I don't know you, sir," she said, her voice firm, although the trembling in her hands betrayed the fact that he frightened her. She glanced around, seeking a way out, but he had her trapped between the statue and a hedge.

"No, of course not. But I know you. I ought to. Bonnange has described you often enough. I came to see if he'd lied about his sweet mistress, Elina. And now I see he hasn't."

Through her fear, she dimly heard his words. "You're lying," she protested. "He hasn't spoken of me. He couldn't have. I'm not his mistress, and I don't believe he would tell anyone I was!" The stranger's words had raised some doubts in her, but she quickly squelched them.

The stranger paused in his advance, studying her as if weighing her reactions. "I see," he said with a shrug. "I should have known René lied. All that talk of how you pleasured him in bed, of what a tempting witch you were." He sighed. "Anyone can see you're not the whore he painted you to be."

"He didn't call me a whore," she murmured in disbelief.

The stranger cracked a grin. "No, no, not in so many words. But I'd find it hard to consider a woman who'd leave one man's bed for his killer's bed as anything but a whore. Tell me, dear girl, what does he do to keep you here, if you're not his mistress? Does he give you money to keep you quiet about that Yankee's murder? Were you there that night perhaps?"

"No, no," she cried, "and he didn't kill my brother!"

The stranger laughed smugly. "If you say so, *ma jolie fille.*"

"I'm not your pretty girl! You can't say such things to me. I don't even know you! Give me your name, sir, so I can tell René which of his friends has been spouting tales about him!"

"I don't think I'd be wise to give my name to a spiteful little whore like you. You know in your heart my 'tales' are true. Do you like your rutting stud's looks so much that you'd ignore the truth?"

She shook her head helplessly, wanting to escape the man's taunts, unwilling to believe his words. Surely René wouldn't have boasted of his conquest even before he accomplished it!

Yet why would this stranger tell her such lies? What purpose could he possibly have for doing so? And how did he know so much about her if René hadn't told him? No one knew her first name or knew she was at Cour de

Cyprès—that is, unless René had indeed told someone other than the magistrate.

One of the servants, she thought in desperation. Of course, one of the servants had told this man of her.

"If you don't leave this instant," she told him, trying to make her voice sound bold, "I shall scream until someone hears me. We're not so far from the house that I wouldn't be heard."

"Relax, *Mademoiselle* Wallace," he said, backing away a few steps. "Don't be so nervous. Bonnange should have said you were a touchy thing. Why, the other night when we played cards at his sister's and the ladies were off chatting, he boasted to me and my friends that you were the boldest filly he'd ever rode."

Her heart sank. René had gone to Julia's just two nights before. She remembered it clearly because Louis had entertained her by teaching her faro. She glanced up into the stranger's face and shuddered. How could she bear it if this man told the truth? How could she endure being simply the object of René's desire and never anything more?

"You ought to be a little nicer to me," the stranger commented as he saw confused emotions play over her face. "After all, you may need me someday."

"Never!"

He shook his head, but his lecherous gaze never stopped roaming over her body. "You will, I assure you. René changes mistresses as often as he changes his shoes. He's easily bored."

She digested this in silence, trying to hide the way his words cut at her heart.

"Lately he's been toying with a little mulatto lightskirt he found in town while he decides whether to keep you. Rest assured, my dear, you'll be needing another protector before long. And when you do, just come to me. I'll be more than willing to take Bonnange's place."

Suddenly he stepped forward and caught her hand, bringing it to his lips. She snatched it away, but not before he'd pressed a disgustingly wet kiss on it.

The touch of his clammy hand on her own had snapped her out of her disquieting thoughts. "I won't listen to your lies another minute," she hissed, determined to escape him. "Now let me pass, or I shall be forced to scream."

With a mocking bow, he stepped aside, waving her past him. But as she passed him warily, he slapped her hard on the rear. "Don't forget, my sweet," he cried after her as she fled the garden. "Just look for me at Orleans Hall any night of the week. I'll be delighted to 'play stud to your mare,' as our good friend René puts it."

She rushed to the house, clutching her hands over her ears in an attempt to drown out his crude words, but his last taunt stuck in her mind. It drummed insidiously through her thoughts, reminding her that the stranger had simply voiced her own fears.

The tears rolled down her face as she stood on the gallery, hesitant about whether to climb the stairs. The stranger had known her name, had known about Alex, had known so many things he shouldn't have known. To her knowledge, René hadn't even told her half brother, Francois, her first name, yet this man had known it. And no matter what she told herself, she knew that none of the servants knew her last name—none except Louis. And somehow she couldn't see Louis revealing anything about his master, even to his fellow servants.

Yet she couldn't imagine René's describing her in such coarse terms, either. She couldn't believe it of him. No, they were lies, she tried to assure herself, nothing but lies!

Still, even if all the stranger's words had been lies, she feared that soon they'd become truth if she allowed René to make her his mistress. Soon he'd tire of her, soon he'd seek others. Then how could she endure it?

She hugged herself, feeling painfully small and alone. Oh, what was she to do? What if their lovemaking had changed nothing for him? What then?

"Damn you, René!" she cried into the beginning winds of a storm. "Damn you for doing this to me!"

Then she turned her face into the rapidly rising wind, praying desperately that it would drive René from her soul.

Chapter Sixteen

Love is like war: you begin when you like and leave off when you can.—Spanish Proverb

Shaking uncontrollably, René sat up in bed. Already the nightmare was fading. He could only dimly remember that it had something to do with Elina and a runaway horse. He did remember that in the dream he couldn't save her. He shuddered and turned to his side, expecting to find her. But the bed was empty.

His body went rigid in alarm as he realized he'd slept the afternoon away, and the sun was sinking. He scanned the darkening room. Her clothes were gone.

"*Sacre bleu!* She's fled," he said aloud, his stomach lurching at the thought. He swung his feet over the side of the bed, and one foot dragged something to the floor with it. Only then did he see her corset, which lay hooked under his foot. A long sigh escaped him.

She wouldn't have gone far, he realized, not without her only corset. He smiled wryly. Sweet modest Elina. It wasn't likely she'd set out on foot for the big city half-dressed. She fancied herself too much of a lady for that.

Then his eyes went to the red stain on the bed. In some respects, she certainly was a lady, he told himself. Gingerly, he touched the spot. There was no question that before he'd taken her, she'd been an innocent.

He felt a surge of gladness at the thought that she hadn't lied about Wallace. The man must have been her brother as she'd claimed, for what man could have been as close to Elina as Wallace had obviously been and not have taken her at the first opportunity? Still, in the gambling world, which Elina and her brother had apparently inhabited, there must have been other men she'd fancied.

He shook his head slowly. None of it made sense, unless her story was the plain unvarnished truth.

He slid from the bed, determined to find her and get some answers to the questions that plagued him. As he dressed, he mocked himself. His little siren had thoroughly bewitched him, or he wouldn't even be considering she might be telling the truth. For God's sake! he thought, suddenly remembering how he'd met her. Her virginity proved nothing, except perhaps that Wallace had been waiting to offer her innocence to the highest bidder and hadn't yet found one high enough.

And yet . . . and yet even that seemed absurd. Why hadn't Wallace just married her off to a rich suitor? Even more curious, why had she hung on tenaciously to her ridiculous story when all she had to do was take René's money and leave town? And why *was* she a virgin?

Burning to know the truth, René strode through the upper floors of the house, his disappointment growing when he couldn't find her. The sound of servants bustling about drifted upstairs.

Of course, he thought, she must have been starved. She'd had no lunch, and it had been some time since breakfast. She had gone in search of food, that was all.

But when a thorough search of the dining room and outdoors kitchen turned up nothing, he questioned the servants. No one had seen her.

Grimly, he walked through the house yet again, his temper rising. Where the devil had she gone? And why had she left his bed?

Gradually, his suspicions of her began to poison his thoughts, try as he might to ignore them. Perhaps she *had* fled. Perhaps she'd purposely allowed him to seduce her, hoping to lull him long enough for her to make her escape.

He swore under his breath. That was absurd. She'd had plenty of chances to escape before, but she hadn't, precisely because she knew she couldn't travel to town without a horse and her terror of horses kept her from trying that avenue.

His eyes darkened until they were almost black as he realized he'd spent half an afternoon teaching her how to ride, how to relax on horseback.

"I'll wring her sweet neck if she even attempted it!" he muttered in anger, starting out the door toward the stables.

But he hadn't even left the gallery when a movement on one end of it caught his eye.

He whirled in that direction just as a familiar slight form turned toward him. Relief flooded through him as he glimpsed Elina's face, but the wretched misery written there stopped him from rushing to her.

Then she noticed him. Her eyes brightened, but only for a moment. The light of the dying sun had long before been obscured by the mounting black thunderclouds, but enough light was left for him to see the way she withdrew from him.

Her reaction infuriated him. He hadn't known what response she'd have to their lovemaking, but this wasn't the one he'd expected.

In his fury, he spoke heedlessly. "Where the hell have you been?" he growled, stepping forward to clasp her arm

265

as she seemed about to back away.

Elina stared up into his angry face, frightened by his quicksilver changes. How could a man be so gentle one moment and so hard the next? Her breath was still coming quickly from her confrontation with the stranger in the garden, and now she had to contend with René's unpredictable temper. Still, her heart gave a strange leap at the realization that he'd been worried about her.

"I—I needed to be alone," she murmured as she searched his face for some sign that the stranger's words had been untrue.

Her solemn perusal of him seemed to unnerve him.

"Don't ever leave me like that again," he told her, his fingers tightening around her arm.

The authority in his voice and the possessive way he held her instantly brought her fears to the fore. Perhaps he did see her as chattel. Did he now assume she was his to do with as he wished? Had she no say in the matter?

She spoke coldly, her chin rising with pride. "I was unaware, *monsieur*, that I couldn't go for a walk without your permission."

"Damn it, Elina, you know that's not what I meant!" His other hand snaked out to encircle her waist. "But I woke to find you gone. What was I to think? I feared you'd left for good."

She thought his tone betrayed some caring, but she was afraid to believe that after what the stranger had told her. "Would it have mattered to you if I had left?" she questioned, only half attempting to hide the pain in her voice.

The frown he wore deepened. "Would it have mattered to me?" he asked incredulously. "You can ask that after this afternoon . . . after—"

"After you bedded me?" she burst out, the stranger's words still ringing in her ears. "Yes, I could ask it. Isn't that all you've desired? To make your conquest and to bed me without wedding me?"

She faced him in defiance, her muscles trembling with the effort of not showing him how much she hurt, how much the stranger's taunts had wounded her.

His hands released her suddenly. She rubbed the sore place on her arm that he'd left behind. He stared at her, shaking his head in disbelief.

"*Mon Dieu*, is that what you think of what we shared this afternoon? Is that all you care about—the proprieties?"

"No . . . yes . . . You don't understand." Her voice dropped to the merest whisper. "Tell me, René," she said achingly, hoping against hope that the strange man had been wrong, that René wasn't what she feared he might be. "What future do we have together? What do you plan for me now?"

He glowered as he stared into her pleading eyes. "It should be clear to you. You've said you have nothing. It need no longer be that way. I'll take care of you, *chérie*. God knows Wallace did a bad enough job of it, even if he was your brother."

She felt she had to defend her poor dead brother. "Alex wasn't accustomed to having me with him in gambling places. What happened on the boat had never happened before. That's why I didn't know what to do."

He raised one eyebrow. "You seemed to learn fairly quickly what was expected of you. You behaved like a professional."

"Appearances are deceiving," she bit out.

"Yes, they are. Which brings me to the one question I want answered. Why are you still an innocent? It seems like a brother of Alex's caliber would quickly have seen the advantages of selling his sister's body to the highest bidder."

His horrible insinuations cut her to the quick. "Alex would never have let a man touch me except in marriage."

"That may be. But he would have made sure he got a pretty price for you from any husband-to-be, I'll wager."

She visibly recoiled from the painful reminder that Alex really had intended to find her a rich suitor if they couldn't find their papa.

"I've already told you why I remained an innocent," she said wearily. "Papa accepted none of my suitors. If you can't believe that, I've nothing more to say to you."

"There's nothing to believe. You've still given me no proof of your identity. But I'm willing to ignore your claims for the present for one reason and one reason only. I want you, Elina. And I'm more than happy to be your protector if that's what it takes to have you."

His cold voice gave the lie to the passion of his words.

"You're not offering to be my protector. You're offering to make me your mistress. Or, to put it more plainly, your fancy woman, your whore, your—"

"No!" The look he gave her would have chilled the sun. "It's not the way you make it sound. I could never consider you a whore."

"To me being a mistress is the same as being a whore," she stated flatly, blinking back the tears that sprang to her eyes.

"That only proves you know nothing about being that kind of woman. Whores have none of the freedom given you. They must service whichever man offers them money, because that's the only way they can eat. What we just did together wouldn't be possible between a whore and a customer. Only a free woman can make love with such genuine passion. Mistresses at least are free to choose their companions."

She paled at his graphic descriptions, but felt she had to make him see how she viewed what he offered. "Freedom? Is that what a mistress has? A mistress must provide affection and attention whenever her man wishes it, regardless of how she feels at the time. Yet you call that freedom! You offer me the privilege of being your lapdog." She said the words scornfully, her hands planted on her hips. "Being a mistress is little better than being a whore, except that mistresses are probably better paid. But a whore isn't required to give her affection to her customer, only her body."

René gazed at her in blank astonishment. His expression made it clear he'd never thought about the things she'd said. He'd merely assumed that any woman of her class would be pleased to be the mistress of a man who treated her well.

"It wouldn't be like that with us, *chérie*," he assured her. "I care for you. Surely you know that. Can you truly say you'd hate being my mistress?" His hands slid once again around her waist, pulling her resistant body up against him. "I want you with me, sweet eyes," he murmured as he nuzzled her ear. "What more can you want than that?"

She fought down the sparks of desire while he tried to stoke her passion with caresses, his lips travelling hungrily over her neck and shoulders.

"No," she whispered, a tear sliding down her cheek. "No," she said more firmly, pressing him away from her.

His eyebrows drew together coldly as he allowed her to push him away. "What do you want then? Money? I'll keep you handsomely. I'll give you whatever your heart desires."

Her heart sank. He really didn't love her or even care for her—not as she wanted him to care for her. It was as the stranger said. He wanted her only as a conquest. "You spoke of freedom. That's what I want—true freedom," she told him in desperation. "Now that you've had what you wanted from me all along, release me. You've proven no one will believe me. You've taken my innocence as you've so longed to do. Now, please, just let me go!"

"You want to leave after what we've just—" he began.

"Yes, yes, of course I do! What more could you possibly want from me?" she cried, but nearly lost her resolve to fight him when she saw the look of utter desolation shadowing his face.

"What more?" The bitter low laugh he gave was like a caustic knife twisting in her breast. Without warning he gripped her arms, jerking her up against him so his face hovered a mere inch from hers. "What more?" he repeated. "Perhaps I want to soothe this fever that has invaded my body, that won't let me breathe without thinking of you. Perhaps I'm hoping I can become so drunk with your presence I'll grow sick of you and be able to cast you aside."

She strained away from him, unbearably hurt by his own voicing of her fears that he would discard her eventually, but his hand slid to clasp her waist so she couldn't move away. Deliberately, she ignored the seductive torment of his presence.

"You want to display me like some trophy," she protested. "I can almost hear you boasting to your friends, 'Look, see whose innocence I took this week. Whose shall it be the next?' "

His eyes widened in shock; then his expression turned grimly suspicious. "Is that what this coyness is about? *Mon Dieu*, but I'm a fool! I should have known you'd use this against me. I should have known you wanted me to seduce you so you could cry rape! Did you think that would help your cause? Did you really think you could have your revenge that way? Or were you hoping I'd get you with child, so you could reach your fortune in one easy moment?"

Her teeth clenched in rage, she swung the flat of her palm at him, taking him unaware. Yet, aside from the loud crack that reverberated off the walls, there was scarcely any evidence she had hit him, for he didn't even flinch.

"You enjoy striking me, don't you, *chérie*?" He spoke the endearment sarcastically. "First, the whiskey bottle and now your wicked hand. Is the whip to follow?"

All the color drained from her face at his painful reminder of what he'd told her about the Creole women with their whips. "I hate you," she whispered in hollow despair. "But there'll be no whip. Next time it will be a knife, for I swear I'll kill you, René, if you don't let me go!"

"I almost believe you would," he muttered as he stared into her green eyes, blazing with the cold fire of emeralds. "So I'll just have to watch my back, won't I, *ma petite menteuse*?"

"How dare you call me a liar!" she cried. "You who promised me—" She broke off as she realized he'd promised her nothing. It was she who'd expected him to be faithful, she who'd thought he truly cared for her. He'd never offered her anything but money and a position as his mistress.

"Yes?" he asked, his face a grim mask. "What have I promised that I haven't given you?"

It was on the tip of her tongue to let him know just what she thought of his boasts to his friends, but she couldn't bear to be humiliated any longer. To have him admit that the stranger's words were true, or worse yet, to make up more lies in an attempt to prove they weren't was more than she could stand.

"You promised to give me what my heart desires," she said lamely, then allowed the words to tumble out as she grew more determined. "All right then, my heart desires to be free, to be away from here. Will you give me that?"

A muscle worked dangerously in his jaw as he stared at her with menacing eyes. "You ask for what I cannot give."

"*Will* not give," she sobbed. Something within her broke then as she realized he had no intention of releasing her, regardless of what she said, regardless of how much she claimed to despise him. And she knew she couldn't bear to stay and let him destroy her.

"What is it you want to hear?" she begged. "Do you want to hear me say I lied, that the whole story was a lie? Is that what you want? Would that set me free?"

His unsmiling face grew even stonier.

"That's what you want, isn't it? You want to prove me a liar, regardless of what the truth is. All right, then. If you'll release me, I'll say what you want to hear to anyone you wish." She swallowed, the words almost too painful to say. Then she continued in a whisper, "I—I'll write a confession and sign it if that's what you want. It doesn't matter anymore. Nothing matters except that I be free! Nothing! I'll say truth is lies and lies are truth if that will set me free."

"Yes, lies come easily to you, don't they?"

"No! But they come easier than being your mistress would!"

Visibly, he recoiled from her words. His fingers dug into her tiny waist as he stared at her with anger. "Yes, I can imagine how wretched that would be. No gamblers to entice, no rich men to fleece. Sheer hell. You'd be forced to endure my lascivious attentions—the attentions you seemed to revel in but a few hours ago. You'd be forced to take the gifts I'd shower you with. How terrible to have your every desire satisfied!"

"Desires, yes. But what about needs? You don't offer what I need," she cried, her hands pressing hard against his chest in desperation. His nearness was suffocating. It reminded her of how easily she'd given herself to him that afternoon. She dropped her eyes from the all too tempting beauty of his face.

One of his hands left her waist to grip her chin and force her head up. Her eyes wouldn't meet his, but were drawn to his lips, which seemed so terribly close to hers.

"What exactly do you need?" he asked her.

She struggled to keep her breathing even as she felt the seductive net closing around her again. "I need nothing from you! I want nothing from you!"

"So this afternoon was a farce? When you said you wanted me, you lied?"

She couldn't speak the lie, so she nodded instead.

"Look at me, Elina!" he demanded, his fingers tightening on her chin. "Look at me and say you don't want me, that you hate me. Say the words, Elina!"

Slowly, she brought her gaze up to meet the bright feverish black eyes that commanded the truth. For long moments, she stared, trying to will the words to leave her mouth, but unable even to whisper them.

His slow smile chilled her. "You've cried 'wolf' once too often, sweet eyes. This time I'm going to prove to you that you want me, that your desires are as intense as mine."

"No-o-o—" she murmured just once before his lips swooped down on hers and his hands crushed her up against the thundering strength of his body. His mouth fed on hers with savage determination, his tongue demanding entrance. And though her mind fought the insidious cravings he raised in her, her body was not so brave. She weakened, and with a groan, he buried his tongue deep inside her, searching her mouth with thorough possessiveness.

She didn't want the pleasure that stole through her, she didn't want its tenuous fingers clutching at her heart, but nonetheless it was there. The sweet, musky taste of him, the feel of his day's growth of beard rasping against her skin combined to overwhelm her senses.

Then he was lifting her in his arms and striding into the house. Broken free from his lips, she came alive, determined to fight. She writhed against him, but he refused to release her. She struck out with her feet but hit only air. Her hands beat on his chest, but he was either impervious to pain or took it well, for the rigid set of his face betrayed nothing.

"*Monsieur*, is something the matter?" Louis's voice inquired with concern as they were about to reach the stairs leading up.

René whirled to face his servant and Elina chose that moment to struggle from his arms. She fled down the hall, not daring to go anywhere near the upstairs bedrooms.

"Nothing I can't handle, Louis," she heard René growl as he followed close behind her.

In desperation, she darted into his study, intending to escape through the doors into the garden. She stopped short in the middle of the room as she saw that the doors to the gallery were closed and locked. She'd forgotten that the

273

servants locked them all at night.

Swearing softly, she pivoted toward the door that led to the hall, but she wasn't fast enough, for René was already in the room.

He slammed the door shut behind him. His fierce expression filled her with more fear than any threats might have done. She backed away from him, her eyes searching for some means of escape.

"Don't overexert yourself, *ma petite*," he said cuttingly. "You'll need your strength for what's to come."

She continued retreating until her back met the cold hard glass of the windows. "You'll have to force me this time," she asserted as he began to close the distance between them.

He paused in his advance to give her a cruelly mocking grin. "I've never needed force before," he assured her. "And I won't need it now."

His words stung her, for they reminded her that he'd had little trouble seducing her earlier. What's more, there'd been others before her, and from those women he'd learned skills of seduction she couldn't begin to withstand.

They wouldn't bring him success this time, she told herself as she slid along the glass doors, circling the room while he took his time approaching her.

Suddenly she pushed herself away from the doors in a foolhardy dash toward the hall door, but he easily caught her, his hands closing like vises on her shoulders.

"Please, René, don't!" she cried as she fought to escape, but his arm held her so close that her arms were pinned between their bodies.

"After tonight, you shan't deny ever again that you want me, sweet eyes," he promised before his lips took hers.

Then his mouth was plundering every part of her—the slight swell of her cheek, the delicate skin of her eyelids, then the place at her temples where her pulse beat. This time, his lips were far from gentle. They pressed against her silken skin as if to brand her everywhere they fell, to make certain she knew to whom she belonged.

She twisted her head, trying to escape his grip. She thought she'd found success but his hand imprisoned one wrist while his other hand clasped her other wrist. He forced her arms behind her, pulling her up against his body.

"Ah, *chérie*, this is where you belong," he murmured, his body molding against hers until she could feel every inch of him, even the growing hard bulge in his trousers that signaled his arousal.

"No," she denied, but even as she said it, her blood was racing through her, pounding so loudly in her temples that she felt certain he could hear it.

She tried to retreat from the intimate touch of his body, but the backs of her knees met the edge of the settee forcefully, making her lose her balance and fall across the cushioned bench.

René followed her until she lay beneath him, her arms pinioned under her. He stared down into her green eyes wild with a mixture of desire and fright. Her wind-tangled hair framed her face, the rich auburn curls setting off her creamy skin.

The sudden warm glint that lit his eyes made her muscles tighten in fearful anticipation. She swallowed convulsively and his lips swooped down to kiss her throat, as if to catch the movement.

Then with a groan, he was kissing her throat lower and lower as his hands swiftly worked loose the buttons on her jacket, exposing the white linen of the shirt she'd borrowed from him.

She struggled to pull her arms out from under her, but the weight of his body on hers wouldn't let her. His hands moved to the top button of the shirt, and then he stopped as he realized the shirt was his.

"You hate me so much, you wear my clothes?" he asked insolently.

"I wish now I hadn't!" she spat, then immediately wanted to take back the words as she realized the double meaning behind them.

He chuckled, having not missed her slip. "Indeed. That's one wish I'm more than willing to grant." Then his hands gripped both ends of the collar and pulled them apart, splitting the shirt open as buttons popped everywhere.

"You bastard," she whispered as his gaze raked her upper body, now clad only in her thin chemise. Unwillingly, she felt her nipples tighten into rosy nubs under his gaze. She blushed, hoping her chemise kept him from noticing her response, but her hopes were fruitless, for his mouth closed eagerly over one breast, sucking it so hungrily through the cloth that she felt desire once more swirl over and through her.

"I won't allow this," she murmured, more to herself than to him.

"You already have," he whispered in response before his hand jerked down the neck of her chemise, baring the other breast. His mouth covered her protesting lips as his fingers worked their conjury on her breasts, teasing them unmercifully until a moan erupted low in her throat.

Then he shifted above her, raising himself on his knees as he straddled her. In one quick motion, he lifted her skirt and chemise, so her legs in their pantaloons were exposed.

She knew instantly what he intended as his hand slid into the slit of her pantaloons. "If you touch me there, I'll die," she sobbed, even as she felt his fingers dance lightly over the soft mound.

"The only death you'll find tonight is *la petite mort, bien-aimée*," he muttered thickly, making her wonder what "the little death" was.

Then one finger buried itself in her velvety wet warmth and began to stroke her until she understood. She feared she would indeed die but not of shame. Every muscle in her body tautened as he brought her hunger to a fever pitch, never quite feeding it enough. Her blood thundered in her ears as she arched to meet the hand that tormented her, trying to find the fulfillment she craved.

Suddenly his body no longer hovered over hers, for he'd moved lower. She half rose, freeing her arms. Then she saw his head settle between her legs and her hands went to his hair.

"No, you mustn't!" she cried, attempting to pull his head away from her, but he ignored her, his mouth closing over the delicate skin.

Warm, it was so warm, she thought, her fingers slowly loosening their grip on his hair. Then his tongue began torturing her as it had her mouth and breasts, coaxing from her a gasp of pure delight as he nipped and kissed the tender folds until every inch of her skin tingled with excitement. Her hands reached for his head, pressing him shamelessly closer as his mouth stole her very pride with each caress.

When he'd brought her to the brink of madness with his exquisite manipulations, he raised his head and slid up over her. He eased himself down on top of her, his hips grinding between her legs so that despite the fact that he was still fully clothed, she could feel the full extent of his desire.

"Now tell me, Elina," he commanded, his eyes in the lamplight mesmerizing her. "What do you need now? Is it your freedom you require?"

"Please . . ." she murmured, the place between her legs burning with the ache to know more.

"Shall I set you free this very minute?" he demanded, rubbing his loins suggestively against her.

"No . . . I want . . . I want . . ."

"Yes? What is it you want? Tell me, *chérie*, tell me what you need if not your freedom," he hissed as she turned her head away from him in shame.

"I need you!" she cried out, half sobbing, her longing to feel him inside her so great that her pride seemed at that moment a useless appendage worth abandoning.

277

"And God help me, but I need you," he muttered before his lips captured hers in a soul-burning kiss. In moments his trousers were unbuttoned and he was sliding inside her honeyed warmth.

She sighed inaudibly as he began to move, his strokes bringing her the relief his mouth and hand had denied her. Blindly, she tore at his shirt, wanting to feel his chest against her skin. He helped her frantically, crushing her to him when the hated shirt was finally open.

"*M'amoureuse*," he whispered against her ear, then swirled his tongue inside the sensitive shell.

In spite of her dazed state of being, Elina heard the words and nearly sobbed aloud. He called her his "lover," not his "love."

"You're a fiend—" she told him, but he cut off the words with his mouth as his body gyrated against hers, his thrusts escalating and with them, her response.

As her need increased, she strove to pull him closer, more fully into her. Her legs wrapped around his waist and he groaned in pleasure. Then her hands cupped his buttocks, feeling the muscles go taut as he neared his release. Her own body quivered as shock after shock of bliss rocked her, bringing her to a crescendo of pleasure. As the pulsing of her lower body matched the rapid pulsing of her heart, she pressed him against her, instinctively wishing her heart could enfold him as tightly, so he could never escape.

And in that moment, she knew she loved him.

Then he gave one last thrust and found his own pleasure. For a moment, they lay silent, their bodies entwined. His head lay in the curve of her neck as he gasped, until at last his breathing slowed.

Even as she lay beneath his warm body, her own body curving into his, her mind began to rouse from its drowsy contentment to face her bitter new realization.

She loved him. She must have for quite some time. That's why she'd felt no shame at giving herself to him and didn't regret even this last joining.

In despair she realized that René had proved to her more than what he'd set out to prove. Not only did she need his body, she also needed his love. He'd demonstrated forcefully that she could no longer survive in his presence, not when her body betrayed her at every turn. She'd meant not to give in to him. She'd meant to be aloof. But every time she'd reached to push him away, she'd found herself clutching him close instead.

Now even more than ever, she couldn't stay, she told herself, her heart lurching at the thought of leaving him. She couldn't bear to watch him make a mockery of her love by treating her daily as nothing more than the soiled dove he'd termed her at first. Tears began to course down her face. It would happen again if she stayed. He would take her soul and trample it over and over until she had no more soul left.

He rose up on one elbow, startling her from her bitter thoughts. At the sight of her tears, he frowned and for a moment, she thought she glimpsed a stark pain in his eyes.

"You didn't really want me to set you free, did you? You must realize that now," he told her as he lowered his head to kiss away a tear that trembled on her cheek.

"No," she murmured. It was true. She didn't wish it. Nonetheless, she had to escape.

He sat up on the settee and drew her up to sit beside him. His face seemed clouded as he stared at her tearstained face. "*Chérie*, I'm sorry, but I had to make you see—"

She slid away from him, refusing the arms that tried to draw her close. She stood, drawing his shirt closed over her disheveled clothing and jerking her skirt down. Like a mechanical toy, she began to walk toward the door of the study.

"Where are you going?" he demanded from the settee.

She couldn't bear to face him. "I'm going to my bedroom. I—I would like to be alone now," she stated, her tone

279

emotionless, although her conflicting feelings were tearing her apart.

"Elina—" he began as he rose to his feet.

"Please?" she asked in a pitifully small voice. He stepped forward to clasp her arm. She half-turned toward him, her eyes lifted to his in a guileless appeal. "Please?" she repeated.

His expression became grim as he gazed at her damp face and the tears that threatened to brim forth from her wide, pleading eyes at any moment.

"I had hoped . . . Oh, hell! I had hoped you would share my bed now." His hand slid down to clasp hers. "I want to wake up to find your sweet body next to me, to have that brilliant smile shine for me in the morning . . ."

"Please stop . . ." she choked out, his tenderness undoing her more than his harsh words ever could. She tried to remind herself that his tenderness was a sham, but her heart didn't want to believe it. "I need time to . . . to adjust to the change," she managed to say, desperate for something that would appease him, so she could slip away to nurse her wounds.

He looked as if he were about to protest. Then he seemed to think better of it, and his hand dropped hers.

"Thank you," she said, turning to go.

"But don't take too much time, sweet eyes," he said, his tone soft as butterfly wings.

"No, not much time," she whispered, not daring to look at him again for fear he'd see she was lying, that she had no intention of moving into his room, no intention even of staying with him at all.

And without even a last look at his dear face, she took what was left of her wounded pride and left the room.

Chapter Seventeen

The rabbit says: Drink everything, eat everything, but don't tell everything.—Creole Proverb

Elina halted opposite René's window, cursing the fact that he was still awake. She could see his silhouette from where she stood on the gallery.

He'd been pacing the floor ever since he'd come upstairs. While she had moved around her room gathering her few belongings, she'd heard his steps move ceaselessly from one end of the room to the other and then back again.

Once in a while he'd paused, and she'd known he was standing in front of the portrait of Papa and his family. She had forced herself not to imagine him in there alone, forced herself to ignore the insistent voice within her that urged her to throw away her pride and to join him.

But she'd known she couldn't. And now, as she stood in the darkness watching his silhouette move back and forth behind the curtains, she wished once more she could find some reason to stay. Her heart thudded loudly in her ears as silent tears rolled down her cheeks.

She was doing the right thing, she reminded herself, rubbing the tears away with one fist as she recalled the stranger's words and René's own harsh ones. She'd never convince René that she was a Vannier, and at the moment, she no longer cared if she did. There was more at stake now than her pride and her inheritance. Staying would mean letting him break her heart, and that part of her was already too badly bruised for her mental well-being. Leaving him was her only recourse.

She forced herself to slide past his room, her back against the railing as her bare feet moved. The long skirts of her riding habit tripped her up for a moment and she stumbled, but she caught herself before she hit the floor.

As if René sensed her presence, he stopped his ceaseless pacing and seemed to turn toward the windows. She held her breath, her hands trembling so badly she nearly dropped her small bag of clothes and her boots. But then he threw himself down on his bed and she relaxed slightly. Inch by inch she felt her way down the railing until she was clear of his room. Then outside the next room, the room where she'd painted, she halted.

The curtains in that room weren't drawn, so she could see it clearly. The open door that separated René's room from the studio allowed the lamp from his room to shine in, bathing part of the studio in a soft glow. From where she stood outside the window, she could just see her unfinished portrait of him. For a moment, she gazed at it, fervently wishing she could slip inside and take it with her, but she knew that was impossible.

Besides, she thought stubbornly, after the way he'd deceived her, the way he'd used her, she shouldn't take any remembrance of him. It would only cause her more pain. Yet it wasn't pain she remembered now, but the whispery touch of his lips on her mouth, and the savage glory of his body thrusting into hers.

Stop it! she told herself firmly. She mustn't let him dominate her thoughts this way. For her own survival, she had to escape his accusations and make a new life for herself.

The overcast sky made the night darker than usual, except for the occasional shard of lightning that briefly lit up the night. She knew she was insane to leave when a storm was brewing, but the sky had been dark for hours and nothing had happened. She could only hope the storm would hold off until she could reach New Orleans.

More important, she had to pray René wouldn't look for her until morning. She needed plenty of time to find her way into the city. Although she knew she had little chance of escaping him, she had to try. Otherwise, she'd never be able to face herself.

She tossed her bag and boots to the ground. Then, as quietly as she could, she threw her leg over the railing and reached for the sturdy oak limb that leaned up against the gallery. It had been a long time since she'd shinnied down a tree. Even as a child she'd only done it once or twice when Alex had dared her to.

But tonight she had little choice. René had locked her door to the hall as usual, although not the door that led into his room. The door to the gallery was always kept locked, so that was of no use to her. But the windows were left open at night to offer some respite from the heat. She had escaped through the window, hoping she might be able to reach the oak tree that grew beside the house.

Now perched precariously on the wide oak limb, she wondered if she'd lost her mind. Even if she reached the ground in one piece, she'd have to walk miles into town in the dark. She wasn't even certain she could find the road.

And once in town, what would she do? She had no money, no place to go.

She refused to think about that. Somehow she'd find someone who would help her, who would give her a place to stay in exchange for her willingness to work. Surely someone could use an educated, hard-working woman.

Carefully, she crept along the limb to the trunk of the tree, telling herself she had no choice. No matter what the consequences of her rash escape, she couldn't stay and let René trample her heart.

What she was about to do was probably foolish, she knew. Most people undoubtedly had all of their work done by slaves. Few would wish to hire servants. But perhaps she could find some position to sustain her until she could either prove her claims or leave New Orleans.

With that hope urging her on, she slid down the tree trunk to the ground. Her skirts caught and tore on the branches, but she didn't care. She'd made certain to carry an extra change of clothes in her bag. Besides, she could always mend the riding skirt.

After putting on her boots, she brushed the twigs and leaves off her clothing and picked up her bag, then looked up one more time at the house where she'd lost her innocence. Then she turned away resolutely and strode down the alley of cypress trees in the direction of the road to town.

As she walked down what she thought was the right road, her mind played over and over the events of the day. How gentle René had been that first time he'd made love to her, she thought, a lump forming in her throat. She could scarcely believe that the René she knew and the René the stranger spoke of were the same person. She had to admit, however, that the last time they'd made love—when he'd forced her to admit her desires—he'd proven he was heartless.

Lightning split the air somewhere close by, warning her that she must hurry. But even as she quickened her steps, the storm broke. Sheets of rain beat both her and the road, turning the dirt thoroughfare into a mire. She wished she'd brought something, anything, she could use to shield her body from the rain. Her Spencer was little help and she hadn't thought to bring a hat. Grimly, she pressed on, remembering all too clearly her mama's admonitions against walking in the rain. "You'll catch a chill," Mama had always said.

But as she struggled along in the downpour, she realized she had something else far more important to fear than a chill. Through the blur of the rain, she realized she could no longer tell where the road stopped and the ditch began. Nor did she know if she were walking in the right direction. Had she taken a turn down one of the many driveways to neighboring plantations?

She was soaked to the skin and in spite of the warm night, her skin was beginning to feel cold. Still, she pressed on, hoping she wasn't unknowingly walking into the swamps.

Her skirts became heavier as they soaked up the mud, making each step more and more agonizing. Her steps slowed.

Then what she thought was the road narrowed, and she began to panic. Was she already lost? How was she to find her way into the city in such driving rain? What was she to do now? She couldn't stop and wait for the rain to end. It could last all night. She had to put as much distance as possible between herself and René's plantation before morning. Otherwise, he'd find her easily.

It was also dangerous to stay out in the wet weather. The storm was worsening, the lightning flashed around her, and she realized she'd best find some shelter immediately.

That's when she noticed the dim light. She couldn't tell how far away it was, but she could see it through some trees.

Shelter! she thought. The dull aching despair in her heart lifted a fraction at the sight.

Eagerly, she stumbled toward the light, despite her sodden skirts and boots. As she neared the warm glow, she realized with some misgivings that it belonged to a massive plantation house much like René's, although his was more imposing.

Still, she worked her way toward it gratefully. Perhaps the owner wouldn't mind sheltering her for a short while, she thought with a sudden surge of optimism as she approached the house. Perhaps she could even ride into town the next day with anyone who might be going there. At least she'd be safe from René for a while. He wouldn't think to look for her here.

The thought of René's waking and finding her gone gave her a momentary stab of guilt. Then she stiffened her shoulders with determination. She was doing the right thing. Surely the fact that the house had appeared to her at such an opportune moment proved that.

Yes, it was a good sign, she told herself, thrusting all thoughts of René out of her mind as she struggled the last few steps toward the light. At last the fates were on her side.

Julia couldn't sleep. She knew why. Her conscience was plaguing her again. She'd thought that time would soothe the ache Philippe's betrayal had brought, but time had only worsened it.

She walked to the window, drawn by the storm. She stood there for a long time, lost in thought. Then her eyes were caught by the sight of a lone figure emerging from a stand of trees. The rain had let up somewhat, allowing Julia to make out the shape of a girl. The poor thing was stumbling blindly forward and, from what Julia could see, was completely drenched.

Instinctively, Julia's heart went out to the bedraggled girl.

"Probably some beggar," she said aloud, but still the girl drew her interest.

When the girl began to approach the side of the house, quite clearly headed for the lights still on in the outdoor kitchen, Julia decided to find out more. Perhaps her action was prompted by her conscience, heavily laden because of her broken promise to Philippe. Perhaps it was simply her desire to escape her room and the accusations that always seemed to await her there. But whatever the cause, before she could stop to think about it, she had dressed and was walking downstairs.

She felt quite silly as she opened the door that led to the outdoor kitchen. From where she stood, she could just see the figure of Cecile, the cook, through the windows. The girl sat huddled at the table as Cecile offered her something to drink. The cook clearly had matters under control. Why should Julia bother to find out about some beggar girl?

She didn't know. But in moments she'd straightened her shoulders and under the covered walkway crossed the short distance to the kitchen.

Both Cecile and the girl glanced up as Julia entered. Cecile's face showed mild surprise, but the girl's face was expressionless, as if she were uncertain what welcome she might find.

"The poor girl, she got caught in the storm, *madame*," Cecile said. "But I told her we wouldn't put her out, not on a night like this."

"Certainly not," Julia said, flashing the girl a reassuring smile.

The girl smiled back tentatively, and when she did, her whole face seemed to light up. Julia quickly took in the fact that her clothing, though soaked and muddy, was of good quality. She didn't look like a beggar, not at all.

"Why don't you get the girl some food?" Julia told Cecile, who quickly began to do her mistress's bidding.

"I—I'm sorry to be so much trouble," the girl said through chattering teeth. "I'll leave if you wish. It's just that I had hoped to reach my destination before the storm broke. Then it began pouring and I—I saw your light—"

"No trouble," Julia said gently. "You mustn't worry about it at all. And we won't even think of letting you go back out in that dreadful rain."

"That's right," Cecile put in. "You listen to *Madame* Vannier and rest yourself. Let old Cecile take care of you."

The girl's face suddenly went very pale. "Vannier?"

Something in the way the girl spoke the word sent a chill through Julia.

"Yes. And what's your name?"

The question seemed to make the girl even more distraught than she already was. Strange emotions played over her face, bitterness and pain among them. She seemed to be struggling within herself, trying to make some decision.

At last her face cleared. "My name's Elina. Elina W–Wallace," she stammered.

Elina, Julia thought, her heart suddenly feeling cold and dead. She'd heard *that* name before. It was engraved on her conscience. Still, it had to be just a coincidence. Why would Kathleen's daughter be in New Orleans? She questioned the girl, even while a vague uneasiness sat at the back of her mind. "Tell me, Elina. Where were you going on a wretched night like this?"

The girl hesitated before replying. "New Orleans," she said at last.

"*Mon Dieu!*" the cook burst out. "It's good you came here instead."

The girl looked from one face to the other in confusion. "Wh–why?"

Julia's expression turned grim. "Because at the moment the city is a dangerous place to be. I left my townhouse because the yellow fever has come, and only those who can't leave New Orleans have stayed to greet it. You wouldn't want to go there now, child. Already the death toll is at 400, and many more are sure to die before summer ends."

The girl's face stiffened, and her eyes fell to her hands. "I had hoped to find work there," she said in a voice that threatened to break any moment. She looked up at Julia, who regarded her with sympathy. "I'm sorry. I didn't mean to burden you with my troubles. Thank you for giving me shelter. As soon as the rain stops, I'll—I'll be on my way."

"And where would you go?" Julia asked as Cecile shook her head and clucked her tongue at the girl's foolishness. "Where are you from? Could you return to your home?"

The girl's eyes darkened. "I'm from Missouri, but—but there's nothing for me there. I'll find somewhere to go, however. Don't worry about me."

Missouri? Julia thought. Julia's hand tightened on the edge of the table. The girl was from Missouri, just like the temptress and her daughter. And Wallace had been Kathleen's maiden name, Julia remembered now. She had noticed the name in Philippe's will in particular, because it was American, not Creole.

Her heart twisted inside her as the truth became obvious. The coincidence was too great. This Elina and the temptress's Elina had to be one and the same.

Julia gazed at the girl once more. Elina's features and coloring were certainly not those of her father. *She must resemble her mother*, Julia thought. Beneath the table, she clenched her fists in both anger and pain. The girl was beautiful. No doubt her mother was, too.

But what on earth was the girl doing in New Orleans? Had her mother brought the entire family to seek out their father? And if so, why was Elina alone?

"Are you running away from your family?" Julia asked with a sudden harshness in her voice.

"No!" Elina answered, looking as if the question wounded her. "No, of course not. My family is dead." She paused, seeming to deliberate over what to say. "Mama died a few months ago and—and Papa, too."

Julia felt as if she'd been struck. Dead? Her rival was dead? She felt relieved even as she began to want to know more. She wanted to ask the girl so very much.

How had she known her father was dead? And was it possible that she knew . . . Julia paled as she realized the girl must know everything about Julia, about the bigamy, for Elina had reacted strongly when Cecile had spoken the Vannier name. What's more, Elina hadn't given her name as Vannier, although Julia knew that Philippe had given his other children his name.

Julia sat very still, uncertain of what to do. Was the girl here because she knew everything about her father's other family? If so, why hadn't she spoken a word about it?

A sobering thought occurred to Julia. Perhaps the girl thought that Julia didn't know of Kathleen's existence. Yes, that was the only explanation.

Julia's insides twisted as she realized Elina was trying to protect her feelings, trying to shield her from the knowledge that her husband had been a bigamist.

Her guilt overwhelmed her. She had ignored the promise she'd made her husband, but this slip of a girl was showing her kindness. And because of Julia's refusal to tell the truth, Elina had suffered. Had the temptress died of a broken heart? Was Julia somehow responsible for that, too?

Then something else occurred to Julia. There'd been a son. What of him?

"Don't you have any other family—brothers or sisters whom you might go to?" she asked with deceptive innocence.

Elina's luminous green eyes brimmed with tears. "My brother was killed shortly after he and I arrived in New Orleans," she said in a voice that was barely a whisper.

Julia struggled not to show her emotions at hearing that Philippe's other son was dead. How had that come about? she wondered. Undoubtedly, he and Elina had come to New Orleans looking for their father, Julia thought, striving to keep her face expressionless. Instead, they'd discovered that Philippe had betrayed them, had lied to them. And somehow the boy had been killed, leaving Elina alone to deal with all that pain.

Then Julia's own pain came back to her. Philippe had lied to her, too. He'd betrayed her, too. Did that mean she must suffer the scandal that would ensue if the girl's story became known? Was her life to be further destroyed because of his foolish act?

And what would Francois do and say? she thought with sudden dread. He'd be destroyed by the knowledge that his father had sired other children with whom he'd have to share his inheritance.

Then Julia thought of René, newly arrived from England and forced to face the threat of scandal. Her heart told her that none of that would matter to her brother, but the part of her that wanted things to remain the same said it would change his standing in New Orleans society forever. If this girl was given her rightful place. . . .

No, Julia thought, *I can't allow it.* She choked back the guilty confession she wanted to make to the girl. She couldn't risk the Bonnange and Vannier family names by revealing the truth. She just couldn't!

A small voice within her told her this was her way of punishing Philippe for his perfidy. But she ignored the voice with determination.

For whatever reason, she told herself, the girl was keeping quiet. Perhaps she wanted it that way, Julia reasoned. Well, Julia would keep quiet, too. She'd do what she could to help the girl, to enable her to leave New Orleans. She'd make certain the girl's needs were met, though she'd have to do it in such a way that Elina didn't suspect Julia knew the truth.

But Julia just couldn't bear to see the temptress's daughter destroy everything the Bonnanges and the Vanniers had striven so many generations to attain. She wouldn't allow it!

"Listen, child," she told Elina, her mind made up. "You can't leave with no position to go to. You'll need funds to leave. You strike me as a good girl. Perhaps I could give you some money to—to help you find a way to another city. You could go to Natchez maybe and find a position there."

The girl lifted her head regally and fixed her with a cold, proud stare.

"Thank you, *madame*, but I can't take your money. But don't trouble yourself about it. If you don't mind, I'll just rest here until the storm has passed and then continue on the road. I'm sure even with the yellow fever in New Orleans, I could find work somewhere."

Deborah Martin

Julia became alarmed. Go to New Orleans? The girl couldn't do that. She'd die for certain! Julia might have prayed at times that her rival's family would just disappear, but she never would have wished upon them the kind of painful death yellow fever brought.

"Don't be silly!" she said in a voice unduly harsh. "You can't go to New Orleans!"

"Then I'll find somewhere nearby—" the girl began.

Julia blurted out the first thing that came to her. "No, you won't. If you must find a position as a servant, you can work here for me."

Elina rose from the table, genuine alarm on her face. "No, I don't think that would be wise. I couldn't ask you to provide a position for me."

Once Julia had embarked on her course, she couldn't turn back. She hadn't meant to make such an offer, but the girl's proud refusal to take money had prompted her to do so. She couldn't chance the girl's going to New Orleans. She'd never live with that guilt. Even sending the girl off to another town without funds seemed too cruel for words. At least with the girl under her roof, Julia could keep an eye on her and perhaps convince her to take money eventually. Besides, it would give her a chance to learn more about the temptress.

"I want you to stay," she told Elina. "You seem more than willing to work for your keep. You can cook, can't you?"

"A little, *madame*," Elina said with uncertainty in her voice.

"What you don't know, Cecile can teach you. You're just what she's been needing. Now that Cecile is getting older, she requires some help in the kitchen. I've been intending for quite some time to find her a helper . . ." She flashed the cook a warning glance when the woman started to open her mouth. "And I'm sure you'll be just perfect. So don't you think it would be best if you stayed?"

Elina bit her lip and then slowly nodded her head.

"Good. Then it's settled. We can discuss the details in the morning."

"Yes, *madame*."

The quiet sadness in that soft voice was nearly Julia's undoing. For a moment, she almost regretted her decision. Then she made herself ignore the girl's bedraggled clothing and her hair, still damp from the rain.

"We'll speak again tomorrow," she said curtly.

Then she swept out of the kitchen, forcing herself not to take one last look at Philippe's daughter—her enemy's child.

Elina stared blindly at the ceiling as she lay in the small room Cecile had brought her to. It was little bigger than a closet, connected to Cecile's larger room in the slaves' quarters. But the room was clean and neat, with a certain hominess to it that Elina found disarming.

If only it didn't belong to Julia Vannier, Elina thought bitterly.

How could it have happened? Were the fates playing a cruel joke on her? The house was supposed to be her salvation not her prison. Yet she felt imprisoned. Despite her brave words to *Madame* Vannier about going on to New Orleans, she knew she wasn't about to risk dying of yellow fever. But she'd been so afraid to stay. What if René found her there? After all, *Madame* Vannier was his sister. He visited her often.

I'm a servant now, and I'll be working in the kitchen out of sight, she told herself. *There's no reason for him to cross my path when he comes.*

Still, she felt terribly uneasy. But what choices had she? How many other plantation houses would hire a servant of whom they knew nothing? Where could she go with no money? Here she'd at least be able to save money for passage to some other city.

As far as proving her claims was concerned, she no longer knew how important that was to her. She didn't have the will anymore to take on René and his entire family. And after meeting his sister and witnessing her kindness, Elina didn't feel she could destroy the woman's life in such a manner.

It was time Elina put the past behind her. She must accept that Papa hadn't really cared for his family, for if he had, he would surely have provided for them. No, she must reconcile herself to his betrayal and make her own way in the world.

Tears slipped from her eyes. She couldn't! She couldn't reconcile herself to what he'd done! In truth, that was why she'd stayed, why she'd accepted *Madame* Vannier's generous offer despite all her misgivings. Somehow, she knew within herself she needed to discover why Papa had done such a thing. What had made him marry Julia Bonnange when he'd already had a wife and family? Why had he chosen to torment two women so needlessly?

Elina had to know. Yes, she thought, she *had* come upon the house at an opportune time, for it would now provide her with the chance to put her past to rest. She would stay and see what she could learn about Papa and what he'd felt for his other family.

And perhaps in the process she would also have a chance to sort out her own feelings for René. With vivid clarity, she saw his face as he had looked before she left, his eyes dark and inviting, even while he struggled to grant her request that she be left alone for the night.

No! she thought in despair. *I won't have you haunting me, too.* But as she fell into a troubled sleep, the image of his face lingered. His voice whispered deep into her consciousness, "Now you're mine, *ma petite chérie.* Never forget it."

Chapter Eighteen

Where there's a good bed, there's good housekeeping.
—Creole Proverb

"She's gone," Etienne announced to Francois with a cocky grin. "The girl has fled. Evidently, she left the same day I encountered her."

"You're absolutely certain?"

"Absolutely. My house slave, Jean, has a sister who works at Cour de Cyprès. She told him that René has been half-mad since his Elina left two days ago. He and his men have searched for her, but she has apparently disappeared."

Francois settled back in his chair, relaxing for the first time since he'd seen his half sister at his uncle's house.

"Indeed. Well, that's certainly good news. Now we need not worry about his hunting down Wallace's killer, need we? Well done, Etienne. I shan't forget this."

Etienne raised one eyebrow. "You might repay me some of the money you owe me."

Francois scowled. "In good time, my friend. My investments are bound to pay off soon. Then you'll get your money."

Etienne gave a shrug that brought a smile to Francois's face. Francois knew his friend wouldn't press him. Etienne realized exactly who held the upper hand in their relationship.

"I wonder where she's gone," Francois said idly. He hoped she'd fled to her home in Missouri.

"If she goes to New Orleans, it will be bad for her," Etienne replied. "With the yellow fever now rampant, she'd not survive long."

Yellow fever. Francois had forgotten about the disease raging through New Orleans. He felt the only moment of guilt he'd ever felt in his life. Then his eyes narrowed. Why did he care what happened to her? As long as the bitch was out of his life, it mattered not if she died. Of course, if Uncle René were to find her body or learn Francois's part in her mad flight. . . .

That didn't bear thinking of, he told himself, trying to ignore the stab of fear that pierced him at the thought of what his uncle's response would be if he discovered the truth. If that ever happened, Francois would be as good as dead, plain and simple. Uncle René wasn't likely to allow such an action to go unpunished.

But Uncle René would never find out. Why should he? Francois thought, his face brightening. Etienne was a master of deception, and Francois had covered his tracks well. *I need worry no longer,* he reassured himself.

"We have searched everywhere, *monsieur*. You and I have been over the roads three times at least, and the men have combed the fields for miles around. We have found nothing," Louis told his master in a voice of trepidation.

René stood motionless, his eyes riveted on the half-finished portrait of himself as if he hadn't heard a word. The dark half-moons under his eyes showed his lack of sleep. Wearily, he ran his fingers through his hair.

Louis stepped closer and raised his voice. "You are exhausted. We all are. You *must* call off the search, *monsieur*."

"No!" René's body was suddenly alert, tensed with anger as he rounded on his servant. "We'll not stop searching until she's found!"

"But we've gone nearly as far as the city. We've been over the entire countryside. The city is all that's left. But the men will go no further, certainly not into the city proper. They do not wish to venture into the bad air and catch the yellow fever. Do you expect them to risk their lives—"

René's entire body stiffened as he spoke through clenched teeth, "No. No, of course not. I'll go alone."

"*Monsieur!*" Louis protested. "You mustn't! To enter the city now is to invite death!"

"But if she's there—" René began.

"She would not be so foolish. She must have heard of the yellow fever. The *mademoiselle* is an intelligent woman. She would not venture into a diseased city."

"The *mademoiselle* never does what she should," René bit out. "She's liable to have decided to brave it alone. I can't take that chance."

"But, *monsieur*—"

"I'll discuss it no further, Louis. Saddle Savage for me."

Louis's face was a grim mask of disapproval. "Suppose she's not there. Then you have thrown away your life for nothing!"

"Saddle my horse!" René commanded.

As his servant turned stiffly toward the door, René stared after him with a frown on his face. Throw away his life for nothing? The man didn't know what he was talking about. If René didn't make sure she was at least safe from the yellow fever, he'd go mad.

For he'd driven her away. He knew it as surely as he knew he had to find her. He'd taken away her pride and left her nothing with which to protect herself. What choice had he given her? Admit her desire or be conquered—that was what he'd told her. And certainly she'd admitted it. His loins hardened just at the thought of that night, of her wildly tempestuous response to him. Oh, yes, he'd proven his point. But at what price?

In silent anguish he stared at the half-completed painting of himself that dominated the room. The insolent grin and wicked eyes were his, that was certain.

"You're a stupid fool, you know that?" he said to the image. "After all these years, to allow a woman to rip you up inside like this—"

He stopped, angry at himself for speaking such thoughts to an inanimate object. Yet still the painting held his gaze. He could almost see Elina working over her canvas, paint on her hands and smock, and a smile on her face that was by turns sweet, then teasing, then unconsciously sensual. Damn, but the woman knew how to raise an ache in him he'd never thought it possible to feel.

"*Sacre bleu*, sweet eyes, where are you?" he demanded aloud of the empty room.

If he found her . . . No, *when* he found her, he would somehow convince her to ignore his overbearing nature and stay. But first he'd take her over his knee and . . . No, he thought grimly, not that. When he found her, he'd wrap her in his arms and hold on tight. For without her. . . .

With that thought unfinished, he whirled away from the mocking image of himself and left the room.

That same mocking image was seared into Elina's mind. It troubled her thoughts as she worked with Cecile in the kitchen, stirring the roux for the gumbo. Although it had been six days since she'd left his house she could still see René's face and body as she had painted it. The firm jaw, the hint of laughter in his eyes, the body that seemed relaxed although beneath that veneer lay the tension of a coiled spring.

What was he doing now? she wondered. Had he been alarmed to discover she was gone? Had he even bothered to search?

Of course he had, she told herself. His pride was wounded. He wouldn't take her escape lightly. But once he searched the roads and found nothing, what would he do?

He'd remember her as a woman he'd enjoyed for one afternoon and night, she thought bitterly. After all, that had been all he wanted—her compliance. He'd certainly had that. Her eyes welled with tears as she thought of the way she'd allowed him to steal her pride. Her hands went still while she strove to contain her emotions.

"Keep stirring, *ma petite,* keep stirring! We mustn't make the roux to burn," Cecile cautioned in her heavily accented English. Most of the time she and Elina spoke Creole French, but occasionally Cecile would practice a bit of her limited English on her new helper.

Reminded of where she was, Elina heeded the old slave's advice immediately. She thrust all her painful memories from her mind and concentrated on her work. She stirred the roux with small quick strokes, careful not to let any of the oil and flour mixture splatter onto her hands. Once the roux had begun to brown, it was as lethal as hot tar and stuck to the skin in much the same way. She'd discovered that the hard way the second day she'd been at the Vannier house when a drop of it had hit her hand, raising a blister the size of a pea.

She had to admit, though, that the gumbo made from the roux was worth all the trouble. Elina never seemed able to get enough of the rich, thick dark liquid, made even thicker by a healthy spoonful of fragrant ground sassafras leaves.

The gumbo had been only one of many new things she'd encountered during her first week at *Madame* Vannier's. Elina hadn't lied when she'd told *Madame* Vannier that she knew a bit about cooking. Elina's mama, who'd not been from a particularly wealthy family, had felt it important that her daughter learn the rudiments of cooking. But the simple chicken stews, beef pies, and country breads Elina had learned to cook couldn't begin to compare with the richly sauced meats, spicy thick bisques, and delicate pastries the Creoles loved. Each day Elina found herself being expected to make exotic creations that were commonplace in the Vannier household, but strange and wonderful to her.

It wasn't just the type of food, either, but the quantity that astounded her. Never had Elina seen so much food. Even though the *madame* was often the only Vannier in the house, other people always seemed to be around at mealtimes. Elina was fast learning that Creoles were very sociable. Not a day passed that someone didn't come to visit and to commiserate with Julia Vannier over the loss of "our dear departed Philippe."

But Elina wondered about what effect those constant visits had on her papa's wife. Outwardly, *Madame* Vannier generally seemed perfectly composed, the gracious hostess to a fault. She certainly kept the house running efficiently. She treated her slaves with kindness and respect. She didn't seem to want for anything, either, evidently content to manage her estate and to entertain her friends.

Given all that, Elina wasn't certain why she always felt as if Julia Vannier was simply keeping up appearances. Perhaps it had something to do with the one or two times Elina had seen a look of utter misery on her face.

What could be making the woman so miserable? Elina wondered as she continued to stir the roux. Did *Madame* Vannier miss Papa so terribly much? It was hard to believe, but she was beginning to think that might be the case. For some reason, she'd assumed that Papa's other wife would be a cold woman, concerned only with money and position. When she discovered Julia Vannier was as warm and compassionate as Mama had been, she was disappointed. She wanted to hate the woman who'd shared Papa's heart, but now she found she couldn't, particularly when the woman seemed so unhappy at times.

Cecile cried out, startling Elina out of her thoughts.

"What's wrong?" Elina asked in alarm.

Cecile muttered a series of Creole oaths that surprised Elina with their vehemence. "Like *une bêtasse*, I have burned my hand," Cecile said, shaking her head as she dug up a fingerful of butter from the dish sitting on the table and swabbed it over her palm. "Such a *stupide* behavior! And just when I was going to carry to *madame* a soothing treatment."

Cecile glanced woefully at the heavy tray with its pot of sassafras tea and its cloth soaked in cold, scented water. "*Madame* finds it so difficult to sleep these days. I thought perhaps my special treatment would help her take a short *siesta*."

"Perhaps someone else could administer it—" Elina began.

"Yes, *chérie*, of course!" Cecile responded. "I would be more than grateful."

"I—I didn't mean me," Elina was quick to add. "What do I know of how to give such a treatment?"

Cecile laughed. "Oh, don't worry. Such a simple thing it is to do. She just drinks the tea while you press the cloth to her head. I promise, the mix of cold and hot will confuse her body, and so it will sleep."

Elina smothered a laugh. "I don't know if I should . . ."

Cecile's face fell. "Yes, of course not. I forget sometimes that you are not a slave. Such acts are beneath you."

"No!" Elina protested, moving immediately to take the tray. "No, that's not why. I'm just not sure . . . Oh, never mind. I'd be happy to administer your treatment. You rest until I get back, and don't use that hand."

Cecile dropped into a chair gratefully as Elina whisked out of the door, carrying the tray.

Elina found her way through the house slowly. Since she'd come, she hadn't had much chance to see any rooms but the ones surrounding the dining room. As she walked up the stairs to the second floor, she gazed about her with avid interest. So Papa had had two homes—this plantation and the townhouse in New Orleans. These were the places he had come to when he'd claimed to be on a buying trip.

The thought troubled her, but not as much as it might have. She'd become accustomed to thinking of Papa's having two lives. Lately, she'd become curious about what Papa's other life had been like. Had he spent most of his time in the stables as he had in Creve Coeur? Or had he reigned supreme in his flawless mansion and his elegant townhouse enjoying his domain while entertaining his Creole friends?

And had he and Julia Vannier shared the same love he seemed to have shared with Mama? That was the question occupying her mind as she sought out her mistress's bedroom.

The house seemed laid out much like René's, so Elina felt certain she could find the bedroom. Besides, with all the doors open to allow the air to circulate, it was a simple matter of peeking in doors until she found *madame*.

In moments, she'd stopped before the entrance to a luxuriously appointed room. Before a mahogany dresser sat Julia Vannier who stared at herself as if to root out some hidden flaw. Her hair was down and she wore a dressing gown. Clearly, she'd planned to take a *siesta*, even if she couldn't sleep.

Disturbed to find her own hands trembling, Elina called out to the woman who both fascinated and terrified her. "*Madame*?"

The woman gave a start and then stared at Elina's image reflected in the mirror. For a moment, a look that strangely resembled guilt flashed over her face. Then it was gone.

"Yes?"

"Cecile burned her hand, so she asked me to come give you the treatment."

"The treatment?" Julia Vannier asked with a frown.

Elina stepped a little farther into the room. "Yes, *madame*. The—the tea and the cold cloth."

She smiled. "Ah, yes. Cecile's cure-all for insomnia. Do come in. She'll be disappointed if I don't take the treatment."

Elina entered. Julia Vannier gestured for her to set the tray down on a table beside the bed, and Elina did so. *Madame* then rose from the table and climbed onto the bed, leaning back against the pillows and fixing Elina with a curious stare.

"Will you administer it then?" Julia Vannier asked.

"I suppose. She said to have you drink the tea and then put the cloth on your head."

The older woman laughed. "She forgot to tell you the most important part, of course."

"*Madame?*"

"You're to brush my hair." When Elina looked bewildered, she added softly, "It relaxes me. Whenever I am troubled, Cecile gives me sassafras tea, places a scented cloth on my head, and brushes my hair. I suppose she didn't tell you about the brushing because she worries that such duties are beneath you. She's convinced you're a lady of quality."

Elina knew of Cecile's opinions. But she'd made a point not to encourage them, because she'd wanted to remain as unnoticed as possible in the Vannier household. She could only escape New Orleans without René's finding out where she'd gone if she kept people from paying attention to her.

"Cecile has funny ideas sometimes," Elina murmured as she poured a cup of tea and brought it to her mistress.

"Quite true. But Cecile is not completely wrong. I can see you were gently bred. The way you talk, the way you stand, the way you move—all of it shows me that. So tell me, dear child, was your family wealthy?"

Elina bit her lip nervously as she picked up the cold cloth and the brush and approached the bed. "Once."

"Did they lose their fortune? Was your papa a wastrel?" Julia Vannier asked as she turned to her side to allow Elina access to her hair.

Deborah Martin

Elina could have sworn the woman's tone was laced with bitterness as she asked the question, but she knew Julia Vannier couldn't possibly know who Elina's papa was. "No," Elina answered in as calm a voice as she could muster. "Papa was a good provider. He was a—a merchant." That was true, though he dealt in horses rather than goods. "But once he . . . once he died, nothing was the same."

Elina sat down on the edge of the bed, laid the scented cloth across *madame's* forehead, and began to brush the woman's long dark hair, wishing she wouldn't ask so many questions.

"Did your papa die heavily in debt?"

Elina sighed. "No. I'm afraid my brother was entirely responsible for placing us in debt. But all that's in the past. Now that they're all dead, none of it is of any consequence."

Julia Vannier fell silent at that statement.

For several minutes, Elina pulled the brush through her mistress's rope of hair.

It's so different from Mama's auburn hair, Elina thought as her fingers worked loose a tangle. Julia Vannier's hair was rich and dark, like molasses. It reminded her of someone else's hair, which was also a deep, shining brown. René's.

Her hands paused as she remembered fleetingly how René's hair had felt between her fingers. Then she thought of that rich hair framing his handsome face. She could almost picture him staring at her with a dark passion in his eyes.

How she missed him! If she'd known just how much leaving him would wound her, would she have done it?

Of course she would have, she told herself sternly. Wasn't it better to experience a little pain now than a great deal more pain later when he cast her away?

Yes, she thought. Yes, she'd done the right thing.

With resolve, she began stroking the older woman's hair with the brush once more.

"That feels so good," Julia Vannier murmured. "I do believe I was in more need of Cecile's treatment than I realized. And you administer it so well."

"I'm glad to be of some aid," Elina said politely, her mind far away, drifting to memories of René and their last ride together. Absentmindedly, she began to rub the *madame's* temples as she'd done for her mama so many times. Elina could feel Julia Vannier relax under her fingers.

Then the woman sighed contentedly. "You make me feel so calm. I haven't felt that way in a great while. I've had so many matters to think about. Between my son and my brother and . . . and other things, I've not been able to rest very easily."

The mention of René made Elina sit up straight. Only with an effort did she refrain from asking what Julia Vannier's brother in particular had done to disturb the woman.

"In any case," the *madame* continued, her voice suddenly a fraction harsher as if she were angry with herself for saying so much, "I don't wish to bore you with an old woman's complaints. So why don't you tell me how you came to be in New Orleans?"

Elina forced herself not to protest against her mistress's innocent question. After all, the woman was simply attempting to make polite conversation.

"My brother and I came after Mama died . . ." she began with hesitation, wondering how much she should reveal. What did it matter? she thought. Julia Vannier would never guess the truth. "Papa had come here on business and we hadn't heard from him. Then our farm . . . our farm burned to the ground, so we *had* to come. We came here in search of him, only to discover he was dead."

Julia Vannier was silent for so long that at first Elina worried the woman had read between the lines and seen the reality of what Elina had only hinted at.

The *madame's* next words startled Elina. "Did your mama's death have anything to do with your papa's absence?"

Elina paused. Then she said, almost bitterly, "Yes." Her eyes filled with tears as her hands mechanically brushed the woman's hair.

"She must have loved him very much," Julia Vannier whispered.

"Yes," Elina said again. Why did this woman have to be so perceptive and so understanding?

"Have *you* ever been in love?" *Madame* asked abruptly.

The question startled Elina. How should she answer? Would it be wise to confide in the sister of the man Elina loved? What did it matter if *Madame* knew the truth? She'd never know just whom Elina loved. "Yes, I've been in love," Elina murmured.

"Did your love make you . . . make you act in ways you knew were wrong?"

Elina felt a chill grip her as she began to wonder if the woman knew more about her and René than she revealed. "I—I suppose."

Julia Vannier sighed. "So I'm not the only one then."

Even as Elina felt relief that *Madame* knew nothing after all, she wondered what the woman had done that was so terrible. How could this demure matronly woman possibly have a skeleton in her closet? And had Elina's papa been the one for whom Julia Vannier had behaved wrongly?

"I loved my husband," the woman said, as if to explain something. "I loved him so very much. But . . . but he was often gone for months at a time. And when he was here, he was often delightful—a good companion. Yet sometimes it was as if his mind were occupied elsewhere. At those times, my heart twisted for him. I could not talk to him. He was a proud man. Still, I knew he had problems. When he was like that, I wondered if he even knew I existed."

A storm of emotions rose in Elina's breast. She, too, had experienced Philippe Vannier's strange moods. How often had his long absences made her fear that he no longer loved her and Alex and Mama? The feeling would evaporate when he returned, bearing gifts and flashing his indulgent smile.

Yet after he'd been home for some time, he would suddenly become distant for no clear reason, forcing her doubts to the surface again.

She'd never dreamed he might have been the same with his other family.

"I'm sorry," said *Madame* Vannier as Elina remained silent. "This treatment seems to be making me into a jabbering old fool. I didn't mean to burden you with my troubles."

"I don't mind," Elina said, surprised to find it was true. She was beginning to see Papa through Julia Vannier's eyes and what she saw somehow set her at ease, even while it made her anger against Papa grow even hotter.

"Let's speak of something else," *Madame* Vannier said with determination. "Tell me of your family. Your mother sounds like . . . like a lovely woman. What was she like?"

Elina's fingers fell still as she thought of her parents, but the *madame* didn't seem to notice. "Mama was a kind woman. it was hard for her because—"

She broke off, realizing she'd already begun to tread dangerous ground. Then she told herself not to worry about what she said. Many men were away often That's why it had been so easy for Papa to conceal his other family. No, Julia Vannier would never connect her husband with Papa.

"It was hard for Mama because Papa was often gone attending to business affairs. I never heard her complain about it, but I know it bothered her that he had to travel so much."

The woman was curiously silent, and Elina plunged on. She felt an absurd urge to tell her side, even if Julia Vannier didn't know the significance of it. "Just as you missed your husband, I missed Papa when he was gone. Sometimes I'd almost hate him for tormenting Mama with his absences, but I—I always forgave him when he returned. My brother, however, wasn't so accepting. Papa wouldn't let Alexandre accompany him on his trips, and Alexandre resented Papa for that. So Alex turned to gambling: I think he did it as much to anger Papa as to make money."

Elina began to plait *Madame* Vannier's hair in a loose braid.

"It's strange, isn't it," Julia Vannier said, "that sons will go to such extremes to make their papas notice them. My son . . . my son, Francois, is like that. I don't believe you've met him, have you? No, of course not.

"At any rate, every time Philippe spoke to him, he took offense. And every time Philippe left, Francois made some grand gesture to demonstrate his disapproval. One time he fought a duel with the son of Philippe's best friend. Another time, he gambled away his entire month's allotment in the space of one night."

"My brother and Francois sound alike," Elina said without thinking.

Madame Vannier gave a forced laugh. "Yes, they do, don't they?"

The heavy awkward silence that ensued after that statement made Elina uncomfortable. She was tiring of watching what she said, of gauging how much was too much to reveal. She wished she could just blurt out the truth and endure the consequences.

Only one thing stopped her—René. To destroy his sister with such knowledge would be tantamount to destroying him. She couldn't hurt him that way, no matter how much he'd hurt her.

"Francois refuses to take any responsibility for the estate," *Madame* Vannier suddenly said, her tone forced, as if she were telling her confidences against her will. "Philippe never could mold our son into the man he should have been. I'd hoped after René returned that Francois would learn some responsibility from his uncle. But René's as bad as Francois sometimes."

"I'm sure your brother doesn't mean to worry you," Elina said politely.

"Perhaps not," Julia Vannier replied with a snort. "But just today I learned that he went into New Orleans a few days ago, knowing about the yellow fever and knowing how dangerous the city is these days. I was astonished! How could he be so irresponsible? If anything ever happened to him . . ."

Elina's heart froze in cold terror at the thought of René in disease-ridden New Orleans. "Why did your brother do such a foolish thing?" she asked in a pained whisper.

Madame Vannier shrugged her shoulders. "Who can know? But I heard from one of the slaves that René was pursuing some mistress of his. It's possible. Still, I can't imagine René's being so enamored of a mistress that he'd risk his life for her."

Elina scarcely heard that last sentence. Her blood was thundering in her ears, and she felt as if she'd just been struck. Oh, God, surely he wouldn't have put himself in such danger for her!

Yet she knew instinctively that he had. René had taken the chance that he might contract yellow fever to look for her in the city. He must care some, she thought with a little thrill, to risk so much. Oh, but it was such a foolish risk and all because of her leaving him. Guilt gnawed at her. Still, how could she have ever guessed he'd do such a thing!

"He'll no doubt be fine," Julia Vannier stated flatly, oblivious to the effect her words were having on Elina. "When my parents died of yellow fever, several of the others in the household had it as well. Only René managed to escape being stricken, although he sat beside their beds night and day. It was as if he were invincible. And I suppose he still is, for he came back yesterday without a trace of fever. Nonetheless, I worry about him."

Elina's dread lifted a fraction as she realized he'd returned unscathed. Yet the fever could still strike him, she told herself. It would take a day or two more for them to be certain he didn't have it. Oh, how would she endure the waiting? And what if he did fall ill?

The other woman's soft voice intruded on Elina's thoughts. "I love my brother so much. He's a good man, but he can be trying. Why are men like that?"

Elina managed to say normally, "Who knows?" but inside she felt twisted with worry.

"Such recklessness! He should know better. When he comes to dinner tomorrow evening, I shall have to be most firm with him."

Elina's pulse quickened. René was coming! Of course, she mustn't allow him to see her, but *she* could see *him*, if she were very careful. He would pay little attention to the servants and certainly not to the kitchen help, who could take a quick peek into the dining room when his back was turned.

Then she would know for certain he was safe. She knew she couldn't rest until she determined for herself that he had survived his visit into the city.

"You know, dear Elina, I believe I *am* beginning to feel tired enough to rest. So if you would be so kind . . ."

"Yes, yes, of course," Elina said as she slid off the bed, her step light at the thought that she would see René soon.

"Thank you, child. For everything. For listening to me babble. I—I don't deserve it."

Elina wondered what she meant, but she merely answered, "Rest well, *madame*."

Only after she'd left the room did she realize that Julia Vannier had never confessed exactly what horrible act she'd committed for the sake of love.

Chapter Nineteen

Mothers make children, but not children's hearts.
—Creole Proverb

The sounds of chatter and tinkling glasses filtered out into the sultry night air. Elina paused in her walk from the house to the kitchen and glanced back in the direction of the sounds. Julia's dinner guests stood just on the other side of a set of open glass doors. Elina ducked her head quickly as she caught sight of René. But in her one glimpse of him, she could tell he was oblivious to the activity going on outside the house.

She stepped back into the shadows and looked once again through the open doorway. René was staring down into a beautiful Creole woman's face, explaining something to her as she drank in every word. Elina felt a stab of jealousy. Angry with herself for caring so much, she muttered under her breath one of the Creole curses she'd picked up from Cecile.

She watched them both, unable to draw away. He seemed

as handsome as ever. If he had the fever, it certainly wasn't noticeable, she thought, relief coursing through her. His skin did seem paler than usual and there were dark smudges under his eyes that she'd never seen before. Still, he didn't look so much ill as he did tired.

He turned slightly away from her, blocking her view of his face. But she could see his companion's face. The woman's simpering smile told her quite well that he was voicing a compliment.

Elina's hands tightened on the empty tray she held as a sudden pang of yearning shot through her. If it could only be her smiling up at him. For once, she'd love to have him pay her polite compliments, talk to her as if she were of his own class. But he'd never do so, never! He was too aware of how he'd met her to give her the chance to be anything more to him than a moment's diversion.

A soft sigh escaped her lips. She'd never be free of him, not if she stayed near New Orleans. She'd always remember his lips pressed to hers, as long as she breathed the same air as he did and her feet trod the same ground.

Long after he'd left the room and passed on into another part of the house with his companion, she stared at the window with an aching frustration seeping through her. She wished she could simply run after him, simply ask to be taken back. But, no, that would be the utmost in foolishness.

After standing there riveted a few moments more, she forced herself to turn away from the window. She wouldn't put herself through this again, she vowed. If it took her all year, she'd save her money until she had enough to leave New Orleans forever.

She'd only walked a few steps when a voice stopped her.

"You there! Come here!" the faintly familiar male voice commanded from somewhere behind her.

She paused, an unsettling feeling growing within her as she half-turned in the direction of the voice. She could not see who spoke, for he stood in the shadow of a nearby oak.

"*Monsieur*? Are you speaking to me?" she asked of the darkness, not quite facing the voice.

"Yes, of course. Who else? Come here. I've a sudden urge to look over *Maman's* new servant. I'm surprised she didn't mention you. But apparently, *Maman* keeps a few secrets from me. Why, I wouldn't have known about you at all if Cecile hadn't told me."

With those words, the man stepped away from the tree. The light from the kitchen shone directly on him. Elina could see the lustful gleam in his eye as he took in her rounded hips and small waist. She kept her face averted as dismay made her blood freeze. Francois! Until now she'd successfully avoided him. He lived in a bachelor house on the outskirts of the plantation and came to the big house only for dinner. Well, she certainly couldn't let him see her now. He knew of her relationship with René and was sure to tell his uncle where she could be found!

He mistook her averted face for reticence and moved closer. "Any servant in this house serves not only *Maman*, but me," he cautioned. "So if you wish things to go easy for you, you'll not be so shy with me."

She had to get away, she realized, before he moved any closer. "Excuse me, *monsieur*," she murmured, "but I have duties in the kitchen."

She began to edge toward the nearby building, hoping Francois wouldn't follow her. To her consternation, he moved quickly to block her path. She turned aside, but he easily caught her arm and swung her around.

"Don't play the coquette—" he began as he grasped her wrists with malicious glee. Then his smile faded as he caught sight of her face illuminated in the lamplight that streamed from the kitchen windows. "*Merde!*" he hissed. "It's you! What are *you* doing here?"

She swallowed hard at the ugliness in his voice. His

hands tightened on her wrists so that she feared he'd break them.

"I—I work for your *maman*, as you said," she whispered, forcing her voice to remain even. "I'm just a servant, no more. I promise I'll do my work and not disturb you. But please, *monsieur*, don't tell your uncle where I am!"

The expression on Francois's face deepened her uneasiness. His eyes glinted like two steel knives that would have sliced her in two if they could have. He released her so abruptly she stumbled back a step.

"Tell my uncle? I don't intend to do such a thing, that's for certain," he sneered.

She stared at him, a quizzical expression on her face. "Thank you, *monsieur*, for—"

"What will it take to make you leave here and find some other place to work?" he interrupted. "Money? Is that what you desire? Come to my house tomorrow, and I'll give you however much you need, so long as you leave immediately!"

His words took her by surprise. He didn't know who she was, so why was he so concerned about her presence in his mother's house?

"I—I don't understand. Why do you want me to leave? What does it matter to you if I work here?"

Francois clenched his fists at his sides, although his face smoothed out, betraying none of his agitation. When at last he answered her, Elina had the distinct impression he'd meant to say something else entirely.

"My uncle is besotted with you. Did you know he'd gone into New Orleans looking for you?" He didn't stop to let her answer. "Yes, you drove him to do such a foolhardy thing. *Nonc* René could easily have contracted yellow fever. He may still. Is it any wonder then that I wish you gone? You're a danger to this family. You're a whore, and I won't have *Nonc* René and *Maman* seduced by you into doing anything else rash."

Elina's temper began to rise. How dare he call her a

whore! He knew nothing about her, nothing! Her body shook with the desire to blurt out the truth so he would know just whom he accused. But she hesitated, wondering what that would accomplish. Francois clearly disliked her. Unlike his uncle, he might wish to take violent steps to eliminate her if he knew just what a threat to his inheritance she was.

So she controlled herself, although her hands trembled from the effort of it. "I am no whore," she bit out. "Nor do I extort money from people for any reason. I don't want your money, so you'll have to endure my presence until I can earn enough money to leave. As long as you mention nothing to your uncle, I don't see why I can't continue as a servant here."

"No reason? No reason!" His rage was so great, he pounded his fist into the nearby oak tree.

Inwardly, Elina quaked at the reaction she'd roused in him, although she stood her ground. "I think I'd best return to my duties," she whispered, now wishing only to escape him. She backed away, but his hands were on her shoulders in seconds, his fingers digging painfully into her flesh.

"You gambler's slut!" he hissed. "A whore, that's what you are! You're not fit to be *Maman's* slave, much less her hired servant! Well, you foolish girl, by the time I'm through with you, you'll be glad to take any money I offer and put as much distance between you and me as possible!"

Without warning, he struck her full across the face so hard she fell to her knees. In shock and anger, she lifted her hand to her lip and felt the sore place, then tasted the blood seeping into her mouth where her teeth had cut into her lip. He raised his hand again and her eyes widened in terror.

But the blow never came.

"Francois!" a voice spoke sharply from somewhere near the house. "If you strike that girl again, you'll have to deal with me."

Elina's ears still rang from the force of Francois's blow,

yet she recognized the voice. Evidently, Francois did as well, for he froze with his hand in midair.

"René, dear," a young woman's voice said petulantly, "must we involve ourselves in disputes over the slaves?"

Both René and the woman stepped into the light, and Elina sucked in her breath as relief and trepidation coursed through her. Belatedly, she ducked her head so he wouldn't see who she was. Fortunately, René's eyes were on Francois.

"Go back to the house, Solange," René said in steely tones.

"You said we could go for a walk—" she began.

"No, I did not. You threatened to swoon if I didn't take you out of all that heat. Well, now you've taken the air, so I suggest you return to the house."

René's "suggestion" was clearly a command. The woman made a tiny moue of protest, but she didn't stay.

René turned his attention back to his nephew. He spoke quickly as if the activity of speaking was the only thing keeping him from resorting to physical violence himself. "I thought Julia had spoken to you about beating the slaves, Francois. She'll have your hide for disobeying her, and I'll take what's left of it when she's through!"

Francois stood motionless, suppressing his anger only with difficulty. "This is not your concern, *Nonc* René," he ventured to say, but the black scowl he received in response to that statement was enough to make him fall silent.

Elina wished she could just melt into the darkness, but now René was staring at her and holding out his hand to help her rise, still apparently unaware of who she was.

Afraid to make him notice her any further, she took his hand and allowed him to pull her to her feet. "Thank you, *monsieur*," she murmured. Then she dropped his hand, turned, and began to walk toward the kitchen, hoping René would merely think she was eager to escape Francois and wouldn't take much note of her. But she realized her hope had been futile when she heard him whisper her name behind her.

"Elina!" he repeated, his voice a mixture of relief and wonder. Then "Don't you dare move another step!" he clipped out, the words hard-edged stones.

His voice turned her knees to wood. She stopped, then slowly pivoted to face him. Even in the dim lamplight, she could tell he was blazingly angry, angrier than she'd ever seen him. But his fury didn't wound her nearly so much as the distrust she detected in his eyes.

Francois took advantage of his uncle's distraction to back away, but René's voice stopped him as well. "We're not through yet," René snarled at his nephew, his eyes never leaving Elina's face. "I wish to know why you were beating my mistress."

Elina bristled at his reference to her as his mistress, but Francois stood stock-still in alarm. Then Francois's face flushed as his uncle's words drove him to retort, "I won't have your whore living under *Maman's* roof. I asked the bitch to leave, but she refused. So I merely tried a different method of persuasion."

Without warning, René turned on his nephew, clutching the young man's shoulders as he slammed Francois up against the oak tree. "If you ever call Elina a whore again, I'll kill you. And I don't want you to so much as brush against her sleeve without her express permission! Is that fully understood?"

"Y–yes," Francois managed to choke out as the blood rapidly drained from his face.

"Then get out of my sight before I use your 'different methods of persuasion' on you!" René commanded as he dropped his nephew to the ground.

Francois rose on shaky knees, his eyes darting from his uncle's face to Elina's. Then casting a look of humiliation and anger in Elina's direction, Francois slipped away into the darkness.

Elina's heart began to race as René turned his attention to her. She forced herself to stand her ground. His eyes raked over her, taking in the coarse servant's clothes she wore and the tray that had fallen to the ground near her.

"So you've been here all along," he said at last, his eyes locking with hers.

She jerked her gaze away from his face, unable to endure the accusation and hurt in his eyes. "Yes," she said faintly.

Her refusal to say any more seemed to enrage him.

"I should have known you'd come here," he growled. "When you found I wouldn't accept your claims, I suppose you decided to try out my sister instead. Have you sprung your story on her yet, or are you biding your time gathering information before you attempt to destroy her life?"

Her head snapped up as outrage flooded over her. "I came here to escape you and for no other reason, I assure you! If I'd known whose house this was, I would've braved every snake in the swamp to avoid coming near it!"

He laughed harshly. "You'll understand, I'm sure, that I have trouble believing that."

"You would have preferred I'd gone to New Orleans looking for a position? I almost did, you know." A look of horror passed over his face, but she continued blindly, her desire to set him straight too strong for her to stop. "I only stayed because your sister insisted I do so. But, unlike you, she offered me a *respectable* position, and under the circumstances, I felt compelled to take it!"

He closed the distance between them, his face an implacable shield against her words. "You had no reason to leave me," he stated with deadly firmness.

"No, of course not."

He stopped, the sarcasm in her voice seeming to affect him.

Uncaring, she taunted him, "I'd forgotten the many options you gave me. After all, I was perfectly free to stay and let you use my weaknesses to degrade me even further."

His hand leapt to encircle her wrist before she could even move. "Did you really find our lovemaking degrading?" he demanded, jerking her toward him.

"I—" she began, wanting to lie to him, to hurt him for his accusations. But the lies caught in her throat.

Her silence gave him his answer. He pulled her resisting body up against his.

"That night I kept waiting and waiting for you to come to me," he stated, the pain in his voice piercing her like shards of glass, "but you never came. Then when I found you gone—" He broke off as if angry at himself for saying so much. "Suffice it to say, it was then I realized you'd played me for the fool."

"Oh, no," she retorted, straining away from the arm that now clasped her waist so tightly. "You're the one who played me for the fool, boasting to your friends about your conquest even before the deed was done! You were so sure of me, weren't you? To you I was simply a gambler's slut, as my dear half brother put it. Well, I won't be your—your whore!"

That last she could hardly choke out. And one look at his face told her he wished she hadn't. His stormy visage matched the tension she could feel rising in the arms that held her immobile against him.

"If you ever use those words to describe yourself again, sweet eyes . . ." His ominous expression told her quite clearly what he would do. "*Mon Dieu,* I don't know where you've heard these incredible lies about me, and frankly, I don't care. Such lies aren't worth discussing. But what *is* worth discussing is the matter of what I want from you."

She opened her mouth to tell him she didn't care what he wanted from her because he wasn't going to get it. But he silenced her with a glance that held so much naked longing that she shuddered against her will.

"I don't want a whore," he whispered, his voice spilling over her like satin covering a burn. "And God forgive me, but I don't even care that you've been attempting to destroy me for something I didn't do. If I thought you'd really tell my sister your insane story about being Philippe's daughter deliberately in revenge for what you believed I'd done to your brother—"

A sob of protest escaped her lips. She couldn't believe he still thought her capable of such deep hatred.

He glanced at the pain on her face. "Well, it doesn't matter," he continued enigmatically. "You see, I'm willing to put all of the past behind us if you can do so as well. And surely you can. I can't help but believe you found as much fulfillment in our lovemaking as did I—"

She stiffened at his reminder of just how much she'd given him.

He deliberately ignored her reaction, although his voice seemed more taut as he went on. "Elina, I want you in my arms, in my bed, in my life. I can't stand another week of wretched nights! God, I need you! You must return with me. Now! Tonight!"

The abrupt shift in his tone of voice from incensed to passionate temporarily threw her off guard. How could she think when his hand was now traveling down over the curve of her hip, crushing her skirt and petticoats as it cupped her and pulled her against him?

Then his mouth came down on hers without warning, as if he were searching for some soft place to insinuate himself. And immediately he found it, his tongue easily parting her lips to slip inside.

At the intimate intrusion, she raised her hands to thrust him away, but they moved further up of their own accord, stretching to clasp his neck and then caress his hair. He moaned, the sound echoing deep within his throat as his mouth pressed harder against hers.

Then as the passions they'd held in check exploded into being, the two of them transformed into two ravenous creatures, half-mad with their desire to rediscover each other's bodies. Her hands clutched his head as if afraid he'd be dragged from her arms before she could have enough of him. And his hands roamed her freely, roughly caressing each part in a blind attempt to mark her forever as his.

His mouth devoured hers, and she felt a rising tide of sweetness within her that blotted out all the warnings her mind was giving her. He wanted her. He hadn't said he loved her or that he wished for anything more than he'd wanted before. But he'd said he needed her.

The rest of it didn't matter, her body said, even while her good sense screamed that it did. Nothing was of any consequence as his hands swept over her body. She was hungrily aware of every inch of him from his taut muscles discernible even through the layers of his coat and shirt to the hardness between his thighs that betokened his longing for her.

"You will return with me, won't you?" he murmured against her ear, his breath warming her cheek.

The sound of his voice, so demanding and so sure, brought her halfway out of the haze of sensuality he'd created around them. "And return to what?" she whispered. "A few months as your mistress? More accusations and suspicions about who and what I am?"

"Don't talk of the suspicions. They don't matter. And I promise we would have much more than a few months together. I don't ever intend to let you go."

"But I *would* be your mistress," she said, fearful that he might confirm all her fears.

"You would be the woman I cared for. Don't make it sound so sordid. I want you. You want me. That's all that matters."

Don't listen, she told herself as his mouth came down on hers once again. She roundly cursed the weakness that made her turn to pudding whenever he touched her. But she knew if he continued to hold her, to whisper endearments in her ear, she would break down and do what she'd sworn not to.

Then just when his hand cupped her breast, eliciting a low moan from somewhere deep within her, a voice behind them made them both start.

"René, what's this Solange tells me about Francois's

beating the . . ." The voice trailed off as Julia Vannier came face to face with René and Elina, still locked in a close embrace.

René's arm clasped Elina's waist and their bodies were pressed so close together that no one would have been able to mistake what they'd been doing. Elina felt the color rising throughout her body and was sure her embarrassment could be seen even in the dim light. She tried to extricate herself from René's arm, but he wouldn't release her, although he did allow her to put some space between them.

"Elina?" *Madame* Vannier asked, her voice both shocked and amazed as her eyes went from her brother's rigid set expression to Elina's pained one.

"I'm afraid there's been some error, Julia," René said with apparent calm, although Elina could tell he was somewhat disconcerted to have his sister discover them in such a compromising position. "I realize Elina's been performing the duties of a servant here, but I'm afraid that's over. She belongs with me, where she'd been before coming here. She left when she shouldn't have, and now she's returning with me."

"She's—she's your mistress?" Julia Vannier asked incredulously, her eyes darting to Elina's for an answer. Then she answered her own question. "You're the woman he went to New Orleans in search of. Of course, I see it now. You *are* his mistress."

The woman's words brought Elina to her senses. She couldn't bear to have Julia Vannier think badly of her, not when she had been so very kind. And after two weeks of being treated like a respectable young girl, Elina was loath to be branded as René's mistress.

"No," Elina answered, trying to force René's hands from her waist. "No, I'm not his mistress."

Madame flashed her brother a searching look as his eyes narrowed and came to rest on Elina's face. Then she, too, turned her gaze to Elina. "So do you indeed wish to leave my employ and go with my brother?"

Elina took one long look at René, at the blinding need that shone in his eyes as his dark face commanded her to say yes. Then she reminded herself of the accusations he'd made when he'd first found her and of what he'd make of her if she went with him.

"N–no," she murmured, turning her eyes from his face, although she could hardly ignore the tensing of his hand on her waist. "I wish to stay here—if you'll let me," she told the woman.

"Of course you may stay," *Madame* Vannier said, her voice filled with something that sounded almost like self-loathing.

"Julia, for your own good, stay out of this," René warned, still refusing to release Elina.

"Please understand," Julia Vannier told her brother earnestly, "she came here in desperate straits and I took her in. She's . . . I . . . Well, I've become attached to her. I don't wish to see her forced to leave even by you before she's ready to go. She's just an innocent, René. Surely you can tell she's too well-bred for what you seem to be offering her."

That statement enraged René. "That 'innocent,' " he ground out, "was helping her gambling brother cheat when I met her. Then she soundly knocked me over the head with a whiskey bottle before absconding with all my money! Don't tell me what she is, dear sister. You don't know the truth of the matter!"

"You have no right to tell her those things!" Elina choked out, wrenching herself away from his arms while he concentrated on his sister. "You *know* why I did what I did! Isn't it enough that you've convinced the magistrate I'm a liar and a cheat? Must you tell everyone the sordid tale?"

Instantly, the anger left René's face to be replaced by a look of pure regret. "Sweet eyes, I'm sorry—"

"No, you're not," she accused as she moved further away from him. "You want to blacken my name, so I'll have no other choice but to take what you offer. You don't want to give me any choices. You never have!"

Julia Vannier watched the two of them, guilt and horror alternately suffusing her face.

"I did give you a choice once," he said harshly, "and we both know what choice you made."

Elina flushed, unbearably aware that he was referring to the first time they'd made love.

He continued, his voice becoming firmer as he saw the confusion in her eyes, "After you made that choice, there was no turning back, *ma petite*. You can't escape me now and there's no use in trying."

"I won't be your mistress," Elina said, faintly at first and then with a pleading note, "I won't!"

"René, love," Julia Vannier interjected, "can't you see the poor child is distraught? Leave her be for now. Just go. Don't torment her anymore." *Madame* Vannier stepped forward to stand between her brother and Elina.

René stared at his sister, his face a stony mask. "Julia, I'll leave if you wish it, but you've lost your mind if you think I'll let her go." His tone contained just enough bitterness to make Julia's face fill with uncertainty. "Elina belongs with me," he asserted. "I know it and she knows it. I'll be back for hcr, and I guarantee the next time we meet she'll make a better choice."

Then his gaze rested on Elina, who trembled at the blatant hunger and determination that shone on his face. "*Au revoir*, sweet eyes," he murmured. Then he was gone.

The second he was out of sight, the tears began to flow down Elina's face. Julia Vannier stood beside her with a pained expression on her face.

"I—I'm so sorry," Elina stammered between sobs. "You've been too good to me to be repaid in such a way. I know you won't want me to remain after what he's told you. I—I'll get my things."

She turned toward the slave quarters and the tiny cabin she shared with Cecile, but *Madame* Vannier stopped her.

"Please," she said, her hand trembling as she restrained Elina. "Please, don't go."

"You mustn't worry about me. I'll find another position. But I wouldn't wish to cause a rift between you and your brother after you've shown me so much kindness."

"No!" Julia Vannier retorted with sudden harshness as Elina began once again to move away. "You mustn't go. Not until you've heard the truth."

Elina turned around slowly, her eyes searching *Madame* Vannier's face.

The older woman flashed Elina a look of sad desperation. Then she gave a sigh that seemed to well from deep inside her. "I'm the one who should be sorry, Elina," she said. Then in a tone full of bitter self-reproach, she added, "It's time you learned just how little kindness I've shown you. Once you know the truth, I fear you'll find it hard to forgive me."

And with those enigmatic words, Julia Vannier led Elina to the house.

Chapter Twenty

A man who prides himself on his ancestry is like the potato plant, the best part of which is underground.
—*Spanish Proverb*

Elina's face mirrored her incredulity as she sat in Julia Vannier's bedroom, trying to assimilate the strange story René's sister was telling her of Papa's deathbed confession. As the bits and pieces fell together, her emotions churned within her. Anger against Papa warred with both anger and sympathy for Papa's betrayed wife. After all, Elina well knew the feeling of resentment that had turned *Madame* Vannier into a woman who'd break a vow in order to punish her dead husband. And yet. . . .

"You're young," Julia Vannier was saying, "but not too young to understand."

Elina couldn't ignore the note of desperation in the other woman's voice. But her head ached from the tug of war her mind and heart were playing with her emotions. She had to fight the urge to leave and never come back.

"I can understand your not wanting to fulfill Papa's last wish," Elina said slowly. "I could have even understood if you'd refused to shelter me that first night. But once you knew me . . . once you . . . you . . ." she trailed off as two fat tears rolled down her cheeks.

Julia Vannier moaned in dismay and reached for her, but Elina pushed her away, not quite ready to let the woman comfort her.

Madame Vannier's face clouded over. "What I did was wrong. I freely admit it. But if you only knew how many hours I spent agonizing over my silence, wondering why I couldn't find it in me to tell you the truth . . ."

"And why couldn't you?" Elina asked, her resentment making her blunt.

"Because a part of me saw you as her. You don't look so much like Philippe, which means you must look like her. And . . . and you're beautiful, so much more lovely than I ever was. I kept seeing Philippe in her arms, arms that are like yours, taut-skinned and sweet as the arms of the young are. It was too hard to bear, the idea that she kept his heart for so long with her looks. Some days I wanted to hate you for being like her but I couldn't. I'm not certain why. Yet I—I also couldn't bring myself to tell you. Please try to understand."

"*Madame* Vannier—"

"*Non, non.* You must call me Julia. After all, you and my brother are clearly very . . . close. And I feel as though I've known you far longer than a few days. You're everything I would want a daughter to be. Did you know I used to wonder what Kathleen's daughter was like? From the moment I learned of her and you, I envied Kathleen for having a daughter. And now that your *maman's* gone, it would please me if you'd call me Julia."

Elina hesitated. But the look in *Madame* Vannier's eyes reminded her so much of the haunted look her mama used to wear that she couldn't refuse the request. "Julia," Elina said aloud.

"I'm sorry about your *maman*," Julia whispered. "I truly am sorry. I know that by not telling her the truth I may have caused her death."

Elina glanced at Julia with pity in her eyes as she was struck with the realization that Julia had probably felt tremendous guilt for a very long time.

"I don't think it would have mattered," Elina assured Julia, a sudden protective feeling for the poor woman assailing her. This *was* René's beloved sister after all, and for his sake Elina felt compelled to ease her pain. "In the last few years, Mama had been very ill," Elina said, her eyes dark with pain as she remembered her mother. "She always pined for Papa, just as you did. Who knows? Perhaps knowing he had another wife would have done as much to kill her as not knowing where he was."

"He loved her very much, didn't he?"

"He must have loved you as well," Elina said with a tinge of bitterness in her tone, "or he wouldn't have left us for months at a time to stay here. He would have stayed with us."

This time Julia looked more thoughtful than guilty. "Perhaps. Who can say what might have happened if your papa had made a choice? But he didn't."

"No, he didn't."

"He loved us both—even me he loved in his own fashion," Julia added in complete honesty. Then she sighed. "But she was his light. He only remained with me to protect his family's good name. At the beginning, oh, I suppose with the optimism of youth, he thought he could keep both families without risking anything."

"What would he have risked by not marrying you? He really loved Mama. Besides, she was his first wife."

Julia's shoulders sagged, and her eyes became weary. "She was, that's true. Before he died, he told me the whole story of how and when they met. He married her without anyone's knowledge while he was visiting St. Louis. When he returned here, he was cautious, especially since his father had just died. He didn't tell his *maman* about the marriage. First he came to see me and broached the subject of breaking off our engagement."

"And you refused," Elina stated.

"Of course I refused! I had always loved him. Foolishly, I thought if I married him, I could make him love me. And to make matters worse for him, our two families sided with me. When at last he told his *maman* he would not marry me, she threatened to disown him. And she would have. With her husband dead, she had complete control of Philippe's inheritance. She was the daughter of a Spanish grandee and she was a tyrant. She made Philippe believe that family name, family pride, was everything."

Elina couldn't stop the acrid words that sprung from her lips. "And the riches Papa would have been denied probably influenced his decision as well."

Julia's expression quickly turned fierce, reminding Elina briefly of René. "How little you knew your papa if you think that! Don't you see? He loved your *maman* too much to have her spend her life in poverty with him!"

"She wouldn't have cared!" Elina cried.

"Perhaps not. But he would have. *Maman* Vannier truly would have left him penniless if he had defied her. A hard woman, she was. In his place, what would you have done?"

"He could have . . . have divorced Mama," Elina said painfully, "and spared us all this torture."

"Your *maman* was pregnant by that time. Would you have had him abandon her with an unborn child? As I recall Philippe's telling me, she had only her elderly mother who was near dying. How would your *maman* have made a living for you?"

"He should have stayed with Mama then! He should have given you and his family pride up!" Elina cried, now beginning to feel trapped by Julia's practical appraisal of the situation. Against her will, Elina was being forced to see that her papa's actions couldn't easily be condemned.

Still, how could Julia be so understanding of him? Didn't the woman want to strike out, to curse her husband for betraying her?

A cold chill gripped Elina suddenly. Yes, Julia had wanted to strike out. And she had—by refusing to accept the other family's very existence.

As if Julia could sense the direction Elina's thoughts were taking, the woman said softly, "You see, I, too, wanted to hate him, to hurt him. But I always knew that would accomplish nothing. I've thought it over so many times. And the more I think the more I know your papa did what he thought was best at the time. Later I believe he regretted it. But by then . . ."

"By then it was too easy just to accept the state of affairs," Elina finished, a trace of anger still lacing her words.

"Yes. Too easy. And so hard. At the end, he told me he wished he'd had a chance to ask his children's forgiveness. He didn't want you to hate him, but he feared you might. You don't, do you?"

Elina sat very still, no longer certain what she felt. She couldn't accept what Papa had done. He'd hurt her family too badly for her to see it as anything but wrong. She couldn't even understand his motives completely, for she couldn't help but compare him to René, who'd given up the only life he'd ever known to make a new one when he'd witnessed injustice being done.

But the truth was, she couldn't stop loving Papa, either.

"I don't hate him," she murmured, knowing it was true.

Julia heaved a heavy sigh. "Good." Then she asked softly, "And me? Do you hate me?"

"I don't hate you, either. Though I do wonder why you finally chose to tell me the truth. And why tonight?"

Julia flushed guiltily. "When I saw you with René, when I realized that he had . . . had taken advantage of your situation, I couldn't continue the masquerade. That would have been more of a burden than my conscience could have borne."

"Did he—did he also know from the beginning who I was?" Elina asked with a sinking feeling in her stomach.

"No!" Julia hastened to assure her. "No, of course not! If he had known, he would have made me act more responsibly. René never knew any of this."

Elina felt immeasurably relieved to hear that René had truly been unaware of her real identity. At least he hadn't lied about that.

"And now," Julia continued, "I *will* do just as my brother would have urged me to do had he known the truth."

Slowly, Julia stood and walked to a chest of drawers. She opened one of the drawers and removed a sheaf of parchment paper. With a grave look on her face, she returned to where Elina sat and without a word handed her the papers.

"What's this?" Elina asked as she stared at the papers in her hand.

"Your papa's will."

Elina sat there in stunned amazement, at first only able to stare blindly at the carefully penned sentences. Then the tears began to fall again.

With a growing bewilderment, she studied the pages. What she found there stunned her. Not only had Papa acknowledged the existence of both families in his will, he'd also provided for both. He'd split his estate evenly. To each wife, he'd left a fourth and the remaining half he'd ordered divided between his three children.

So he *had* loved them! she thought with a sudden leap of joy. And he'd cared enough to provide for his family—for both families!

"You see? You needn't worry about working for me anymore," Julia murmured. "Once we combine all of your papa's holdings, including whatever monies he has left in Creve Coeur, I'm sure we'll find there's plenty to take care of all three of us."

"Yes," Elina said in wonder as another thought occurred to her. "Why, I could even return to Missouri if I wished. I could rebuild the farm or build another home or—"

Julia's face fell. "Yes, you could. If that's what you want."

Elina glanced at Julia in surprise. "That isn't what *you* would wish? I can't believe you'd want me to remain in New Orleans, where I would always bring back painful memories for you. And people would talk if I used my real name. After all the trouble Papa took to protect his family's pride and good name, I wouldn't wish to destroy it now."

"You have a right to proclaim the truth to the world if you wish. And once René knows the truth—"

"No!" Elina said with a force that surprised even herself. Then she added more gently as she saw Julia's expression of surprise, "He mustn't hear this from you."

"Why not? Elina, you must let me tell him! Any fool can see he loves you. And once he knows that you're not some gambler's sister but Philippe's daughter—"

"That's just it," Elina protested. "He *does* know." At Julia's look of surprise, she related everything that had happened from the time she and Alex had left Creve Coeur until she'd found herself a prisoner in René's house. She left out the details of her relationship with René, but she could tell from Julia's expression that the other woman had guessed the truth. "So you see, he does know who I am. He simply refuses to believe it," she finished, uncertain what reaction to expect.

But Julia merely sat up straighter, a new eagerness in her eyes. "Oh, it's far better than I thought! I'd begun to despair that René would ever find anyone who would love him for himself, someone whom he could love. And now, at last, he finds someone of whom even I could not disapprove!"

"Julia! I hit him over the head with a whiskey bottle! I lied about my name, I let my brother steal his money . . ." She added with more anguish, "I accused him of killing my brother, for heaven's sake! He doesn't love me. He never will, I fear. He merely wants to punish me for what I did."

"That wasn't a desire for revenge I saw in René's eyes tonight, I assure you. He risked his life for you by going into New Orleans. He would never have done so for a mere mistress. No, you may not see it, he may not acknowledge it, but my brother loves you. I know real love when I encounter it. The question is do you love him?"

Elina wanted to deny that she did, to put an end to Julia's insane matchmaking. But she found she couldn't. "Yes," she finally whispered.

Julia smiled broadly. "Then you must tell him the truth. I know he will marry you."

"You don't understand, Julia," Elina said with pleading in her voice. "If I tell him the truth, he'll feel obligated to marry me. He still fears I'd bring scandal to your name."

Julia frowned. "If I'm not concerned with scandal, why should he be?"

"He's more afraid for you than you'll ever know. Besides, even if I tell him the truth—that I'd never reveal our secret, that I have no desire to—he wouldn't believe it. He doesn't trust me. And I won't have him marry me solely to protect his family."

Julia looked perturbed. "But, Elina, you ask a great deal of him if you want him to marry you without any proof that you aren't a liar and a thief. You want him to trust you when you say you're not marrying him for *his* fortune."

"I believed him when he said he didn't kill Alex. I allowed him to—to take my innocence because I believed him. But now, I have to know that my faith in his feelings for me wasn't misplaced. I must know he loves me despite his misgivings, Julia, I must!"

Julia sighed and gathered Elina against her breast. "I understand, dear. I truly do. I'll hide the fact that I can confirm your identity, at least for a while. But in return you must stay with me here until René has had a chance to show he loves you."

"I can't impose on you forever," Elina protested.

"Don't worry. I'm certain you won't be here long." Julia's slow smile gave even Elina some hope. "Besides, this will allow you to observe New Orleans society. You might find it pleasurable here once you become acquainted with us all. You might want to stay anyway. I know what we'll do. We'll inform everyone that you're one of Philippe's distant cousins come to visit. Then you can use your real name. And tomorrow we'll go to the solicitor immediately and establish an account for you drawn on Philippe's estate."

"But what will you tell René?" Elina asked worriedly. "He'll wonder why you've sheltered me and why you're introducing me into polite society."

"Oh, yes. My thickheaded brother. Don't worry. I'll think of something that won't raise his suspicions." Then Julia grinned. "This may be amusing, no? He and Philippe always told me what to do, how to spend my money. They've always tried to protect me, even when I didn't wish to be protected. Well, now my brother will discover what it's like to have me making my own decisions. And since that decision will involve keeping the woman he wants from him, it will be quite a pleasure to see my self-sufficient brother squirm for a change. Oh, yes, this shall be very enjoyable. Very enjoyable indeed."

Francois stormed into the Pannetrat bachelor house and roused Etienne from his bed in a fury.

"What in God's name is wrong with you?" Etienne grumbled as he watched his friend pace the room.

"That bitch! You got rid of her all right. She went straight to *Maman's* to work as a servant!"

"So? At least she's out of René's hair."

"Not anymore. He caught me trying to 'persuade' her to leave."

Etienne sighed. "You see? I told you that you should let me attempt my more effective methods on her in the first place. Women like that only understand force."

"I offered her money, but she wouldn't take it."

"Of course not. Why should she take a paltry sum from you when she could bleed her lover for everything he'll give her as long as the infatuation lasts? No doubt she was already contemplating returning to his comfortable bed. Now you've merely pushed her into his arms. They're probably even now working out their differences. And if she tells him about my conversation with her—"

Francois drove his fist into a wall in pent-up frustration. "You didn't give her your name, did you?"

"Of course not. But one description and he'll figure it out."

"Damn! I must get her away from him somehow!"

"It's a bit late for that now. The only thing we can hope for is that he doesn't suspect the real reason you're trying to get rid of her. I think under the circumstances you'd best lay low for a few days."

Francois nodded. "Yes. I must see which way the wind blows before I make any further moves. In a week or so, if we hear nothing about the murder being pursued, then we can return and find some other way to wrest her from Uncle René's arms."

"We?"

"Do you wish to remain and endure Uncle René's questioning about why you lied to Elina?"

Etienne scowled. "No, certainly not. What about Alcide?"

"Leave him here. He knows nothing beyond what happened the night of the murder and I'd rather keep it that way. The less he knows, the less he can tell if he's asked. And the only way René will ask him about the murder is if he knows something already that will condemn us. No, I think we're safer leaving him here and implying that nothing is out of the ordinary. Besides, my uncle will become more suspicious if we all leave at once."

"True," Etienne said as he climbed out of bed and began to dress. "Well, let's at least go somewhere minimally enjoyable, shall we? I have this friend in Natchez . . ."

Francois relaxed as Etienne's voice droned on. Perhaps matters weren't as bad as he had thought. After all, Elina and his uncle might be so busy sorting out their differences that they wouldn't be able to give him much thought. In the meantime, he and Etienne wouldn't be here to answer any questions his uncle might have or face his anger. And in a few days, who knew? His uncle's righteous indignation could fade, lulled by the comfort of having his mistress back.

Then Francois could strike, and this time his wretched half sister would learn that it didn't pay to cross him.

Chapter Twenty-One

It is better to weep with wise men than to laugh with fools. —Spanish Proverb

René couldn't help the excitement that coursed through him as he rode toward his sister's plantation. *You're acting like a besotted fool!* he told himself, but he knew he really didn't care. He'd begun to accept that Elina haunted his days and nights, that he didn't want to be away from her for any reason. Now all he had to do was convince her of that.

He thought of the last time he'd seen her. Unwillingly, he remembered Francois's raising his hand to strike her. "If I ever discover where my snake of a nephew has run off to," he murmured aloud to himself, "I'll make him regret he ever touched her."

René's blood still raged at the thought that Francois had tried to beat Elina. The man had gone too far this time. And for what reason? None that René could see. Francois had never been so concerned for Julia's welfare before. It would have been more in character for Francois to reveal to

337

René where Elina had been hiding than to try to drive Elina away. And Francois's lame excuse that he'd been trying to protect his uncle and mother just didn't ring true.

Yet what other reasons could Francois have had? Had hatred for his uncle made Francois strike Elina? Or did the man have some other reason entirely for wanting her out of his way?

René then remembered the strange way his nephew had behaved when he'd seen Elina the first time. The man had deliberately provoked her anger, deliberately made her suspect René had killed her brother. Why had Francois done that? It was as if he feared her, as if she could somehow hurt him.

René's blood went suddenly cold. Could Elina have told Francois the same story she'd told René? If so, she might have convinced Francois that she would inherit some of Philippe's wealth. That would have made Francois determined to ensure she never told her story to anyone. Elina might even have told Julia her story, which would explain why Julia was protecting her for fear of Elina's spreading her tale.

But that would make Elina more devious than René had previously thought her capable of. Somehow, René just couldn't believe she was that manipulative. Her story had been concocted in the heat of vengeful anger. But he could swear she no longer desired revenge or even believed he'd committed the murder. Of course, she had every reason to still suspect him. The real murderer had never been found and she might think. . . .

That was it! he thought, leaning forward in the saddle eagerly. The real murderer! What if the real murderer weren't some stranger, but someone with a tendency to lose his temper, someone who often killed in anger. Someone . . . like Francois.

René's eyes narrowed. What a possibility! Yet it explained Francois's odd behavior. René forced himself to remember every encounter he'd had with his nephew since the murder.

Francois had provided an alibi, but one supported only by his friends, men who lied as easily as himself. With growing anger, René remembered how Francois had boasted of his uncle's having fought a duel, even when René had expressly told him not to speak of it.

"Damn him!" René shouted aloud, spurring his horse on. Now it all made sense. Alex had tried his tricks on Francois and lost. Francois had shot in anger. And as usual he'd been too cowardly to stay and face the consequences of his actions.

Then he had used to his advantage the circumstances that painted René as the killer. The scheming bastard had certainly done his utmost to keep people from suspecting the real murderer!

It was all a theory, René well knew. Any judge would immediately question the patness of his solution. It *was* an incredible coincidence that Francois should meet up with Alex the same day René had. But René felt certain his hypothesis was rooted in reality. Now he needed proof. Unfortunately, Francois had conveniently left town after striking Elina. Even his servants didn't know where he'd gone.

But there were other ways of finding the necessary proof than questioning Francois. René knew exactly how to get what he needed. He'd have to visit Etienne and Alcide, probably Alcide. Alcide was the weak one. He'd break down and tell all at the merest threat from René.

René reined in at his sister's stables, more eager than ever to see Elina. Now he could at last present her with something she would value—the name of her brother's alleged killer. With her doubts about René's role in her brother's death removed, René might have a chance.

Then another thought sobered him. If he told her, she was liable to do anything in her quest for revenge. No, he couldn't tell her and risk her unpredictable reaction to the truth. If she tangled with Francois again, before René had any facts to support his supposition, Francois might dispense with her as he'd dispensed with her brother.

Nor could he make such accusations against his own nephew without solid proof. After all, René had Julia to think of. If René were able to prove that Francois had killed Elina's brother in cold blood, Julia would have to be told. Then . . . What? Would Elina demand complete satisfaction? Frustration ripped through René at the realization that his nephew had forced him into an untenable position.

For the time being, he must keep his suspicions secret and search for Francois. At least he could find his nephew and make certain the man didn't attempt to harm Elina anymore. But before René set off in search of his nephew, he would see what Elina could tell him to confirm his conjectures. And when he finally had all his evidence, somehow he would see to it that Francois got his just deserts!

He dismounted, taking with him the rolled-up canvas he'd had strapped to his saddle, and strode toward the house. The slave who greeted him told him Julia was in the kitchen.

Julia whirled as he entered, but she didn't seem entirely surprised to see him.

"Good morning," he said, irritated to find that no trace of apprehension marred her face. He'd hoped to intimidate her a bit into letting him see Elina, but clearly she felt not the least intimidated.

"I suppose you wish to see Elina," she replied matter-of-factly.

"I could be coming to see you."

"You could be, but you're not, are you?"

At any other time he might have smiled at her perception, but at the moment he was more concerned with finding Elina. "No," he replied, his face serious. "I've come for Elina."

"And if she doesn't wish to see you?"

He resisted the urge to swear. "I never thought to find my sister keeping my mistress from me. To be honest, I never thought to find my sister anywhere near a mistress of mine."

"She's not your mistress," Julia said with a certain petulance.

"Only because she won't let me provide for her. In every other sense of the word she is."

Julia flushed as his meaning struck her, but her embarrassment didn't seem to stop the anger that flared in her eyes. "I can't believe my own brother could be so crude and unfeeling! Can't you see she's a gentle girl with delicate sensibilities? If you treat her like some—some *demimondaine* accustomed to such ways, she'll break. Perhaps not now but someday. Then what will you have?"

Julia's words made him far more uncomfortable than he dared admit. "You act as if she's an innocent," he reacted by saying, "as if she's not the liar I know her to be! You know what she's done yet you defend her. Why, Julia?"

For a moment he could have sworn he saw guilt flash across her face, but it was gone so fast he knew he must have imagined it. She opened her mouth to say something, then closed it.

When she spoke again, he felt sure she did not say what she'd intended. "Unlike you," she said with a certain dignity, "I accept that people sometimes act in ways distasteful to them in order to survive. I'm aware of the circumstances surrounding her and her brother's encounter with you. To be truthful, dear brother, I feel sorry for her. I know how single-minded you can be when you've been wronged. I can't say I blame her for wishing to protect her brother from you."

René's temper flared at that. "*Mon Dieu*, Julia, I can't believe you'd defend her! I've known you to take in strays, but never willingly to aid a known liar and cheat!"

"You keep saying she's a liar! But I've never seen evidence of that!"

"You have no idea what she's capable of," René ground out, but the words were like ashes in his mouth. Even he was having trouble painting Elina as the black schemer he still feared she might be.

"Perhaps you're right," she retorted. "But I do know that when she came here, she was tired and scared. She didn't even want to stay. I forced her to. And since she's been here, I've found myself enjoying her company a great deal. I've been so very lonely, René. You don't realize how hard it's been with Philippe dead. Francois is never here, and you're so often busy restoring the plantation—"

At his scowl, she placed her hand on his arm. "I understand," she whispered, "really, I do." She sighed. "But sometimes I need someone to talk to. She's been like . . . like a sister or even a daughter to me. She's eased my pain. I don't care what she did in the past. In the present she's a very sweet, dear young woman, and I refuse to see her destroyed simply because you can't control your desires!"

His body went rigid at his sister's uncharacteristic bluntness. She dropped her hand from his arm.

"What are your plans for her?" he asked in clipped tones. "How long do you intend to support your new companion?"

He instantly regretted the harsh words as he saw that they had hurt her.

She looked down at her hands. "Elina wishes to leave New Orleans as soon as she . . . ah . . . earns enough money to do so."

"That's absurd!" he exploded. "She can't leave! I won't allow it! The only place Elina is going is to Cour de Cyprès!"

Julia continued to avoid his eyes. "She has the right to go where she wishes," she ventured.

"And I have the right to keep her from leaving! Where is she? She must be made to see what nonsense she's planning! Where is she, Julia?"

Julia lifted her eyes to his face, her expression bland. "In the arbor. She's sketching. Did you know she was an artist—"

He was gone before she could finish her sentence.

He found Elina perched on the edge of a stone bench in the secluded arbor nearest the river. She had her back to him and was staring intently into space, her fingers resting on the sketchpad. As he saw how quiet and still she sat, his heart twisted with an intense desire to sweep her into his arms. He controlled the impulse only with an effort.

"*Bonjour*, sweet eyes," he said softly as he moved up to stand beside her.

She glanced at him with surprise, and for a moment he thought he glimpsed pleasure in her expression. Then it was gone, and the face she presented to him was unsmiling.

"I brought you something," he said. He unrolled the canvas he'd had tucked under his arm and laid it across her lap.

She looked down at the painted canvas. For several long moments she stared silently at the unfinished portrait.

"I was hoping you'd finish it for me," he told her. "You left before it was completed."

She shuddered at the implied accusation in his words. "I didn't want to leave," she murmured, her fingers tracing the line of his jaw on the painting. "But I had to."

It took all his endurance not to take her in his arms and kiss all her objections away. But his limited control didn't keep him from toying with a stray lock of her hair that had escaped the loose chignon at her neck. He noted with pleasure that the touch of his fingers brushing her skin made her blush.

"Why did you leave?" he asked. "When you left my bed the first time, I would have sworn you were content. But when you returned from your walk, you seemed entirely discontented, even angry. Why?"

His fingers began to stroke her neck, and she drew in her breath sharply. As if to take her mind off his caress, she spoke quickly. "When I was walking, I met one of your friends who was skulking around Cour de Cyprès. I suppose he was looking for you. I never asked. He said he

wanted to see the mistress you'd boasted of. He told me . . .
things that made me feel so . . . dirty. I couldn't stand it."
She craned her neck up to look at him, her green eyes dark
and soulful. "Don't you understand? I can't be that kind of
woman for you, René! I just can't!"

He stared down at her, barely controlling his fury at the
unknown man who had told her such lies. "I don't want
you to be that kind of woman. I've never thought of you
as such. And I assure you the man couldn't have been a
friend of mine, for I've told no one about you."

Her eyes searched his face. It wrenched his insides to
see the uncertainty written in her expression. But at last
her face cleared, and she seemed satisfied that he told
the truth.

"Who was he if he wasn't your friend?" she asked.

"I don't know. What did he look like?"

Haltingly, she described a man who was certainly Creole, but unlike many Creoles, was blond. René's fingers
closed unconsciously on her shoulder as he realized she
was describing Francois's friend, Etienne Pannetrat.

Of course! he thought in anger. He should have seen
Francois's devious hand in it all. Francois wouldn't want
Elina to prod René into finding out who her brother's killer
really was. And what better way to dispose of Elina and her
questions than to feed lies to her?

"Who was he?" she repeated.

"A friend of Francois's," he said mechanically, his mind
already racing ahead to what he was going to do when he
got his hands on Etienne.

"Francois's?" she said in confusion. "Then Francois . . .
Why? Why is he so determined to drive me away? I don't
understand his hatred. Did you know he offered me money
to leave New Orleans?"

"When?"

"Two nights ago, right before you saw us. I refused."

"Which must have been why he struck you," René bit
out.

"Yes. He said he didn't want me in the same house as Jul—...as *Madame* Vannier." She sat very still for a moment. Then she added, a note of despair in her voice, "Is that why *you* don't want me staying here? Because you don't want a woman 'of my kind' to be a companion for your sister?"

"No!" he said harshly, his speculations about Francois fleeing his mind. "No," he repeated, circling around in front of her and pulling her to her feet. The portrait slid to the ground between them. Both ignored it.

"You don't belong here," he murmured, gripping her hands tightly. "You belong with me."

She lifted her chin with pride. "You mean to say I'm suitable to be your mistress, but not your sister's companion."

"*Mon Dieu*, Elina, you know that's not what I mean! I want you to be *my* companion, not my sister's. I want to be near you every day, for hours at a time. It's not enough to catch glimpses of you at my sister's house." His voice deepened. "I want to watch you shed your clothes every night as you transform into that passionate, sensuous creature I made love to a week ago."

Her eyes went wide as a soft blush stained her cheeks. He pulled her to him, kicking the canvas from between them. "I want to own you," he told her earnestly. "And failing that, I want you to own me. I don't even care which it is, as long as you stay with me."

He pressed a kiss to the corner of her mouth, then covered her lips with his own. He could feel her hesitation in the quivering of her mouth. Then she swayed unsteadily against him, and he lost all control. He crushed her to him, his loins growing heavy as she responded to his unbridled embrace.

The feel of her fingers winding in his hair drove him to insanity. He kissed her with passionate eagerness, his hands roving over her, trying to mold her body to his. When his lips left her mouth, she was gasping and her eyes desire-glazed. His hand covered her breast as he lowered his mouth to her neck. He nibbled at the sweet ivory skin, and

Deborah Martin

she made a noise in the back of her throat that heightened his desire to a fever pitch.

If he wasn't careful, he would take her right there on the ground. Reluctantly, he tore his mouth away from her. "Come with me," he whispered. "Come home with me now."

Her lips formed the word no, but she didn't pull away. He pressed his advantage, pulling up her skirts and undoing the one ribbon that held up her drawers. His hand pushed the silken material down over her hips, then slid to caress the sensitive skin between her thighs.

"No," she whispered, her eyes widening as he took bolder liberties.

"Let me touch you, *chèrie*. I want to so very badly," he murmured, slipping one finger into her moist warmth. When she sucked in her breath and arched into his hand, he buried his face in her hair. The soft scent of lilac clinging to her auburn tresses undid him.

With a groan, he pressed her backward until she lost her balance. She clutched at him and he lowered her to the ground.

"René!" she protested, but he smothered her protest with his lips as his hand, still under her skirts, began to tease her, gently at first, then with increasing roughness until she was rocking against his hand in a steady rhythm. Her head tossed against the summer grass, and he showered her neck with rough kisses until she began to clutch his shoulders with a feverish strength that only intensified his desire.

Then he slid down the length of her body until his mouth was at the place between her legs. At the first feathery touch of his lips on the sensitive skin, her eyes flew open and she tried to push him away.

"Relax, *mon amour*, don't be ashamed," he whispered, scarcely conscious of the words he spoke. "I must taste you, or I'll go insane. You yielded to me before. Yield to me again."

She shook her head no, but when he persisted in what he was doing, the expression in her eyes grew wild. Her first soft moan led to others as he continued tormenting her with his mouth. At last he could take no more.

"*Mon Dieu*, sweet eyes, I can't wait any longer," he murmured. In moments, he'd shed his trousers and positioned himself between her thighs.

"I have missed you so much," he whispered as she gazed up at him, her face suffused with the warmth of the pleasure he'd been giving her. "Let me show you just how much."

And with that, he buried himself in her tight sweetness. As she strained up against him mindlessly, he began to move in her.

"*Mon amour, mon amour . . .*" he muttered over and over.

And all at once they were no longer two enemies, two strangers. Nature seemed to conspire to make them one, to whisper that they belonged in this naked joining amid the pagan profusion of the flowered arbor. Together they melded into one, and he shuddered as he reached his fulfillment, his pleasure increasing to dizzying heights as he felt her reach hers.

In the aftermath, he hovered over her, afraid of giving her all his weight, but she clutched him so tightly he couldn't keep from resting on her. When her breathing had slowed, he slid off to lay beside her on the grass. His hand stroked her flushed cheek, and she turned toward the caress.

"You see?" he said as he studied the expression of rapt fulfillment on her face. "You want this as much as I do."

She blushed profusely, although she didn't deny his words. "Is it . . ." she paused, dropping her eyes from his in embarrassment. "Is it always so . . . so . . ."

"Glorious?"

She gulped and nodded, the color rising even higher in her cheeks.

He smiled, his thumb rubbing her lower lip idly. "No. Not for everyone. But for us, *ma petite*, I know it will always be so. We have something special between us."

She gazed up at him in earnest attention, her expression suddenly painfully serious. "How special?" she whispered.

He pressed her back against the grass, his eyes darkening with passion. "Come with me, and you'll discover it yourself. I'll make you happy. Today should prove to you that I can. You won't regret becoming my mistress, I swear."

His words made her wince, as if he'd inflicted some bodily pain. Blindly, he went on, only half realizing he'd blundered. "And whatever you want, you can have. I don't care. I'll give you anything your sweet heart desires."

"Not anything," she whispered, her face a mask of despair. "There is one thing you refuse to give me."

Mechanically, she pulled down her skirts and twisted away from him. He reached for her, but she thrust his hand away and stumbled to her feet.

Her abrupt dismissal of him infuriated him.

"And what is that one thing?" he asked as he rose to his feet in a surge of anger and jerked on his pants. He was certain he knew exactly what she wanted. "My inheritance? Or is it my name you covet? You think I should make you my wife, don't you?"

He could tell from the sudden paleness on her face that his biting tone had hurt her more than his words had.

"No, no, of course not," she choked out. "I haven't forgotten my place. I'm not suitable to be the wife of a rich Creole planter. After all, you must ensure your place in New Orleans society by marrying someone of your own class!"

Her oblique reference to his earlier scorn for New Orleans Creole society stung him. "And, of course, your motives for wishing to marry me are entirely pure. It would have nothing to do with your present state as a penniless woman!"

Instantly, he cursed his quick tongue. He hadn't meant to be so blunt. He wasn't even certain he believed what he'd said.

But clearly she thought he did. Her face went ashen. "I wouldn't marry you now if you begged me to," she said, her tone deadly quiet. "Why would I wish to be the wife of a man who thinks me a liar and a cheat and the worst sort of schemer? Somehow I'd managed to forget what your true opinion of me is. I shall not make that mistake again."

When she whirled away, he caught her arm. "You ask too much of me, Elina! You ask me to destroy my family in order to marry someone whom I fear I can't even trust!"

She surprised him by laughing, but the laugh was low and bitter and the face she turned to him mocking. "I don't ask anything of you except that you leave me alone. As for your sister, she doesn't enter into your feelings in this matter, as you well know. In your heart, you know I could never hurt your sister. No, it's your pride that's at stake here, your damnable pride! It won't allow you to act on whatever true feelings you have."

Then she looked at him, an expression of anguish growing on her face. "Then again," she whispered, "perhaps I'm merely telling myself lies. Perhaps you really have no feelings at all. Perhaps Francois's friend was right and you've merely been entertaining yourself with me. Is that it? Are you angry only because your toy has been taken away?"

She stared at him in open defiance, ignoring the increasing pressure he was unconsciously placing on her arm.

"You know better than that. And I could ask the same thing of you. After all, you refuse to be my mistress, but you wish to marry me. What am I supposed to think that says about your feelings for me?"

She flinched, but didn't turn away. "It says I love you too much to endure being your plaything. And it appears I'm to be cursed forever for loving a heartless man!"

With that she seemed to lose control. A sob escaped her lips as she flung herself away from him and fled toward the house, leaving him to stare after her in stunned amazement.

"Damn you for that, sweet eyes!" he cried aloud. "Damn you!"

Chapter Twenty-Two

Everyone believes in friends until he has had occasion to try them.—Creole Proverb

She loved him, René thought in shock as he watched her go. He'd wanted her love for so long, though he'd never admitted it before. But as much as he wished to call her back, he couldn't. Too many uncertainties stood between them, too many lies and half-truths.

Or were they lies? Could Elina have always been telling the truth? He murmured a low curse. He couldn't stand not knowing if she were telling the truth. Was she really Philippe's daughter or just a clever actress?

The more he delved into the matter of her brother's death, the more he began to doubt his earlier assessment of her. Too many questions were still not answered to his satisfaction. If Francois had killed Alex for cheating, for example, he wouldn't have left the scene. Why should he? No man would have arrested him under such circumstances. And the coincidence of Francois's having met up with Alex the same day René had still bothered René, making him wonder if there *were* another explanation.

What if Alex really had been Philippe's son? And what if he'd somehow discovered who Francois was? It was conceivable that Alex might have gone to confront his father's son, to see for himself the evidence of his father's betrayal.

If Alex had actually told Francois the truth, Francois certainly wouldn't have stood for it. Francois would never have allowed his father's fortune to be split. The man was too greedy to give up any part of his inheritance.

If matters had fallen as René thought they might have, then Elina's story made much more sense. Of course, that also meant that Francois possibly had killed his own half brother in cold blood.

That was the key question. Had Francois killed to ensure Alex's silence? And if he had, what did he intend for Elina? René had to find his nephew. That was paramount.

René strode for the stables, his head spinning with questions. But he didn't ride for Cour de Cyprès. With Elina's words ringing in his ears, he rode hard toward the Pannetrat family's bachelor house. It was time he heard the truth about Alexandre Wallace's death, and he'd only get it from Etienne and Alcide.

Knowing if Elina had been lying to him about her identity had become more necessary than ever, now that she'd made her declaration. He no longer wanted to believe she had lied, for if she had, it made everything else false. And how could he believe her false? Not when he loved her so much.

And he did love her. He knew it now. He'd known it from the moment she'd fled, but he'd refused to admit it to himself. In the past week, however, it had become quite clear to him that he couldn't live without her, and pretending he could wouldn't change that. But he couldn't marry her not knowing who and what she was. He mustn't. He had Julia and her reputation to consider. His sister needed her station in society now that she had no husband to protect her. And if Elina spoke the truth, if Elina truly was Philippe's daughter, René might have to ruin that for Julia. René would have to ensure that Elina's rightful place was given to her. No, he couldn't take such a chance without being certain.

And yet . . . The images that the thought of marrying Elina brought to mind—of him dancing with her at one of the many society balls, of her painting a portrait with her hands as bedaubed with paint as the canvas, of her with her belly heavy with his child—those images were beginning to make him weaken, to make him believe it no longer mattered.

How ironic that she'd achieved her revenge at last, he thought. Finally, she'd found the one vulnerable place in his defenses where she could slip the knife in. His heart.

He swore as he drew up in front of the Pannetrat bachelor house. He must know the truth. He had to know!

He pounded on the door, oblivious to the noise he was making.

"I wish to speak with Etienne or Alcide," he told the slave who opened the door, a man named Jean whom René knew because Jean's sister worked for him.

Jean regarded René with an arrogance slightly tempered by wariness.

"Master Etienne is away on business."

"And Alcide?"

Jean looked uncomfortable for a moment. "He is ill."

"Unless he's near death, I wish to see him," René demanded.

The black man stiffened, his eyes not meeting René's. René didn't move. Since Jean's sister worked for René, Jean was unlikely to antagonize René if he could avoid doing so.

"Sir, you must return later," Jean murmured, twisting his hands nervously. "I cannot show you in. The master is in bed ill and left instructions that he is not to be disturbed. I must not disobey his command."

"Fine," René said, shouldering his way past the slave. "I shall show myself in."

As René strode down the hall and bounded up the stairs, Jean followed, begging René not to go any further. But Jean didn't touch René. It was good he didn't, for René refused to stop, driven on by his desire to learn the truth.

It took him only moments to find the bedrooms. He dismissed the door at the back, for it would be the one that led to the master bedroom, the bedroom Etienne would occupy. He stopped instead outside the door beside it. When he heard moans coming from behind the door, he didn't stop to think, but opened the door and charged in.

What he saw stopped him cold.

The girl whose body was entangled with Alcide's buried her face in Alcide's shoulder, but not before René recognized her.

"Maria," René said none too gently, "I think you'd best take your clothes and go. I wish to speak with your brother."

Alcide's face turned several shades of red as he sat up in bed and drew the covers over himself and his sister.

"Get out!" he shouted. "You have no business here! Jean! What are you doing, ignoring my orders? Show Bonnange out!"

Jean, who stood cringing behind René, began to slink away.

"Jean!" Alcide shouted.

René's low laugh with its hint of mockery drew Alcide's attention.

"Go," Alcide murmured to his sister. "Get your clothes and go."

For a moment, Maria hesitated, looking from her brother to René. But when Alcide pushed her away, she drew the sheet up around her and fled.

"What do you want?" Alcide asked as he left the bed and fumbled around for his own clothes. He'd clearly given up on throwing René out, once he realized he couldn't force his slave to do it.

"I'm looking for my nephew."

"Francois? I don't know where he is."

"And your brother?"

Alcide shrugged. "Who knows? The two of them often leave town together. What business is it of yours?"

Alcide's nonchalance infuriated René.

"Francois murdered someone, perhaps with you and your brother's help," he said bluntly, deriving a cold pleasure from the way Alcide's head snapped up. "I thought you might tell me just why he killed Alexandre Wallace."

Alcide paled considerably before he regained control of himself. "This . . . this Wallace," he asked. "I don't know anything about Francois's killing someone named Wallace. Who is he?"

René had trouble controlling his temper as he stared at the obstinate man who stood before him. "I think I should remind you, Alcide, that your sister's betrothed and I have been friends for some time. And he'd be none too happy to hear that his beloved Maria's brother had prepared the way for him, if you take my meaning?"

That simple statement was enough to throw Alcide into confusion. "He wouldn't b—believe you," Alcide stammered.

"Yes, he would. He's never known me to lie."

Alcide sat down on the bed slowly. "You can't do that to Maria!" he said, his voice now pleading. "She's got to marry him, she's got to! We need his fortune!"

René felt sorry for Maria's poor betrothed. "What do you know about Wallace's murder?" René pressed on coldly.

Alcide's face filled with fear. "My brother will k—kill me if I tell you anything."

"And Maria's betrothed will kill you if you don't."

Alcide stamped his foot in exasperation. "Damn it, René! He was just a miserable card cheat! Why do you care what happened to him?"

"I was blamed for it—or didn't you know?"

Alcide jumped up and began to pace the room. "No one arrested you. No one would dare."

"No one would have arrested Francois either under the circumstances. Unless, of course, he *didn't* catch Alexandre cheating. Did Francois have some other reason for killing Wallace? Could it be the three of you conspired to kill the poor man just for sport?"

René was simply throwing out possibilities to provoke Alcide into telling the truth, but his words had the intended effect.

"It wasn't like that at all!" Alcide blurted out. "Etienne and I had nothing to do with it! Nothing!"

"Are you saying Francois killed the man himself?"

"I—I . . . I cannot say more," Alcide murmured, turning his back on René.

René grabbed Alcide's shoulder and whirled him around. "You *will* tell me what happened, Alcide, if I have to beat it out of you!"

Alcide's eyes widened in terror. "Etienne and I weren't even in the room! It isn't our fault!"

René's hand dropped, and he gazed at Alcide in surprise. "Why weren't you in the room? If you were all playing cards and Francois caught Alexandre cheating . . ."

Alcide stood motionless and silent as René's eyes narrowed.

Unless . . . unless this had nothing to do with card playing. Unless Elina hadn't lied when she had said Alexandre hadn't gone out that night intending to gamble. René clasped Alcide's shoulders and pushed him against the wall. "Were you playing cards with him that night?" he demanded. "Were you?"

"N–no."

"What happened? Tell me all of it!"

"L–let me down," Alcide croaked out. "I'll tell you what happened."

René released Alcide who collapsed against the wall. "It

355

wasn't anyone's fault," he whispered. "It wasn't. This man Wallace said he wished to talk to Francois alone."

"Why?"

"He never said."

René's brow clouded. What could Wallace possibly have wanted to discuss with Francois except their father? That was the only answer that made sense. "What happened then?" he persisted.

"We left them together and Wallace locked the door. When we returned, there was a shot and then a few moments passed. Then there was another. After that, Francois opened the door to let us in. Wallace lay there dead."

René felt his blood run cold.

"What reason did Francois give for killing Wallace?"

"He said the man fancied he had some grievance against Francois's papa. Francois said Wallace attacked him, forcing him to protect himself. I know that's true! The man had a gun, and it was there in plain view. He must have shot at Francois, forcing Francois to fire back."

"Had Wallace's gun been fired when you entered the room?" René asked.

Alcide thought for a moment. "I don't know," he answered. "We didn't question Francois. We were too concerned with trying to decide what to do with the body."

But René didn't need an answer. The gun found on Wallace had been René's and had still contained its bullets. So unless René was mistaken, Francois had shot a man twice in self-defense without the man's firing a single shot.

Any doubts René might have had before about what had happened that night vanished now. While Elina had waited in her hotel room for her brother to return with Philippe, Francois Vannier had killed his own half brother.

Elina daubed idly at the portrait in front of her, still not quite satisfied with the way it looked.

"What do you plan to do with it when you're finished?" Julia asked from behind her.

Elina jumped, then released a long ragged sigh. "I'm sorry. I didn't see you enter."

"What will you do with it?" Julia repeated, moving to look over Elina's shoulder.

Elina stared at the canvas, an urgent longing twisting her insides. "I don't know."

"You never really explained to me how you came to be painting René's portrait, dear, or why he brought you the unfinished portion."

Elina gave Julia a bittersweet half-smile. "Who knows why he brought it? To torment me, I suppose. The portrait was part of a bargain we made. He'd let me use the materials for my own uses if I'd also paint his portrait. He wanted it to be for you."

"Really?" Julia said with a hint of sarcasm in her tone.

Elina's rueful smile brought a smile to Julia's face. "No, I think it was just his way of keeping me in his presence."

"My brother's a fool. The best way to keep you is to marry you. He should know that!"

The smile left Elina's face. "He won't ever marry me, Julia. It's useless to think so. And I'm not even certain I want him to. He'd be an infuriating husband, the sort of man who always wants everything to go his way."

"I see. And other men are not like that, are they? Your father, for example."

Elina frowned. "René is different from Papa. I don't believe he would ever have done as Papa did."

"No, of course not. I loved your papa with all my heart, but he was sometimes afraid to resist the dictates of society. At home he often railed against the narrowness of his fellow Creoles. But in public . . ."

"Yes, I can guess. He was the same with us."

Julia put her arm around Elina's shoulder sympathetically. "Give it time, dear. All of it. The hurt subsides eventually, though it never disappears. In the meantime, don't paint all men with the same brush. René is stubborn and proud, but he loves you. I know it."

"He . . . he hasn't come here since that day a week ago," Elina choked out as a sob seemed to stick in her throat.

Julia's face turned grim. "I know. But he hasn't been at home, either. I went to Cour de Cyprès one day and asked for him. Louis told me he was away."

Elina bit her lip hard, trying to keep the tears from flowing.

"Listen," Julia murmured, clearly aware of Elina's distress. "Brooding over that painting won't raise your spirits, but I have the perfect thing for doing so."

"Wh–what?" Elina asked shakily.

"The Rivieres are having a small supper tomorrow evening. There will be dancing, and those men who are *bon famille* will most assuredly be there. I was invited long ago, and I'm certain they'd be delighted if I bring my house guest—Philippe's long lost cousin."

Inwardly, Elina groaned. She didn't feel like dancing. She wasn't certain she'd ever feel like it again. She wanted to be as far away from men as possible. She wanted to sort out her thoughts alone, to decide what to do with her life. "I don't know how wise that would be—"

"Nonsense! It's just what you need. You need to be reminded of what a lovely woman you are and of where you belong. It will be good for you to forget your past for a while. You can start afresh."

"But aren't you afraid—"

"That you'll start the tongues to wagging? No. I trust you to be discreet. If you wouldn't even tell me the truth when you first met me, then you're certainly not going to tell anyone else, are you?"

"You know I wouldn't!" Elina cried.

"You see? I have nothing to worry about."

Elina tried another tack. "What about a gown? There's no time before tomorrow to have one made."

Julia grinned mischievously. "Ah, but my brother already had gowns made for you, didn't he?"

"Julia!"

"I told you I went over to his house. While I was there, Louis gave me the dresses René had ordered made for you. At least three of them would serve well as ball gowns."

Elina grimaced. "I won't wear them."

"Why not? If it makes you feel better, you can pay the dressmaker yourself and leave René to guess who paid those bills. You'd enjoy thwarting him that way, wouldn't you?"

Elina smiled slowly in spite of herself. She *would* enjoy taking that away from him. It would make her feel less like his mistress and more like her own woman. And she had to admit that the thought of wearing one of those gorgeous dresses and for once looking like the woman she was brought up to be was tempting.

But that didn't mean she wanted to go to the ball.

Blindly, she searched for another excuse and found one, blurting it out without thinking. "What about Francois? What will he say when I arrive at the ball as Philippe's cousin? He doesn't know the truth yet, does he?"

Julia's face sobered, and she turned away to stare back at the house that rose magnificent and white behind them. "No," she finally said. "I haven't told him. He hasn't been here to tell. He, too, has disappeared. He often goes on trips without telling me, but this time . . ." she paused and sighed. "I don't know when he'll return. But I won't lie to you, Elina. When I do tell him, he won't be happy to hear he must divide his inheritance with someone else."

Elina could easily guess how Francois would feel when he heard the truth. How could he accept as his sister the woman he'd gone to such lengths to drive away? He hated her. Still, even now it struck her as strange that he should hate her so much, not knowing who she was.

And his reasons! He'd said he cared for his mother and his uncle. Yet the one time she'd met him he'd been tormenting his uncle. And he never seemed to show any concern for his mother. So why did he detest Elina for supposedly "ruining" Julia's and René's lives?

"Sometimes I wonder," Julia broke into Elina's thoughts. "Sometimes I think perhaps he has already guessed the truth about who you are. Why else would he wish you to leave? Is it possible René told him of your claims?"

Elina shook her head no. Francois *had* acted like he knew, but he'd never intimated that he did when he was around René. She still remembered the first time he'd met her—the odd way he'd looked at her, the oblique questions. She hadn't been able to shake the feeling that he knew more than he said.

But how could he have known if René hadn't told him? Not unless. . . .

Unless he'd met her brother. Her heart began to hammer. What if Alex had heard about Francois the night he'd gone searching for their father? What if he'd confronted him and. . . Her blood ran cold. What if the two brothers had met, both intent upon gaining their father's money, both with good reason to hate each other, and both armed with deadly weapons?

"What's wrong?" Julia asked, her eyes intently studying Elina's face.

"Nothing," Elina managed to say. But everything was wrong. She wanted to deny the possibility that Francois had killed Alexandre. She couldn't believe her own flesh and blood would do something so wicked, knowing what he was doing. How could it be?

"You're not getting ill, are you?" Julia persisted.

Elina forced a smile to her face. "No, of course not. I—I was just thinking about how hard it will be for Francois to accept my presence." And how hard it would now be for her to accept his, if indeed he were guilty.

Another thought struck her. If Francois had murdered Alex, René couldn't have been guilty. She didn't know whether to feel relieved that René had been firmly exonerated in her mind, or destroyed to realize that Alexandre might have been killed by his own brother.

Of course, she couldn't know what really happened. Given Alex's temper, who knew to what extent he'd provoked Francois? And had Francois and Alex fought? Her head ached with the effort of thinking through all the possibilities in an attempt to find some way of believing both brothers innocent of wrongdoing.

Still, she reminded herself, if Francois were guilty, he'd done something far worse than just committing the crime by trying to cover up his part in what had happened that night. What's more he'd even gone so far as to implicate his own uncle. She could never forgive him for that. Never!

"Don't worry about it," Julia said, sliding an arm around Elina and making her wonder if Julia had any idea that her son had committed such a crime. Julia's next words confirmed that she did not. "Francois won't like it at first, but he'll accept it eventually. I know he will. He'll probably be glad to have a sister."

Elina choked back the hysterical laugh that rose to her lips. Far from being glad, Francois might even be capable of wanting her dead as well. Until now, he'd merely tried to frighten her away. But what if he did more than that?

Then again, she told herself, once he realized that Julia and the solicitor knew the truth, he'd have to admit defeat. With everyone aware of her true identity, he'd have no choice. That gave her some solace, but not enough to make her feel safe.

"You're brooding again, dear," Julia stated flatly. "It isn't good for you to dwell on this so. My brother is all kinds of a fool, but he'll come around. In the meantime, you simply must make an effort to show him that you belong in his world, that you would make him a suitable wife."

Still reeling from her realization, Elina wasn't in the mood to temper her reply. "René's probably not even planning to be there. Besides, I don't intend to parade myself in front of him so he can choose me to be his wife the same way he chooses his horses by assessing their walk and the fine qualities of their teeth."

Julia's face went stony, and Elina instantly regretted her words. "Oh, Julia, I'm sorry! But your brother has had his chance, and he's clearly not going to take it!"

Julia softened a bit. "Then we must find you someone else, mustn't we? You need someone to take care of you— a husband. If you don't want to attend for René's sake, at least attend for mine. I'm tired of staying at home and dwelling on past mistakes. I may be in mourning, but I don't have to lock myself up forever. Philippe wouldn't want me to. I'll wear my mourning ball gown and watch you enjoy yourself."

Elina's face clouded. "I wanted to wear mourning," she whispered, "but I never got the chance."

Julia reached out and stroked her hair. "That's as it should be. You're young and pretty. You've mourned more than enough in your heart. Now's the time to put it behind you. Besides, if you attend as Philippe's cousin, people will wonder why you're in mourning. No, you should go just as you are. For my sake, do go. I feel so responsible for the position in which you find yourself now. If I had only—"

"No! Don't blame yourself." Elina sighed. Julia's plea seemed so earnest, although Elina suspected that the guilt in her voice in this case had been calculated to persuade Elina. "I'll go," she agreed. "But I won't promise to enjoy it."

Julia's answer to that was a secret little smile.

Chapter Twenty-Three

Try to reason about love, and you will lose your reason.
—French Proverb

Elina gazed around the crowded ballroom lit with hundreds of candles. Despite her doubts about coming, she found herself looking forward to the evening. She couldn't help but be entranced by the gracious women and handsome men who flitted in and out of the elegantly appointed room.

What was more, she'd been stunned to discover that they accepted her as one of them. Julia had been right. No one had questioned Julia's story that Elina was Philippe's young cousin. And Elina's excellent French had evidently satisfied them that Elina was French enough to be acceptable. Once they'd determined that her breeding was above reproach, everyone had treated her as the well-bred young woman she was. The dancing had scarcely begun, but already several men had asked for the privilege of dancing with her.

In fact, the evening was going so well Elina wasn't certain whether she wanted René to appear. She ached with her desire to see him, to determine if her declaration of love had touched his cold heart at all or if it had driven him to wish to be free of her. Yet she knew that when and if he came, nothing would be the same.

She almost feared he might expose her. She didn't think she could bear that. If he treated her publicly as if she were his mistress, if he humiliated her in that way, she would simply have to leave New Orleans. She couldn't rise to the battle anymore. For too long she'd deluded herself that he cared for her. His continued absence showed he didn't. And if he returned only to humiliate her, she'd be forced to cut him out of her heart forever—if she could.

She turned her attention to the young gentleman who was twirling her around the floor with expert grace. His smooth good manners and correct smile were ingratiating, but she couldn't stop comparing him to René. In spite of herself, she began wishing he were a bit older, a bit more . . . daring.

Firmly, she clamped down on that thought. She wouldn't let René ruin this night for her.

"I never realized *Monsieur* Vannier had cousins outside of Louisiana," the young man murmured. "And certainly not such lovely ones."

"My . . . er . . . cousin had more skeletons in the closet than you can imagine," she said flippantly, flashing him a smile even as she wondered what he'd say if he knew the truth.

The young man laughed and tightened his grip on her waist a fraction. "I see his wit runs in the family."

"Yes," she said, but this time her smile was decidedly forced.

The next two hours went on much the same. It was delightful to be courted by the men who thought she was nothing other than a lovely *demoiselle*. Flirting and smiling, she whirled around the floor in the arms of one darkly handsome Creole man after another. They paid her lavish compliments on the gown of daffodil crepe de lisse trimmed with black velvet that René had purchased for her. They admired her hair, piled high and ornamented with combs.

She knew she should have been thrilled by all the attention and the compliments, particularly since her papa had given her few chances to be courted. Nonetheless, she couldn't keep her mind on her surroundings. She kept finding herself watching for René, hoping she might glimpse him.

And after a time, she also grew tired of masquerading as her father's cousin, of fielding the myriad casual questions about her family, her parents, her "cousin" Philippe. At least with Julia and René she could be herself. René might not believe her story, but at least she didn't have to pretend to be someone else with him.

The dancing had just stopped and she and her partner had been joined by other couples, when she suddenly became aware that her companion's attention had been arrested by something or someone behind them. Her skin began to tingle in anticipation, as she sensed rather than saw who had entered the room.

Her companion's next words confirmed her fears. "*Mademoiselle* Vannier, is there some reason *Madame* Vannier's brother is presently staring at us with murder in his eyes?" Her dance partner smiled genially, though his smile faded when she blushed in response to his comment. "Don't tell me you've made a conquest of the notorious Bonnange," he said with a mixture of jealousy and disbelief. "Though it's odd that he's here. Bonnange has always avoided these gatherings. To be perfectly honest, he doesn't seem glad to be here now."

She knew she shouldn't glance behind her, that she should just ignore her body's craving to see René, but in spite of her better judgment, she turned to meet his gaze. What she saw there sent a frisson of terror and excitement down her spine, for he was regarding her with an expression of impassioned anger that she knew she'd never seen before.

Deborah Martin

The minute her eyes locked with his, he started toward her. She stood motionless, incapable of moving away. Then he was stopped by the same voluptuous Creole woman who'd held his attention the night of Julia's dinner.

That broke the spell. Quickly, Elina turned back to her partner.

He saw the expression of dismay on her face and asked, "Shall we dance again?" Immediately, she acquiesced, hoping somehow that in the arms of another man she might keep from noticing René and Solange.

But as Elina mechanically went through the steps, she couldn't resist stealing a glance in René's direction. Solange still gripped his arm possessively, but he stood there seemingly oblivious to the woman's presence. His eyes followed Elina around the room.

Try as she might to ignore it, the familiar rush of elation flooded her at the sight of him watching her, looking so stunningly handsome in his dress suit of black superfine and tight black kerseymere trousers. She hated herself for the pleasure she derived from seeing him, but secretly she was delighted by the scorching heat in his eyes as they followed her every step.

His gaze seemed to devour her, noting every inch of her appearance. She was instantly glad that she'd worn the ball gown and that she could hold her head high amongst the reigning Creole beauties. Still, despite the obvious admiration in his expression, the anger on his face didn't fade at all. If anything, it worsened as the dance went on.

Once the dance ended, he strode toward her again, apparently not at all concerned that Solange still clutched his arm. As he reached them, Elina's partner greeted him congenially. René's cool reply evidently curbed her partner's urge for conversation, for he mumbled some excuse and fled.

When Solange cleared her throat, René seemed to become aware that she still held his arm. "*Mademoiselle* Lambert, this is—"

"*Mademoiselle* Vannier," Elina hastened to say. At his

lifted eyebrow, she added, "I'm Philippe Vannier's cousin."

He smiled, although the smile seemed to have a certain mocking quality. "Yes," he said to Solange, his eyes boring into Elina. "*Mademoiselle* Vannier is my dear departed brother-in-law's cousin. So you'll understand, won't you, if I must do my duties as a distant relative and dance with her."

This last was more a command that Solange release his arm than a request. Solange hesitated at first, but as she realized that neither René nor Elina seemed the slightest bit aware of her existence, she withdrew to seek a better companion.

"I don't wish to dance with you," Elina murmured as soon as Solange was out of earshot.

"But you will," he stated flatly as the music began and he took her in his arms.

She tried to hold herself stiffly away from his body, but he refused to allow her even that. His hold on her was blatantly intimate, forcing her to relax against him or stumble. Unwillingly, she permitted him to mold her body to his, all the while cursing the weakness in her that made her revel in the feel of his strength meeting her softness, his arms bowing to her gracefulness.

"You look very lovely tonight," he murmured, his eyes traveling over her artfully dressed hair and rouge-less face before dropping to her low-cut gown above which peeked two creamy white half-moons.

When she reddened instantly, he smiled. Then his eyes returned to her face. "You seem to have most of the men in the room enamored of you. I've been bombarded with questions about Philippe's cousin from the moment I arrived."

She ignored the jealousy in his tone. He had no right to be jealous after the way he'd avoided her for the past week.

Deliberately, she made her tone light. "I must say Creole men are the handsomest I've ever seen. And such excellent dancers!" she exclaimed, pasting an artificially bright smile on her face.

Although René's expression remained carefully bland, his hand tightened on hers almost instinctively. "I see you missed me terribly. Is this what you've been doing while I was gone? Dancing every night away in the arms of these witless fools?"

Her contrived smile faded as she seethed with barely controlled fury. "If you had wished me to restrict my activities, *monsieur*, you should have stayed nearby, instead of galloping about the countryside visiting friends, or whatever it was you were doing."

Instantly, she hated herself for revealing how much his absence had upset her. Her anger with herself only heightened when his scowl softened and he smiled.

"So you did miss me, did you?" he said, a hint of smugness in his voice as his anger seemed to fade.

She lifted her chin stubbornly. "No, not at all."

"I missed you."

The bald statement, spoken with sudden tenderness, made her gaze at him in suspicion.

"I doubt that. You probably managed quite well without me."

His eyes trailed meaningfully down over her clothing. "You as well, it appears. You didn't even wait for my return to begin wearing the gowns I bought for you."

She stiffened. "They're not *your* gowns anymore. I paid *Madame* Laplante for them with my earnings."

He chuckled. "Did you now? If that's the case, my sister must be incredibly extravagant with her servants."

Despite the logic behind his words, they angered her. The icy glare she leveled on him wiped the smile from his face. "Forgive me. I'd forgotten I can't practice my deceptions on you successfully. Everyone else here may think I'm a well-bred young woman with impeccable credentials, but you and I know better, don't we? We both know I'm a liar, a cheat, and a thief. Tell me, when do you plan to expose my thievery—before or after supper is served?"

Her taunts seemed to affect him profoundly, though not in any way she would have expected. His eyes darkened with pain. "Have you done something I must expose?"

"No!" she protested, hurt that he could turn her words into a guilty confession.

"I must confess to being a little curious. If you so fear being exposed, why are you here at all?"

His direct question disconcerted her. She held her head high. "Since you've probably already decided why I'm here, I'm sure you have a better answer for that than I do," she said with a great deal of sarcasm in her tone.

His expression became grave. "Well, either you are trying some new scheme to gain money or a wealthy husband or . . ."

She dropped her eyes, hardly able to bear what other despicable conjectures he might conjure up.

"Or you've told my sister the truth and she believes you."

Elina's head snapped up. She wasn't certain she'd heard him correctly. "Wh—what truth?"

"That you're Philippe's daughter. That you came here looking for him and found his other family instead."

"Are you saying . . . you believe it's the truth too?"

"Yes," he replied with quiet confidence.

Her eyes narrowed. "What has made you change your mind? Have you found some proof for my claims?"

His eyes searched hers. "No concrete proof. Or rather, very little. But the proof I do have is irrevocable. It's you."

Her whole body tensed with expectation. "Me?"

"You. I've tried for weeks to reconcile the two images I have of you—one of a scheming liar who concocted a wild story to revenge herself on me and the other of a giving, innocent, sweet woman who for the first time in her life had been left without family or friends all because she

369

trusted her father. I've given up trying to hold on to the first image. I've decided to trust the second one."

She could hardly depend on her voice to be even. "You believe me," she whispered.

"Yes."

By this time he'd danced her right out one of the double doors and onto the balcony that was thankfully deserted. She scarcely noticed where they were, however. She was shaking from the havoc his words were wreaking on her emotions. Upon first seeing him at the ball, she'd expected his wrath, his displeasure, perhaps even his public rejection of her. But she hadn't expected this.

He stopped dancing, forcing her to stop, too. But when she sought to pull away from him, he only clasped her more tightly.

"Please, Elina," he whispered in a voice hoarse with emotion. "I need you to love me. I know you think I'm heartless. I know you don't quite trust me. But I can make you happy, I swear. I love you."

Her bitterness over his unexplained absence still rankled enough for her to say accusingly, "You love me? Then why did you disappear without a word for a week? Why did you leave me to believe that my declaration had driven you away?"

Her voice broke on that last phrase, and his guilt-stricken face tightened in alarm. "Oh, God, sweet eyes," he murmured, drawing her unwilling body against his. "Is that what you thought? What you said couldn't possibly have driven me away. I had longed to hear you say those words for so long. And when you did, it confirmed what I already really knew—that I couldn't live without you. But I also knew that until I resolved some of my doubts, we had no hope for a future together. So I went in search of Francois's friends and managed to get the truth out of one of them."

She drew back from him, her eyes widening. "All this time you've been with Francois?"

"No, but not for want of looking. After what Alcide told me, I tried to find him—"

"What did Alcide tell you?"

René stared beyond her.

"Francois killed Alexandre, didn't he?" she whispered.

René's eyes snapped back to her in surprise. "Yes. How did you know?"

"It's the only sane reason Francois could have had for wanting me gone."

René's face grew grim. "I think so, too. I suppose your brother learned the truth from someone in town and went to confront Francois with it."

She nodded. "That's why the papers disappeared."

His eyes narrowed. He'd clearly forgotten about the papers. "Yes. That makes sense. If Alex showed Francois papers, then Francois would have been forced to believe Alex was Philippe's son. I suppose after Francois . . . I suppose he destroyed them."

She shuddered against him, and he tightened his grip on her with a fierceness she could feel. Her heart was aching at the misery her brother must have experienced before his death, but more than that it hurt her to realize just how much Francois hated his own siblings.

How could Francois be Julia's son? Their reactions to the truth, although similar, had still been very different. The same was true of René.

Suddenly, she remembered why they'd begun discussing Francois in the first place. "Why did you want to find Francois?" she asked timidly.

"When I went to see Alcide, I thought I just wanted to know the truth. I think by then, however, I'd already decided I had to believe you.

"But once I realized how treacherous Francois was, I couldn't rest until I knew it all. I had hoped to get the whole story from him and ensure he didn't try anything else against you. It was to be my way of atoning for everything I'd done to you. I feared that unless I could demonstrate

371

how completely I believed you, and could show to what lengths I was prepared to go to make amends for what you've been forced to endure because of me and mine, you wouldn't marry me."

"Marry you?" she asked, not quite certain she'd heard him right.

"Immediately, if not before," he said, some of his natural domineering nature coming to the fore.

"All your objections are gone?"

He nuzzled her neck, then kissed it gently. "Every single stupid one."

"What about Julia? Aren't you worried about what this will do to her?" she asked perversely, remembering why he'd said he couldn't marry her before.

His face grew pensive. "Yes, I am. But she'll have to accept it. I don't know how she'll take it. I'm not even certain how to tell her about . . . about Philippe."

"She knows."

"Oh? Did you tell her?"

Elina couldn't meet his eyes. "I didn't have to. She already knew."

"What?"

"Papa told her everything before he died. He even left a will providing for us. But—but she couldn't bring herself to act on it until I showed up on her doorstep."

She lifted her eyes to his, startled by the intense fury in his expression.

"How long have you known that she knew?"

Elina trembled under his angry glare. "Since the night you found me at Julia's."

His lips tightened.

"Listen, René," she said softly. "You mustn't be angry with Julia for not telling you—"

"Julia? I'm not angry with Julia. Why didn't you tell me? Why did you let me continue to wonder who you really were? If you had just told me—"

"You would have demanded that I marry you out of some

sense of duty. I would have never known for certain how you really felt, if I mattered enough to you to make you forsake it all."

His anger seemed to lessen somewhat, though his face still held a trace of bitterness. "Was it so important to you?"

"My father married your sister out of a sense of duty, knowing he loved Mama, knowing what he did was wrong. It caused us all incredible pain. I had to be sure, don't you see?"

"And now?" he asked, his eyes darkening as they lingered on her face. "Are you sure now? Will you marry me, sweet eyes?"

She took one look at the earnest pleading in his eyes and nearly said yes. But she had to know something first. "Your deciding that I was telling the truth didn't make you feel you ought to marry me, did it? Are you marrying me because you feel guilty for what happened? Because you needn't do so, René. Julia has taken care of giving me my part of Papa's inheritance, and I can always continue on as Papa's cousin until I wish to leave—"

"Over my dead body!" he thundered. "I refuse to spend one more evening watching you in the arms of some other hot-blooded Creole who's likely to attempt seducing you the moment he gets you alone! *Mon Dieu, chérie*, I love you, but one more night like tonight will be the death of me! Either you marry me, Elina, or—"

"Or what?" she finished, her doubts laid to rest by his outburst.

His eyes glittered with the beginnings of passion as his arms stole around her waist again. "Or I'll carry you off to Cour de Cyprès and make you my prisoner until you accept my proposal."

"That sounds perfectly . . . mm . . . terrifying," she murmured right before his mouth captured hers.

The purest pleasure she'd ever known filled her body with heat. He wanted her, and not just for what her body could provide him! That knowledge served as an aphrodisiac more potent than any shellfish. She clasped his body tight in restless wanting, and he responded by molding her to his length.

After one long breath-stealing kiss, he tore his lips away from hers to ask, "Do you wish to remain for supper?"

"What?" she asked, still dazed with the renewed delight of having him caress her.

He took one look at her upturned face, her eyes dilated and wide in the moonlight and her lips parted, and he found his answer.

"I shall tell Julia you're not feeling well and that I'm taking you home."

As the meaning of what he was saying sank in, she blushed. "And whose home are you taking me to, *monsieur*?"

"Ours."

At his answer, she smiled softly, instantly forgetting any protest she'd had.

The next half-hour passed in a blur. Elina had not needed to pretend to be ill. Her flushed face and distracted manner had made the host and hostess believe René when he made his excuses. As for his sister, he hadn't been able to find her, but he'd left a message stating that he was taking Elina home.

Moments later, he and Elina were in his carriage.

Elina suddenly felt inexplicably shy. Never before had she purposely undertaken to behave scandalously.

To cover her embarrassment, she asked René, "What is to become of Francois?"

René released a long sigh. "I don't know. He should be prosecuted for your brother's murder, I suppose. But I'm not certain, *chérie*, if I could be the one to reveal his treachery. I don't know how Julia could endure it."

"She doesn't know what he's done," Elina said. "It would destroy her to learn of it. I can't bear thinking that his crime might go unpunished, yet . . ."

"Yes?"

"He is also my brother, after all."

René drew her into his lap, cradling her head against his chest. "Don't think about it now, sweet eyes. We'll sort it out later. I'd much prefer discussing our wedding."

Her heart gave a tiny leap at the thought. She still couldn't believe he actually intended to marry her.

"How soon can we marry?" he continued.

"Let me see," she said slowly. "We have invitations to send out, gowns to order, a wedding banquet to plan . . ."

He groaned. "I can see you're already making me pay for my past transgressions."

"All in all, six months at the very least," she said with a wicked grin.

"We'll elope," he said, and at her burst of laughter, he insisted, "I'm serious. If I have to carry you off secretly to the parish priest, I shall. But I'm not waiting six months to make you mine, sweet eyes, so you'd just as well put that idea out of your head."

"We'll see," she murmured, but anything else she might have said was forgotten as he captured her lips with his own.

In a short period of time, they'd reached Cour de Cyprès. Elina slid off René's lap, but before she could protest, René had bounded out of the carriage and lifted her in his arms.

"This time, *mon amour*, I intend to make it clear what your place is. Once you cross that threshhold, you're mine."

"I'm already yours," she whispered as his chocolate-brown eyes played over her face.

Her words spurred him on. He was up the steps in a few quick strides. Then without even setting her down, he opened the door.

As he carried her through the house, Louis came out of the dining room and stared at them in astonishment.

"Say *bonjour* to your soon-to-be mistress," René said with a nod toward his gaping servant.

Elina hid her face in René's shirt, unable to face Louis

and the knowing expression that was sure to cross his face once he glimpsed hers.

"Now say *au revoir*," René continued as he began to climb the stairs with her in his arms.

And despite her acute embarrassment, Elina did not protest.

Chapter Twenty-Four

Grab for too much and it slips away from you.
—Creole Proverb

Exhausted, René and Elina lay sprawled across his bed, their bodies languidly entangled. She trailed one finger along his belly, laughing when he caught her finger and moved it lower.

"I can't stay," Elina murmured. "You know I have to return to Julia's."

He ignored her comment, choosing instead to press her back against the mattress. "Julia never returns home until the wee hours of the morning."

"It *is* the wee hours of the morning," Elina replied with a woeful expression.

"Nonsense," he murmured, smothering her weak protest with his lips.

A sudden knock at the door made them both start.

"*Monsieur?*" a voice that was unmistakably Louis's asked.

Deborah Martin

René directed a murderous glance at the door. "Whatever it is, Louis, it can wait!" he shouted.

"*Madame* Vannier is downstairs," Louis replied.

As René swore, Elina wriggled out from under him.

"Tell Julia I'll be there shortly," René called, then turned to find Elina gathering her clothes together. "Where are you going?"

"Please, René, I know it seems silly, but I can't let her think . . . I don't want . . ."

"I understand. But what do you intend to do?"

"Sneak back to Julia's, of course, while she's here," she said as she began to dress. "If you'll just keep her occupied, I'll slip out the back and walk there. I've walked there before. If you delay her long enough, I can reach it before she returns home."

René's eyebrows lifted in an expression of wry amusement. "I hardly think I can occupy her with chitchat while she's worried about you."

"If you tell her we're getting married, she'll start discussing wedding plans. I promise you, you'll have to throw her out long before she'll tire of the subject."

He grinned. "I dare say you're probably right about that. But don't walk. Take Monique."

Elina stared at him in surprise. "Ride? At night? By myself? You must be mad!"

René frowned. "Yes, I suppose I must. All right then, ask Louis to accompany you. I'll use some excuse to send him back to you once I get downstairs. He'll be more than happy to escort you to Julia's, I'm sure."

"I can just go myself—"

"If you don't allow Louis to accompany you," he said smoothly, "I'll carry you downstairs right now. I wonder what Julia would say to that."

Elina threw a pillow at him, but she was smiling. "As you wish. I'll take an escort. But, remember, don't let her go for at least an hour."

She was starting to open the door, when René slid from

the bed. "Wait, *mon amour*," he commanded. Then he pulled her to him for a long, probing kiss. "Just so you won't forget me," he murmured as he lifted his mouth from hers.

"Never," she whispered. Then she smiled and slipped out the door.

As she walked down the stairs, she heard Louis in the parlor, trying to calm an irate Julia. Quickly, she crept the remaining steps and walked toward the back of the house. Only when she'd escaped out the back without being seen did she sigh with relief.

But her relief was short-lived. She'd managed to walk only a short distance from the house to wait for Louis to join her when Francois stepped out of the shadows.

"How very good of you to oblige me by coming out here," he said with a grin. "I wasn't too happy to arrive in town and go to *Nonc* René's in search of you only to learn you were at the Riviere's ball. Nor was I happy when you left with *Nonc* René and returned here in his protection. Still, I followed the two of you on the chance that I might catch you alone. And I see Lady Fortune has stood me in good stead."

Elina felt a cold dread squeezing her heart. "What do you want?" she asked, inching back toward the house.

"Just a few words with you," he said, motioning with his hand. From out of the darkness came the man she'd talked with in the gardens. "I'm sure you remember Etienne," Francois continued. Etienne moved up to stand behind her, blocking her way to the house.

"Now, my dear Elina," Francois went on, "once again, I offer you money to leave here. If you're wise, you'll take it and run as far away from Cour de Cyprès as you can." With that, he pressed into her hands a very heavy bag of coins. "It's all gold," he told her.

She glanced down at the bag in horror, then dropped it at his feet. "You can keep your money. I don't intend to leave."

"Then I'm afraid I must force you to leave," he stated.

Before she could even scream, Etienne's hand was clamped over her mouth. Then she felt something sharp against her side, and she groaned, for she had no doubt it was a knife.

Etienne's low chuckle sent a chill through her. "Come now, my lovely. Francois and I plan to make certain you're on the next ship leaving for Europe. But you won't make it that far if you make a single noise, for I swear I'll kill you if I have to."

She wasn't certain he would, but she had no desire to test his sincerity. So when he dropped his hand from her mouth, she said nothing.

Slowly, Francois and Etienne maneuvered her through the grounds. The knife that Etienne continued to hold pressed against her side stuck her often enough to make her thoroughly convinced of their intention to force her to leave, no matter what.

When she realized they were moving toward the stables, she felt her panic rise, but she strove not to let them see her growing fear.

Only when they stopped at the stables and she saw their two horses saddled and ready did she panic. She had to do something! Otherwise they would be far away with her in their power before René even realized she was gone. But what could she do with Etienne holding a knife against her side?

She watched helplessly as Francois mounted his horse.

"Shall she ride with you then?" Etienne asked.

"*Non*. I don't want her near me," Francois said in disgust.

Etienne's low chuckle made Elina's skin crawl. "I assure you I have no such objections to the little filly's nearness."

His comment made her worry she might have to deal with more than just their kidnapping her. She could only hope her half brother wasn't so wicked as to allow Etienne to act on his desires.

Etienne lowered the knife for a moment. Then he swung her up into the saddle with ease. Despite the waves of terror threatening to engulf her, she realized this was her chance to make herself heard, while Etienne's knife was not at her back. Screaming would do her no good. This far from the house no one would hear. Instead, she tried another tack.

"Francois, I can't believe you would do this to your own sister," she cried, fearing his reaction yet hoping to make him realize how serious his action was. Making him see the folly of his ways was her only chance. Perhaps if he would acknowledge her as his own flesh and blood, he might consider how extreme his actions were.

Her words got a reaction but not from the person she'd expected it.

"Sister?" Etienne asked, his hand on the saddle behind her as he prepared to mount. "What is she talking about, Francois?"

Breathlessly, Elina rushed on, "I'm Francois's half sister. His father had two legitimate wives, one of them my mother. Even Francois's mother knows. Why else do you think she'd taken me in? Ask him. He knows I'm telling the truth."

Francois had grown incredibly still.

"Francois!" Etienne barked. "Does she lie? Is she your sister?"

"What does it matter?" Francois asked, throwing Etienne into confusion.

"I—I don't know. It's just that . . . your sister. *Sacre bleu!* If even your mother really knows—"

"Etienne, don't be a fool!" Francois commanded. "She's lying about *Maman*. Surely you realize that. *Maman* would have told me if she'd known of Papa's indiscretions."

"So she is your sister then? Doesn't that affect you? I mean, if something should happen to her on the ship . . ."

"You're acting as if she should mean something to me. She's American, don't you see? She's René's mistress, a whore! Shall I take such a sister into my bosom, allow her to take half my inheritance?"

Etienne's face hardened. "No, no. I guess not."

Etienne prepared to mount again, but before he could hoist himself into the saddle, they heard thundering hoofs approaching. Francois wheeled his horse around to face the coming rider.

"Alcide! What the hell is he doing here?" Etienne muttered.

The man pulled his horse up abruptly in front of them. "Jean told me you'd both arrived in town. He said you'd come to Bonnange's . . ." he began, then trailed off as he saw Elina perched on Etienne's horse. "Oh, no. I was afraid you'd do something foolish. You both must leave at once. Bonnange knows."

"What does he know?" Etienne demanded as his brother fell silent, out of breath from his mad ride.

"He knows . . . he knows Francois killed that Yankee Wallace. And I don't think he believes it was accidental."

Etienne dropped the reins to Elina's horse and turned on Francois. "You see! I told you this was a mistake. Now your uncle will hound us. We can't take her now. We'll be lucky if we escape from here with our lives!"

"If we allow her to stay, he'll follow us to the ends of the earth. His pride will not allow him to let her brother's death go unpunished." Then Francois smiled slowly, a cold bitter smile. "But without her, he has no case. It is his word against ours that I had reason to kill Wallace."

Elina saw the sudden steely glint in Francois's eyes and shuddered. In that instant she knew. Without a doubt, he planned to kill her. In the split second when she realized his intention, she made a decision. She had to take her chances on the horse or die.

The hard kick she gave Etienne's horse sent the animal off like a shot. At first all she could do was close her eyes and hold on. Then as she put some distance between her and Francois, she leaned low in the saddle, clinging to the pommel for dear life. Behind her she could hear Francois shouting curses, but she could scarcely take them in.

For now her fear had taken over. Once again she was at the mercy of the beast she hated most. Once again she was in danger of being thrown and trampled.

She gripped the pommel in desperation, half wanting to simply stop the horse and get off. But then she would die, for Francois definitely meant to kill her.

Her only choice was to ride, to control the animal while gaining as much distance as she could. But to do that, she had to reach the reins. She looked down to see them trailing, then swallowed convulsively as she glimpsed the dark ground passing below her at an alarming rate.

"René, my love," she whispered. "Where are you when I need you?"

Suddenly it was as if she could feel him behind her as he had been the last time they'd ridden together. His hands had clutched her body tightly, his lips had brushed her hair. She clung to that memory in desperation, willing herself to feel his body against hers, to feel his strength and love empowering her to overcome her fears.

Then she remembered René's voice saying, "You must be at one with the horse, mold yourself to him." Her terror abating a fraction, she forced herself to relax, to think of herself and the horse as one creature. At first, all she could feel was the furious beating of her heart and the tensed muscles in her thighs and hands.

But as she began to make herself concentrate on her surroundings and note the speed at which they were moving as well as what part of the plantation they were passing through, she found her fear subsiding a bit. With determination, she strove to force her fear into the background, to ignore the fact that she was on horseback.

Several tense moments passed during which she struggled with herself. But between her greater fear of Francois and the power that the knowledge of René's love gave her, she at last began feeling her limbs yield to the motion of the horse. The jolting gait slowly became a rocking one as her body adjusted to the horse's rhythm.

Then to her alarm, the horse began to slow as he tired. Certain that Francois couldn't be far behind her, she started to spur him on. Then she stopped. The reins. She didn't have the reins.

Her blood pounding, she bent over, straining to reach the leather thong that flapped just beyond her reach. Steadily, she inched her left hand forward until the leather brushed her fingers. She caught at it and missed, swearing under her breath as she did so. Then she caught at it again. This time, her fingers closed around the rein.

With a cry of triumph, she repeated the process with the other rein. In moments she had both.

In spite of the danger that surrounded her and her fear of her half brother, she felt a thrill of satisfaction when at last she knew she had the means to control the horse.

Casting a glance behind her, she thought she saw a rider. Quickly, she pressed the horse's flanks with her knees. Her major concern now had to be escaping Francois.

As best she could, she glanced around her. They were galloping through fields bounded on the left by a dark line of trees. Her only hope was to move out of the open fields where Francois could find her easily and into the trees.

With the surest hand she could manage, she tugged on the reins, relieved when the horse obeyed her direction.

"If I ever get through this alive," she muttered to the tossing head just in front of her, "you shall have all the apples and celery and whatever it is horses eat that you could possibly stomach."

The sky was beginning to lighten in the early hours before dawn. As the horse thundered closer and closer to the trees, Elina suddenly realized that the trees didn't look quite as a forest should. They seemed spindly, lacking much greenery. They rose like ghostly fingers out of the ground, a mist hanging low around them.

Only when the horse tore down a steep incline onto marshy ground did she realize the forest was really a swamp.

Then she tried to stop the horse, but she'd scarcely begun tugging frantically on the reins when the horse hit a boggy area and stumbled.

As the horse fell, bringing her down with it, all she could think was that she wasn't ready to die. That was her last conscious thought.

René focused all his energies on appeasing his irate sister. "I told you, Julia, she's not here," he asserted once again.

"Have you any idea how much trouble I had getting her to attend the ball at all? Then you have to spoil it all by—"

René's patience was at an end. "I'm going to marry her. Will that make any difference in the scolding you seem bound and determined to give me?"

Evidently, it did. Julia stopped short. Then her eyes narrowed in suspicion. "Have you told her this?"

"Of course," he said with irritation. "If you'll just calm down, I might give you some of the details."

Julia assumed her most dignified expression. "If you think you're going to pacify me by telling me you plan to do the right thing by her after all this time, it won't work. I don't care what she says. You need to know the truth. She's Philippe's legitimate daughter and she deserves better than this."

"I know," René said quietly. "I know all of it. I told you we're to be married."

Julia wasn't quite convinced. She glared at him suspiciously. "If so, you shouldn't have carried her off like that. She's got a right to her place in New Orleans society. You've put that child through hell, dear brother. I simply won't stand for your ruining her reputation by keeping her here until the wedding, if that's what you intend. She left with you, so I know she came here. Where is she?"

René was about to retort when Louis entered the room, pushing in front of him a trembling Alcide Pannetrat. A cold dread gripped René. Louis was supposed to be escorting Elina to Julia's house. And what was Alcide doing here?

"Tell him," Louis urged Alcide. "Tell him or risk both his and my wrath."

René knew before Alcide could even speak. "Where's Elina?" he demanded. "Who has Elina?"

"No—no one," Alcide stammered. "Not yet anyway. She rode off before Francois could stop her."

Julia gasped as René's eyes darkened in rage. "What is Francois doing here and what does he intend?" he demanded.

Alcide gulped and stared from Julia to René.

"Answer me!" René shouted.

"H—he and Etienne returned from their trip and came here to persuade her to leave. But it all fell apart. Now Francois's after her. Etienne and I tried to reason with him, but he's determined to kill her, since she knows he killed her brother."

"Francois killed Alexandre?" Julia asked, the blood draining from her face. "René, what is he talking about?"

René spared only a second for his sister. "I'll have to tell you everything later, love. I'm sorry, but I can't stay now." Quickly, he went to his desk drawer and withdrew his pistol.

"Don't hurt Francois!" Julia cried out as she saw the gun. "Please, René, he's my only son!"

René turned to look at his sister, taking in her terrible distress. "I won't hurt him. But I can't let him hurt Elina, either. You do understand."

She nodded, although the tears streamed down her face.

René wheeled around and hastened to the back of the house. Louis thrust aside the cringing Alcide and followed.

"I sent a groom after Francois," Louis said as he quickened his pace to keep up with René. "With my age, I was afraid I wouldn't be able to catch them. But the groom is young and he's armed."

"Has someone saddled Savage?" René asked.

"Yes. Now that daylight is breaking, you should have no trouble following three horses' tracks."

René's blood began to race in fury. Three horses! Elina was on one of them. Elina who was terrified to ride a sedate mare, who feared even touching a horse. *Mon Dieu*, could she control the horse at all?

He had to pray she could. Otherwise, if Francois reached her before René could. . . .

"Hold on, sweet eyes," he murmured as he raced to the stables. "Please hold on, *mon amour*!"

Elina's head cleared very slowly. A heavy weight crushed her leg and her hand lay in something wet and slimy. She opened her eyes.

No wonder her leg hurt her. The horse had fallen across it. The horse didn't seem to be dead yet, but clearly it was hurt, for it thrashed occasionally, soft whimpering neighs coming from it. She stroked the poor suffering creature, speaking to it with a gentle voice.

"How noble of you," a sarcastic voice said from somewhere close by.

She followed the sound of the voice to find Francois sitting on a dead log not far from the edge of the water where she lay.

"Help me," she called to him.

His answer was to smile, and in that smile was such venom that she shuddered.

"Help you? Why should I? I couldn't have wished for a better situation. I had hoped you wouldn't even regain consciousness, but since you have, I suppose I must find some other way to send you to your death, a way that can't be attributed to me."

As he stood, her stomach knotted with fear. "Why are

387

you doing this?" she asked in a whisper. "Papa's estate is large enough to support us all comfortably. I don't even want his money. I never did. And now that René and I are to be married—"

Francois laughed harshly. "That's just it, dear sister. My uncle has become thoroughly bewitched by you. He'll do anything you ask as long as you're alive to ask it. He'll never forgive me for killing your brother and keeping you from him. But he can hardly blame me if you're found dead in the swamps, pinned under your horse. My inheritance will still be all mine, and *Nonc* René will have nothing to prove that I killed anyone—neither your brother nor you."

"It won't work, Francois," she said, forcing as much coldness into her voice as she could. She knew that appearing unafraid was the only way to make him doubt the practicality of his plan. "By now I'm certain your two friends have told him where we've gone, and he'll be following behind us."

Francois grinned diabolically. "The only one following us was a mere groom whom I dispatched with only one bullet. I'm saving the other for you, though I'd rather not kill you that way." His smile broadened as his eyes turned to something beyond her. "Ah," he continued, "it appears Lady Fortune is still with me."

As best she could, Elina twisted her head to see what he was looking at. At the sight of the alligator sliding slowly through the water, she went numb. She'd never seen such a creature, but she'd heard of them. René had told her stories of the terrifying power they wielded. The reptile's eyes seemed to be assessing her plumpness as he leisurely closed the wide distance between them, and she shivered at the thought that his jaws might soon close on her.

In desperation, she tried to wriggle from under the horse, but the horse was too heavy and she wasn't strong enough to budge it.

"If you don't mind," Francois said as he stood, "I believe I'll watch from a distance. I wouldn't want our friend there to mistake which of us is his intended victim."

"Francois," she cried. "You could kill him with your gun. You must! My father was your father. Can you ignore the blood that runs in both of our veins? We're Vanniers—both of us! How could you kill another Vannier?"

For a moment he paused, but she never got the chance to find out if he had changed his mind, for suddenly another voice broke the stillness.

"Elina! Where are you?" René's voice rang out from very near.

Francois froze.

"I'm here!" she shouted. "Over here!"

"Quiet, you bitch!" Francois hissed. Swiftly, he pulled his gun and lifted it to her head, but he was too late. His eyes glittering with fury, René stormed through the cypress into the small clearing.

"Put down the gun!" René commanded as he took in the situation at a glance. "You don't dare to kill her here before my very eyes!"

"Don't I?" Francois replied. His face hardened in a stubborn expression that Elina recognized. Alex had often had such a mulish expression when cornered. Francois steadied the gun on her with grim determination. "I shan't let your mistress twist your mind into believing that I killed her brother, *Nonc* René. I know what she's about. You've let her looks blind you to the truth, but she's a liar and a cheat and—"

"She never told me you killed her brother. Only you have mentioned that. I didn't even know you knew that Wallace was her brother," René said with an outward calm, although Elina saw the dangerous glint in his eyes.

Francois grew pale. "That sniveling card cheat pulled one trick too many, so I shot him in self-defense when he shot at me."

"With my stolen gun. Did you know I found it on his body? He'd never fired it. How odd that you shot him twice to protect yourself without his ever firing a shot. I know it all, Francois. Every treacherous act you committed in your attempt to keep Elina and her brother from being acknowledged. So there's no point in continuing this. Put the gun down." When Francois continued to hold his aim steady, René pulled his own gun. "Don't be a fool," he hissed. "If you even attempt to shoot her, I'll be forced to fire."

Francois pivoted to face his uncle and turned his gun on René. Then he laughed mockingly. "Shoot me? I doubt that, *Nonc* René. You're too loyal to family for that. You'd never kill your own nephew, never. But you see, I have no compunctions at all about killing you. What's an uncle to one who's already killed his brother? Nothing. I'd as soon shoot you as live."

"Would you really?" René said in a commanding tone as he moved closer to his nephew. "And how would you face your mother with the news of her brother's death?"

That gave Francois pause, and René moved closer, holding out his hand as he did. "Don't act in haste and ruin your future, Francois. There's no reason to compound your crimes."

Francois's hand had begun to waver until René said the word "crimes." Then he steadied it on his uncle again. But by that point, René had come close enough to reach the pistol. In moments, he had Francois's wrist gripped and his gun hand forced down.

"Drop the gun!" he commanded.

Francois dropped it onto the boggy ground, and René released his wrist.

But without any warning, Francois brought his knee up, catching his uncle in the chest. The blow seemed scarcely to faze René. He swung for his nephew's jaw, but Francois feinted to the side. In that moment, Francois slid on the slick ground and landed in the water.

He came up sputtering and stood in the water, ready to lunge for his uncle, but by that time the alligator had whisked through the water to come up behind him. Elina screamed as it opened its massive jaws and clamped down on Francois's leg. René fired twice at the reptile, but the alligator, though wounded, thrashed backward, dragging the screaming Francois with him.

In seconds the reptile had pulled his victim down into the murky waters of the swamp. The waters roiled in bloody turmoil, the green algae floating on top agitated from the desperate struggle taking place below the surface. One final thrash disrupted the water and then all was still.

The blood tinging the muddy water soon dissipated, leaving no trace of the violence that had marred the swamp's quiet. Only the horror on Elina's and René's faces remained.

Elina shuddered and then dissolved into tears, her body shaking from the terror she'd witnessed. No one deserved such a death, she told herself, not even her poor wretched half brother.

René was beside her immediately, his face a grim mask of concern. "Don't cry, sweet eyes," he murmured, cradling her head in his lap, though he, too, seemed unable to cast aside the image of his nephew's final moments. She could see his own horror reflected in the haunted sorrow of his eyes.

Then he turned to the task of freeing her. Silently, he worked to thrust the horse aside. Once he'd pushed the horse off her, he helped her to her feet, his arm tightening around her waist as she stumbled. To her relief, her leg wasn't broken, only numb and bruised. Gently, René led her to the very log Francois had been sitting on.

After he seated her, he went to examine the horse. The poor creature had not fared well. As René checked him, he lay there whimpering.

"His leg is broken," René said quietly. Elina's stomach lurched as she realized René would have to return later to put the horse out of its misery.

Suddenly it was all too much for Elina—the chaos and death.

"I'm so—so very sorry about Francois," she stammered,

the vision of his dying still vivid in her mind. "If only I hadn't come here—"

"I would never have known you," he finished for her, deliberately leading her away from the horse and up the steep incline to higher ground. "Francois would have come to a bad end regardless. You mustn't blame yourself for his death. He would have killed you if he'd had the chance."

She knew that was true, yet it didn't lessen her guilt.

"But if you hadn't come," he continued, "my life would be as meaningless as it was before I saw you standing at your brother's side on that boat. For my sake, sweet eyes, you must not blame yourself." He turned her toward him as they reached firmer ground. Gently, he clasped her chin, lifting her face to his. "Because without you, my love, I'd just as soon not live."

She stared up into the face she loved. René was right. After what they'd seen and what had happened, their love was the only thing that mattered.

"I love you," she whispered as her heart swelled with emotion.

He smiled and planted a soft kiss on her lips, his eyes giving her a look of burning love that filled her with awed delight. "I hope so," he murmured. "I've been accused of murder, braved yellow fever, and challenged my own nephew because I love you. After all that, I think I deserve to see those sweet eyes shine for me every morning. Don't you agree?"

She smiled. "I do," she murmured as she drew his mouth down to hers. "I definitely do."

Epilogue

What you lose in the fire, you find in the ashes.
—*Creole Proverb*

Elina stared at the two gravestones, one for her brother, the other for a brother she'd scarcely known. She and Julia kept both graves clean and tidy, leaving flowers weekly. Elina was glad that Alex's body had been brought here and that the two men had been buried beside each other. She liked to think that in the grave the brothers were making their peace with each other. Perhaps together their spirits could even learn to forgive the father who'd made them what they were.

No, she thought. She couldn't blame everything on Papa. After all, she'd had the same father and she was as different from her two brothers as left from right. They'd made their own choices, lived by them, and died by them.

Yet they'd caused so much pain in the process, she thought as she remembered how Julia had mourned her son's death. René had felt so guilty at first about indirectly causing Francois's death. But with time, the guilt and pain were beginning to heal. Julia had lost herself in the wedding preparations and then in getting the newlyweds settled, while René, of course, had lost himself in Elina.

"How are you feeling?" René asked as he came up behind her and encircled her waist with his arms.

"Fine. Cecile's special tea has kept me from feeling too ill," she murmured, turning away from the graves to face him. Slowly, they began to walk toward the gates of the family cemetery.

He clasped her close at his side and placed his free hand over her barely rounded waist. "Julia's not certain whether to tell the child she's his aunt or his stepgrandmother."

Elina laughed. "His? What if it's a girl?"

His brown eyes glowed with a warmth that seemed often to fill them lately. "If it's a girl, then Julia will be in trouble. She's counting on your having a boy, so she can give him all my old baby clothes." His face darkened. "And Francois's, too."

Elina stopped and faced him. Her fingers swept up to smooth away the frown on his face. "This child will have a life much different from Francois's, for its father won't have to keep any secrets from him or her."

His eyes twinkled mischievously. "And suppose I start spending half my months away on business trips?"

She smiled coyly, twining her arms around his neck. "Then I'll just have to come after you and hit you over the head with a whiskey bottle. Knock some sense into you."

He laughed and drew her up against him. "I can see I had best keep my liquor locked up."

"No," she murmured, her face growing serious. "Just stay close by and keep saying the words that make me trust you."

"What words?" he teased, then pressed a kiss on her cheek as she flashed him a mock glare. "I love you, sweet eyes," he murmured against her ear. He held her closer as he added, "I'll always love only you."

There was no need to say more.

PREFERRED CUSTOMERS!

Leisure Books and Love Spell
proudly present
a brand-new catalogue and a
TOLL-FREE NUMBER

STARTING JUNE 1, 1995
CALL 1-800-481-9191
between 2:00 and 10:00 p.m.
(Eastern Time)
Monday Through Friday

GET A FREE CATALOGUE
AND ORDER BOOKS USING
VISA AND MASTERCARD

 LEISURE BOOKS 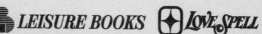 *LOVE SPELL*